"You are strong, Maggie . . ."

". . . Hell, you're the strongest woman I know, and I was raised by an Army wife."

She smiled.

"Look at you," he said, reaching out and cupping her cheek. A frisson of electricity shot through her, and she wanted so badly to close her eyes, to embrace the feeling, but she couldn't look away from him. From the way he touched her like he wanted to know all of her—the good, the bad, and the beautiful. "You're amazing," he whispered, leaning forward, his lips brushing against hers.

He kissed her like it was the last thing he wanted before he left for war. Like she was air and light and sound . . .

By Tess Diamond

DANGEROUS GAMES

Coming Soon

SUCH A PRETTY GIRL

DANGEROUS GAMES

TESS DIAMOND

AVONBOOKS

An Imprint of HarperCollins*Publishers*

This is a work of fiction. Names, characters, places, and incidents are products of the author's imagination or are used fictitiously and are not to be construed as real. Any resemblance to actual events, locales, organizations, or persons, living or dead, is entirely coincidental.

First Avon Books mass market printing: April 2017

ISBN 978-0-06-265580-6

17 18 19 20 21 QGM 10 9 8 7 6 5 4 3 2 1

For my man in blue.

ACKNOWLEDGMENTS

Most grateful thanks to Tessa Woodward, Heather Martin, and everyone else at HarperCollins for all their hard work. Thank you to my agent, Rebecca Friedman, for making my dream come true. And lastly, thank you to my family for all your support and love.

CHAPTER 1

"We have to be quiet."

Her sister's voice trembled, but her bound hands were steady, pressed against Maggie's shoulder. In the darkness, Erica's touch anchored and soothed her. But it couldn't drive away the fear, thick in the back of her throat. The ropes looped around her wrists, pulled punishingly tight, rubbed her skin raw with every movement. She tried to hold back a sob, but the noise bubbled to her lips. She pressed them tight. Quiet. They had to stay quiet.

"Be calm, okay? Just stay calm, Maggie."

The girls huddled together, knees pulled up tight to their chests, as if making themselves smaller would help. The room was barely bigger than a closet, stuffy and stale as she breathed in, desperate for fresh air, for light. Anything but the endless darkness and rising heat.

"What does he want?" Maggie whispered to Erica.

"I don't know," Erica said. "We just have to wait and see."

"I want to go home." Hot tears trickled down Maggie's face when she blinked. She couldn't stop them. "What are Mom and Dad going to do without us?"

"We'll find a way out," Erica promised, cradling her as close as their bonds allowed. "It'll be okay, Mags. But we have to stay calm."

Maggie closed her eyes tightly, her heart drumming in

her chest, almost drowning out the sound of footsteps. A soft, once-harmless sound that now made her stomach twist.

He was coming.

The doorknob rattled.

Maggie whimpered, drawing closer to Erica.

He was here.

MAGGIE'S FEET POUNDED the pavement, her breath coming fast as she pushed into her fifth mile. Sweat trickled down the back of her oversized tank top as her feet struck the trail with hard-won precision. Slowing down wasn't an option, even as her lungs ached and her calves burned. In fact, the pain helped—it drove away the memories. Just for a little while, sure . . . but it was something. And she'd take a brief reprieve over nothing any day.

It was late spring, and she'd gotten up early to run, escaping the afternoon mugginess that began to set in at this time of year. The fruit trees that lined the park's running trail were in the final stages of bloom. Splashes of pink and white blossoms blurred as she sped past them.

She ran without music, alone with her thoughts. Sometimes it was a great combination.

Other times . . .

Well, everyone was running from something, she figured.

She felt a buzz against her arm and slowed to a stop, pulling the phone out of her armband. Panting, she wiped sweat off her face before looking at the screen. She'd been so wrapped up in her run that she hadn't noticed Paul had called. With more than a bit of dread and a lot of guilt, she keyed in her passcode and listened to her ex-fiancé's voice mail.

"Maggie, it's Paul. I'm just calling again about the things your left at my place before you went to Africa. I've boxed them all for you. Let me know when you want to pick them up. Or I could leave them with the doorman. Just let me know what you prefer. I . . ." He paused. "Take care," he finally said.

Maggie's stomach twisted, a spark of long-buried hurt and dread coming back to life at his hesitant, careful tone.

She shoved the phone back into her armband with a little too much force. She couldn't deal with him right now. He'd want to talk about why they broke up again, slog through the whole sorry mess. Paul was a good man and a great FBI agent, even if his by-the-book attitude sometimes frustrated her. When it came to playing by the rules, Maggie would abide by them best she could, but in a choice between rule breaking or saving a life, she'd choose the life every time—to hell with everything else.

It hadn't been right between her and Paul. She had loved him—she still loved him—but she hadn't been in love with him. It had taken her much too long to realize that, and she regretted that more than anything. But she wasn't sure he'd reached the same realization yet. She could hear a trace of hope in his voice.

He'd emailed when she'd been in Chad, working with the Clean Water Initiative to dig wells and provide better access to clean water for the people in the area. She'd emailed back a few times, but when she returned home he'd given her space, like the gentleman he was. She'd been back for almost six months now, and this was the first time he'd called.

She checked her watch. Time to head home. Turning toward the park exit, Maggie broke into a slow jog down the running trail. The scent of apple and cherry blossoms was thick in the air after last night's spring storm as she rounded the curve toward the iron gates leading out of the park. As she approached them, she saw an older man standing at the park exit waiting for her and came to an abrupt halt, her sneakers skidding on the pavement and dread coiling in her stomach like a rattlesnake. He waved in greeting, walking up to her. The dim morning sunlight shone off the bald spot on his head, and his gray suit blended with the cloudy day.

"Hey, kid," he said, smiling affectionately.

"What are you doing here, Frank?" Maggie demanded, hands on her hips. There was a time she'd never have dared speak to her mentor in that tone. But things were different now. He was no longer her boss, and her FBI days were well behind her—she'd quit more than two years ago. It wasn't as if she hadn't seen Frank since she quit the Bureau—she had. Before she left for Chad and after she came back, every month or so, he'd call her up for lunch. She'd go, and they'd talk about everything but work. It was an unspoken agreement: He wouldn't push, and she'd keep showing up for lunch.

This felt different, though. All her instincts—the ones she'd buried, the ones she ignored, the ones that had failed her—roared to life.

"Maggie, I need you to come in," he said in his gravelly voice. "A freshman girl from the Carmichael Academy's missing, and I'm putting together a team. I want the best—and you're the best, kid."

A jolt of fear surged like an electric current through her limbs. Maggie backed up, as if putting distance between them would lessen her panic. She couldn't. She *wouldn't.* Not after . . .

Just stay calm, Maggie. Her sister's voice echoed in her head.

"I meant it when I said I was out for good, Frank," she said harshly. "I'm done with negotiating, and I'm not coming back to the Bureau. Not after Sherwood Hills. Never again."

Frank's face—which had always reminded her of a bulldog—softened. "I know how hard Sherwood Hills was for you. We can't win 'em all. But this girl? We can get her back safe and sound. *If* we have your help." He reached into his pocket and pulled out a photo, pressing it into her hand. Maggie told herself not to look. Not to see the girl's face and imagine her lost or afraid. Not to worry that she was hurt—or worse. She couldn't invest in another case like this. Not again. But the photo in her hand tugged at her like a moon with its own gravitational pull. She pressed her lips together and looked down. A beaming girl clutching a lacrosse stick stared up at her, blond hair cut in thick bangs across her forehead making her look younger than fourteen.

Once upon a time, Erica had been a baby-faced fourteen. To Maggie, she was forever fourteen: ageless, frozen in time.

Would this girl become forever fourteen to *her* loved ones?

Maggie winced at the thought. Her fingers tightened on the edges of the photo, and she had to catch herself before she crumpled it.

You could help, a traitorous voice inside her whispered. She tried to block it out. Unfortunately, Frank was harder to ignore.

"Why don't you come in, just to listen?" Frank pleaded as Maggie continued to stare at the girl's face. "You can throw the team some advice if anything jumps out at you. If you want to bail, I'll have someone take you home. Favor paid. Promise."

Maggie traced the corner of the photo. "I can't," she said. What if it happened again? What if she lost control of the situation? What if this girl died too?

"Come on, kid. You owe me," Frank said softly. "I cleaned up the mess at Sherwood Hills. I didn't make a fuss when you quit on me. I've given you space, I've given you time. But now I'm calling in my favor. I need you on this. You're better than the guys they have me working with since you left."

"I'm sure whoever you chose is very good," Maggie said.

"Kid, you've got a once-in-a-lifetime kind of talent," Frank said. "They can't compare."

"But I failed," Maggie said, unable to block out the memories of Sherwood Hills. She could still hear that gunshot. It echoed in her dreams. She'd never be free of it, just like she'd never be free of that empty room that haunted her.

"You think I've never messed up?" Frank demanded with an edge to his voice. "You think I've never failed? You think all my cases ended with the victim safe and the criminal behind bars? Come on, kid," he scoffed. "I taught you better than that. But when I failed, I picked myself up and went back to my damn job because I knew it was bigger than me. This is bigger than both of us—a girl's life is at stake. Again. And I trust you—I *need* you—to guide us through. We need that special Maggie magic."

Maggie looked up at him. When she'd been a green negotiator with no field experience, he'd taken her under his wing. He'd handpicked her at Quantico. He'd seen her potential and nurtured it. He'd trained and mentored her. He'd helped make her great at her job. It wasn't his fault that she'd screwed up so badly. And it wasn't this girl's fault either.

Dammit. She was stuck between a rock and a hard place. She owed him. Not just for cleaning up the mess she left behind, but because he'd played a huge part in making her *her*.

"Okay," she said reluctantly. After all, she could leave at any time. The second it got too hard, she was out. "But just to observe. I'm not taking the lead, and I'm not coming back to the Bureau. This is an unofficial favor."

"As long as I can use your expertise, you're as unofficial as you like," Frank said, his craggy face breaking into a big, warm grin. He gestured toward the iron gates. "Let's get going."

Maggie took a deep breath and followed Frank through the gates and out of the park, trying to ignore the faint sensation of rope tightening around her wrists.

CHAPTER 2

Four hours earlier . . .

Jake jerked awake, staring up at the ceiling. Every muscle in his body was tense, ready to explode into action. He counted two heartbeats, his breath coming slow and steady as his eyes adjusted to the darkness. He didn't reach for the Glock in its holster on his bedside table—he wasn't the kind of man who pulled his gun unless he meant to shoot.

Instead, he rolled out of bed, his fingers curling into fists. Not as deadly as a gun—most of the time. It depended on how pissed—or how desperate—he was.

Something had yanked him out of sleep. A sound? He craned his neck, listening for the noise. Then he heard it: the crunch of footsteps on gravel.

Someone was there.

He checked his watch. It was two a.m. That meant bad news.

Clearly, his vacation was over.

Jake grabbed a pair of pants, fastening the Glock in its holster onto his hip. Pulling on a t-shirt, he was halfway down the stairs before the knocking started.

He opened the door to find General Hoffman, his military handler. The tall man had salt-and-pepper hair and deceptively kind eyes. Looks aside, he was a hard son of a bitch whose recruits were unfailingly loyal to him. Just because he was tough didn't mean he wasn't fair.

The general had been more than fair to Jake, even though, three years ago, their partnership had started off a little rocky. The last thing Jake had wanted was to be taken out of the action and corralled into some desk job or, worse, be trotted out for events in his dress uniform, medals on full display for everyone to see.

Instead, he'd been handed a unique opportunity. The Rangers had prepared him for almost anything, and his work in the Middle East had given him valuable knowledge of the players there and in DC. So the Army took him out of the war zone and put him to work on DC's more . . . sensitive problems. From money laundering to blackmail to kinks he didn't even know existed, his last three years in DC had been interesting, to say the least. But in his heart, he was still a soldier—and with one foot in civilian life and the other in the military, life was a balancing act he was still trying to figure out.

Serving your country comes in many forms, the general had told him when he'd handed him his first assignment. *You're good at this, O'Connor.*

And that was true. Jake was good—in fact, he was the best. Discreet and efficient, he had gained a reputation for getting difficult things done right the first time around with little fuss.

If he wanted them to send him back to the desert, he probably should have done a crappier job, he thought with a bitter smile as he squared his shoulders and snapped a salute.

"General," Jake said. "Good morning, sir."

General Hoffman nodded, stepping farther out on the porch. Jake followed, arms at his sides, waiting.

"We've got a situation," the general said. "I've just received word that Senator Thebes' daughter is missing."

Jake frowned. "How long has she been gone?"

"They're not quite sure," Hoffman replied. "There seems to be some confusion as to where she was supposed to be after school. The parents thought she was staying overnight with a student who boards there. Her friend thought she'd gone home. All we know is she left school, but she never made it to lacrosse practice."

"Shit, that's almost twelve hours already," Jake said.

"Which is why I'd like you to step in to assist the senator," General Hoffman said. "His security is decent, but they're not equipped to handle what's to come."

Jake rubbed at his chin, his fingers catching against his stubble. "So what are we thinking? Ransom demand within the next six hours?"

"That's my take," the general said grimly. "The FBI's been alerted, of course."

"Just what I need—a bunch of suits messing things up," Jake said, shaking his head.

Hoffman's stern face broke into a ghost of a smile. "You'll play nice, O'Connor. That's an order."

"They're a pain in the ass, and you know it," Jake said. "But I'll play nice. Give me ten minutes."

The general nodded. "I'll be waiting outside."

Jake hurried back into his house, getting dressed quickly. Gone were the days of weather-worn fatigues and pounds of sand in his combat boots. Nowadays, he wore Armani and Hugo Boss. It helped to fit in with the security details surrounding the men he worked with these days, but most of the time, he'd be happy to trade the monkey suit for seventy pounds of gear on his back.

After straightening his tie, he tucked a knife into one boot—he refused to wear those shiny, slick dress shoes with no tread; screw fashion—and slipped a .380 Beretta, so small it looked like a toy, into the holster on his left ankle. His Glock stayed on his hip, with two extra clips in his inner jacket pocket.

No matter where he was, how he was dressed, or who he was looking for, he was a soldier first and foremost. And that meant being prepared for anything.

Hoffman was waiting on the curb with two SUVs. Jake got into the first one, and the general handed him a file.

"Read it over, and tell me what you think," he said as they made their way through the night. This time of night, there was less traffic—but the city never really slept.

Jake flipped through the file, landing on a paper listing the senator's possible enemies. "You sure this is about him?" he asked. "The mom—his wife—she's old money. She's a Rockwell—practically American royalty."

"We can't know for sure until a ransom for Kayla is issued," Hoffman explained. "From what Peggy could pull on Mrs. Thebes, though, she seems harmless. No known enemies. She's well liked in her circles . . . on the Children's Cancer Society's board, and she instituted an award-winning equine therapy program for at-risk youth."

"Does the kid work with her on that?" Jake asked, shifting through the file, trying to find the info. He paused at a photo of Kayla—God, she couldn't be more than fifteen. She looked impossibly young, beaming up at the camera, her blond hair like a halo around her face. He could taste a familiar bitterness in the back of his throat. He hated cases with kids. There was so much at risk.

"I think so, yes," the general said.

"I wouldn't rule out the wife as the ransom target," Jake said. "Not this early."

"You think some juvenile delinquent kidnapped the girl?" Hoffman asked, skepticism laced through his voice.

"I think we don't know a whole lot, and focusing on one parent over the other is a bad idea this early in the game."

"Logic says they're after the father. He has all the power and prestige—he's a senator. And he's running for reelection next year."

Jake scanned the list of the senator's known enemies. "I see his opponent is at the top of this list," he said.

General Hoffman's eyebrows drew together in a dark line. "Politics is a dirty game, son."

"Don't I know it," Jake said.

After all, political optics were the whole reason he was working a cushy assignment dealing with . . . unique situations among the DC elite instead of leading a team of Rangers, like he'd been trained to do.

Fate's tricky like that.

A STRING OF SUVs was already parked in front of the senator's mansion as they headed through the gates and down the driveway.

"Looks like the Feds are here," Jake said as the general slowed to a stop behind a car with government plates. He swung out, and the two men walked up the steps.

"Frank Edenhurst will be running the show with the Feds," the general said. "He's a smart guy. Impress him, and he won't get in your way."

"Got it," Jake nodded.

"And don't spook the parents—the mother's hysterical, supposedly."

Jake raised an eyebrow. "Wouldn't you be?" he asked.

Hoffman sighed. "There's a reason I didn't have kids, O'Connor. Now let's get to work." He reached out and rang the doorbell.

Jake straightened his suit, and the door swung open.

Time to enter the fray, Jake thought. He pasted a calm, controlled expression on his face and stepped inside the mansion.

CHAPTER 3

Frank's car was black and nondescript on the outside, all luxury on the inside. Maggie settled herself in the plush leather seat, suddenly aware that she hadn't showered or changed. Her t-shirt was sweaty, but she knew better than to ask Frank to make a stop at her place. Time was crucial.

Uncomfortable, she shifted in the seat as Frank started the car, pulling into the early morning traffic. Falls Church wasn't large by any means, but it was close enough to DC to house the political elite in search of a quieter family life. The bumper-to-bumper commute was considered a fair price to pay for the privacy the quaint town afforded.

Frank let her have a few minutes of silence as they drove—and Maggie was grateful for it. She needed to collect herself, so she stared out the window. Falls Church was postcard charming, with beautiful colonial architecture and dozens of shops, bistros, and charities to keep the politicians' better halves occupied. The elite private schools housed Yale and Harvard's future students—and the country's future politicians and CEOs. If you lived here, you were either someone with power or a member of their family. The kidnapped girl attended the Carmichael Academy, so she was definitely the child of some bigwig. That could make the case easier—or much, much harder. Powerful people had connections, but they also tended to have secrets to protect. From affairs, blackmail, and gambling debts to underhanded business deals, Maggie had seen enough lying to last her a lifetime.

"Your purse and coat are in the back seat," Frank said.

Maggie turned to look. Sure enough, her leather satchel was sitting on top of her peacoat, the engraved brass buttons gleaming against the rich crimson wool.

"You broke into my car?"

"Just a little," Frank said. "Gotta keep my skills sharp."

Maggie rolled her eyes. Frank's fondness for lockpicking and safecracking was legendary at the Bureau. "You could've at least brought my go-bag from the trunk," she muttered. Wearing jogging clothes in the tension-filled environment that was a hostage negotiation was not ideal. In fact, she was pretty sure she'd had a nightmare like that before.

"You still keep a go-bag packed?" Frank asked. "You *sure* you don't want to come back?"

"Don't read anything into it," Maggie ordered, folding her arms across her chest. Dammit, she never should have mentioned it. "It's just a habit. So . . . why don't we talk details?" she said, concentrating on the wood-grain dashboard instead of looking at Frank. It was so polished she could practically see her reflection in it. "What are we dealing with? What's the time frame so far?"

"Her name is Kayla; she's fourteen. Parents thought she was staying the night at school—about half of the kids who go there are boarders. But around midnight last night, they realized she wasn't at school. The friend she said she was staying with in the dorms doesn't know anything—or at least, she's not talking."

"Are you sure it's a kidnapping?" Maggie asked. "Have you been contacted about a ransom? Do you have video of an abduction? Witnesses? Why isn't this being treated as a runaway case?"

"Kayla is Kayla Thebes," Frank said.

That made Maggie look up and concentrate on Frank for the first time.

"As in *Senator* Thebes?" Well, that certainly upped the

stakes. The senator's reach was long and powerful. Quite a few people wanted him to consider a presidential run in the future, and he had a chance at the nomination if he played his cards right. He was handsome, charismatic, happily married, and had served in the Senate since taking over his late father's seat in his early thirties.

If it got out, this case was big news.

"Yep. *That* Thebes," Frank said. "By all accounts, Kayla's a good, obedient kid. Doesn't fit the runaway profile. Add in the fact that she's a senator's daughter—"

"And it'd be risky to treat it as anything other than a kidnapping," Maggie said.

Frank grinned at her. "Back to finishing my sentences, kid? Just like old times."

Maggie shot him a look. "I'm coming to observe, Frank," she reminded him. "It's just a favor—not a way to get me back working for the Bureau."

I don't want to disappoint you again, she thought.

"Whatever you say." He waved off her protest, turning onto a sycamore-lined street and taking a sharp right into a gated driveway. A man in a suit was standing outside it, and when Frank flashed his credentials, he spoke into his radio, and the spiked wrought-iron gate creaked open. The driveway was long and curving, the senator's mansion coming into sight around the final turn. A luxury estate with massive marble columns standing sentry in front, it was both classical and timeless, the many gabled windows glittering in the rising sun. The expansive green lawn was pristine, bordered by neatly manicured topiary spheres lining the front walk. A few black SUVs were parked outside—the kind the local PD and FBI like to use when they don't want to call attention to themselves. Frank pulled up behind one, and Maggie unbuckled her seat belt, getting out of the car. She tried the best she could to hide the way her legs trembled, and she clenched her fists, counting to five before turning to close the car door. Running a hand over her hair, she tried to smooth the unruly curls that had started to frizz up out of her braids.

"You look fine, kid," Frank assured her brusquely. "Let's go."

Maggie took a deep breath, and they walked up the marble steps to the entrance in silence, but as soon as the ornately carved front doors of the mansion opened and they walked down the foyer into the entrance hall, she found herself in the middle of chaos.

Police swarmed around the room, clogging the double staircase leading to the family's living quarters upstairs. FBI suits milled about, half of them on cell phones, the other half grouped together, their heads bent and faces grim as they discussed options. Security, their sunglasses off for once, hurried in and out of the room, talking urgently into their sleeves. Maggie caught snatches of coded language through the crackles of radios. One FBI agent was sweating profusely, arguing on the phone with someone as a police officer tapped him on the shoulder, trying to get his attention.

Maggie looked over at Frank, and he nodded his permission. This was her favorite thing about him—his ability to silently understand her without a word. She wanted to see Kayla's room without interference or influence. She needed to get a feel for the girl before she started asking the family questions and they clouded her impressions. Teen girls were notoriously secretive, but one of the best places to get a glimpse of Kayla's inner life would be her bedroom.

Maggie headed for the double staircase and slipped upstairs into a long hall, leaving the noise and rising tension behind. Someone had to control the situation downstairs. That kind of frenzy was just going to stress the family out and make them question law enforcement's ability to handle the situation.

This isn't your case, she told herself firmly as she focused on the hallway in front of her. Photographs in antique frames lined the wall, many in black-and-white, depicting what looked like a very happy family. It was practically a timeline of Kayla's life, from a blue-eyed baby with cornsilk hair asleep on a bearskin rug, to a wobbly toddler taking her first steps into her mother's waiting arms, to a grinning kindergartener in a miniature school uniform, her plaid tie askew. There she was as a middle schooler playing lacrosse with her father, her ponytail flying behind her . . . riding horses as a teenager with her mother in muddy knee-high boots, waving at the camera.

Maggie opened a few doors before she found what had to be Kayla's room. The walls were painted a soft blue, and her bedroom window was still half-open, the ruffled ombré curtains moving slightly in the breeze. A heart-shaped collage of photos—not nearly as polished or professional as the ones in the hallway—hung over her bed, where a huge stuffed tiger was lying between two silver tasseled pillows. Maggie stepped up to the collage, examining it closely. Typical teen stuff: selfies at various places, snapshots of Kayla and a brunette girl wearing a little too much eye makeup, Kayla with her lacrosse teammates, Kayla at summer camp, Kayla hugging the neck of a beautiful chestnut mare, a few of Kayla and boys, but most of them with her girlfriends.

Maggie moved deeper into the room, opening the mirrored closet doors dotted with little Post-it reminders like "Dinner w/ Mom on Wed" and "Stable—clean out Star's stall/6 a.m." She rummaged through Kayla's clothes—a mix of designer jeans, casual tops, dresses, and school uniforms—and bent down to flip open a few shoeboxes stuffed in the back of the closet, but they contained only more photos and trinkets—the normal things you'd find in any teen girl's room. In fact, Kayla seemed to be on the innocent side, Maggie thought cynically. There weren't even any hidden birth control packs or condoms. No love letters or notes either—though she was sure times had changed since her own teen years. They probably did everything online or through phones these days.

She rose from her knees and walked over to Kayla's desk, which was more a vanity than a study center. Lipsticks, blushers, and eye-shadow pots were strewn everywhere, covering the stack of notebooks and textbooks for school.

There was a space for a laptop next to the mason jar full of pens and makeup brushes, but it was missing. The FBI probably already had their techs going through it for clues.

Maybe Kayla had been lured away by the kidnapper online, not knowing she was heading into a trap. Fourteen is a dangerous age for a girl—old enough to attract unwanted attention, yet young enough to be easily tricked into trusting the wrong person. Had some adult won her trust only to betray it in the worst way? What was their aim? It had to be something to do with the senator or his wealth. It was too coincidental otherwise, a senator's daughter getting kidnapped for any other reason.

A floorboard creaked behind her. Maggie whirled, her hand going to her hip to a gun that wasn't holstered there—and hadn't been for years.

Some habits are hard to break.

A man was standing in the doorway—not even standing; no, he was *slouching* in the doorway, leaning against the doorjamb like a sheriff in an Old West saloon. His hair was jet-black and parted neatly on the side, but his green eyes simmered with a dangerous, intriguing energy. He was tall and broad shouldered—and entirely too relaxed, given the situation.

He was also possibly the most attractive man Maggie had ever seen in her life, but that certainly wasn't going to sway her.

"Can I help you?" she asked, an edge in her voice.

"I was just about to ask you the same thing," he said. "What are you doing up here?"

Maggie raised an eyebrow. "Are you FBI?"

He shook his head. "I'm advising Senator Thebes on security."

Was he from the private sector? Just what she needed—an overpaid Neanderthal getting in her way. Maggie bit her lip, frustration mounting inside her. Guys like this just made trouble for her. They were almost always all about going in hot instead of trying to defuse the situation as much as possible.

"If you're not FBI, I don't have to answer your question," she said coolly. "FBI has jurisdiction in this case."

"Are *you* FBI?" he asked. "I don't see a badge. You guys usually love flashing your badges."

Maggie gritted her teeth. She could still feel the absence on her belt, the weight that should be there, her credentials that she'd worked so hard for—and walked away from.

"I guess you'll have to find out," she said, brushing past him in the doorway, ignoring the electric prickle that went down her spine as they touched.

"Looking forward to it," he drawled behind her, not moving from his place in the doorway.

She shot him an irritated look over her shoulder, hating that she couldn't resist one more look at him. He was still standing there, all loose and grinning at her as if they were in on a joke together.

Who in the world was he? She didn't remember him, and she thought she knew all the major players in the private security sector. Senator Thebes would only hire the best—so why didn't she recognize him?

She knew things would have changed in the years since she left the FBI, but it was odd to feel so out of place. She took a deep breath, pausing at the top of the stairs to gather herself. She needed to put her game face on. She was about to walk into a situation that had already had more than twelve hours to spiral into panic and chaos. She would need to take control. Immediately.

After a few deep breaths, Maggie put the man upstairs out of her mind and walked back downstairs, where Frank was waiting at the landing.

"Anything pop out at you?" he asked in an undertone.

"Seems like a nice girl. Sporty. Likes makeup. Closer to her mom than her dad, if the collage in her room is any indication, but that's pretty typical, especially for an only child," Maggie replied. "No boyfriend, unless she's keeping him from the parents."

"How likely is that?" Frank asked earnestly.

Maggie had to smile; sometimes she forgot Frank had

never had children. Teen girls were probably as much of a mystery to him as astrophysics was to her. "Well, she's a teenage girl, and she's pretty. And there's nothing like forbidden young love."

Frank shook his head. "Kids these days."

"You tell 'em, Grandpa," Maggie said sarcastically. "Are you going to take me to the senator?"

"This way." Frank led her through the entrance hall into a smaller one off the marble foyer that was richly furnished in dark blues and greens. The entire north wall of the room was a floor-to-ceiling barrister bookcase, with glass protecting what looked like a comprehensive collection of legal texts. In front of the book wall was a mahogany desk and a well-worn leather chair.

When Frank closed the door behind them, the senator, a tall man with silver hair and a strong jaw, turned from the bay window, looking troubled.

"Frank," he said, relief on his tired face. "You're back." His gaze flicked to Maggie, and he frowned a little as if he was confused. Maggie tugged at the hem of her shirt, shifting from foot to foot. What if he dismissed her because she looked like she'd just rolled out of bed?

"I brought someone to meet you," Frank said. "Maggie Kincaid, this is Senator Thebes."

"It's nice to meet you," the senator said, holding out his hand.

Maggie shook it. "I apologize for my appearance," she said. "Frank caught me when I was out running, and when he filled me in on the situation, we felt it was best to get here as soon as possible."

"Of course," the senator said. "I'm sorry, I'm not sure what you do . . ."

"I trained Maggie, Senator," Frank said. "She was my protégé, though I'd say the student has surpassed the master at this point. She's graciously offered to lend a hand."

"Thank you," the senator said, looking at her with a tight smile. "Any help we can get . . ." He trailed off. "Kayla's our world," he blurted out, an edge of panic shaking his voice. "We need her back. Her mother needs her back."

"I understand," Maggie said. "Can you sit with me?" She gestured to the two oak-and-velvet armchairs near the fireplace.

He nodded, taking a seat. Maggie did as well and smiled at him—not too broadly, but with some warmth. Handling the relatives and friends of victims had always been harder for her than negotiating with the kidnappers. She had to stay in control for the loved ones because everything else in their lives was suddenly so wildly out of control. She was the touchstone.

It was a lot to live up to. A lot for someone to be. That was why Sherwood Hills had hit her so hard. It was the main reason she'd left the Bureau—the emotional toll was too great. It had taken pieces from her, pieces she wasn't sure she'd ever get back. Pieces she wasn't sure she could sacrifice anymore. Yet here she was, right back where she'd told herself she'd never be again.

You can leave at any time, she told herself firmly. She pulled a pen and notebook out of her purse, flipping it open in case she needed to write something down.

"I'm going to ask you some questions about Kayla," she said, waiting a moment for the senator to gather his thoughts. "Is she a happy girl? Have you heard about any trouble at school? Maybe with one of her girlfriends? Or a boy?"

"Kayla's very happy," Thebes said. "She has so many friends. Everyone loves her at school, at the stables, on her lacrosse team. She was voted MVP last year. We were so proud."

"What about boys?" Maggie asked. "Does she have a boyfriend?"

The senator shook his head. "There've been boys in the past, of course. She's a pretty girl, like her mother. But there hasn't been anyone serious yet—at least, not that I know of. You know how teen girls are," he said. "She probably wouldn't want to share anything too personal with her old dad. It isn't cool."

Maggie was about to ask about Kayla's regular schedule when the door opened, and a beautiful woman with thick blond hair pulled into a French twist came into the room. A wave of Chanel No. 5 tickled Maggie's nose as the senator got up and hurried over to his wife, whose blue eyes were glimmering with tears. "I've called all her friends," she said to him, her voice rising in near panic. "Nobody's heard from her. Oh, God, Jonathan—what if she has an attack?"

Maggie rose from her chair. "What do you mean, an attack?"

"Kayla's diabetic," the senator explained. "She's insulin dependent."

"It's usually very manageable," Mrs. Thebes said through her tears, turning to Maggie with a forced smile. "She's always been so good at dealing with it. She's never let it hold her back. But this kind of stress? Even if she has her regular shots, she could go into shock. And if she doesn't have her insulin?" Mrs. Thebes shuddered, her shoulders shaking underneath her cream blouse, unable to utter the answer as she began to weep into her husband's shoulder.

"Without her insulin, she could go into a coma," the senator said softly, holding his wife tight, as if to shield her from his words. "She could die."

Mrs. Thebes cried harder, sagging against her husband.

Maggie stepped back, moving to look out the window, trying to give them some privacy.

Talking to the families was always a reminder—a reminder of what her own parents had gone through, a reminder of her sister never coming home, of those ropes tight around Maggie's wrists. These tense personal encounters had always been the hardest part of her job: raw, agonized emotion, pouring out at her. But being a great negotiator was about separating yourself from emotion. Being the calm in the storm. The guiding light at the end of the tunnel.

She needed to stay in control if she had any hope of helping anyone.

There was a knock at the door, and an agent poked his head in. "Agent Edenhurst, we're all set up in the library."

Frank, who had stationed himself near the door, nodded, motioning to Maggie.

"Senator, Mrs. Thebes, we should go into the other room. To wait for a phone call."

"Of course," the senator said. With Mrs. Thebes still gripping his arm as if it were her lifeline, he led her through the door and down the hall, into the library, where floor-to-ceiling oak bookcases filled with antique books and curios lined the walls. Hanging above the fireplace was an oil portrait of Mrs. Thebes in her younger years, her blue eyes enigmatic and her smile teasing as she posed in a garden of night-blooming jasmine. Kayla looked just like her mother.

Agents buzzed around the room like bees at a hive. Laptops were set up on a folding table with techs pounding on them, ready to trace any call that came in. Field agents were tensed, waiting for the phone to ring. Until then, there was nothing they could do but wait. And when what you do best is action, waiting is agony.

Maggie caught sight of a head of auburn curls, and frowned. No . . . it couldn't be . . . But it was. *Jackson Dutton* was the best Frank could do? On a case like this, with its potential to become so high profile? Jackson Dutton was a third-rate negotiator; way too tightly wound. They'd been in the same class at Quantico and had worked together a few times after graduating. Maggie had spent most of their training wondering when he'd snap. And in her third year of working for the Bureau, she'd been there when he'd lost his temper during a fifteen-hour standoff, yelling at the victim's abusive boyfriend who was holding a gun to her head, which unnerved the man so much that he nearly pulled the trigger. After that, Maggie had never trusted him. She didn't like abusive men either, of course, but negotiating couldn't be about the negotiator's feelings. The moment that feelings get involved, the more dangerous it becomes for the hostage.

She knew that all too well.

What in the world was Frank thinking by bringing Jackson in? Maggie turned to go and ask him just that, but instead she collided with a broad chest. Caught by surprise, she rocked back, almost losing her balance. A hand shot out, steadying her.

"Easy," said a deep voice.

She looked up, and the warmth that surged through her when their eyes met made her catch her breath. There he was again—the man from upstairs. His eyes crinkled as he flashed her a smile.

"You okay?" he asked, with a hint of a twang.

Maggie nodded.

"Seems like you and I keep running into each other," he said. He looked over her shoulder at Frank and the senator talking together. "So you *are* FBI. Let me guess . . . shrink? One of those behavioral analysts who catches serial killers?"

"Hostage negotiator," Maggie said.

He whistled, and she couldn't tell if he was impressed or sarcastic. She felt unsteady, like the floor beneath her was being dragged away. She couldn't quite read him—and it made her nervous. "That's a big job," he said.

"For such a little woman?" she asked, her eyebrow arched sarcastically. She'd heard it before, countless times.

But instead of a sneer or male posturing, there it was again: that killer, crooked smile that tilted his lips with such charm. Her stomach flipped.

"In my experience, underestimating a woman—of any size—who works in law enforcement is a really bad idea," he said. "They tend to be the kind of women who can ruin a man—in good ways and bad."

He'd surprised her—this mystery man whose name she had yet to discover—maybe hidden depths lay beneath the macho cowboy exterior. She hadn't been surprised by a man in a long time. Something sparked in her, and her heart picked up, fluttering in her chest.

She needed to say something, not just stand there staring at him like an idiot. She opened her mouth, but before she could reply, the library phone on the desk rang.

Maggie's head snapped toward the sound, her whole

body stiffening. Everyone in the room froze, the chatter coming to an abrupt stop, like a record cut off midsong. Every eye focused on the phone, waiting as it rang again.

The flash of warmth she'd felt down to her toes vanished as Maggie moved forward, just two steps, a compulsive movement she couldn't stop. She forced herself to stop, to hold back. She needed to *think*, not react.

"Okay, everyone," Frank's gruff voice rang out with authority, breaking the silence. "It's showtime. Keep a lid on it. Start tracing as soon as the line's picked up. Senator, come on over here. You're going to answer like we talked about, okay?"

Mrs. Thebes made a small noise in the back of her throat, sinking into a chair as the senator strode over to the desk, trying to look confident.

"Just like we talked about," Frank repeated soothingly. "Calm. No attacks. Let him lead. Let him talk as much as he wants. No interruptions. Let him tell us what he wants."

The senator's hands shook as he picked up the phone, his voice unsteady as he said, "Hello?"

Silence.

Thebes looked at Frank desperately, who made a "go on" gesture.

"Do you . . . do you have my daughter?"

Silence again. The senator looked desperately at Frank, and Mrs. Thebes pressed her fist against her lips, trying to stifle her sobs.

"Please, just . . . tell me what you want. I need my baby girl back."

Maggie's fingers twitched as the silence stretched through the room again. She wanted to reach out, grab the phone, and take charge. Get whoever was on the other side of the call to talk. She knew she could do it.

She could always get them talking.

Then, a computerized voice rang out into the room: "I know you're not alone, Senator. I want to speak to whoever's in charge."

Maggie's stomach tightened as she looked over at Jackson Dutton, who stepped forward. Frank held out a hand, stopping him, and gestured to Maggie, his eyebrows raised in a silent question.

Maggie hesitated. If she took the phone from the senator, that was it. There'd be no turning back. She'd be in it for the long haul, until the very end—however messy or deadly that end was. She would become the point of contact—the lone voice that could bring the kidnapper to justice and get Kayla back safe and sound.

Was she even any better than Jackson? He'd let emotions bleed in the last time she'd worked with him, but she'd done the same thing at Sherwood Hills. She hadn't managed to be calm or objective then—and look what had happened.

Was she ready for this? Would she ever be?

Could she live with the risk of failing again? But if she turned around and left now, could she live with the knowledge that she was tossing Kayla Thebes' fate to a shaky negotiator with a temper problem?

Frank snapped his fingers.

Maggie glanced over at Jackson once more. Annoyance played across his face, his ego obviously bruised by Frank so blatantly favoring Maggie in front of everyone. He'd be unfocused and hurt the entire time he talked to the kidnapper. He might snap again.

She couldn't let that happen. She was going to have to be better. Better than him *and* better than the person she'd been at Sherwood Hills.

She took a deep breath and strode over to the desk, holding out her hand for the phone.

The senator gave it to her, and with a firm, steady grip, she raised it to her ear.

"This is Maggie Kincaid speaking," she said. "I'm in charge."

CHAPTER 4

Hello, Maggie," said the kidnapper, the voice so digitized that it was impossible to identify anything—gender, age, or accent.

"Can I ask who's speaking?" she asked. Build familiarity first. It helps establish a bond.

There was a pause. "You can call me Uncle Sam," said the kidnapper.

Great. A grandiose self-image. Never good when it comes to hostage negotiation. Those types are liable to end it in a spray of bullets if they don't get their way.

"It's nice to meet you, Sam," she said. "I'm wondering if Kayla is okay. I'd really like to talk to her."

"Kayla is indisposed at the moment," Uncle Sam said.

Mrs. Thebes sat straight up at that, looking worriedly at her husband.

"What does that mean, exactly?" Maggie asked. "Is she hurt?"

"She's a little tied up," Uncle Sam said, and Maggie frowned. Was that an attempt at humor? Who *was* this guy? What did he want?

"Has Kayla had her insulin? You know she needs it, right? I'm sure you do, Sam. You seem to have put a lot of thought into this." She decided that with the ego he seemed to be displaying, the flattery route would be the best way to establish trust. He might be the type to look down on her because she was a woman. It was pretty damn common, really.

She'd lost track of the times that male unsubs—the FBI's term for an unknown criminal subject—underestimating her smarts had helped her in a case.

"You won't be able to trace me," Sam said. "Don't bother trying. I know all about Kayla's little insulin problem, rest assured. She's being taken care of—for now. And I'm sending proof of life to the senator's cell phone."

Maggie hit the mute button so the kidnapper couldn't hear them and looked over to the senator, whose phone began to buzz in his pocket. He pulled it out, his mouth tightening to a thin line as he held it out to Maggie. Kayla looking pale and scared, her bangs plastered to her forehead with sweat, her hands cuffed, was holding that morning's edition of the local newspaper. Mrs. Thebes rushed over, but as soon as she caught sight of her daughter, bound and clearly terrified in the photo, she sank backward, nearly falling. One of the cops rushed forward, supporting her. "Mrs. Thebes, maybe you should go lie down," he suggested gently.

She shook her head. "That's my little girl!" she whispered, straightening in the cop's hold, grim resolve settling across her pretty face.

Maggie stared down at the photo, tapping her fingers against her collarbone, one of the stupid nervous tics she'd never been able to shake. She was running out of time; the kidnapper would expect a response soon. This person was smart, with an ego. Someone who expected her to play by his rules. She could play along—for a while. Feed his ego, let him get really comfortable with his supposed superiority before yanking the rug out from underneath him. It might work.

Or it might not. Maggie took a deep breath. Instead, she could throw him totally off-kilter, putting him on the defensive immediately, scrambling, so he'd make a mistake.

Otherwise, he might not make any mistakes. This guy had thought things through. He'd kidnapped a high-risk target with a high-risk illness. While Kayla's diabetes could definitely work in his favor by motivating her parents to give him whatever he wanted, it also was a huge gamble to kidnap a girl who might go into a coma or die if you didn't get her the right dosage at the right time.

Maggie had made up her mind: It was time to change the game.

She hit the mute button on the phone, turning the sound back on.

"I just got the photo, Sam," she said. "Thank you for sending it."

"You're wel—" he started.

"There's just one problem," Maggie interrupted. "That photo isn't going to work for me. It could easily be Photoshopped, and we really don't have time for the FBI techs to analyze it, do we? We both want this over in a timely manner, I'm sure. So I'm going to need you to send me something else, just so we're all comfortable and sure Kayla's there with you. I want you to send me a video file of Kayla reading the first page of *Crime and Punishment*."

"You aren't in control here, Maggie," said the kidnapper. "I have the girl. I've given you proof. Now it's time for *you* to give *me* something. I know how you people work."

Maggie ignored the fact that everyone in the room—agents, cops, the Thebeses, Frank—was staring at her, waiting for her to cave. "Your proof isn't good enough, Sam," she said. "Send me the video. Until you do, this conversation's over."

Before the kidnapper could protest or bargain, she hung up the phone.

"What in the hell are you doing?!" The senator loomed above her, filling her space with his fury. Maggie stood her ground, because retreating wasn't an option with a man like him. His eyes glowering, he turned to Frank. "Edenhurst, you said she was *good* at her job. She's supposed to keep the psycho calm, not antagonize him!"

"Senator, please," Frank said, grabbing his arm and pulling him away from Maggie. She breathed a little easier as soon as he was out of her space. "Maggie knows how to handle unsubs. You need to trust her judgment."

"This is insanity!" Jackson Dutton jumped in. Of course

he did. Maggie glared at him, forcing herself to take a deep breath before she did something rash. "She's making bad decisions already. What if the guy decides to just slit the kid's throat?"

Mrs. Thebes whimpered, grabbing the arm of her chair tightly, her perfectly manicured nails digging into the expensive wood.

"Dutton, shut up!" Maggie snapped. "I needed to shake things up. This person, whoever it is, has thought this out. He's prepared. He's miles ahead of us. He's prepared for this for who knows how long. We needed time to catch up—now we have it. I got it for us. You two—" she pointed at a couple of agents standing near the cherrywood bar at the far side of the library "—search the house for anything that might be missing."

"Dutton!" She snapped her fingers at Jackson. He wasn't the greatest negotiator, but she knew he was good with families. "Question the family and staff again, find out if anything unusual has happened recently. Amy—" she singled out one of the few female agents in the room "—go with Dutton."

Next she turned to the short, stocky man standing next to Jackson. "Matt, I need you to go to Reed Park." She handed him her keys. "My car is parked in the north lot. Drive it to Kayla's school. I'll take one of the FBI SUV's. I'm going to have a little talk with her friends."

"What if he calls back while you're gone?" asked a tech.

"Then you forward the call to my cell phone and record everything," Maggie said.

For a long moment, everyone in the room hesitated, all eyes zeroed in on Frank, waiting. Maggie found herself looking at him as well, almost in supplication. She needed him to have her back. She was right about this—she was sure of it. She could barely breathe as she waited—what was she going to do if he didn't support her call?

Frank gave her a long look, and then suddenly clapped his hands. "You heard her—so get to it!" he barked to the agents. "Kincaid is lead on this. You do what she says—right away."

A flurry of activity rippled through the room as the agents ran to do Maggie's bidding. She watched them hurry through the door, out of the library, Jackson scowling as he left.

"You really want to be the one to go question the kids at the school?" Frank asked her in an undertone. "I can send someone else so you can stay here to field the calls."

Maggie shook her head. There were a lot of negotiators who preferred to stick to home base, glued to the phone and the techs who monitored every call. They sent agents out to do the legwork of the case while they focused on waiting for the next call. While she appreciated this school of thought, it had never been her style. Especially when technology allowed her to negotiate from anywhere if need be.

She liked to get her hands in the muck of the case, in the minutiae of the victim's—and the unsub's—life and mind. The only way to do that when time was limited was by putting shoes on the ground.

"If he abducted her from the school, I need to get a feel for the space. And if it was someone she knew, there is no one who'd know more about a teenaged girl's life than her friends. I'm pretty sure I can make it back before he calls again. This guy's on his schedule, not ours. He won't call back until he's good and ready."

"He'll probably make us wait for it," Frank growled. "Show he's in charge."

"He seems the type," Maggie said. "I'll be right back," she told Frank. Before he could protest, she'd hurried away through the door, which she closed behind her.

The foyer was empty and blessedly quiet. The only sound was her breath, and she hated how quick it came. How fast her heart was beating.

She looked down, realizing she was rubbing her wrists, the phantom feeling of tightening rope building with each breath. When the sound of a floorboard creaking spiked her childhood fear, she froze. She couldn't stop her knee-jerk reaction to reach for her weapon—but one no longer sat holstered to her hip.

"You're making a big mistake," a voice said behind her.

CHAPTER 5

Maggie turned around, a glare already twisting her face.

There he was again. The senator's security expert. Mr. Tall, Dark, and Handsome. Irritation flared through her. She'd made it clear she was in charge, but here he was, already questioning her.

Typical.

His beautifully cut suit did nothing to hide the bulk of his muscles. His brilliant green eyes and dark hair gleamed in a stunning contrast that caught a woman's eye. This close, with no distractions, she saw that his nose was just a little crooked, like it'd been broken and badly reset. Instead of marring his looks, it added to them . . . just the suggestion of danger, of roughness. Coupled with the smooth, low voice that carried that hint of twang, and most women would be weak in the knees. A rugged type. If she was a betting woman, she'd put her money on him having a pair of well-worn cowboy boots in his closet. The thought shouldn't be so appealing—or so sexy—but it was.

Maggie barely resisted the urge to pull on her jacket to hide her running clothes and run a hand through her hair. Her blond curls were French-braided into pigtails, of all things. It was the best way to keep her hair tidy during a run, but she couldn't deny that it looked ridiculous in this context. She should have made Frank stop at her house to change—but then she would have missed Uncle Sam's first call.

Her chin tilted up. Ignoring the tightening in her stomach that had nothing to do with the stress of the case and everything to do with how well he filled out that suit, she looked him up and down. "And what mistake would that be?" she demanded, trying to muster an icy tone to mask her embarrassment—and her attraction.

"Every hour that goes by, there's a greater chance of something going wrong," he said. "Especially with Kayla's diabetes. The kidnapper could panic and react. Badly. You don't need to play power games with this guy or go interview her teenybopper friends about boy bands and lipstick. What you need to do is arrange a ransom drop as soon as you can, and then send me in solo to handle it. This ain't a tea party, Goldilocks."

Well, there went that burst of attraction. Maggie drew herself up to her full five foot three and stared him dead in the eye. "I know this *ain't* a tea party," she said, emphasizing the grammatical error. "But it also isn't a poker game, as you seem to think. This is *life*. Kayla's life."

"I am well aware of the risks here."

There was something in his voice, some hint of deep, dark sadness that made her straighten. That made her pause for a moment.

That made her soften, just a little.

"I'm here to do a job, just like you are," she said. "You're here to advise the senator. I'm here to negotiate with the kidnapper. And negotiation is about staying patient and in control. Waiting for the moment the kidnapper makes a mistake, and then using it to our advantage to get the hostage out with the least possible risk."

"What if he doesn't make a mistake soon enough?" he demanded. "Sometimes great risks mean great reward. Sometimes it's a choice between a live kid and a dead one. Which one do you prefer, Goldilocks?"

Maggie flinched. She told herself he didn't know. That he couldn't. But it didn't lessen the hurt. The memory of Sherwood Hills, of the blood on the mall floor, flashed through her mind.

She couldn't think about it. She had a job to do.

"I'm not going to let anyone go off all half-cocked, guns ablaze, into a contentious situation, *cowboy*," she snapped. "I don't gamble with human life. And neither will you or anyone else as long as I'm in charge. Is that clear?"

He stared at her for a beat and then shrugged.

The thin thread of patience inside Maggie frayed. *"Is that clear?"* she repeated, her voice low and threatening.

The man smirked, his upper lip curving in a way that would devastate some women. Well, not her. She wasn't going to be swayed by a pretty face—no matter how sinful the grin. He stared at her with those gleaming, cocky eyes as if he was sure he'd get her to cave. "Yes, ma'am," he drawled, the twang in his voice deepening with sarcasm.

That thin, patient thread, the one that she tried so hard to maintain, broke. "Who the hell *are* you?" she demanded.

He rocked back on his heels, his hands in the pockets of his well-cut suit. "Jake O'Connor," he said, holding out his hand.

Maggie almost ignored him, but then she decided she was going to take the upper hand—literally. She reached out, stepping closer, getting into his space as her hand clasped around his.

The second she touched him, she knew it was a mistake. His skin against hers sent a crackling spark through her, like flashes of lightning before a storm. She swallowed, her mouth suddenly dry.

His hand squeezed hers before dropping it, and she felt it down to her toes, a jolt that seemed to wake her whole body.

"Who do you work for, exactly, Mr. O'Connor?" she asked, half-worried that her voice would crack as she pulled her hand away. She shouldn't have gotten so close. She could feel the heat coming off his body. It made her want to lean forward, to let him envelop her. She shook her head. What was she thinking about? She was on a case . . . not on the prowl.

"That's classified," he replied smoothly. "But feel free to ask any of your contacts. I have an excellent reputation. I'm sure they'll sing my praises."

"Confident, aren't you?" she asked.

Now that she wasn't touching him, it was easier to ignore the attraction that flared every time their eyes met, and instead to focus on her anger about his defiance.

"What gave you the idea you could speak to me the way you did, especially with my people in the next room?" she asked.

"As I understand it, Ms. Kincaid, you don't work for the FBI anymore."

"It doesn't matter who I work for," Maggie said, bristling. "I'm in charge. You will follow my orders. In fact, I don't need a Neanderthal like you anywhere on my team," Maggie said. "You're dismissed. I don't need your assistance on this. Go guard Mrs. Thebes. Make her some sweet tea. That sounds like a perfect job for you."

"Nice try, Goldilocks," he said, unperturbed. "You're not my boss—and I have my orders. So you're stuck with me unless you want to go argue with the senator instead of spending our time searching for his kid."

Maggie frowned. He was right, dammit. She didn't have the time to extricate this jerk herself—and she wasn't sure she could convince the senator to send him away. More likely she'd just piss Thebes off, and he'd put O'Connor in charge—or worse, Jackson Dutton. She was stuck with both of them.

"Just stay out of my way," she warned him. "I'm sure you're very good at your job, but I'm trained specifically for this type of situation. You aren't."

"I've dealt with hostage situations before," O'Connor said.

"Have you done it outside of a war zone?" Maggie asked.

He looked down. His silence was her answer to a few questions, including the crew he worked for. Some branch of the military, clearly.

"In a situation like this, we need one person in charge,"

she said. "One touchstone. I am the touchstone, not you. You get me, O'Connor?"

He looked her up and down, like he was thinking about touching *her*. He flashed her another one of those my-way-or-the-highway smiles that made all those sparks she'd tamped down fly free. "Got it, Goldilocks."

Maggie pulled on her coat, heading toward the front door and calling over her shoulder, "And O'Connor? If you call me *Goldilocks* again, you're going to find out just how well I scored on tactical training at Quantico."

She marched out before he could reply, but out of the corner of her eye, she caught the wry smile on his face as he watched her leave.

CHAPTER 6

Jake watched Maggie stalk out of the foyer, and shook his head slowly, trying but failing to suppress a grin of reluctant admiration.

That was one hell of a woman. Stubborn as a mule and cute as hell.

He couldn't stop himself from watching her leave, his eyes lingering on her curves. She had the kind of body that could break a man. Those twin braids of hers gave him the irresistible urge to tug on the ends. He wanted to unravel them, letting the curls spring free and wild around her heart-shaped face.

She was everything he liked in a woman, with so much fire in her blue eyes that it made his blood go hot at the challenge she embodied. She carried her strength like she'd earned it, and he wondered what she'd gone through to gain that kind of power.

"It's O'Connor, isn't it?" asked a voice behind him.

Jake turned. Special Agent Edenhurst was standing there, looking at him so closely that Jake had to wonder if he'd overheard their conversation.

"Yes, sir," Jake said, holding out his hand.

Agent Edenhurst took it, his eyes narrowing. "You trying to steamroll my agent?"

Jake raised an eyebrow. "Ms. Kincaid isn't an agent anymore."

"Technicalities don't change who a person is," Edenhurst said. "You of all people know that."

A chill went down Jake's spine at the knowing expression on the old man's face. Was he imagining it—or did Edenhurst know the truth?

His last covert operation had been completely off the books. A one-man mission into hell. He still woke up nights covered in sweat, the smell of blood-drenched sand fresh in his mind.

He shook off his paranoia. He had a job, and he certainly wasn't going to let his past get in the way—even if Edenhurst did know more than he should.

"She seems to think she can just talk this guy into giving up," Jake said. It seemed ridiculous to him, no matter how strong she'd come off when she'd engaged with the unsub. In his eyes, this was a cut-and-dried scenario. There was no need to draw it out. They just had to get the ransom ask, agree to a drop point, and make the exchange.

"And you doubt her?" Edenhurst asked.

"In my experience, talk's cheap," Jake said. "It's action that gets the job done."

"Let me give you some advice when it comes to Maggie," Edenhurst said. "For your benefit—and hers. Don't underestimate her. She'll prove you wrong every time."

"I'd like to see that," Jake said, and he was surprised to find that he was telling the truth.

Maggie Kincaid interested him. She was steely and strong, and she obviously had a take-no-prisoners attitude that was a little unusual for a woman. But much like his fellow female soldiers, the women of the FBI were a different breed. It took a special kind of woman to not only work in a male-dominated field, but succeed in it.

She'd obviously earned Edenhurst's respect. Which, if Jake's sources were right, wasn't exactly easy.

Maybe he'd let her play it her way while he set things in motion to take over if the situation went bad.

"I hope we'll be able to work together amicably," Edenhurst said, smiling mildly at him.

"Of course," Jake said, smiling back just as passive-aggressively. He could play polite—for now. He just had to make sure he had the senator's ear. "If you'll excuse me. I'm certain the senator is wondering where I am."

"Don't let me keep you," Edenhurst said.

Jake walked back into the library. The senator was still there, but his wife was nowhere to be seen.

"Did Mrs. Thebes go upstairs?" Jake asked.

The senator nodded. His skin looked as gray as his hair, and the deep grooves around his mouth betrayed his anxiety.

"Let's go somewhere private and talk," Jake suggested.

The senator nodded, following him like a child lost in a crowd. He felt a twinge of pity for the man—this was every parent's worst nightmare.

Thebes' office was across the hall from the library, and Jake closed the door behind them, sitting down in one of the chairs facing the desk.

"What do you know of this Maggie Kincaid?" the senator asked as soon as he sat down.

"Our paths have never crossed," Jake said. "She left the FBI two years ago—right around the time I got back to DC."

"I want to know everything," the senator said. "Who she is. Where she went to school. Why she left the FBI. Why she's back now. Why Edenhurst brought her in."

"He seems to think she's an asset," Jake said.

"And what do you think?" the senator asked.

Jake hesitated. Maggie had taken control of the negotiation with the confidence of a seasoned veteran. She'd taken a risk in forcing the unsub's hand to give her proof of life—but it was clearly a calculated risk, even if he didn't agree with it. "I'll need to do some recon before I can give you an informed opinion," he said, finally. "Give me a couple of hours."

"Thank you, O'Connor," the senator said, a tremulous smile on his haggard face. "I'm very grateful the general saw fit to send you to me."

"I'll get to work," Jake said. "And get you the info you need."

THE SENATOR HAD given him a small office on the second floor. It was quiet and out of the way of the FBI, which is what Jake wanted at the moment. The agents would do their thing—follow the rules and methodology—and he would do his.

He settled himself behind the small desk set under the room's one window. It overlooked the back lawns, where a lush rose garden was in bloom.

Jake dialed a number, put his phone on speaker, and leaned back in his chair as the phone rang.

"Hey, boss, what's up?" chirped a bright voice. "Heard you got sent over to the senator's. You find the kid yet?"

"Not yet, Peggy," he said. "I need you to do a basic rundown on someone for me."

"Who are we digging the dirt on?" she asked. He could hear a rolling sound, and knew from experience she was pushing her office chair back and forth between the two lab tables she used instead of a desk. His assistant wasn't exactly the normal kind of office aide. Peggy could file papers and organize a schedule with the best of them. But she could also hack into the Pentagon, put together an M15 blindfolded, and had patented several new poisons and their antidotes during those six weeks she decided to dabble in chemistry.

Übernerd is how she liked to put it, with a wide smile.

She also happened to be General Hoffman's only daughter, which was the main reason she was working with his team of problem solvers instead of heading up her own think tank or designing defense systems.

"Her name is Maggie Kincaid," Jake said. "Until two years ago, she was a hostage negotiator with the FBI."

"Okay, good, good," Peggy muttered as he heard her begin to type. "Okay . . . Margaret Elizabeth Kincaid. Thirty years old. Father deceased. Mother living. Looks like she was recruited right out of college—she went straight from Harvard to Quantico."

"Tell me about her cases," Jake said.

"Hmm, let's see . . ." More clicking and tapping. "There it is!" Peggy crowed triumphantly. "So, she did a year in the New York field office and then was transferred to DC at the request of Frank Edenhurst."

"Pretty sure that's her mentor," Jake said.

"That'd make sense. He recommended her for the New York assignment. His letter's glowing. She was also the first agent he chose for his DC team when he was given leave to form it."

"Any red flags?" Jake asked. "What's her success-to-failure ratio?"

"She spent five years with the Bureau," Peggy said. "Pulling up her cases without casualties now . . . oh, wow!" She let out a low whistle. "Damn, this woman's *good*. She's had only five casualties in all the cases she's headed up. And just one of them was a victim."

Jake straightened in his chair. "When was the victim killed?"

"Almost two years ago," Peggy said, confirming his suspicion.

"That was the last case she worked, wasn't it?"

"How'd you know?" Peggy asked.

"Just a hunch," Jake said. "All right. So she's good at her job."

"Looks like she's the best," Peggy said cheerfully.

"But her last case . . . she had a loss," Jake said, mostly thinking out loud. Peggy was a good sounding board. "Maybe it broke her?"

"It's always hard when it's kids," Peggy sighed.

"The victim was a kid?" Jake asked.

"Yeah. A teenage girl shot in a mall. God, how horrible." Peggy shuddered. "People suck."

So Maggie failed to save one girl, and now she was determined to save this one. Was that why she was so stuck on doing things her way?

Or was she just stubborn?

"You there, boss?" Peggy asked.

"Yeah," he said. "Just thinking. Keep digging. You find anything relevant, send it to me."

"I'm on it," Peggy said. "Anyone else I need to keep track of?"

"You've got the names of the senator's staff I sent over?"

"Yep. Nothing's popped up on any of them yet. I'm running them through all my systems."

"Okay," Jake said. "Do me a favor. Run a check on the senator too."

"You think he's crooked?" Peggy asked, sounding surprised.

"No," Jake said. "But it's becoming clear he's the likely target here. There might be no reason why other than he's rich and powerful."

"But there could be more to it," Peggy finished his thought. "And it could give us a clue. Makes sense. Okay. I'll get back to work. Hope you find the bad guy soon."

"Yeah," Jake said, thinking about Kayla's diabetes. "So do I."

He hung up, leaning back in the chair, musing. He stroked his jaw. He hadn't shaved that morning—he'd have a five-o'clock shadow by noon.

The additional proof of life Maggie had demanded had given him and her time—but it might also give him information. He needed a way to find Kayla—some clue to her location. Without it, he was dead in the water.

He needed a clue—if it wasn't found on the video Maggie demanded, he would need the kidnapper to reveal it somehow, unknowingly.

Jake smiled ruefully.

It looked like he might need to cooperate with Maggie Kincaid after all.

CHAPTER 7

It was dark. Kayla couldn't see anything. The rough hood he'd pulled over her head brushed against her lips as she inhaled sharply, unable to quiet the pounding in her chest.

How could she have been so stupid? She should have noticed. Listened to her dad. He was always saying she needed to be more aware. She always ignored it. She'd been ignoring everything he said lately. She'd just been . . . God, she'd been stupid. *So* stupid.

She shifted on the rough concrete, her right shoulder throbbing dully. As she sat up, a sharp pain pierced her calf—a charley horse from sitting crumpled on the ground for so long. Biting her lip, she stretched out her leg, whimpering in relief as the cramp eased. Her knees were sore, raw, like the skin had been scraped off. She stretched her cuffed hands, blindly searching her skin before finding an oozing wet patch that made her flinch when she touched it. For some reason, the blood—it had to be blood—on her fingertips suddenly made things very real. Kayla gulped, her fingernails digging into her palms.

She tried to push the hood off her head, but there was a drawstring pulled tight around the neck, and her fingers were stiff and clumsy from the lack of circulation.

Okay. Okay. She couldn't panic. She needed to concentrate on something else. She closed her eyes, trying to forget the hood over her head, even as the thick fabric scraped her lips. She tried to ignore her aches and pains—and the strangling sensation in her chest as she realized it had been hours since her last insulin shot.

Don't panic, she told herself sternly. *Think about something else.*

She thought about Mom braiding her hair the mornings before horse shows. The light tug of her mother's fingers moving nimbly, gently, to put every hair in line. No matter how many times Kayla tried, her French-braiding sucked, so Mom always took over. She had never told her mother, but Kayla liked that time in the mornings the best. Sometimes they talked; sometimes they didn't, but it was just her mother's presence that made Kayla feel safe. Loved.

Oh, God, why haven't I ever told Mom that? What if I don't get a chance to? What if he's going to kill me and is just waiting for the right time?

Mom must be so worried. And Dad . . . I should have listened to him. Stupid, stupid, stupid!

Kayla shifted on the concrete, trying to find a more comfortable position. She winced, her back and legs aching as if she'd spent the whole day running suicides. She awkwardly rose to her feet, the combination of cramped muscles and darkness almost making her topple over. The pleated folds of her school skirt flapped against her thighs, and she breathed a sigh of relief to know she was still dressed in her uniform. She wasn't stupid—she knew there were sickos out there. At least whoever had her hadn't done anything—so far.

She stretched her hands out blindly in front of her, shuffling forward. Her fingers hit something smooth—a wall. She moved forward too fast, her feet catching against a heap of . . . something on the ground. Down she went, her bound palms scraping onto the rough concrete floor in an effort to brace her fall. Her cheek slammed into the ground, and for a moment, she lay there, dazed and coughing. She rolled to her side, still coughing, and reached out, making contact with a cool, slippery material. She had tripped over a sleeping bag tossed over a mattress pad. With a shaky breath, her cheek hot and sticky with tears, she got back on her feet, continuing to trace the room, trying to find a way out. Finally, on the farthest wall, her hand touched a door frame. Kayla scrambled for the doorknob, but it was locked. Dead-bolted, she realized as she reached up, feeling metal. She banged on the door, over and over, but the solid wood didn't even budge.

"Let me out of here!" she yelled, until her voice was hoarse and her hands felt bruised. She collapsed on the makeshift bed, breathing hard. Her mouth was so dry. When was the last time she drank something—when Becky offered her that extra bottle of water before practice? It seemed like years ago.

She straightened, remembering something. She'd taken the water, but she'd *told* Becky. Before she ditched lacrosse practice, she'd told her where she was headed. Becky would say something, right? People had to be looking for her by now. Becky would tell. It's not like she's any good at keeping secrets even when you wanted her to.

A little bit of hope ignited in Kayla's chest. Becky *would* tell someone. They could get, like, surveillance video or something. Everyone was probably searching for her right now.

But just as she began to breathe easier, the sound of the door unlocking and swinging open filled her ears. She cringed against the wall, turning her head back and forth, trying to trace the sound of footsteps as they came closer and closer.

The hood was roughly torn from her head. A sudden burst of light filled her eyes. Tears flooded them, tracking down her cheeks as she blinked furiously, trying to focus on the blurred figure standing in front of her. Gloved fingers gripped her chin painfully, tilting her head to the left, then the right, as if he was checking something. Her eyes finally adjusting to the light, now she could see he was wearing a black mask that covered his entire face, with a gray hoodie pulled tight around his head, obscuring his hair. God, who was this guy? What did he want? Maybe she could, like, talk him down or something. Make him think of her as a person. That's what you were supposed to do, right? Kayla tried to think hard back to all those crime shows she and Becky used to watch, even though her mom had disapproved.

"Who are you?" Kayla asked shakily. "I'm Kayla. I guess you probably know that. Please. If you just call my dad . . . he'll give you whatever you want—just call him." She took a breath and willed her voice to remain steady. "Really, I *promise* there won't be any trouble. Just call him and ask. He'll get it for you."

The man—her kidnapper—stepped forward, and Kayla shrank against the wall, scrambling back into a corner as he advanced, digging into the pocket of his hoodie. A grip of panic seized her chest. This was it. He was going to pull out a gun or a knife and kill her. Kayla opened her mouth to scream, to plead for her life. But the sound died in her throat when she realized he wasn't holding a weapon. He wasn't going to kill her. At least not yet. He gripped the purple pouch from her purse that held her insulin, pulled out a needle and a vial, and filled it in front of her.

"Wait a second," Kayla said slowly, unable to tear her eyes away from the needle. Oh, God, what if there was an air bubble? What if he didn't know how to administer insulin? The only person other than her doctor she'd ever trusted with her insulin shots was her mom. Her dad didn't even do them when she was little—he had a thing about needles, so Mom had been the one to teach her.

What if whatever he was putting in the needle wasn't insulin? A new kind of fear flooded her. Those vials could just *look* like her meds.

Her eyes widened in horror as he tapped the side of the syringe and checked for air bubbles, and then stepped forward, the needle held aloft.

"Wait!" Kayla said, but she knew it was no use as he pinned her against the wall with his free arm. She tried to fight him off, but he was so much stronger, his arm like an iron band pressing her down onto the concrete. He pulled up the hem of her shirt and she kicked out wildly, catching nothing but air, screaming as the needle jabbed into her hip and he pressed the plunger, injecting her with what she prayed was insulin.

Then he stepped back, placing the pouch in his hoodie pocket, and grabbed a video camera from the backpack by the door.

Kayla barely had any time to glance around the room—no windows, gray walls, concrete floor—before the kidnapper threw a book in her lap. She looked down at it, confused. *Crime and Punishment.*

"Read," he demanded, pointing the camera at her. His voice sounded funny—too deep and hoarse, like he was trying to disguise it.

She pulled further into herself. "Okay," she whispered. She didn't want him to shove her against the wall again; her collarbone still ached from the impact. It was awkward to open the book with cuffed hands, especially because she was still shaking in fear, but she managed to flip to the first chapter. She took a deep breath and began to read, the words cracking in her dry throat as she forced them out. Glancing nervously at the camera, she finished the first page, turning to the second. She was about to continue when he lowered the camera, shutting it off. He moved toward her, and she tried not to flinch as he pulled the hood back over her head. The last things she saw before everything went black were his brown leather tasseled shoes, polished to a high shine.

CHAPTER 8

By the time eleven o'clock rolled around, Maggie was out of her running clothes and had changed into a dark blue pencil skirt with a crisp white oxford tucked into it. She'd furiously undone her braids, still stinging from O'Connor's idea of a nickname. Goldilocks indeed. She'd show him. She tried to finger-comb her curls into some sort of order, but ended up twisting her hair up into a (somewhat) neat bun. Her spectator heels clicked on the black-and-white tile floor of the entryway of the Carmichael Academy.

The academy was surrounded by seven-foot fences and guarded by a gate that was on par with the one at Quantico. The perfectly manicured lawn sprawled over fifteen acres, affording the college-size track, tennis courts, lacrosse fields, and stables the utmost privacy for the children of DC's elite. The series of brick buildings that made up the actual classrooms had stood the test of time, and the main building had an honest-to-God *turret*.

"If you'll just wait," said the security guard who'd led her into the building, "I'll let Miss Hayes know you're here."

Maggie took a seat, trying not to fidget as she went over the pieces she had so far. A highly organized unsub with a big ego and desire for control was never a good thing. They must have been tracking Kayla outside of school, because there was no way they would have been able to bypass the academy's security. To get through the gates, Maggie had been asked for three forms of ID, and they'd video-called Frank to verify her identity.

"Miss Kincaid?"

Maggie looked up to see a thin woman with a long face and silver hair pulled back in a tight bun standing in front of her. "I'm Miss Hayes, the headmistress."

"Please, call me Maggie." Maggie held her hand out, but Miss Hayes didn't take it. That was when she knew this wasn't going to be easy. People who ran this kind of place were notoriously protective of their students—and their rich parents.

"Shall we talk in my office?"

Maggie followed her inside a windowless room that was as dour and depressing as a principal's office should be. There were no photos on the wall, but instead, a towering oil portrait of a grim-looking man with gray muttonchops glowering down from above the desk.

"I understand that you're a hostage negotiator," Miss Hayes said. "That means you deal with criminals to release the people they've abducted?"

"Among other things," Maggie said. "It also means I'm in charge of this case. So I need to know everything I can to get Kayla home safe. That's where you come in."

Miss Hayes' pinched mouth twisted, and she bristled. "You must understand that at the Carmichael Academy privacy and safety are paramount."

Oh, boy. If there was one thing she had no patience for, it was people trying to claim "privacy" in the face of a crisis involving a child. If Miss Hayes wanted to pay hardball, Maggie would step up. And she'd win.

"I agree that privacy and safety are very important," Maggie began. "But one of your students isn't safe right now. She's in a lot of danger. So you're going to cooperate with me. I need Kayla's full school schedule, and you're going to call Kayla's friends in here so I can talk to each of them."

"Before we even think about doing that, I need to call their parents for permission," Miss Hayes said.

"I need you to do what I ask. Now." Maggie smiled, pleasantly, with just an edge of threat. "I don't think the parents of your students would appreciate knowing your security is so lax that students can easily skip class and leave the grounds. I'm sure Mrs. Thebes is very well connected with the other Carmichael mothers. Just a few phone calls from her, and you might have a public relations problem on your hands."

"That's not true!" Miss Hayes exclaimed angrily.

Maggie shrugged. She was done playing nice and waiting around. She may have bought some time from Uncle Sam, but she knew it wasn't much. She wasn't going to sit around patiently until Miss Hayes got with the program.

"We don't know, do we?" she asked. "Kayla could have been abducted on school grounds. I could get forensics out here. I bet the parents picking the kids up in a few hours would *love* to see FBI agents crawling around your school turned crime scene—that'd make a great photo op. Or maybe she skipped class and was taken after she'd left the grounds, and your security is so lax she was able to leave campus without permission. Until I have a better picture of her day and her state of mind from her friends, I won't know for sure. So maybe you should get the girls so I can speak with them—unless you want to spend the next few days dealing with angry and worried parents, and maybe some curious reporters too."

Miss Hayes' sharp cheeks had turned bright red with suppressed anger, but she picked up a phone, punching a few buttons. "Glenda," she said briskly, displeasure dripping from her voice. "Please get Bree Lawson, Becky Miller, and Adrianna Sussman out of class and into my office."

"Feel free to stay as I talk to the girls," Maggie said as Miss Hayes glared at her across the antique desk that took up much of her office.

"I wouldn't dream of leaving," the woman replied stiffly.

A few minutes later, an aide ushered three teenagers into the office. They crowded close together as they looked at Miss Hayes and then Maggie suspiciously.

"Girls, this is Miss Kincaid," the principal said. "By now, you've heard about Kayla, I assume?"

The girls nodded. The redhead sniffled, wiping at her eyes.

"Miss Kincaid would like to ask you some questions."

"Come sit down," Maggie said, gesturing to the uncomfortable-looking antique settee in the corner. She moved her chair so it was facing them, her back to Miss Hayes. "I know Kayla's mom called you girls earlier to ask if you knew anything, but I wanted to ask some more questions she might not have thought of. Can you give me your names?"

"I'm Bree," said the redhead. "Kayla's mom said it was a big secret. That we couldn't tell anyone. Does that mean you too?"

"Well, I already know Kayla's missing," Maggie pointed out. "And I'm working the case. So it's safe to talk to me. But please, don't talk about it with anyone else. No social media, okay?"

The girls nodded.

"I appreciate that," Maggie said.

"Do you know anything?" Bree asked.

"Not yet," Maggie said. "That's why I'm here. So you girls, the people closest to Kayla, can help me. Can you tell me if Kayla seemed nervous at all yesterday? Or upset about something?"

"She was fine," the petite blonde who looked like a teenage version of Tinkerbell piped up. "She was a little stressed about the algebra test because she'd stayed up late mucking out Star's stall—that's her horse."

"And I saw her at PE," said Bree. "Becky did too," she said, nodding to the quiet brunette who was hanging her head, refusing to meet Maggie's eyes. "Kayla seemed totally okay. She said something about the test not being as hard as she thought. She seemed relieved. I was too because I had to take it after lunch. I don't think I did very good."

"We all had lunch together," Adrianna said. "Just like always. It was totally normal."

"Who would do this?" Bree asked.

"We don't know yet," Maggie said. She couldn't help but look at the quiet girl, Becky. What was she hiding? "Girls, I asked Kayla's parents if there was a boy in her life. They didn't think so. But I know it's not always cool to be up-front with your parents about that stuff. I used to lie to my mom about boys all the time. So . . . was there a boy she was seeing? Maybe someone she didn't want her parents to know about?"

The girls shifted in their seats, looking nervously at each other.

"I really need to know," Maggie said. "It could be important. She might've been with him or told him where she was going."

Adrianna sighed mightily, her blond bangs fluttering in the gust of air. "She started seeing Lucas Birmingham a few months ago. He's a junior and, like, kind of a bad boy, I guess. Kayla knew her mom wouldn't be okay with him, and her dad would probably blow a gasket, so they kept it quiet."

"Adrianna!" Becky hissed, glaring at her.

"What?" Adrianna demanded. "We have to tell her the truth! She's in charge. And anyway, maybe Lucas knows something! Kayla could, like, die, Becky. She's diabetic. She needs insulin, remember? And that's, like, if she wasn't human-trafficked or something."

Bree burst into tears at the thought. Maggie barely resisted the urge to glare at Adrianna. Instead, she looked over to Miss Hayes, who was not impressed with her or the girls.

"You don't think that's what happened to her, right?" Bree asked through her tears.

"I'm not sure, honey," Maggie said gently, grabbing a box of tissues from Miss Hayes' table and handing them to her.

"Miss Hayes, where's Lucas now?" Maggie asked.

The principal turned to her computer, typing in something. "He's in the gym."

"I'd like to talk to him," Maggie said.

"Very well. Girls, go back to your class. You can follow me, Miss Kincaid."

The girls trooped out and scattered while Maggie followed the principal through the halls of the academy, which looked more like a museum than a school. Austere oil paintings of what Maggie suspected were notable former students—or perhaps very rich donors—hung on the walls, and trophies rested in antique, ornately carved cases. Everything spoke of wealth, control, and history. The gym was across a brick courtyard with a burbling fountain, in a large stone building that was more modern in design than the rest of the school.

When they entered the building, they found students taking turns on a climbing rope. When the gym teacher—a short man with legs like tree trunks—caught sight of Miss Hayes, he hurried over, a look of apprehension on his face.

"Miss Hayes, what can I do for you?"

"We need to talk to Lucas," Miss Hayes told him.

Maggie was already walking toward the group of teens. A few of them had caught sight of her and were whispering among themselves. Halfway up to the high ceiling, the boy climbing the rope looked down, his eyes meeting Maggie's.

"Oh, my God, Lucas!" shrieked a girl as the boy lost his grip on the rope, sliding down a few feet before recovering.

"Dude, be careful!" a boy shouted as Lucas swung back and forth, unable to tear his eyes off Maggie.

She beckoned with two fingers, her face stern and all cop. This wasn't going to be too hard. She could intimidate a dumb teenage boy in her sleep.

Lucas, his blond surfer-boy locks swinging, finally looked away and slid down the rope to the floor, rubbing his hands against his gym uniform as he ambled toward Maggie.

"Rope burn's not fun, Birmingham," she said. "You should be more careful. You need to come with me."

He squared his shoulders, all teenage-boy cockiness,

magnified tenfold by privilege and money. "Who're you? If you're a cop, you've got to tell me. And then I'm calling my father's attorneys. I don't have to talk to you without them."

"Someone's mighty defensive." Maggie folded her arms across her chest, staring him down.

"What is it? Got some weed in your locker? Worried I'm here to bust you?"

He frowned, looking over his shoulder at the rest of his gym class.

"Let's go into the hall," Maggie said. And the kid nodded, following her out of the gym.

"So you're not here about the thing at the mall?" he asked sheepishly.

"What thing at the mall?"

"It was just a prank some guys and I pulled. Shoplifting stupid stuff. You know."

"A prank," Maggie echoed.

"It wasn't a big deal! It wasn't even a lot of stuff."

"How about we put aside your 'prank'—for now," Maggie said. "And talk about Kayla."

He rubbed at the back of his neck, looking confused. He was obviously not the brightest bulb. "Kayla's missing," he said. "Adrianna told me."

Maggie made a note to get one of the FBI techs to shut down Adrianna's social media accounts right away. Some teenagers needed to be saved from themselves. "Yes, that's why I'm here."

"I don't know where she is," he said earnestly, sounding believable. "I'd tell you if I knew. I've been kind of worried about her lately."

"Why were you worried?" Maggie asked.

Lucas bit his lip.

"I can always inform the local PD about your little shoplifting spree, Lucas," Maggie reminded him. He looked down and scowled. Then he sighed and started talking.

"Kayla and I, we've been dating a while, you know? We've gotten close. Shared stuff."

"All boyfriend-girlfriend and Facebook official," Maggie said. "Got it. But why have you been worried about her?"

"Well, a couple of weeks ago, she showed up to one of our dates really late. I was kinda pissed because we missed the movie, but then she started crying. Really hard. I've seen her cry at those stupid mushy movies she makes me watch, but nothing like this. She didn't want to talk about it at first, but she was so upset she finally caved. It was her dad again."

"Again?" Maggie interrupted.

Lucas shrugged. "I know they put up this great front, the senator's all family-friendly and crap. And Kayla and her mom are tight for real. But Kayla and her dad? They're always fighting. Like, our entire relationship, she's had issues with him, and he didn't even know about me! And that night she was all upset, it was because of him. She kept saying he was a liar, but I couldn't get her to tell me what he was lying about. So I just tried to, you know, be there for her. She didn't talk about it after that night. I brought it up once, but she told me to drop it, so I did."

"Can you remember anything else she said?" Maggie asked.

He shook his head.

"And the day she disappeared, she seemed normal?"

He nodded. "We met up between third and fourth period, like we always do. Her history class is right next to my English class. We walk together. She seemed fine. She said she'd text me after lacrosse practice, but she didn't, because . . ." He trailed off.

"Okay," Maggie unfolded her arms. "You really should put something on those," she said, gesturing to his rope-burned hands.

"You're gonna find her, right?" he asked as she turned away. "And she's going to be okay?"

Maggie looked over her shoulder, the earnest worry in his face made her heart twinge. He wasn't the brightest, but she could sense that he had a good heart. He cared about Kayla . . . maybe even loved her. She smiled as reassuringly as she could at him.

God, she hoped so. She couldn't lose another one. She just couldn't.

As MAGGIE MADE her way down the academy's steps and toward her car, the worry started seeping in. Kayla's world was becoming real to her. On one hand, that was good. It gave her focus. Understanding. But it also made it harder to keep feelings at bay. This was a teenage girl. She had friends and a reckless boy who seemed to truly care about her. She had an entire life that she'd been ripped away from—that might be cut short. She was somewhere out there, alone and terrified, wondering if anyone was going to save her.

Maggie knew all too well that sometimes you had to save yourself, but she'd be damned if Kayla Thebes would have to. She was reaching for the keys in her purse when she heard a voice behind her.

"Miss Kincaid?"

Maggie turned. The quiet brunette from the office who had chastised Adrianna for spilling the beans—Becky—was standing at the top of the staircase. She hurried down after Maggie, her saddle shoes echoing with each step.

"Becky, right?" she asked.

The girl nodded, looking nervous.

"You were the friend that Mrs. Thebes thought Kayla was staying with last night," Maggie said.

"That's right," the girl said.

"You said you didn't know anything about her staying over."

"I promise, I didn't," Becky said. "I had no idea she was gonna tell her mom that. Honestly, if she had told me, I would've gotten her to come up with a better lie. She should've known her mom would call the head of the dorm to check in."

Maggie suppressed a smile. "Okay, so you didn't know she was gonna lie. But you do know something else, don't you?"

Becky took a deep breath. "I saw her before she disappeared. It was right after school. We play lacrosse together and we were going to practice. But she told me she was going to Sutton's—that's the ice cream place on Maple Street. We're not allowed off campus without an authorized adult, but there are ways to sneak out, even here."

"Can you take me to the shop?"

Becky nodded. "Miss Hayes gave me permission."

Maggie's face must have showed her surprise because Becky smiled. "My dad donated, like, an entire wing. She's nice to me."

"That makes more sense," Maggie admitted.

"She's not all bad," Becky said. "I think she needs, like, a life outside of the school, though. Desperately."

Maggie smiled. "Work shouldn't be everything," she said, uncomfortably aware of how hypocritical that statement was, coming from her.

The girl followed Maggie through the parking lot. Maggie unlocked the car door for her, slipped behind the driver's seat, and started the engine. Nodding at the security guard, who hit the buzzer, she drove through the opened gate and out of the parking lot, taking Becky's directions. Ten minutes later, she pulled up in front of a small building designed to resemble an old-fashioned ice cream shop, complete with old-timey lettering and an antique carriage with horse outside.

"I know it's cheesy-looking, but the ice cream's awesome," Becky said, getting out of the car. "And Kayla loves it because Mr. Caldwell stocks more than one kind of sugar-free flavor at a time."

Maggie followed her inside, pausing in the doorway for a moment. The black-and-white checked floor was polished to a high shine. Classic white iron parlor chairs and round tables filled the lobby. A smiling man was dishing out ice cream over the brass-trimmed glass counter, chatting with customers, as "The Man on the Flying Trapeze" rang out from the player piano. The oak barrels of saltwater taffy and other hard candy along the far wall of the shop looked exactly like the ones at the candy store where Maggie's mother used to take Erica and her when they were little. Erica had loved taffy. Their mother always warned them it would ruin their teeth, but Erica said it was worth it.

The summer they were taken, Erica was supposed to get braces. She'd agonized over it, begging their mother not to make her.

You'll thank me when you're twenty, Mom had said. But, of course, Erica never got to turn twenty. She didn't even get to fifteen.

"Miss Kincaid?" Becky asked.

Maggie looked away from the candy barrels, concentrating on Becky. "Sorry," she said. "What was that?"

"Kayla didn't say who she was meeting," Becky said. "I just kind of assumed it was Lucas. They can't really hang out at her house. But I guess it wasn't."

"Are you sure she was meeting someone?" Maggie asked. "Did she ever come here to be alone?"

Becky shook her head. "She said she was meeting someone. Kayla's not really an 'alone' person, you know? Except when she's at the stables. She likes people. She likes to be in the center of stuff. She has a lot of energy."

Maggie nodded, taking another look around the shop. "Why don't you order something?" Maggie said, handing her a ten-dollar bill. "I'm gonna check some stuff out."

Becky took the money and walked up to the counter, and Maggie turned in a slow circle, getting a feel for the shop. No visible cameras. Only two customers, a mom and her young daughter poring over the ice cream selection. She walked over to the large picture window, peering across the street at the dry cleaners and the vintage clothing boutique. No security cameras evident. Plus, the old carriage provided a convenient obstacle to visibility. The horse hitched to it was asleep on its feet, its head drooping toward the ground. Not even an avalanche would wake it.

Kayla would have been comfortable here. It was one of her regular hangouts. Her guard would be down. It was the perfect place to snatch her. It was as good as being invisible.

The unsub wasn't just smart—he was professional.

That could be useful, especially in light of Kayla's diabetes. He had probably prepared for it—a comatose hostage isn't nearly as useful as a healthy one.

But it also meant he'd be harder to negotiate with, which made it harder for Maggie to find a crack in the unsub's exterior.

Pros don't make mistakes.

Maggie was going to have to trick him into making one.

CHAPTER 9

When Maggie pulled her car up to the front steps of the Carmichael Academy to drop Becky off, it was nearly two o'clock. Her shoulders were aching with residual tension, and she'd give up the contents of her bank account for a long bath and a toffee chocolate bar. But she didn't have time to unwind—she needed to get back to the senator's estate and run her theories by Frank.

But first there was Becky, who had spent the entire drive back to school staring out the window, trying hard not to cry. Maggie didn't have a lot of experience with teen girls other than having been one once upon a time, but she knew the panic of fearing for the safety of a missing loved one. Knowing they were in danger—or worse, that they might be dead—and not being able to do anything about it. The helplessness could choke you, consume you, until you were only a shell of the person you once were.

Maggie reached out and squeezed her shoulder. "This isn't your fault, Becky."

"I should've made her go to practice with me," the girl said, her voice quavering. "Told her not to skip."

"You did the right thing, telling me where she went," Maggie said. "It's going to help a lot."

Becky looked at her, her dark eyes desperate for any speck of hope. "Really?"

Maggie smiled reassuringly. "Promise. Now get back to class before Miss Hayes gives me detention."

That made the girl crack a smile. She got out of the car and hurried up the steps. Maggie took a moment to reach over and grab her purse from the back seat.

Someone knocked on the passenger window, startling her. A man bent down, and a flash of frustration shot through her when she saw who it was. Paul Harrison, her ex-fiancé. Guilt snaked through her irritation, and she gripped the steering wheel until her knuckles turned white. What in the world was he doing here?

She pushed the button to roll down the window, leaning out. "Paul, I'm a little busy right now. We can talk about my picking up my things later."

Paul smiled—that easy, comforting smile. It was so familiar, one of the traits that had drawn her in when they first met. Well, that and how he had tried his hardest that day to save both the hostage and the distraught heroin addict who was holding her at knifepoint. Although he wasn't a seasoned negotiator, he'd formed a connection with the junkie in the fifteen minutes he'd spent trying to talk her down. He was in over his head that day, but he'd tried his best before Maggie came in to advise. His resolve and ingenuity had always been admirable. And he was easy on the eyes, if you liked the Captain America type—blond, blue eyed, complete with a dimple.

Paul was safe. Comforting. But he hadn't been able to understand the darkness in her. He'd seen it and he wanted to banish it, to love it away, not recognizing that it was the core of her: Good or bad, it made her who she was.

"I'm not here about your stuff, Maggie. Frank brought me in."

Maggie had to admit that it was the right choice, even if it made things awkward for her. Paul's attention to detail and rules made him a favorite among the more by-the-book agents, but his doggedness was what Frank—and Maggie—admired in him.

"Did Frank send you to keep an eye on me?" Maggie asked.

Paul shook his head. "Frank wouldn't do that, Mags. I

came to interview school security and brought a tech to look at video footage. How about that Miss Hayes, huh?" He mock-shuddered. "What is it about disapproving principals that makes you feel sixteen again?"

Maggie smiled reluctantly. "She was pretty scary."

"Mind if I catch a ride with you?" he asked. "The tech is still going through the videos."

She wanted to say no because she knew it would be awkward—she'd make it awkward. But that would be rude. She didn't mind being rude to Jake O'Connor—he deserved it, questioning her with such assured arrogance. God, who did that guy think he was? He'd seemed almost amused by her stern warnings. And she'd be rude to Jackson Dutton any day of the week—that man needed his ego punched down to size. But Paul didn't deserve her rudeness, especially not after she'd broken his heart. She could still see the look on his face when she'd ended their engagement. It wasn't even a surprised expression—that's what made her feel most guilty. It was just a sad resignation that had told her he'd seen the signs maybe even before she did, but was willing to keep fighting.

She wasn't.

"Get in," she said.

As they drove through the academy's gates, Paul bent over to fiddle with her radio, and she had to bite her tongue, recalling their old playful bickering about music in the car. She hated the radio when she drove and fought the urge to remind him. There was no point in picking a fight now.

Maggie turned off the tree-lined, secluded road that surrounded the academy. The main street leading through town was a riot of colors this time of year, bright greens and pinks from the magnolia trees and their blossoms. In a tradition going back many years, every spring the brass statues in town—most of them historical figures—would be festooned with May Day ribbons. As Maggie drove past Reed Park, she could see a few pink and blue streamers draped over the shoulders of the statue of George Washington near the west entrance.

"Did you get anything useful from security?" she asked, desperate to break the awkward silence that had settled in.

"None of them saw anything unusual yesterday," Paul said.

Maggie switched lanes. As they drove away from the academy, the traffic thickened, making her slow to a crawl. She stared straight ahead, but out of the corner of her eye, she could see Paul looking at her closely. She couldn't stand the silence. "What?" She winced at the frustration that bled into her voice. She was being so unfair to him.

"I'm just wondering if you're okay," Paul said softly. "Teenage girl, kidnapping . . . I'm sure it brings up bad memories about . . ." He hesitated, and Maggie braced for what he was about to say. What she knew he was about to bring up, what he couldn't *help* but remind her of. He spoke out of concern, maybe even love—but what he didn't realize was that Maggie couldn't talk about what happened when she was young. Not like this. She had to keep those fears buried deep in the dust of her memory.

"You know," Paul finally said. "Your childhood. The unanswered questions. Your sister."

It felt like a brick slamming into her chest. Even though she knew it was coming, the word spoken out loud turned her cold. Paul was one of the few people in her life who knew about her childhood. She hadn't hidden it from him, but the few times he'd tried to get her to open up, she'd shut him down. About a month after he proposed, he'd stopped by her brownstone without calling, only to find her drunk, a photo album spread across her coffee table. Her own private version of a memorial service, an unofficial event she held every year, on the day that she'd lost—*left*—Erica. She'd broken down—and shouldn't you be able to break down in front of the man you're going to marry? That's what she told herself at the time, but the discomfort at being so vulnerable settled in her chest and stayed there.

He'd said all the right things. He'd made her tea and held her as she cried. He'd gone through the childhood pictures of her and her sister, and tried to comfort her. But she couldn't shake it: the feeling that even though he was doing all the right things, it wasn't right for *her.*

He understood her grief, but he didn't understand her anger or her guilt. Those were messier emotions, harder to hold and harder to heal.

She needed them. That was the one thing she couldn't admit to even him. She *needed* the anger. She *needed* the guilt that thrummed through her, faster and stronger than her own blood. That was what fueled her. That made up the core of who she was—and if she had let him, he would've tried to melt it. To replace it with love and happiness. A house with a yard and a dog and a white picket fence. And she'd been too scared to let him try. Too scared to hand over that much trust. Too scared to bare herself. Too scared to let go of her motivating force; to give up what had become the core of her being.

She should've broken off the engagement then but was a coward. She'd let it die a slow death—they both had.

"I'm not going to discuss my childhood with you," Maggie snapped.

"I'm just saying that this could be traumatic—"

"Paul, you're not my shrink, and I'm not your fiancée anymore," Maggie said, horribly aware of the barely contained anger in her voice. "You need to drop it." Her fingers clenched the steering wheel—otherwise, she was going to lose her temper.

"Maggie," he said gently. "I understand your not wanting to talk about it. Really I do. But I care about you, and I just wanted to make sure you're okay. This is a big case. Are you sure it's the one you want to dive back into negotiating with? Especially one with another little blonde girl? What if—"

"I'm fine, Paul," Maggie interrupted him icily. She had to regain her control, to freeze those emotions before they ran rampant. To go numb. But she couldn't help but mentally fill in that what-if. What if he was right? What if this ended like Sherwood Hills? What if she just wasn't cut out for this anymore? What if she was too damaged to ever be adequate, let alone the best?

Taking one hand off the wheel, she rubbed the skin on the opposite wrist, unable to stop herself.

Paul noticed. "Oh, honey," he said, his voice low with concern.

Maggie quickly grasped the steering wheel with both hands again, her cheeks burning. "I'm fine," she repeated, a note of finality in her voice. She inhaled slowly, counting to ten. In those few seconds, she would bury her panic, find the control she'd had mere minutes ago, and take up the role she'd maintained on the phone with the unsub. "What about the video footage at the school? Did you catch Kayla on any of it?"

"She was everywhere she was supposed to be," Paul said, trying to match the abrupt shift from personal to professional. "And the cameras didn't catch her leaving the grounds."

"Well, she did leave," Maggie said, glad they were back on more solid ground.

She didn't need any concerned ex stirring up memories that could weaken her right when she needed to be stronger than ever. The traffic finally eased, and she pressed on the accelerator, glad to get moving again. "One of her friends confessed that Kayla was headed to this ice cream shop where the Carmichael kids hang out."

"Meeting someone?" Paul asked.

"Maybe," Maggie said.

"What are you thinking for our unsub? Has he done this before?"

"Well, he knows what he's doing," she replied. "He's careful, and he thinks things through. When the ask comes, it'll be a professional setup: wire transfer for a lot of money somewhere untraceable. And there'll be a ticking clock on it. He's not going to give us any more time than he has to. We'll be lucky to get a few hours to get the money together."

Paul looked troubled. "What if there isn't enough time? What are her chances?"

Maggie swallowed, pushing harder on the gas. She didn't

want to answer, but her silence did it for her. With Kayla's diabetes, the kidnapper wouldn't even have to kill her. All he'd have to do is leave her wherever he was keeping her without food, water, or insulin. Without any solid leads on her location, the FBI wouldn't find her in time.

If Maggie couldn't find the fuse to blow this case open soon, Kayla's chances were slim, if that.

CHAPTER 10

"I think setting up a press conference for tomorrow is your best bet, Senator."

Jake watched as Max Grayson, the senator's policy advisor, juggled two cell phones and a smoothie as he paced back and forth. Grayson was short, and he was clearly one of those guys who had a chip on his shoulder about it. Dressed to the nines, tanned to an unhealthy degree, with an ever-present green smoothie in one hand, two cells in the other, Grayson was someone who wanted to be impressive. In Jake's opinion, Grayson was failing, but he'd never had much patience for a big ego. The FBI agents milling about the senator's library dodged the agitated man half-heartedly, annoyed by his restlessness. The senator was seated at his desk, his hand pressed over his mouth, his eyes tired and haunted.

"I know it's gauche to say, but this will work wonders for us in the polls," Grayson continued, oblivious of the dark mood in the room. Jake was thankful Mrs. Thebes had finally agreed to go upstairs to rest. Otherwise, he would have had to find a way to shut Grayson up, and he wasn't inclined to do it politely.

"Max, maybe we can do this later?" the senator said, sounding tired and defeated.

"We need a game plan," Grayson insisted.

Jake shook his head in disgust. "I think the senator's right. Time to take a break," he said. It was an order, but

Grayson's head was so far up his own ass, he didn't know what was good for him. He looked up from his cell to Jake, clearly annoyed by the interruption.

"Senator, it's going to leak anytime," he pressed on, as if Jake hadn't even spoken. "I'm surprised it hasn't yet, considering that negotiator woman went to the school. You know teenagers and social media—no discretion whatsoever. We have to get ahead of this . . . control the narrative."

Jake had to stop himself from snorting. The narrative? *That's* what he called this? It was a crime. A young girl's life at stake, for Christ's sake. Evil men doing evil things. It was simple. Clear-cut. That's why he was so frustrated that Maggie Kincaid wouldn't just take a step back and let him take the lead. She was cute as hell, the kind of feisty that revved him up more than anything else, but damn, she was being stubborn. She was obviously someone who saw the world in a prism of grays, when he knew too well it was stark black-and-white. If she kept up this cat-and-mouse chase with the kidnapper—trying to outsmart him instead of outgun him—someone could get hurt. Kayla could get killed.

He knew how to handle this. Getting the bad guy was what he was good at . . . what he was trained for. At eighteen, he'd sworn an oath to the United States, and he lived by those words to this day. Boot camp hardened him, and he was ready for action soon afterward. His admission to Ranger school shone as one of his proudest moments. He'd dedicated his life to his men, his country, and his honor. On his fifth tour of duty, his squad and the Red Cross workers they were escorting to a refugee camp in northeast Nigeria had caught enemy fire. It hadn't been a routine mission—they'd just been in the area, and his commanding officer liked to help out the camp workers as much as he could. They'd been unprepared for an attack, but Jake had taken charge as soon as the bullets and missiles suddenly started raining down on them.

Quickly pairing his men with the terrified doctors and nurses, Jake provided covering fire as each pair made a run for it. His second-in-command hadn't wanted to leave Jake behind, but he knew there was no choice—the Red Cross workers had to be protected, per Jake's order. And then he was alone, crouching behind an overturned truck, holding off the Boko Haram gunmen with an M320 and not enough ammo.

He knew without a doubt they'd hit the refugee camp next, and the women and children especially would be subjected to unspeakable horrors, so he had to be precise and brutal. The innocent lives at stake were too precious. He'd spent time at the camp, at the makeshift school where kids gathered early every morning, eager to learn. He'd be damned if those bastards harmed any of them.

A nightmare of adrenaline, blood, and terror, it'd been the longest thirty-six hours of his life, but he'd survived—along with his team, the refugees, and all the doctors and nurses. The Army sent him home after that, slapped some medals on him, and paraded him in front of the press. Told him the best way to serve his country wasn't back in action, but in DC, serving the Washington elite. It looked good to have an Army hero working with politicians—a circular image-boost that made the politicians look pro-military—and, in turn, gave the Army the good press it craved.

But then the general had showed up on his doorstep with an offer to join his private team. The operations Jake and his team worked on weren't covert, exactly, but they were sensitive. In need of quick handling before they blew up.

DC was an entirely different type of war zone, but he was good at the job he'd been thrust into—maybe a little too good. Sometimes he wondered what life would've been like if his squad hadn't been assigned the Red Cross escort duty that day. Would he have never caught the general's eye? Would he have been able to go back to his team? He never regretted it—the refugees', his men's, and the health workers' lives were worth everything—but sometimes he couldn't help but wonder at the turn his life had taken.

Dealing with slippery politicos like Grayson was part of his job now, but he didn't have to like it—or hide his dislike when they stooped low.

"This isn't a fucking novel, Grayson," Jake growled. "This is the senator's daughter." God, what the hell was this guy's deal? Jake felt like decking him. He was talking about the kidnapping like it was a campaign commercial or something. The senator was clearly too distraught to put him in his place.

Finally, Grayson had the grace—or savvy—to look a little ashamed. "I'm trying to help."

"What do you think, Jake?" Senator Thebes asked.

"I think involving the press is a terrible idea," Jake said, relieved that the senator was asking for other opinions. If Thebes listened to Grayson, they were in for a hell of a mess. Plus, Maggie Kincaid would get all stubborn and huffy and start issuing more orders. Actually, Jake would enjoy seeing that curvy little spitfire go up against Grayson. She'd eviscerate him with just one look, likely. And good riddance.

"We're walking on a tightrope with this person, Senator, and they can cut it at any time. Because they have Kayla, they have the power. Do you really want dozens of camera crews parked outside? Paparazzi hopping the fence? Nancy Grace speculating about Kayla's chances as the hours tick by? Unless you lie low and wait for the ask, you could turn an already very risky situation into a deadly one. We want this to go smooth—and shouting it out into the world for publicity is the opposite of smooth."

"Controlling the narrative gives us power," Grayson insisted. "And the polls. Really, Senator, you should look at these numbers . . . I think they'll convince you—"

Before Grayson could finish, the door to the library opened, and there she was again, the tiny blonde commander. This morning, when he'd caught her up in Kayla's room, her defiance had amused him. Later, after the first phone call, it had annoyed him.

Now? He had to admit he was impressed. Especially after he'd gone through all the information Peggy had pulled up on her. She was highly decorated, Ivy League–educated, and her success rate was unusually high.

The woman with the golden tongue, Peggy had said, laughing. *That's what they call her. She's kinda mythic in the negotiation circles, Boss. They say she can talk anyone down.*

Should he trust that she knew what she was doing? That this was another case she could add to her list of successes?

Or had that last case—the one where she lost both the hostage and the unsub—shattered her confidence?

He knew better than anyone that faith in yourself was key to this kind of work.

Did Maggie Kincaid have faith in herself? The unshakeable kind that would see Kayla through this safely?

That was what he needed to find out.

Maggie had changed out of her running clothes into a skirt that directed his attention to a killer pair of legs. Well, running *was* good for the body and soul.

Gone were the double braids that had made her look much younger and innocent; her blond curls were pulled back tightly, but they were fighting their way out of the bun in spiky little corkscrews. Jake's fingers itched with a nearly irresistible urge to brush back the little ringlets along her temple. Her skin had been warm when he'd reached out to steady her this morning. Soft against his rough.

He cleared his throat, adjusting his stance. He needed to concentrate on Maggie Kincaid's tactics, not her luscious curves and golden hair. Her insistence on patience might screw them over even more than Max Grayson's crass demand for a sympathy bump in the polls. Too much waiting led to nervous kidnappers. Nervous kidnappers shot first, thought later. He couldn't let that to happen to Kayla.

Jake watched Maggie closely as she turned her head, talking quietly to the agent she'd come in with. He didn't recognize the man from earlier this morning—was she bringing someone new in? The guy was looking at her like she'd hung the freaking moon. Watching him, Jake was strongly reminded of a puppy. Kincaid didn't seem to share the man's feelings. In fact, she looked almost annoyed—and for some reason, that made satisfaction curl in Jake's stomach.

She muttered something to the guy before she hurried over to Senator Thebes, propping her hands on her hips in a resolute stance. Grayson glared at her before going back to glaring at Jake. He probably resented them for putting an end to his political maneuvers. For doing their jobs, essentially. What an idiot. Jake imagined squashing him like a fly and smiled. He probably could.

"Why don't you give us some space, Max?" Thebes asked.

Grayson reluctantly crossed the room to sit in one of the leather chairs, huffily checking one phone, then the other.

Jake was close enough to hear Maggie and the senator's conversation. As he listened, he kept his face impassive, ready to jump in as needed.

"Is there any news?" the senator asked.

"I've spoken to Kayla's friends," Maggie replied. "As well as Lucas Birmingham."

"I don't know who that is," Senator Thebes said.

"Lucas is Kayla's boyfriend of several months," Maggie explained tersely.

So Kincaid had dug up some teenage dirt. Well, Jake hoped the boyfriend had given her some good intel. To find Kayla and get her out, he needed all the information he could muster—even if it seemed innocent or useless.

"I've never heard Kayla talk about a Lucas," the senator replied, looking confused.

"Well, he's heard plenty about you from Kayla," Maggie countered. "My understanding is that they've been keeping the relationship a secret from you and Mrs. Thebes."

Senator Thebes leaned forward. "Out with it, Ms. Kincaid."

"Lucas went into great detail about your problems with your daughter," Maggie said. "About how the two of you were always fighting. And how she discovered something you were lying about that upset her so much she ran to him in tears. He was shaken up by the whole thing."

Thebes straightened in his seat, his face tightening with anger—anger at Maggie. It made Jake take notice. Thebes shouldn't be angry at the woman who was trying to find his daughter, even if she'd informed him of a boyfriend he didn't know about, and even if that boy had said unflattering things about him.

"I don't know why the boy would say that, but none of it's true," the senator said. "I work long hours, but Kayla understands that. It's always been that way. I make sure I have time with my daughter so she doesn't feel neglected. Anyway, I've never heard Kayla mention a Lucas. Are you sure he's not just some boy with a crush who's making things up?"

Jake watched as Maggie Kincaid drew herself up, zeroing in on the senator's face. She hid it well, but her frustration was apparent to Jake. Her eyebrows drew together, a little V forming between them, her blue eyes darkening to a stormy gray. This was a woman who knew when she was being lied to. A woman who wouldn't stand for that nonsense ever, but especially when a child's life was on the line. This was a woman who was going to do all she could to save Kayla's life, come hell or high water.

"Senator, I understand this is a very difficult time," she said. "But I need the whole truth from you. You understand that, don't you? I need to know all of it. Everything. Even if it's uncomfortable or illegal or embarrassing. This isn't about your career or your marriage—this is about your daughter, your baby girl's life. So why don't you tell me what you and Kayla have been fighting about? Have you been cheating? Did she find out? Are there gambling debts? Are you being blackmailed?"

Jake watched as the man's eyes narrowed to slits, his mouth doing the same as he looked down at Maggie, barely restrained fury radiating from him. Jake tensed, stepping forward slightly, just in case he needed to put himself between them.

"I have a wonderful relationship with my daughter," the senator said icily. "This boy, whoever he is, he's mistaken. Kayla and I are very close and always have been. There's been no fighting. And I have never been unfaithful to my wife."

Maggie let out a sigh, and when she looked up, her eyes

met Jake's. The V between her eyebrows deepened. "Why don't you mind your own business, O'Connor?"

He smiled, slow and easy, impressed with her despite himself. "Apologies, ma'am."

She frowned at him, puzzled at the genuine note in his voice. He looked back at her in appreciation. Damn, she was cute when she was fired up.

"I'm going to get some coffee," Maggie said pointedly. "I'll give you a few minutes to ponder what we've talked about, Senator. When I come back, I expect answers, sir. *Real answers.*"

Jake couldn't stop himself from watching her make her way toward the door. Her heels gave her a good three inches, but she was still tiny. Almost fragile-looking. At least until a man caught a glimpse of the steel beneath her soft, curvy surface.

She had a good point about the senator—he seemed more than a little off. It was why Jake had asked Peggy to start digging. He could tell himself it was because Thebes was worried about his kid, but after this exchange and the way he seemed to be open to Max Grayson's terrible ideas about politicizing the situation, Jake was starting to wonder if Maggie's instincts were right. The senator shouldn't be worried about poll numbers or even entertaining his aide's ridiculous press conference proposal. His focus should be on his daughter, and doing everything—sharing every bit of information he had—to get her home safe. If Thebes had been fighting with Kayla over normal teenage problems, the senator wouldn't have denied it the way he did. Had Kayla done something he wanted to hide? Fourteen seemed a little young to Jake for an unplanned pregnancy, but either that or drugs could be possible. Kids—even privileged preppies—got started early these days.

"Wait." The senator's voice rang out through the room.

Maggie turned, a triumphant look on her face that changed as soon as she saw what Thebes was holding.

His cell phone, buzzing.

"It's him," he said.

CHAPTER 11

Maggie strode across the room, taking the phone from Senator Thebes. Her heart was in her throat, residual anger from the man's behavior fading as she projected calm. It was time to be in control.

"What is it?" Paul asked, striding across the room toward her.

"It's a video file," she said. Picking up a USB cable, she connected it to one of the laptops on the desk and pulled up the file on-screen. While everyone gathered around, Maggie hit Play.

It was Kayla, in the same gray room as before. She looked pale and sweaty, her hands shaking as she held the copy of *Crime and Punishment*, reading it in a barely-there voice that cracked and swelled with fear. Maggie carefully studied what she could see of the room behind the girl: blank gray walls, concrete floor, nothing notable. The video went dark for a second and then cut to a masked man's face. He pressed on something near his throat, hidden by his hoodie—whatever device he was using to disguise his voice.

"I've given you proof of life, Maggie," he said. "Now it's time for you to give me something. I want five million dollars. Tell the senator to get it ready, and I'll call back with the account number in the morning."

The video went dark, and Maggie straightened, puzzled.

"What are you going to do about this?" the senator demanded angrily, but Maggie was staring at the computer screen, thinking.

Why would the unsub want to wait until the morning? She glanced over at Jake. His dark brows were drawn together, like he was asking himself the same question. Something was not right here. The kidnapper should be in a hurry. He'd been prepared so far. Careful. He should want to unload Kayla and get the money as soon as possible. He should have had an untraceable account number at the ready—after all, Senator Thebes was the kind of man who could get his hands on five million dollars pretty fast. And the kidnapper had to know that. He'd clearly done his research on the senator and his family.

Why wait? Did he have something else planned? Something she was missing?

"So what do you think?" Jake asked. A little startled, Maggie looked up at him standing next to her. She hadn't even noticed him approaching her. He moved like a cat—silent, stealthy . . . it made her more convinced he was military. She looked at him, the wide shoulders, the arms roped with muscle, the seriousness that always seemed to be in his green eyes. Yeah, definitely military. The man would have seen a lot of action if his eagerness to leap forward and throttle instead of staying calm and careful was any indication.

"It feels a little off, doesn't it?" she asked in an undertone.

"Glad you think so too," he said. "Who waits almost twenty-four hours to get their money?"

"I don't know," Maggie said. "But we're going to find out. Jessa." She raised her voice, addressing the forensic tech whose dyed black hair was spiked all over her head, making her look like a punky Peter Pan. "Get the video file to the lab and have the profilers look at it too. I want to know everything. Clothing brands, paint colors, camera angles, shadows on the wall, reflections—anything you can find. I want to know what device he's using to digitize his voice. I want sound techs stripping down the audio to get me something closer to what he really sounds like. I want everything you can see—if there's a poppy seed in his teeth, I want to know about it. You got it?"

"Got it." Jessa dove toward her computer and beginning to type furiously while pulling up a video-chat with the lab at headquarters.

"Agent Kincaid?" asked a voice behind her. It was strange to hear herself be called that again. Maggie shook it off; she didn't have time to spare. She turned to see a young tech holding his hand up like he was in school, waiting for her to call on him. "I think I found something."

"What is it?" Maggie strode over to where he was seated, peering over his shoulder at his laptop screen.

"A match on the cell phone that took the first proof-of-life picture," the tech explained. "At first I thought he was bouncing the signal and that's why we couldn't get a lot. But then I dug into the metadata and found a name hidden in there: Randy Macomb."

"The pool guy?" Paul and Jake asked at the same time.

The two men looked at each other in surprise. Maggie raised an eyebrow, peering at the tablet Paul held out, where a list of the senator's household staff was on the screen.

"That can't be right," she said, shaking her head. "This guy's a pro, not a pool cleaner. He wouldn't be stupid enough to use his own phone. He'd use burners."

"You're overthinking it, Maggie," Paul said. "Occam's razor, you know? The simplest explanation might be the right one. Think about it: He would have access to the estate, to the senator, to Kayla. He'd know her schedule. He could have a personal grudge—kidnappers are often somebody with a direct connection. You understand that. If he's acting like a pro, well . . ." Paul shrugged. "Maybe he's just seen a lot of hostage movies and he's doing a good impression. And—"

"There's no way an unsub this smooth learns how to kidnap a senator's daughter by watching some movies," Jake interrupted, derision in his voice. "You can only fake so much. This guy's not faking."

Paul looked Jake up and down and sneered, "Nobody asked your opinion, O'Connor."

Jake rolled his eyes. "As opposed to your stellar 'he learned it from the movies' theory? Come on."

"Paul, his opinions are relevant," Maggie said, looking at Jake. He'd spent the morning trying to alpha her, but now he was playing nice. Was it a game? A way to trip her up?

Or was he sincere?

She wouldn't know if she didn't ask.

"What are your thoughts?" she asked him.

"I've met the pool guy," Jake said. "If he's putting on an act, he's the best damn actor in the world. Our guy isn't some sunbaked pool skimmer. He's practiced."

"A freelancer, maybe?" Maggie asked.

"Could be," Jake said. "Wet work pays well, but it takes more talent and a lot more resources and control to pull off a hostage situation."

"And he wouldn't be this careless, leaving the phone metadata behind," she mused.

"No way," Jake agreed. "He wants us running in circles, Kincaid. That's why I want this to be a clean in and out as soon as we nail down the place he's holding Kayla. Sooner the better."

"I think so too," Maggie nodded. "But we need to find Kayla before we discuss extraction—and that'll be *my* call, not yours," she added, just to remind him who was in charge.

He grinned at her, and it made her heart flip. "I know, I know, you're the touchstone."

Surprisingly, she liked this, being able to bounce ideas off someone sharp. She liked it a lot, actually. She used to try it with Paul, but their rhythm was always a bit off. Jake O'Connor seemed to be able to meet her step for step with ease and intelligence. It sent a thrill of excitement and hope through her. She looked over to Paul, who was frowning at the two of them, and her excitement faded as she realized he wasn't convinced.

They'd never been on the same wavelength.

Paul reached out and squeezed Maggie's shoulder. Out of the corner of her eye, Maggie saw Jake shift, his mouth flattening at Paul's casual touch. "Sorry, Mags, but I've got to go after this," Paul said.

Maggie bit the inside of her lip. Of course he did. Paul would doggedly follow every lead, even if his gut was screaming that it was a dead end. "Do what you have to," she said with a shrug, and Paul looked disappointed that she wasn't going to ignore all her common sense and go along with him.

Maggie turned away toward the window as Paul mobilized the cops and several agents, and they headed out to arrest Randy Macomb. It was so frustrating that Paul wouldn't take her opinion into consideration—and surprising how much it meant to her that Jake not only stood up for her, but had met her as an equal, as someone with an opinion to be valued.

She was starting to think she'd been wrong about him. There were hidden depths beneath that handsome face and warrior body. It seemed almost unfair to the women of the world if he had brains behind that brawn.

Maggie shook her head, trying to banish her unbusinesslike distraction. She needed to focus on the case, not think about how Jake O'Connor filled out a suit. Which was hard, because the man in question had just walked over to her place by the window.

"He's wasting time," Jake said behind her.

"I know," Maggie said as she watched the SUVs pulling out of the driveway.

"What's your plan?"

Maggie looked up at him, and the openness in his eyes made her tell the truth. "I'm not sure yet. I feel like I'm missing something."

"Sometimes I think we're always missing something," Jake replied. "Things change fast in situations like these. Once we get the account number, we'll get a location. I can get her out safe, Kincaid, as long as I have a location. I promise."

Maggie couldn't stop the stricken expression that fell across her face. "You shouldn't promise things like that," she said in a hushed voice.

His brow furrowed at the brokenness behind her words, and he stepped forward, reaching out. "Maggie—"

She moved away before he could touch her. She still remembered the warmth of his skin against hers from this morning when she bumped into him. She couldn't have another reminder. "No promises," she said firmly. "Not in this line of work."

Before he could say another word, she smoothed out the wrinkles in her skirt and walked briskly over to Jessa.

"Play me the video again," she ordered.

Maybe this time, she'd see something new.

CHAPTER 12

Jake waited outside of the senator's office, his hands clasped behind his back.

He could hear Thebes' voice talking to one of his policy advisors, but he couldn't make out the words.

Harrison going after the pool boy was a dead end. Jake couldn't believe he'd even bother to follow such an obvious red herring, but the guy did seem a little straitlaced. A rule follower.

His mind wandered back to Maggie, to the haunted expression on her face, and her response to his promise to get Kayla back safe.

He had thought it was odd at the time, but right after Maggie had left the senator's mansion with Edenhurst, Peggy had sent him a complete file on her.

He'd spent an hour inside his temporary office, reading through her life, his heart tightening with each page. When he finally closed the folder, he'd found himself placing the flat of his hand against the file, as if somehow she'd be able to feel it. As if somehow he would make it better.

He hated how intrusive he felt, how he'd read about moments in her life that he knew she didn't share often. But it was the job, he reminded himself sternly.

But *she* wasn't a job. She was . . .

He didn't know what she was. Smart. Beautiful. Infuriating. Intriguing.

Stronger than steel, judging by her past. God, what hell

had been heaped on her as a little girl. To lose her sister like that . . .

"O'Connor?"

Jake looked up, torn from his thoughts. Senator Thebes was standing in the doorway, eyebrows raised expectantly.

"I'm ready for you," he said.

"Of course," Jake said, getting up and following him into the office.

He sat down on the leather chair across from the senator's desk.

"So, what do you think about Harrison and his pool-boy lead?" Thebes asked.

"I think it's a dead end, sir," Jake replied.

Thebes sighed, his face drooping with exhaustion. "You won't be offended if I hope you're wrong," he said.

"No," Jake said. "Any lead at this time would be good," he explained. "I'm just not convinced this is it."

"And the matter we discussed earlier?" the senator asked. "The Kincaid woman? Have you looked into her?"

"I have," Jake said. "All her credentials stack up. And her case success rate at the FBI as a negotiator was much higher than average."

"So she's good," the senator said slowly. "Even though she seems to be gambling with my child's life?"

"According to my sources, she's the best," Jake said. "And there is a level of risk taking in a situation like this, Senator."

"There shouldn't be," he growled. "It's my child's life on the line."

"I understand that," Jake said. "And I think Ms. Kincaid does too."

Thebes' eyes narrowed as he thought, his fingers interlaced. "Why did she leave the Bureau?"

Jake shifted in his seat. He had a choice here. If he told the senator what he suspected—that Maggie's last case, the loss of life, had hit her hard—he was certain she'd be off the case in seconds. Jake would be free to run the rescue operation the way he wanted—the FBI would probably put

Boy Scout Harrison in charge, and he could handle that guy any day.

But something stopped him—and it wasn't his attraction or even his admiration for Maggie Kincaid.

Jake trusted his instincts—they were how he survived in war zones and kept his people safe—and every instinct he had was screaming that Kayla's best chance wasn't him or Maggie—it was *them*. Working together. As a team.

"Her father passed away the winter before she took a leave of absence from the Bureau." Technically, Jake thought to himself, that was the truth. "From what I could gather, it was pretty hard on the family There was a considerable estate to deal with after her father's death. My sources say Agent Kincaid left the Bureau in order to help her mother manage the estate and the charity—the Clean Water Initiative—that her father started."

"So she values family," the senator said.

"She does," Jake said. "I know I was originally skeptical of bringing her in, Senator, but I think Agent Edenhurst pulling her out of retirement might be the best thing to happen to this case."

Senator Thebes stroked a hand over his mouth, the troubled expression on his face not fading. "Let's hope," he said softly. "For my family's sake."

CHAPTER 13

Frank was waiting for Maggie at the entrance of the FBI headquarters, his suit jacket thrown over his arm. From the sixties, the building had a retro feel with its block concrete construction and windows lining the two sides facing the street.

It was strange to be standing on the sidewalk, looking up at it again—she hadn't been back since she quit. Frank had sent over the things in her office at her request.

She'd been avoiding this moment. Having to walk inside, to face who she'd been before Sherwood Hills, and who she was now, after. She didn't want to see her former colleagues, endure the accusatory or, worse, *pitying* looks. She hadn't been able to cut it. Maggie, the most promising student in her class at Quantico, had failed.

The dread churned inside her like choppy waves in a storm. God, she didn't want to go inside.

"Told you I'd get you back here," Frank said, smiling and holding out a visitor's badge.

Maggie took it, clipping it to her blouse, trying to tamp down the apprehension building in her stomach.

"You can have your real one if you want," Frank said. "All you have to do is come back to work."

Maggie shot him a stern look. "No thanks, Frank," she said. "I don't want to be here, and I'm not joining up again. This is a onetime favor, remember?"

"Yeah, yeah," Frank muttered, holding the door open

for her. "Ruin my dreams, will you?" They passed through two metal detectors and a full-body scan before being allowed access to the area where suspects were questioned. As Maggie walked down the corridor, she could feel eyes following her. It made her skin crawl. She tried to ignore it—these people's opinions didn't matter anymore—but then she caught sight of Mike Sutton, one of the SWAT team leaders, standing outside a room up ahead.

Her step faltered, just for a second, before she continued down the hall.

"Well, well, well." Mike turned and grinned at her. "Look who's back in the game."

"Sutton." Maggie nodded curtly.

Mike leaned against the wall, sticking his hands in his pockets. "You in on this one, Kincaid? They actually letting you out to play after the mess you made? Better watch her, Frank. But I guess my boys did all the hard work for you. We took Macomb down in twenty seconds. Smooth sailing. Not like Sherwood Hills, you know? You really screwed the pooch on that one. Good thing the grown-ups were there to take care of this pool guy. Otherwise we'd have another mess on our hands."

Maggie's fingernails cut into the flesh of her palms as she forced herself to stay quiet. She didn't have time for male ego. Mike was the kind of man who enjoyed stomping on people to get to the top—especially the women he had little respect for. She had more important things to do than battle him—she had to find Kayla.

"Sutton, don't you have some paperwork to do?" Frank asked pointedly, glaring at Sutton with a powerful kind of anger.

"Don't worry about it, Frank," Maggie said coolly. "Mike, it was nice seeing you." Without another word, she left him behind, looking bewildered, and strode up to the door of the interrogation suite ahead as Frank scrambled to catch up with her.

Like most of the interrogation suites, there was a soundproof observation room for the agents, a few chairs scattered here and there, with a large one-way mirror cut into the wall, allowing them to watch the interrogation. Paul and several other agents were grouped around the window, watching in silence.

"Who's in there with him?" Maggie demanded, pushing forward to see.

Randy Macomb was a muscle-bound beach boy with a perfect tan. A stereotypical musclehead, he was even wearing an oversized tank top. His thick black eyebrows scrunched up in confusion as the agent inside shot question after question at him, his voice rising with each one when Randy didn't give him what he wanted.

"You liked talking to Kayla, didn't you?" the agent asked. "Thought she was pretty?"

"Kayla's a nice kid," Randy said, eyes widening in horror. "But she's a kid, man! That's sick! I've got a little sister her age."

"You resented working for the senator all the time. I know I would have. All those long weekends he called you in," said the agent.

"My job's the best." Randy shook his head in frustration and glanced at the window, mirrored on this side of the room, as if he expected the senator to leap out of it. "I get to be outside all the time, thinking up lyrics for my songs. It's the life, man! And the senator's a chill guy for an old dude."

"What about Mrs. Thebes?" The agent leapt onto another line of reasoning with such speed that it made Maggie's head spin. Who the hell had taught this guy interrogation?

Dear God. This was embarrassing. And unproductive. There was no time for this with Kayla's life on the line—she needed a *real* lead, not a half-assed interrogation by a guy who sounded like he had watched too many detective movies.

Maggie had had enough of this incompetence. She whirled around and strode to the door, flinging it open before Paul and the others could protest.

Both men looked up when she entered the room. "I can take it from here," she said brusquely to the agent. He glared at her, but she met his eyes coolly, daring him to argue.

"You're in charge," he said, a hint of disgust in his voice as he rose from his chair and left the room.

Maggie sat down across from Randy, smiling gently at him. "Hi, Randy. I'm Maggie."

"I didn't do anything," he said immediately.

"Why don't you just tell me where you were yesterday?"

"I was in Baltimore, visiting my ma."

"Can you prove it? Do you have gas receipts? Bus ticket?"

"Um, you could call Ma."

Maggie looked over to the two-way glass. "Could someone call this guy's mom?" she asked. She turned back to Randy. "What about your cell phone, Randy?"

"I lost it the other day."

"You lost it," Maggie repeated, knowing already that this confirmed what she had suspected all along.

"Yeah, I've been looking all over," Randy said. "I keep having my buddy call it, but I never hear anything." When Maggie didn't respond right away, he said, "Why, do you have it?"

Maggie shot a pointed look at the window. They'd need to follow up on all this, but she knew—and they did too—there was nothing here. They'd arrested the wrong man.

She thanked Randy and left the room, heading out of the suite without saying anything to anyone. She needed to get the hell out of here before she ran into anyone else. Before she was hit full force with bad memories.

"Kid," Frank started to say, but she shot him a quelling look. "Come here," he said softly, pulling her into a side hallway, away from the group of agents who'd brought Randy in.

"We follow every lead—you know that," Frank said, when she crossed her arms, refusing to say anything. "I know it's a pain in the ass, but it's what we do." He looked her up and down. "When was the last time you ate?" he asked, his bushy eyebrows scrunched together in concern.

"Well, I was going to eat breakfast after my run, but this

old geezer accosted me and insisted on cashing in on this favor I owed him," she said dryly.

He grinned ruefully. "Take an hour," he said. "We've got to regroup, anyway. Get some food in you. Then come back and we'll kick some ass."

He was right. She should eat. Damn him.

"Fine," she said. "I'll go get a burger at Sal's. But if there's any movement—"

"You're my first call," he promised.

"I'll see you in an hour," she said.

They parted ways, and she was almost to the elevator when she heard someone calling her name.

"Maggie, wait," Paul called.

Whatever calm Frank had soothed into her disappeared in a second. She turned, frustration mounting. "What?" she asked.

"Don't be mad," he started.

"I'm not mad," Maggie said. "I'm frustrated time's been wasted. Kayla is a high-risk victim. You understand that, right? Her diabetes makes this situation even more dangerous because even if the kidnapper makes every effort to keep her alive, he could screw it up out of inexperience with the disease. It was clear from the start Randy wasn't involved, but you just had to cover your bases. The second you laid eyes on that guy, you should've known. He could barely string four words together without injecting *man* in there. Criminal mastermind, that one."

"We're not all like you, Maggie," Paul said, and it startled her, that for once, he seemed frustrated. He'd been so patient lately. Like he was waiting for her to change her mind and want him back.

"I don't know what that means," she said.

"You're gifted," he said. "A natural. It doesn't come as easy to some of us, the instinct."

Maggie stared at him, horrified. "You think this is *natural*?" she said, her voice lowering, a surefire sign she was about to cry. God, her instinct wasn't natural—it was born out of horrible experience and fear . . . out of blood and terror and loss. It'd been forced on her at twelve, and she'd never recovered that part of her, that innocent part. She had never got her sister back either. And he was telling her this was her *gift*? She felt sick.

A moment too late, Paul seemed to realize his mistake. His blue eyes widened, and he reached forward automatically, but she stepped back, unable to even look at him. "Maggie—"

She held out her hand, stopping him. "I'm leaving," she said.

Maggie turned on her heel and hurried away, thankful that he at least had the sense not to follow.

CHAPTER 14

One eye on her watch, Maggie drove a few blocks down to her old haunt, Sal's Lounge. After parking across the street, she darted down the asphalt, dodging traffic. Sal's was a hole-in-the-wall with a neon sign that sputtered weakly and crumbling concrete block that had seen better days, but Maggie always had a fondness for it.

She hadn't been inside in a long time—she'd taken pains to avoid this part of town—but the long, polished oak bar, well worn and well loved by Sal, the owner, was still the same, as was the low light that was as comforting as it was seedy.

"Maggie." Sal, a broad woman with long silver hair braided down her back, smiled at her. "Long time no see. Jameson on the rocks?"

"Just a burger." Maggie sat down on one of the ancient leather stools, leaning forward, her elbows on the bar. God, this day. When she got ready for her run this morning, she couldn't have begun to imagine Frank would show up and reel her in to work a case that was all too familiar, threatening to shake her hard-won stability. And with Paul and Jake tearing at her emotions in different ways, her nerves were on edge, and she felt like she was falling apart.

Sal slid a glass of water down the bar and Maggie caught it with her hand, taking a long drink. "You on the clock?" she asked.

Maggie nodded.

"I'll get the burger started for you quick, then," Sal said.

"Thanks," Maggie said, absently pulling her hair out of the bun she'd put it in that afternoon on the way to the Carmichael Academy.

"Looks like you're drinking alone." A man with slicked-back hair and an ill-fitting suit sidled up next to her. "I can change that."

Maggie shot him a disgusted look. This was the *last* thing she needed, on top of everything else. "I'm not drinking at all," she said. "And I'd rather keep doing that alone."

"Aw, sweetheart, don't play hard to get." The man leaned into her space, his palm grazing her thigh. Maggie grabbed his wrist in a vise grip, bending it backward—hard. He yelped.

"*No* means *no*," she hissed. "Get lost."

He scuttled away, his tail between his legs.

Maggie took another sip of water. Frank had been right to send her to cool off for an hour. She had had her fill of machismo today. She could practically smell it, sticking to her like a cheap cologne. First she'd had to deal with Paul's stubbornness and Jackson's ego, plus the senator's skepticism and his advisor's naked ambition, only to run right into Mike Sutton's bullshit at headquarters. The only man she wasn't feeling entirely annoyed with right now was Jake O'Connor, though that morning when she'd first met him, if she'd been told she'd feel that way by the afternoon, she would never have believed it. And now . . . how odd it was that she'd felt more comfortable bouncing ideas off him than off people she'd known and worked with for years.

What was his deal, she wondered. When she met him that morning, he'd challenged her and told her she was doing it all wrong, but that afternoon, as soon as she came back from the academy, all of a sudden, he was willing to listen, to meet and even elevate her theories; use them as a springboard. What had changed his mind? Did this case feel as off to him as it did to her?

She'd eat her most expensive pair of heels if Jake O'Connor didn't have some kind of military background.

It was obvious in the way he carried himself; how when he followed her out into the mansion's foyer this morning, he instinctively checked and double-checked visuals of all the exits in mere seconds. Most combat vets do that. All the field agents she knew did it. Hell, she did it too. It became a habit, a part of you, to calculate an escape route, just in case.

Maggie hadn't learned that trick in the FBI or the military, though. She'd learned it the night she and Erica were taken. It was a lesson learned too late, but she'd never forgotten it.

What lessons had Jake O'Connor's life taught him? A man like that, with *that* body, paired with his cocky country-boy-done-good personality, would have gone over well in the service. A natural leader. He wasn't used to taking orders—she figured he was the guy who gave them. She could tell from the way he'd tried to take the reins from her this morning. But then, later, he'd proven to be flexible. Helpful, even.

He was confusing, that's what he was. Confusing . . . and way too attractive. But she was relieved he was on her side, even if he did still want to go rushing in as soon as they found Kayla's location. She could understand that, really. She didn't blame him for it. There were times she felt that way too. She had just learned the hard way to ignore it.

Maggie ran a hand through her curls, taking another sip of water as her phone buzzed. She jumped a little, but then saw it was a text message from her friend Grace, a profiler at the Bureau.

Heard you were at HQ. Where are you now?

Maggie sent her a text back:

At Sal's.

A few seconds later, her phone buzzed.

On my way.

Sal came bustling out of the kitchen then, a basket with a burger and steaming, golden fries in her hand. She placed it in front of Maggie, who took a bite, trying not to moan.

She was so hungry that, by the time Grace arrived a few minutes later, she'd almost finished the entire burger.

Grace entered the bar in a cloud of expensive perfume—the kind that was a scent specially blended for her in Paris—her Manolo Blahnik heels clicking on the bar's cracked tile floor. The guy who'd tried to hit on Maggie—Mr. Handsy—looked up at the sound, his eyes glazing over a little as he took in Grace. Luckily, Maggie had taught him his lesson, so he kept his distance.

Grace Sinclair was the kind of beautiful that got deeper the longer you looked at her. Her black hair was thick and straight, falling to the curve of her waist. Her tall hourglass figure was always clad in the latest designer clothing. It boggled Maggie's mind to think how much Grace must spend on shoes alone. Grace's heart-shaped face was sweet and open—deceptively so. It was one of the reasons she made a fantastic profiler. People underestimated her intelligence because of her high-fashion appearance, and she used that to her advantage. Being one of the few women in the boys' club that was the FBI isn't easy—you have to use every tool and talent you've got to make it to the top. Grace knew that, and so did Maggie. It had bonded them when they met, Grace fresh out of Quantico, Maggie only one year into being an agent.

Grace brushed at the stool next to Maggie before sitting down. Her dark blue linen dress had an asymmetrical neckline that reminded her friend of an alligator's teeth, and the trumpet skirt flared out at the knees, allowing her more freedom of movement as she perched on the stool, crossing her long, slim legs. Her heels seemed lethally high—the spike stilettos so sharp they could pierce a vital organ if the woman was determined to do so.

Maggie knew how determined Grace could be. The first case they worked together was a bank robbery where two unsubs had taken a lobby full of people hostage. Grace was shadowing another profiler who had little respect for her, Maggie, or women in general. He kept cutting Grace off when she suggested something, but instead of letting it cow her, Grace just kept going until Maggie started asking *her* questions instead. Grace had ended up delivering a profile of the unsub's partnership that helped Maggie establish a deep enough connection with the submissive partner that he rebelled against the dominant partner, shooting him and giving SWAT a window of opportunity to move in and get the hostages out safely.

"You and this place," Grace sighed, looking around disparagingly at the shabby, dimly lit dive. "What's wrong with the wine bar on Second Street? They have jazz on Tuesdays."

Maggie smiled. Grace loved jazz. She couldn't even keep track of the number of times Grace—who was as beautiful as she was unlucky in love—had dragged her to some dark smoky hole-in-the-wall to listen to whatever jazz quartet she'd discovered. But as much as she loved Grace, Maggie wasn't going to step foot in a bar where she couldn't get a beer. That was asking too much, even for a good friend.

"Sal's has something better: personality," Maggie insisted.

"So, did Frank put you on a time-out?" Grace asked.

"He ordered me to go eat," Maggie said, dipping a fry in some ketchup. "He caught me in the park early this morning. We've been nonstop since. I made first contact with the unsub, plus interviews at the school, and Paul decided to chase after the wrong suspect even though I told him it was a dead end. So today's been *great*." She stabbed a fry a little too hard into the ketchup.

"I can't believe Frank finally called in his favor," Grace said.

"Yup," Maggie said, ending the *p* with an audible pop.

"Well, it's not like he could cash it in that entire year and a half you were traveling," Grace mused.

"I was helping build wells in Chad, Grace. You make it sound like I was on a vacation."

"Your charity work was incredibly noble and rewarding, I'm sure," Grace said. "But you were running away, and we both know it."

Maggie sighed. She had a point. She had loved her work with the Clean Water Initiative. It had been her father's passion project and it had felt good to continue his work. But she had joined the team in Chad to get away from her life—from her professional and personal mistakes.

"Speaking of why you ran away, how are you and Paul working together?" Grace asked.

Maggie sighed. "Paul plays nice—you know him. Boy Scout, through and through."

"Captain America," Grace said with a smile. Paul was the head of her team and they worked closely together. When Maggie had broken off the engagement and left for Chad, she had felt slightly better that Paul would have Grace and the rest of his team to lean on.

"To a T," Maggie said. "He's been professional, of course. It's that O'Connor character who's being a pain in the ass."

Grace raised a perfectly threaded eyebrow. "*What* O'Connor character?"

"He's some security expert," Maggie said. "Military, I think. Someone sent him in to work with the senator. Supposedly he deals with 'sensitive situations' like this."

"Are you talking about someone from General Hoffman's team?" Grace asked. Maggie perked up, interested. She needed a better understanding of the guy aside from the fact that he filled out a suit in a criminally attractive way.

"I don't know, I might be," she said. "He hasn't been really forthcoming on where he's getting his orders."

"Unsurprising, if the general's in charge. I worked with one of his guys on a serial killer case last year," Grace said. "They have this tech whiz kid who's almost as good as Zooey."

Zooey was the head of forensics on Grace's team. She sang her praises regularly, so Maggie knew she meant business with the comparison.

"So these guys are trustworthy?' Maggie asked.

"They're the best," Grace said. "But they're covert military types. You know how closemouthed men like that are."

"He thinks he should be in charge," Maggie said. "It's so annoying."

"Well, that's stupid," Grace said. "But working together? Might not be a bad idea. He'll probably have decent ideas when it comes to getting Kayla out safely."

"We need some inkling of *where* she is to even start thinking about that," Maggie sighed.

"No luck?" Grace asked.

"Have you read up on it?"

Grace nodded. "Frank sent me over the call transcripts and case file. He asked me to put together a rudimentary profile with what we have."

"Which isn't much," Maggie said.

"I've worked with less," Grace said.

"Does it seem . . . off to you?" Maggie asked.

"Off *how*?" Grace asked.

"I keep thinking it through, but it doesn't make a lot of sense. The kidnapper gave the senator longer than he needs to get the money together. Who does that? Someone green. But everything else this guy's done tells us he's not new to the game. He came prepared to play. He's a pro. Why is he acting stupid all of a sudden?"

"I don't know," Grace said, grabbing one of Maggie's remaining fries, looking thoughtful. Maggie could practically see the cogs in her extraordinary brain clicking along as she pieced together what she knew about the unsub to create an actual personality. "He says he knows about her insulin dependence and he seems to be administering it, so he doesn't seem to be a sadist. Kayla's a tool; she's not his prize. That's very good in a lot of ways. He clearly has an ego, but he's goal oriented, and Kayla's just a step toward that goal. It means the risk of sexual assault or extreme abuse is fairly low—he might not even have the stomach for it."

"Thank God," Maggie said.

"He's obviously trying to take decent care of her so he

can use her to get what he really wants. Or . . . I guess he might even feel guilty. Abducting a kid, especially one who has a serious health risk, is crossing a bigger line than taking an adult."

"That could be it," Maggie said. "But this isn't the guy's first rodeo. I'm not sure he has much of a conscience."

"True," Grace agreed. "His actions—the smoothness of the abduction, the preparation with the insulin, the disguising of his voice, the tech he must be using to bounce his phone signal—speak to experience. But then he gives you a ransom demand, with no account number. That's . . . sloppy."

"Do you think he's just worried we're going to trace the account?" Maggie asked. It was the only logical thing she could think of.

Grace swirled her wine in the glass, staring at the red depths. "If he's sophisticated enough to bounce his phone signal, he should be prepared with an untraceable account."

Maggie sighed. She was right. "The pieces aren't adding up—I try to put it together, but I just can't *get* there. Maybe I'm just too rusty after . . ." She took another swig of water.

"Mags, I'm kind of worried about you," Grace said, her eyebrows drawn together in concern. "You've gone through a lot of changes. You left the Bureau and ended things with Paul. I respect your decision," she added hastily. "I love you, and Paul's a good guy, but I understand why the two of you together didn't work. And I understand why you needed to get away and throw yourself into charity work. But now I see you throwing yourself back into negotiating, all because you owe Frank a favor. It concerns me."

Maggie bit her lip, hating the way it all sounded out loud. "What's your point?"

"It's a lot of chaos and stress," Grace said delicately. "And it's a lot of avoidance. Are you seeing someone? Have you spoken to a therapist about Sherwood Hills? About any of the changes in your life? You know there's no shame in therapy. It can be very useful to help people process trauma and grief. I know you had positive experiences with therapy after, well, after what happened to you and Erica. Maybe it's time to think about finding someone you're comfortable with to talk to."

Maggie drew back from her as if she were burned. Her grip tightened on the water glass so hard she was afraid it'd crack under the pressure. For a moment, all she could hear was her heart pounding in her ears, the screams that echoed through her nightmares. She took a deep breath, forcing herself to answer. "I'm fine, Grace," she said shortly. "Also, no offense, but if I wanted to have a deep personal conversation, I wouldn't do it with a card-carrying member of the FBI . . ." She trailed off, nearly dropping the glass of water as the insight struck her.

"Holy crap," she said. "I just realized something."

"What?" Grace asked.

"The ask, the first ask the kidnapper gave, it's not a real one. He doesn't want money—he wants something else. The money's just a distraction. *That's* why he didn't give us an account number. He wasn't being sloppy—this guy is too good—he was trying to buy time so he can set up his next move. He's working this at different angles. He's going to contact the senator directly to get what he *really* wants. And I bet he'll do it tonight."

She jumped up off the barstool so fast she faltered a bit, then grabbed her coat and phone, tossing some bills on the bar. "I'm out of here. Don't worry, Grace."

Grace shot her a frustrated look. "I'm your friend, so I always worry. Be safe."

Maggie strode out of the bar. She wouldn't make any promises. As long as you didn't make them, you didn't have to break them.

CHAPTER 15

She texted Frank as she drove back to the senator's mansion: Gonna be a little late. Got a lead. Will let you know if it pans out.

Her fingers tapped the steering wheel as she wove in and out of traffic, flashing her temporary pass at the man guarding the gate. She cut the headlights as she navigated the first curve of the senator's driveway, pulling around the back instead of the front, and situated her car so she had a side view of the door and his office windows.

Maggie settled back into the shadows, waiting.

She'd told Grace she was fine, but that was a lie. Even as she watched the video of Kayla today, seeing Kayla squint at the camera, scared but trying not to show it, she could feel the ropes against her wrists again and sense the panic rising in her gut. Grace was right—she probably *did* need to go back to therapy. She'd spent her entire childhood after the kidnapping in therapy. Plus all of high school and most of college. The idea of going back was exhausting. Which was an entirely self-defeating way to think about it.

Maybe it would help with the nightmares.

Almost every night, she was twelve years old again, running back to the shed. As she tossed and turned in her rumpled sheets, her dream self ran and ran, and when she got to the door and pushed it open, she screamed, because all that's left is blood.

Erica's blood.

It splattered the walls and floor of the shed. She'd fallen to her knees, gutted by the sight, and the blood had smeared her clothes, her skin. The coppery stench was so strong she could still almost taste it in her mouth . . . it had stuck to the back of her throat for weeks after. She'd scrubbed her skin clean of the bloodstains, but even all these years later, she could still feel them, somewhere under her skin.

Maggie leaned back against the headrest and closed her eyes, trying to block it out. But that just made it worse.

"We have to try it," Erica said.

"I can't go without you," Maggie begged. She couldn't. She wouldn't. God, how could Erica ask her to do that? What if he hurt her? What if he punished her when he saw Maggie had got away?

Erica pulled her close. "I can't fit, Mags," she whispered against her ear. "I'm too big. It has to be you. We can't just sit here and wait for whatever's going to happen to us. I know you can do this. You just wiggle through and run for help. I'll be here when you get back."

"I don't want to." Maggie's voice was so small as she looped her bound arms over Erica's head for a clumsy hug. "I can't leave you here. What if he hurts you?"

"I'll be fine," Erica reassured her. "You just need to be brave, okay? For both of us."

"I'll try," Maggie said. She had to try. What choice did they have? Her big sister was right, as usual.

Erica smiled shakily, brushing Maggie's hair off her cheek. "We'll do it tonight, after he brings us food, okay? After he leaves, you'll wiggle through and you'll run, Maggie. You run fast as you can and you don't stop for anything and you don't look back for anything. No matter what."

Maggie's eyes welled with tears. She tried to bite them back. She had to be strong. She had to be brave. For her sister and their parents who were looking for them.

Erica squeezed her hands tightly. "It'll be okay, little sis. No matter what happens tonight, you and I are in this together," she whispered.

Maggie had tried to be brave. That day and every day

since. Sometimes she fooled herself into thinking she'd succeeded. But after Sherwood Hills, she couldn't fake it anymore—not even to herself.

She needed help—she knew that. But knowing it and doing something about it were two different things. Who could even begin to understand what she'd been through? None of her friends, no matter how well-meaning. Most shrinks wouldn't be equipped. She didn't even know how to start to get help. And she wasn't sure if she had the courage to start that journey. It was so much easier to just tamp it down, to ignore it. To let the wound fester, but never heal.

Her thoughts were disrupted by a glimpse of movement in the distance. She snapped to attention, peering to her right, where a figure was walking out of a side door. A cloud shifted, spilling moonlight on the man's gray hair.

It was the senator.

Showtime.

Maggie watched as he got into his silver Lexus and began to make his way off the estate via the side road. A familiar feeling started to uncoil inside her: the adrenaline of the chase. Her blood began to pump and her stomach tightened in anticipation. God, she'd forgotten this—maybe a little on purpose, because she'd *missed* it. She'd missed the way every cell of her body and mind felt alive, complete. Missed the way it felt right, as if this was where she belonged, what she should be doing.

As soon as the senator had turned out of sight, she sped down the main driveway after him, managing to get onto the main road just in time to see the Lexus pull out of the ivy-covered entrance and turn left.

She followed a few cars behind, every muscle in her body singing, her heartbeat loud in her ears. Her eyes narrowed, focusing on the Lexus as everything else fell away. Until it was just her and the chase, her and the target, her and the search for answers. Real ones, this time.

The senator drove normally—no speeding, swerving, or urgency. Responsible use of turn signals. For all she knew, he could be headed somewhere totally benign—but she found that hard to believe. He was hiding something—sneaking out in the dead of night made that much obvious.

Someone blared a horn, and Maggie swore, swerving into the right lane to avoid an SUV. For a second, she lost sight of her quarry. She gunned the accelerator, shooting ahead of the SUV that had almost swiped her, her eyes searching the traffic ahead of her. There he was. With a sigh of relief, she settled back in the bucket seat.

After a few miles of stop-and-go traffic through the residential part of Falls Church, Maggie almost relaxed.

The key word here is *almost*. You never relax, not truly. Because that's always when the target acts.

The Lexus, which had been meandering down Washington Boulevard, veered suddenly across two lanes, speeding onto the highway on ramp.

Maggie changed lanes fast, once, twice, nearly clipping a sedan in the process as she sped onto the on ramp by the skin of her knuckles. As she merged into traffic, she thought for a moment she'd lost him. That he'd realized he was being followed. But *there*—four cars ahead, she could see the silver Lexus zooming into the fast lane.

"Gotcha." Maggie smiled. "Let's see where you're going, Senator."

As they made their way East toward DC, she tried to calm her quickened breathing. She had to stay sharp—every minute that ticked by gave the unsub more time to plan, to plot, and to destroy.

CHAPTER 16

Thirty minutes later, Maggie had tailed the senator into the city. He'd parked outside one of the lower-end hotels and walked down the block to that rarity, one of the few remaining pay phones. Pacing back and forth in front of it, he checked his watch every few seconds.

Maggie parked six cars away, reaching into the back seat, where a silver briefcase was resting on the floor. She'd asked Matt, the tech who'd brought her car from the park that morning, to pick up a few things at headquarters while he was at it. You never know when you might need a directional mic to listen in on a conversation. She liked to be prepared, and luckily, Matt had followed through.

This one was the newest model. Maggie slipped the bud headphone into her ear and aimed the small, disc-shaped mic toward the senator just as the pay phone began to ring.

The late-night traffic zipping around her wasn't helping her home in on the call. She fiddled with the dials, raising the mic's volume a little.

The sound crackled through her ear, making her wince at the static, but then it cleared. *There we go.*

"Are you there?" The senator sounded nervous.

"I see you got my instructions," said Uncle Sam—the same digitized voice they'd heard that morning. Maggie's heart began to pound in her chest as she tried to discern the senator's expression from a distance. Was he scared? Angry? Why hadn't he gone to her or O'Connor when Uncle Sam contacted him to set up this meeting?

"We need to talk about this—" Thebes started.

"There's nothing to talk about," Uncle Sam interrupted. "Either you get it for me or your daughter dies."

Maggie frowned, pointing the mic a little higher. Get *it*? What was it? She knew this wasn't about money—but that still left a myriad of government secrets and knowledge the Senator was privy to.

"I can't just waltz into the Capitol and take it!" The senator ran his hand through his hair. Even this far away, Maggie could see his cheeks turning a mottled shade of red. Her triumph, a slow and steady burn, was tamped by what it meant to be right in this instance. The senator was keeping things from her—and this was about much more than money.

"You're a senator—they won't look twice at you," Uncle Sam said. "Stop making excuses. Either you get it, or your pretty little Kayla will go into diabetic shock and die. Maybe I'll dump her body in the swamp. You'll never find her. Your wife won't even have a grave to visit. That'd be a pity, wouldn't it be, Senator?"

"Please," Thebes said, his voice cracking. "What you're asking me to do . . . it's illegal. I'd be arrested. Everything would be ruined. I can give you as much money as you want—"

Maggie's mind raced, her grip on the mic tightening. This was definitely not about money. Then what? What in the Capitol was worth enough to Uncle Sam that he'd kidnap someone? And what the hell was so important to the senator that he was standing firm when a kidnapper had his daughter? When his kid's life was on the line, he was concerned about *legalities*? Maggie felt a flare of anger light in her chest, sparking into a wildfire within seconds. What the hell was this guy's problem? His priorities were all screwed up.

"Do it, or I won't even wait for the shock to set in," Uncle Sam said. "I'll slit her throat."

"But—" Senator Thebes said.

There was a click—and then the dial tone.

"Dammit!" The senator slammed the pay phone down so hard it bounced off the receiver and swung there as he ran an agitated hand through his hair, his feet shuffling like he wanted to pace.

Well, Maggie wasn't going to let any narcissistic indecision enter into this. If she had to fight the senator while she was trying to find Kayla, it'd get the girl killed even faster. Her mind made up, she opened the door and jumped out of her car, striding up the sidewalk. It was chilly outside, and she drew her peacoat tighter around her. She needed answers, and she needed them *now*. She didn't care who he was, how much power he had, or what he'd done to bring this nightmare about. Kayla was more important than all of that.

The senator still stood in the phone booth, his slumped back to her. He seemed wholly defeated, deflated, staring down at the ground like a broken man. Now was the best time to confront him, really, Maggie thought coldly. People don't lie as well when they're distraught. She'd be able to get at some of the truth behind his facade now.

"Senator," she said.

He whirled around, his eyes widening in shock when he recognized her.

"Ms. Kincaid," he said, trying for short and clipped, but the hoarseness of his voice, weighed down with guilt, skewed his aim.

"I think it's time we have an honest talk," Maggie said.

"I think it's time you get in your car and go home," Thebes snapped. "You're off this case. I'll inform Frank immediately."

Maggie drew herself up and stared him down. She knew men like him well—men who thought they could bully and muscle their way out of things. And she knew just how to deal with them.

"Senator, we're going to get in your car, and you're going to tell me what the hell is really going on here. Or I'm going to get ornery."

His eyes didn't just widen, they almost bugged out of his head at her hubris. The senator was a privileged man—a man that not a lot of people said no to.

Lucky for Kayla, Maggie wasn't cowed easily.

"Do you know who I am?" he demanded, stepping toward her, trying to use his height to intimidate. Refusing to flinch, Maggie stared steadily back at him. "I could *ruin* you."

"And I could have you arrested and in an interrogation room in twenty minutes," Maggie said flatly. "Complete with cameras, an official record, and reporters waiting for you on the drive out of headquarters to your very own jail cell. So you might want to think for a second before you threaten me any further. I could ruin *you*, sir. To the point where you'd never recover anything you have. Not your job, not your friends. Your wife would leave you. Your kid—whose life you're gambling with, for whatever reason—won't ever speak to you again . . . *If* she gets through this. You'd just be another washed-up, corrupt politician. You'd never get your shot at the Oval Office. And I'm starting to think *that's* what you care about, more than Kayla's safety. I can't imagine your being so corrupt that you'd risk your daughter's life just to protect your political career."

He stared at her, wordless, furious, practically vibrating with anger. For a moment, she was afraid he might try to hit her, but she continued, heedless. She could restrain him if things got ugly.

"Weigh the pros and cons, why don't you?" she hissed. "Your family . . . your daughter's *life*. If you care about them at all, you'll do what I say."

Maggie folded her arms and settled back on her heels, fixing him with a harsh look. She wasn't going to back down. She wasn't some cowering sycophant. She was Kayla's advocate. Her lighthouse. And she was going to get that girl home.

"Your move, Senator."

CHAPTER 17

Jake swore under his breath, one eye on the monitor set on his passenger seat. A red dot was sitting on Fifth Street and had been for a good fifteen minutes. Wherever the senator had been going, he'd parked his car.

After his second talk with Kincaid that afternoon, Jake had put a tracker on the Lexus. He just couldn't shake the feeling there was something off about this whole thing. And late that night, when he saw the red dot move, indicating that the senator was leaving the house, he knew he was right.

He would have been able to keep on Thebes' tail if he hadn't gotten pulled over for not signaling a turn. The cop had let him go as soon as he flashed his credentials, but it'd given Thebes a head start.

Dammit. Jake wrestled his way through traffic, annoyance growing with each minute that passed. He finally turned onto Fifth, slowing as he saw the parked Lexus with nobody inside. Jake gunned it up the block, and then back down. Then he caught sight of them.

Damn. Maggie Kincaid was standing there on the sidewalk, arguing with Senator Thebes. *Of course* she'd gotten the jump on him. He smiled reluctantly. She would lord this over him, he just knew. At least she'd be cute as hell doing it, he thought, his smile widening. This woman was all passion and trouble. And Jake had always been irresistibly drawn to both. She'd call him on his shit and then some—and you couldn't say that about a lot of women. Especially ones who got caught up in the whole "military hero" thing.

Maggie Kincaid was someone who wasn't going to be impressed by anything that had happened years ago—she was focused on the now. On this case. The more time he spent with her, the more he wanted to. And not just so he could stop her from getting the drop on him.

When he saw Maggie leading the senator back to his car, Jake pulled over and got out of the SUV, walked back down the street, and knocked on the Lexus' tinted window. Might as well make this a party.

The window opened a crack, and Jake smiled neutrally at the guilty-as-hell look on Thebes' face. "Senator," Jake began, "I'll be getting in the back, if you don't mind."

Without waiting for permission, he opened the back door and slipped into the back seat.

Maggie shot him a look that said *"You? Again?"* but Jake just grinned at her. She turned away and continued talking to Thebes.

"You need to tell me what's going on," she insisted, fixing the man with a penetrating glance. "I don't care what it is. I don't care if you've done something wrong or illegal. I'm not a member of the FBI anymore. I couldn't care less about any laws you're breaking or underhanded political deals. I'm not here to punish you—I'm here to save your daughter."

The senator sighed, lifting his glasses for a moment to rub his eyes. Then he started to speak. "There—there are documents that have . . . special . . . levels of classification. Documents that only certain senators on certain committees are allowed to see. Because of their sensitive nature, there's a reading room we use. It's completely private. No notes can be taken; we're not allowed to bring aides or cell phones. He wants me to take a file from that room."

"Well, can you do it?" Jake asked.

Senator Thebes shook his head. "I can't. It's illegal."

Jake frowned, and when he caught Maggie's eye, he saw

that her expression mirrored his. The man's daughter was in the hands of a kidnapper—and he was concerned about breaking a *law*? Something here was off—*way* off.

"Senator, what document does the kidnapper want? What's in it?" Maggie asked.

"I can't tell either of you," Thebes replied brusquely. "Neither of you have the clearance on national security matters such as the ones in that document."

It was a lie, and a bad one. And even if it wasn't, it didn't matter. Maggie took a sharp breath, and Jake could feel anger tightening in his chest. Jesus, did this guy care about his kid at all? If someone had grabbed *his* kid, Jake would move heaven and earth to get her back. And then he'd tear the bastard kidnapper apart with his bare hands.

"That's garbage," Jake said, and Maggie's eyes widened when she heard the disgust in his voice. "If this was a national security issue, there are hundreds of people you could go to for help instead of trying to deal with it on your own. The NSA would be all over it. So would the military and Feds and probably the spooks, incognito."

Thebes glared at him, and Jake suddenly understood. He felt that tightness in his gut that meant he was right. "Whatever's in that file Uncle Sam wants is embarrassing . . . maybe career-ruining. You're just covering your ass."

"Nonsense!" the senator said. "I have no reason to lie. But I have every reason to protect our national security. The FBI is the one that's bungling this investigation." He shot Maggie a meaningful look.

"I'm not bungling anything," Maggie replied angrily. "You're the one who's hiding vital information from the case. You need to get your priorities in check, Senator," Maggie went on. "Are you really going to put your daughter's life at risk because of something that might hurt your career?"

"I have done everything that has been asked of me," the senator said, not meeting her gaze. "We shouldn't even be in this situation. Your techs should have found a way to trace his calls. SWAT should have rescued my baby girl already."

"It doesn't work that way, Senator," Jake said. "Not with this kind of criminal."

But there was a grim resolve in Senator Thebes' eyes as he stared back at Jake. "O'Connor, you're not here to think—you're here to take orders."

He finally looked at Maggie. "I appreciate your insights, Ms. Kincaid. But I cannot break my oaths as a political official and put dangerous information that could risk our national security in the hands of a madman. I have more than Kayla to think about. Getting her home safe is your job. My job is to protect my country's national security."

It was a clear, cold-blooded dismissal. Maggie knew she wasn't going to get any more out of him. Not tonight. She needed to regroup, figure out what this meant. Figure out a way *around* this man who didn't even care if his own child lived or died. She stifled a shudder, realizing that she was facing a man who was even more monstrous than the kidnapper who'd stolen his child—the child he was so willing to toss away to preserve his career.

"O'Connor," the senator barked. "I'm going back to the house. I need my rest. I'll see you tomorrow morning. I've decided to take Max's advice and hold a press conference. It's time to take control of the narrative."

Maggie sighed. "You're making a mistake," she said, pulling the car door open and stepping out.

As soon as Jake had followed her out of the car and onto the sidewalk, the senator backed up the Lexus and screeched angrily away. Jake glanced at her, taking her in as she stood there, furious, her hands on her hips and her blue eyes stormy as she watched the car vanish into the distance. She yanked her phone angrily out of her pocket, dialing a number.

"Frank, it's me," she said into it. "The unsub contacted Thebes privately. This is more complicated than we thought." She paused, listening in the phone, nodding. "Okay. I understand. I'll see you tomorrow morning."

She hung up the phone, glaring at it.

"Is Edenhurst gonna toe the line?" Jake asked. He hadn't

struck him as the kind of man who would acquiesce to the pressure of powerful men, but you never knew.

Maggie snorted. "Frank's too cranky and too close to retirement to play nice," she said. "Thank God. It may be the thing that saves Kayla if her father's going to get in my way like this."

"What's the game plan?" Jake asked.

"The night shift's taken over, monitoring the phones. But our unsub isn't going to call in the middle of the night. Now that we know he and the senator are in contact, that gives us a whole new angle on his calls to us."

"How so?"

"It makes them more like a performance. He's not really making deals or negotiating with me, he's just pretending for an audience. He doesn't think I can give him what he wants—he's convinced only the senator can. Frank wants to regroup in the morning, figure out what this means to our approach to the case."

"Thebes is going to stand in your way," Jake said.

"I know, and it's bullshit," she declared, looking at him like she expected him to argue with her.

But he shook his head in disgust. "I'll say," he replied.

In her surprise, she stepped back, her gaze traveling from his face all the way down to his boots and then back up again. When she met his eyes, he raised an eyebrow, hoping it'd make her blush.

But instead she said, "Well, since we can't do a damn thing about it until tomorrow morning, let's go get a drink."

His fury at Thebes fading for the moment in his shock at her sudden shift of focus, he could feel the beginning of a grin tugging his lips.

"I know a place," he said.

CHAPTER 18

He took her to his neighborhood bar—a quiet haven inside an Italian joint that served the best lasagna he'd ever had. Giorgio's was small and dimly lit with that fifties Old World ambience Jake got a kick out of.

He watched as Maggie took the place in—the candles in wine bottles, the checkered tablecloths, the autographed eight-by-ten glossies of Frank Sinatra hanging on the wall, and Giorgio himself, standing proudly behind the bar, his starched white shirt gleaming in the flicker of the candlelight.

For a second, he thought she'd hate it . . . that the kitsch was too much. Had he underestimated her? Was she the kind of woman who demanded bottle service and Michelin stars?

But instead of looking horrified, her lush lips broke into a wide smile. "This place is *great*!" she said. "Whoa . . . is that a gold-plated meatball?" She pointed to the glass case at the end of the bar, where there was indeed a single golden meatball on a plate.

"It is," Jake said.

"Please tell me there's a story behind it," Maggie said.

"Well . . . it's a gold-plated meatball," Jake said. "That's kind of a given."

She laughed, and the sound tugged at him deep, a soothing balm to his tired soul. "Okay, I've got to hear this," she said as they walked toward the bar.

"Giorgio tells it best," Jake said, nodding to the man behind the counter.

"Jake, nice to see you," Giorgio said. "Who is this lovely lady?"

"Giorgio, Maggie. Maggie, Giorgio."

"A pleasure," Giorgio said, taking Maggie's hand and kissing it with a flourish.

"Maggie was wondering about the meatball," Jake said.

Giorgio's mouth twitched into a smile under his black mustache. "Some things, they are just too perfect to eat," he told Maggie very seriously. "One day, my chef puts this meatball on a plate. And I'm not sure what it was—but I *was* sure in that moment that it was the most perfect meatball to ever exist."

"Without even tasting it?" Maggie asked, shooting a sly look at Jake.

"I didn't have to!" Giorgio declared grandly. "My instincts, you see."

"So you're a man of instinct."

"Always trust your gut," Giorgio said, tapping his rather rotund one. "Anyway, I swept the meatball away, much to my chef's chagrin. She's always arguing with me."

"She managed to stop arguing with you long enough to marry you," Jake pointed out.

"This is true," Giorgio said. "My wife, she has a gift with food. I wanted to memorialize that gift. Give her something special she would have forever. A tribute worthy of her talent."

"So you gold-plated the world's most perfect meatball," Maggie finished.

"For love!" Giorgio said passionately. "And for posterity!"

"He gave it to her for their anniversary," Jake added.

"Oh, dear," Maggie said. "How did that go over?"

"I slept on the couch for only a week," Giorgio said with a grin. "But it's grown on her."

Maggie laughed. "You're a unique man, Giorgio."

"So they tell me," he said, pulling out a bottle of wine

and pouring them two glasses without prompting. "This one—" he gestured at Jake "—he's one of a kind too."

"Is that so?" Maggie asked, turning in her seat to look at Jake, assessing him.

"A soldier's never one of a kind," Jake said. "Just one of a unit."

Giorgio scoffed. "Who else would bother to help me with those delinquents who were tagging the windows of every business on the block? Or drive my bartender home so she doesn't have to walk home late at night? This one . . ." He clapped Jake on the shoulder. "He's one of the good ones. Hang on to him." He winked at Maggie.

"Oh, we aren't—" Maggie started, but she was interrupted by a clattering from the kitchen and a female voice calling Giorgio's name.

"Duty calls," he said with a bow. "Let me know if you two need anything else."

He disappeared into the kitchen, and Jake turned to Maggie.

"So this is your regular place," she said, looking around.

"Yeah, I live a few blocks away," he said. "And they have the best garlic knots."

"Not much of a cook?" Maggie asked.

"Not unless you count grilled cheese," he said.

Her blue eyes softened. "I'm not so hot either," she admitted. She took a sip of wine. "So, we should talk about the case," she said.

Back to business already. He couldn't blame her—time was of the essence—but he'd enjoyed the glimpse of her lighter side as she teased Giorgio. She'd seemed almost relaxed—which was new.

He tried to focus on what she'd asked, instead of all the ways he could get her to relax more.

But she was damn distracting, just inches away from him, her skin glowing in the candlelight, her fingers wrapped around the wineglass. He found himself focused on her nails, of all things, for a moment. He liked that they didn't have any polish on them. She had the kind of hands that had gun calluses. It was an oddly alluring thought, the capability it spoke to.

A strong, deadly woman who would fight for what was right at any cost.

Was there anything sexier?

It didn't hurt that she was one of the most beautiful women he'd ever seen. Skin smooth as cream, and eyes so blue it almost hurt to look in them. Those golden curls he wanted to run his fingers through, drawing her closer, his lips covering hers . . .

"What are we going to do about Thebes?" Maggie asked, breaking his reverie. He cleared his throat, shifting in his seat, uncomfortably aware of where his daydreaming was leading.

"I've got some people," Jake said. "They could hack into his computers. See what he's hiding."

"But we *know* what he's hiding," Maggie said. "Or at least we know what the kidnapper wants—whatever file's in the Capitol. That won't be on his computer."

"True," Jake agreed. "So what do *you* think is the best plan?"

"Our unsub," Maggie said. "*He* knows what's in the file."

"So you want to con him into giving you the information?" Jake asked.

"Why? Do you think it's a bad idea?" Her delicate brows drew together defensively.

"No," he said. "I think it's a good idea. He will get back into contact with us when Thebes doesn't hand over the file. If you play it right, he could be more forthcoming than Thebes."

"It'll be a shaky line," Maggie mused, swirling the red wine in her glass. "I can't push him too much, or seem too eager. If he realizes how in the dark Thebes is keeping us, that's it. He has all the power."

"You can do it," Jake said.

"You think so?" Maggie asked, and there was a vulnerability in her voice that startled him. She'd been so confident, so ball busting so far, he'd almost forgotten what Peggy had told him about her last case.

"I do," Jake said. "You got the drop on me with Thebes, didn't you?"

A triumphant smile spread across her face. "I did," she said smugly.

"Don't gloat," he said.

She stuck her tongue out at him. "It's not my fault I'm clearly a better tailer than you. And faster."

"I got pulled over!" he protested.

"I *don't* get pulled over," she added primly, tossing her head.

He laughed. "You're a piece of work," he said, affection and attraction making him feel loose and happy.

"I try," she said. She checked the time on her phone. "I really should get going," she said. "It's late."

"You good to drive?" Jake asked.

"I had half a glass of wine," she said, rising from the barstool. "I'm fine."

Jake walked her out, his palm coming to rest lightly on her lower back, his heart beating a little faster when she didn't frown or pull away, but instead leaned into his touch.

The street was empty and dark this time of night. Maggie turned toward him, smiling still.

"This was nice," she said. "Maybe you're less of a pain in the ass than I thought."

"I'm shocked that you're willing to admit that," he said.

"I should go," she said, but she didn't move.

He wanted to bend down and kiss her. To grab that tantalizing dip in her waist and draw her close, until he could feel the softness of her skin, the press of her breasts and hips against him. But he knew he couldn't. He knew that if he did, he'd ruin the gentle camaraderie they had found over a gold-plated meatball and a half glass of wine.

And he didn't want to ruin that—for her or him—or the them he was starting to hope they might become in the future.

"You could walk me home," he said with a laugh to tell her he was joking.

"You're a big boy, O'Connor," she said. "I think you'll be safe."

"See you tomorrow?" he asked as she turned and pointed her key to her car, opening it.

"Tomorrow," she said.

He waited until she was in the car and had driven off, her brake lights fading into the distance, before walking back inside the bar.

Giorgio was back at the bar, wiping it down. "You scare her off already?" he asked.

Jake rolled his eyes. "She has an early morning." They both did.

"I like her," Giorgio said with a smile.

"Yeah," Jake said, thinking of how her eyes crinkled when she laughed. The husky, infectious sound echoed in his head. "Me too, Giorgio. Me too."

CHAPTER 19

Frank Edenhurst was a lot of things: a patriot, a crack shot, a damn fine chess player, and a decent husband—or at least, Alyce hadn't complained yet, and it would be thirty-five years in October.

Tactful he was not. Which is why, when Max Grayson sidled up to him in the senator's office, sipping green sludge from a clear glass bottle, and asked him what he thought about the setup for the press conference at the Hale Building, Frank grunted and said, "This is a terrible idea."

"Nonsense!" Grayson replied, almost cheerfully. "It'll poll great, rally the whole country. Foster a feeling of togetherness."

"It will bring attention to something that's still thankfully under the radar and endanger the child's life," Frank gritted out. What in the world was the senator thinking, going along with this sycophant's awful ideas? Grayson obviously had political stars in his eyes, and nothing was more important to him than a leap in poll numbers, not even the life of his boss's daughter. But what was the senator's motivation? After Maggie's encounter with the senator last night, Frank was on high alert. The senator's motivations weren't clear—but the unsub's were becoming clearer now. This was all about the senator. Frank had been monitoring the phones since four a.m., not just waiting for the unsub to call with the account numbers as promised, but keeping track of who Thebes was calling.

So far, Frank had nothing, but that didn't mean anything this early in the game.

"It's only a matter of time until the news breaks, anyway," Grayson said, looking a little annoyed at Frank's obvious lack of enthusiasm. "This way, we control the narrative."

His phone rang. "If you'll excuse me." He nodded at Frank. "You've got Grayson," he said as he walked away. "No, no, I need at least three more cameras at the venue. I want all angles on the senator and his wife. And talk to me about lighting." He snapped his fingers at one of the assistants running around. "Has anyone seen Mrs. Thebes?"

"I don't think she's out of bed yet, sir," the woman replied.

Grayson rolled his eyes and turned back to his phone.

Frank could barely conceal his sneer of disgust. That one was a piece of work.

Speaking of pieces of work, Maggie had arrived, followed by Jake O'Connor. She took one look at Grayson as he paced back and forth, arguing about camera placement and scheduling mic checks, and she pressed her lips together so hard they nearly disappeared.

"Have there been any calls?" she asked Frank. "Did the unsub give us an account number?"

He shook his head, and she seemed unsurprised at the news.

"And they're still going through with the presser?" Maggie asked, her eyes narrowing.

"Looks like," Frank said grimly. "Tried to talk them out of it, but they wouldn't listen. The compromise was that they pushed it back until tomorrow. To give us time to negotiate more."

"Well, let's see about that," Maggie said. Before Frank could stop her, she strode down the steps, snapping, "Grayson!"

The man turned, pointing to his cell and then showing her his back.

Frank winced. Bad move on Grayson's part. Ignoring Maggie was like trying to ignore the sun in a heatwave.

Maggie walked up to Grayson and without missing a beat, she snatched the phone out of his hand. "Hi," she said into it. "Grayson will have to call you back." She punched the screen with a fingertip to hang up and tossed the phone onto a nearby chesterfield couch, where it bounced twice and fell onto an antique Persian rug spread across the floor.

"What the—" Max's ears turned bright red as he sputtered in shock.

Frank shook his head, trying to hide his smile.

"A press conference is a terrible idea," Maggie said. "And if you didn't have your head up your ass, you'd see that."

"This isn't your call," Max snarled. "I don't take orders from you. I work for Senator Thebes, and this is what he wants me to do. Isn't that right, Senator?" he asked meaningfully over Maggie's shoulder.

Frank turned and saw Thebes standing in the doorway, watching the confrontation.

Maggie whirled around, zeroing in on him. "Senator, please think twice about this," she pleaded, an ominous edge in her voice. "Think about what we talked about last night. This situation needs to be kept calm and controlled. Going to the press and whipping up a frenzy will light a fire we can't control."

"She's right, sir," Jake interjected. "Once the press spotlight exposes a negotiation, everything ramps up. Things get much harder. Journalists get underfoot; hell, sometimes they get involved, trying to scoop the story. With all this focus on us, we lose any element of surprise we might have—which is a huge risk from a tactical standpoint."

"The kidnapper could easily panic." Maggie picked up the plea, her voice impassioned. "The whole country will be watching the case. Everyone will be looking for him. That will make him paranoid—and you don't want your daughter's life in the hands of a person who knows everyone's looking for him. We haven't given him any reason to not negotiate with us or to distrust us yet, but a press conference will ruin all that. I warn you, this will blow up in our faces, and there will be consequences . . ." She trailed off meaningfully, fixing the senator with a knowing glance. He avoided her eyes and remained silent.

"The public has a right to know!" Max Grayson insisted, walking across the room to stand next to the senator. "It's a miracle Kayla's friends haven't been tweeting or Snapchatting or whatever the hell it is that kids do about it yet."

"They didn't because we told them not to," Maggie said icily. "They're good kids. They want their friend found. That's more than I can say about you."

Grayson stepped back as if he were wounded. But Frank knew—he could tell from the coldness in his eyes—that it was a performance. He held his breath, watching as Grayson gathered himself. Frank understood where Maggie was coming from, but, damn, if she didn't push the envelope. He agreed that this Grayson character needed to be whipped into shape, but these hardball tactics were something only Maggie would be brave enough to try.

"Of *course* I want her found," Grayson finally said softly. "But we can't count on any kids, good or not. We need to get in front of this, Senator." He placed a hand on Thebes' shoulder. "You're a public figure. This is your job."

The senator took a deep breath, looking at Maggie, then at Jake, and finally Grayson. "You're right," he said. "Let's do it. Is there a speech prepared?"

"You're making a big mistake," Maggie said, her voice low and rough with disgust. Before any of the men could say anything, she stormed out of the library. Her footsteps clipped along, but Frank could see her fury in her balled-up fists and the tightness in her shoulders.

Frank sighed. Maggie had always had a problem with the shaky morality that unfortunately powered most of DC. This instance, more shocking than most, jarred him too: The slimy bastard had just decided to risk his daughter's life for a PR move. But Frank had been on the DC beat long enough and worked with enough crooked politicians to accept it for what it was and work around it.

Maggie never tried to work around it. She'd use nuance and deception only as long as it worked, but when the chips were down, she was open defiance through and through. Especially when something got in the way of saving a life.

God, she'd been the best—a prodigious talent. He'd known it the first time he observed her at Quantico, running through a kidnapping scenario he'd designed to weed out the recruits who would break under the extreme pressure of negotiating. Maggie had a powerful combination of intuitiveness and a steady nerve that was rare not only in recruits, but in seasoned agents as well.

In the final moment, some recruits panicked. Others didn't get more than a few hours in before they lost their temper, or they couldn't maintain the deception necessary to do the job, so that the lies leaked into their voices, dismantling their connection with the unsub. And a few just didn't have the instinct—when to push, when to pull back, when to bargain, when to change the game, when to show authority, and when to show understanding.

During the exercise, Maggie had been the last one standing. A slip of a girl with a curly blond halo of hair and serious, wide blue eyes. She never broke, not even when she sent in the fake SWAT and they reported back that both recruits playing the victim and kidnapper were "dead."

He'd found her on the steps after the class and introduced himself.

"You were very good in there," he remembered telling her.

And he'll never forget what she said back, her chin tilted up and she said, "I did everything right in the simulation, but in real life, they would've died, too."

"Kid," he'd told her gently, "that's this job sometimes."

It was the first lesson every rookie had to learn. And the most important.

She'd taken a deep breath and said, "I know."

It would take Frank a few more days to look at her file to realize how intimately she *did* know . . . and that she was the kind of survivor who would keep rising out of the ashes no matter how many times she was burned.

Today, he'd seen some sparks of life, glimmers of the old Maggie—in the way she'd tossed Grayson's cell, in the icy disgust in her voice when she confronted the senator. It encouraged him more than anything else he'd seen in the two years since she'd left the Bureau. He'd kept tabs on her, of course, but for a long time, he'd feared that losing the girl at Sherwood Hills had broken Maggie for good.

But now, here she was, back in the game and coming out swinging with the kind of fierceness that Frank had only ever seen in women agents. They worked harder because their intuition wasn't clouded by macho power plays—and because they had more to prove.

Maggie always had the most to prove to herself—that's what made her so good. She strove to be better; she never got complacent.

Because she understood the stakes in a way none of the rest of them did.

"Frank, could we have a few minutes?" Senator Thebes asked, interrupting Frank's reverie.

Frank sighed. "Senator, if I were you, I'd listen to the experts on this."

Thebes glared at him. "It's been decided, Frank."

Frank bit his tongue. He wasn't stupid—he could tell something was up. But he knew he wasn't going to get it out of this guy.

Maggie, on the other hand . . .

"I'll be right outside," he said. As he closed the doors to the office, he saw Max Grayson lean toward the senator, probably instructing him about the best lighting angles.

Frank snorted, sitting down in a chair set in a corner that offered a good view of the stairs while remaining partly hidden by a giant fern in an elaborate brass pot.

He'd only just sat down when Maggie descended the stairs, Jake O'Connor right behind her.

"We should talk this over," Jake was saying.

"I'm perfectly capable of handling this," Maggie said. "I don't need an escort."

"I think you do since you seem to have the habit of going off without backup," Jake shot back.

Maggie rolled her eyes. "You're just mad I got the drop on you last night."

"I got pulled over, I would've caught up if it weren't for that."

Maggie snorted. "Like hell. I'm a big girl, O'Connor. I can take care of myself."

"Gonna lone-wolf it, Goldilocks?"

"I told you not to call me that!" she snapped.

Frank watched as O'Connor grinned, his eyes lighting up in appreciation. "Sorry, I forgot."

Frank could see the smile in Maggie's eyes, even if it didn't show in the rest of her face. "Remember better," she said.

She stalked down the remaining few stairs, coming to an abrupt halt when she spotted Frank sitting there.

Frank raised an eyebrow at her, and her cheeks turned bright red as she realized he must have overheard their ruckus.

People fought like that for only two reasons, Frank thought: chemistry or loathing.

From the redness of Maggie's cheeks as she hurried down the hall away from both men, it was definitely chemistry.

CHAPTER 20

Maggie heard the kettle whistle, picked it up, and poured herself some white tea, dunking the teabag and stirring in some honey. Grabbing the steaming cup, she walked out of her kitchen into the living room.

She'd spent the entire day at the senator's mansion, but as the hours stretched with no call from the kidnapper, the tension ramping up with each minute that passed, Frank had finally pulled her aside as dusk began to fall.

"I don't think we're going to be getting a call from our unsub," Frank said.

He was right. But Maggie couldn't decide if this was a power play on the unsub's part, punishment, or performance art. Was he just making them sweat? Or was he faltering, losing his cool when faced with the reality of what he'd done? Or was this all a game, and the real negotiating was going on behind her back between him and the senator?

"This isn't about money," Maggie said, leaning against the library wall, watching the senator and Max Grayson work through his speech for tomorrow's presser. Mrs. Thebes hadn't left her room the entire day. "All his calls—they're a distraction from his real goal. This is about something bigger than a payday."

"Any ideas?"

Maggie shook her head. "None that I'm ready to share," she said. "I can't think in here. There's too much going on. Too many people."

"Night shift will take over in twenty minutes," Frank said. "He's not calling tonight, kid. Go home," Frank said. "Get some sleep. Read through your notes and the case files. Maybe it'll jar something loose. I'll call if anything changes. Meet me at the press conference at ten."

"You sure you can hold the fort down?" Maggie asked.

Frank looked at Thebes, his eyes narrowing. "I won't let him out of my sight."

So Maggie had retreated to her house and searched for a clue, for anything that would tell her what the senator was hiding—and therefore what the unsub really wanted.

Thwonk, her clumsy-as-hell cat, meowed from the couch as Maggie turned up the volume on the TV. She scratched his gray ears, and his yellow eyes slitted in pleasure as he began to purr.

"In other news, Senator Thebes will be holding a press conference at two o'clock tomorrow. As of now, the exact subject of the press conference is unknown, but the senator, a prominent political figure and businessman, is expected to speak on a personal matter."

Maggie jabbed the off button on her remote, settling back on her plain gray linen couch. The senator was worse than an idiot, he was evil—squandering his daughter's chance of survival in favor of his ego and poll numbers. He may not have believed her when she told him, but she knew for certain that any press would only raise tension in any negotiation to come. The attention could squash any hope the kidnapper had of getting out of this unscathed. And while suicide by cop could be common in some of these situations, with Uncle Sam's ego and machinations so far, she had a feeling that wasn't in the cards. Not without bringing Kayla down with him. She shook her head, wondering what on earth Thebes had done that made him so complacent about tossing his daughter's life away.

Maggie sighed, running a hand through her hair, looking around her bare-bones living room. She'd bought the couch and a white chair back in the pre-Thwonk era. Now she kept a throw over them to protect the linen from his shedding. The long, rectangular glass-and-wood coffee table and the TV stand were the only other furniture in the room.

She used to keep a few family photos on the wall, but after the engagement party, she'd moved them to her bedroom upstairs. One of Paul's friends from college had innocently asked where her sister was, and she'd spent the rest of the night with a pit in her stomach, faking happiness and trying not to rub her wrists.

Utilitarian to the core, she never had needed much, so she'd never bothered to do much decorating. It had always bugged Paul—he probably took it as another sign of her inability to commit to anything. How could she commit to him when she couldn't even decide on a color scheme in her own house? The brownstone had character of its own, though, from the graceful wainscoting and ceiling medallions to the 1920s slip-shade chandeliers that were such a pain to dust. She would never replace them because Erica had loved them when they were little girls. There was Kincaid history in these halls. She'd inherited the house from her father, and was all too aware that it should have gone to both her and Erica.

Maggie took a gulp of tea, the faint rose scent helping to mute her bad memories. She needed to focus on the present, not the past. She didn't care what the senator had planned—she was going to keep working and break this case wide open. This one would not turn out like Sherwood Hills: She was going to bring Kayla home safe, whether her father cared or not.

She spread the files out on the coffee table: phone records and a transcript of the interview with Randy Macomb, the pool guy. She flipped open her laptop, pulling up the video Uncle Sam had sent the senator.

She queued up video, watching it on regular speed first. It was hard not to focus on Kayla's terrified face and her squinting eyes as she struggled with the sudden light.

Maggie knew that feeling all too well. All these years later, she could still feel the chafe of burlap against her chin, the constant scream of panic in her core, masked only by a body full of aches and injuries. Bruised kneecaps. Back sore from crouching on concrete all day. The parched pain of thirst in her throat. Maggie looked down, away from the screen, and realized she was rubbing her wrists again.

"Dammit!" Her voice rang through the high ceilings of the brownstone. Thwonk yowled, skittering off the couch at the sudden sound.

"I'm sorry, sweetie," she called after the fleeing cat, but Thwonk had already gone to his favorite hiding spot under her bed.

Maggie let out a deep breath, closing her eyes as she tried to hold it together. "Concentrate," she told herself. "This isn't about you—it's about Kayla."

After another big breath, she played the video again, frame by frame this time. But it was a tight close-up on Kayla, so she could barely see anything about the room the girl was held in; only that the walls seemed to be gray. Kayla's terror made it hard to notice any other details.

She turned on the volume and Kayla's shaky voice stumbling over Dostoevsky's words filled the room. Maggie steeled her heart against it, concentrating on the surroundings. Uncle Sam hadn't been as careful filming the video—she could see more of the room than the original proof of life photo. The walls were gray—but they also looked like they were hastily painted drywall. Maggie noted the seams where the drywall connected in places, where the mud and paint job weren't so great. The video came to an end and she restarted it, going frame by frame, searching again.

Wait—what was that? Maggie squinted to Kayla's left at the dark blur in the corner. She zoomed into the spot, taking a few minutes to clean up the now-pixelated image.

It was just a pile of trash.

Dammit! This time, she managed not to yell it out loud, but boy, did she feel like it. She slammed the laptop shut, leaning back angrily.

What was she missing?

Randy Macomb's phone. She sat straight up. It was gone.

The kidnapper had obviously stolen it so they'd be chasing dead ends instead of him.

But where?

Maggie grabbed her phone, calling the contact number Randy had left with the FBI. It rang and rang, and just when she was about to give up hope, a sleepy voice answered.

"Hello?"

"Randy?"

"Yeah?"

"This is Agent—this is Maggie Kincaid," Maggie corrected herself, gritting her teeth. God, this case—it was bringing *everything* back. "I talked to you yesterday at FBI headquarters."

"The blonde chick," Randy said. "I remember."

"I just need to ask a few follow-up questions," Maggie said. "You said you lost your phone, right?"

"Right."

"Where was the last place you saw it?"

"Dude, lady, I don't know," Randy replied, bewildered. "It's probably stuck under my couch or something, out of juice."

Maggie barely resisted rolling her eyes. "Okay, just do me a favor," she said. "Walk me through that day. You wake up and . . ."

"Check the stats on the net," Randy said. "Do my business, you know."

Maggie did roll her eyes this time. Men.

"I made a protein smoothie," Randy went on, "Got dressed. Called my girl."

"No shower?" Maggie asked, scribbling his answers down on a yellow legal pad, just in case.

"I shower at the gym," Randy said. "Hey, the gym!"

"Is that where you last remember having your phone?" Maggie leapt on it.

"I remember texting a buddy of mine, Tank, right when I was walking in. I bet I left it in my locker!"

"And this was Monday?" Maggie asked, writing *gym* and circling it.

"Tuesday."

"And you're sure you didn't have your phone when you left the gym?"

There was a pause, as if he was trying to think hard and it took a lot of work. "I remember calling my buddy before the gym. Next time I remember needing it, I was home and I didn't have it."

"You went directly from the gym to your house?" Maggie asked. "No stops for coffee or gas?"

"Nope. I went straight home," he said.

"Okay," Maggie said, relieved. At least she had a lead, even if it was coming from a meathead pool guy. "What gym is this?"

"Adonis Lodge, on Fifth," Randy answered.

What a name. Why wasn't she surprised? "Thanks, Randy. You've been very helpful."

"Hey, you're gonna find Kayla, right?" he asked. "'Cause she's a really nice kid. She invited my little sister to her birthday party last year when she found out she was visiting me. They'd never even met, and she made sure my sis had a great time."

"I'm going to try my hardest," Maggie said, her throat tightening at this glimpse of Kayla's good nature. She couldn't make any promises. Not to anyone, not even to herself. "Thanks again, Randy. Bye."

She hung up, staring down at the haphazard notes she'd assembled. She needed to get herself to the Adonis Lodge—and quick. But she'd need help. She didn't speak musclehead.

"Dammit," she swore softly, aware that Thwonk had crept back into the living room during the phone call.

Hating the fact that she would have to ask for help, she keyed in a number, raising the phone to her ear.

"O'Connor," said a rough voice that made her stomach clench.

Dammit.

"It's Kincaid," she said. "I need your help."

CHAPTER 21

Jake sat up in his bed, the sheets pooling at his hips. "What's wrong?" he asked, already swinging his legs off the bed, feet touching down on the floor. Ever the soldier, ready to spring into action.

"There's no emergency," she said quickly. "I was just going through some of my notes. Randy, the pool guy, he said he'd lost his phone."

"Okay," Jake said slowly, still not following why she needed him.

"I walked him through his day, to figure out where he might've lost his phone. I'm thinking he didn't lose it."

"Our unsub took it," Jake said.

"Exactly," Maggie said. "Last place he remembered having it was his gym. But I don't have a badge to sway management into letting me look at the security footage."

"I'll meet you there in the morning," Jake said. "Text me the address."

"Thank you," Maggie said, and she sounded a little surprised he had agreed so readily.

There was a slight pause. "Anyway," she said. "I should get going."

He tried to picture her, then. She must be at home—what kind of place did she have, he wondered. Something cozy and warm? Or did her style slant more modern?

He couldn't quite imagine Maggie living in a house full of softness and pink. She was prickly—in the best way. She wasn't one to have chairs that no one was allowed to sit on or an overabundance of knickknacks.

"Good night," he told her.

"Night," she said.

He stared at the *call ended* on his screen for a long moment, trying to puzzle out the feeling in his chest at her quiet goodbye. There was something about Maggie Kincaid that tugged at him—and it wasn't just that she was one of the most beautiful women he'd ever seen.

Her spirit—that stubborn streak—it made him want to know her. All of her.

He shook his head, trying to drive thoughts of her from his head. It was late. He hadn't slept much since being called in. This was the first time he'd managed to get home to his bed. He should sleep. He had to get up in a few hours. He tossed his phone onto his end table, slouching down in his bed, closing his eyes.

He drifted, and then fell into sleep.

Fell into a dream.

At first, it was just overwhelming sensation. Impossibly soft skin brushing against his, the perfect lushness of firm breasts pressed to his chest, that unmistakable husky laugh as he gathered her in his arms and flipped her over. The sheets tangled around them, her face, flushed and sated and beautiful, coming into focus.

Maggie smiled up at him, and it wasn't that sharp, uneasy smile she'd flashed at the bar—it was the smile of a woman who was safe and happy in the arms of her lover.

"You trying to be on top this time?" she asked, that sweet smile turning wicked.

"Always," he said. And when he bent down to kiss her, she wound her arms around his neck, arching up into him, moaning.

His hands were everywhere—he couldn't get enough. The velvety feel of her skin was like heaven and hell combined. Her head tilted back as his fingers grazed across her pink nipples, and her mouth opened in a gasp as he leaned forward and brought one to his lips.

"You're driving me crazy," she said breathlessly as he dragged his mouth up the slope of her breast, scraping his teeth lightly against the sensitive skin of her collarbone, making her twist in his arms, pressing herself more firmly against him. The friction was maddening—*she* was maddening.

He wanted all of her. Now. Tomorrow. Forever.

"You're driving *me* crazy," he countered, sucking a light mark against her neck.

She pulled away, just enough to scowl adorably at him. "No hickeys!" she ordered. "We are not sixteen!"

He chuckled against her neck, against the slightly reddened spot that said *mine* to anyone who could see. "You make me feel like I am," he whispered.

She grinned, wiggling out from under him, pushing him onto his back on his bed. He let her, intrigued where this was going. She was so bossy—even in bed.

He loved it.

She swung her leg over his waist, her breasts swaying with the movement. His palms itched to cup them, to lightly trace around her nipples in that way that was guaranteed to make her squirm. But as she dragged her nails lightly down his chest, then his stomach, his needs went completely out the window.

This was all about what she wanted.

"I have you at my mercy," she said, with a glowing smile.

"Anything but that," he deadpanned, just to get another laugh out of her. And he was rewarded, that beautiful sound filling his heart and soul.

She bent down, and her lips began to follow the path her hands had forged. His stomach tightened as her fingers hovered over the elastic band of his boxer briefs before dipping inside, pulling them down.

One more teasing look, her blue eyes gleaming, her expression telling him she knew *exactly* what she was doing to him. And then her mouth, that clever, wicked mouth, closed over him.

Jake groaned, the heat of her lips filling his senses.

Beep. Beep. Beep.

His eyes snapped open. Beams of early morning light fell across his empty bed. He was breathing hard, like he was six miles into a run. He leaned over, swiping his alarm off before falling back onto the mattress, trying to sort his thoughts. His entire body ached from the dream-memory of Maggie's touch. It had felt so real.

He wanted to *make* it real.

The realization hit him all at once. He'd known she was attractive, that he wanted her, that if they ended up in bed together, it'd be nothing short of amazing, but this feeling in his chest . . .

This was something more. Something different.

Something special.

And he was determined to pursue it—just as soon as this mess with the senator was resolved.

CHAPTER 22

The next morning, Maggie showed up at the gym bright and early. The Adonis Lodge was aptly named. On her way inside the old brick building, Maggie passed three tall, dark, muscle-bound model types. And waiting for her in the barn-wood–paneled lobby was the tall, dark, muscle-bound security expert who'd been on her mind far too often.

Somehow, O'Connor stood out in the sea of masculine musculature. Maybe it was the depth in his green eyes, or the slight crookedness of his nose—broken in the military or maybe just a bar fight, she figured.

This wasn't a man who'd spend his time calculating grams of protein and counting reps. He had more serious work to do. His body came from his job, from living on his feet and jumping into action. He understood instinct. He listened to it. And he trusted his—maybe more than Maggie trusted her own, after Sherwood Hills.

She hated to admit it, but she needed that confidence right now. Everything about this case was upside down, and it disturbed her more than she liked. More than anything, the senator's choice to have the press conference threw her off. What kind of father would ever choose politics over his daughter? She couldn't help but remember how her parents looked when they'd gotten her back. The relief taking over the agony in their faces . . . the grief when they realized Erica wasn't with her. While clutching Maggie so tightly she nearly lost her breath, her mother had made an inhuman sound, a broken moan that turned into a scream, and her father had crumpled to the ground, his face buried in his hands. It was the first time Maggie had ever seen him cry—but it wasn't the last. *That* is how the senator should have been acting—and the fact that he wasn't set off all sorts of alarms in her.

"Did you decide to start lifting and get ripped?" Jake asked, raising an eyebrow.

Maggie quelled the lame joke with a look. "Very funny." She nodded toward the man sitting behind the rustic wood counter. "I need you to get him to let me look at the security tapes. You speak their language." Maggie gestured to him. "You do all this macho stuff."

"I stay fit." Jake shrugged. "When I was in the desert, staying fit meant staying alive."

Maggie could feel her cheeks turning red. She hadn't meant to insult him. Or maybe she had, a little—he could be so irritating!

"If I talk to them on my own, they're not going to let me see the tapes," she told him. "But they might for you. Do that thing guys do, the buddy 'hey, man' thing."

"You have no idea how guys work, do you?" Jake asked, bemused.

"Do you have any idea how women work?" Maggie shot back.

Jake pulled a shocked face. "You mean you don't live only for designer shoes and pillow fights with your girlfriends?"

That got a reluctant smile out of her.

"Stay here. I'll try to get this guy to talk using my special man powers," Jake said.

If she was another woman, she might have reached out and playfully smacked him for his insolence. But Maggie wasn't that bold. Instead, she watched as he strode over to the antique bar turned into a desk and leaned on it, an easy smile on his face. "Hey," he said.

"You looking to sign up?" The attendant, a few strands

of gray streaking his temples, stood up, clipboard in hand. "I've got some great deals this month, man."

"Maybe," Jake said. "Hey, you a Ranger?" He nodded at the tattoo on the man's forearm.

"Almost twenty years," the man replied proudly. "Busted my knee on my last tour, so they sent me home for good. Taught firearms for a few years before I retired. This is my boy's place," he said, gesturing to the gym. "I help out to keep from getting too bored. The wife likes to keep me out of her hair."

"Fifteen years for me," Jake said. "I'm O'Connor. Jake O'Connor."

"Mark. Mark Radley."

They shook hands.

"So, civilian life, right?" Jake smiled, self-deprecating.

The man laughed. "It's an adjustment. Slow as hell. Makes me miss the desert sometimes."

"I know that feeling," Jake said. "Hey, do you know Pete Complin?"

Mark's face broke into a grin. "Oh, man, Pete's the greatest. Is he still doing those BBQs in the middle of bumfuck nowhere?"

"Last I heard." Jake smiled. "So, look, man, I work security for a senator now. His pool guy has a membership here, and I've got reason to suspect he's stolen some stuff. Nothing huge, so the senator kind of wants to handle it quietly without getting the cops involved, you know?"

"I understand," Mark said. "The bigwigs like their privacy."

"You know it," Jake agreed. "I'm trying to place the guy's whereabouts when the items went missing. I've got his schedule pretty nailed down, but I'm wondering if you'd let me and my assistant—" he jerked his chin at Maggie, who tried hard not to bristle at her new title "—look at your security tapes for Tuesday, around noon?"

Mark frowned. "Those tapes aren't really supposed to be viewed by anyone but staff," he said.

"I get it," Jake said. "Trust me, I do. But the senator's

gonna have my ass if I don't catch this thief. I'm pretty sure it's the pool guy. I just need to confirm he wasn't in your gym around the time the stuff was stolen."

"Okay," Mark said. Obviously the brother-in-arms thing and the authoritative way Jake carried himself had placated him. "Sure. I'll bend the rules to help out a fellow soldier."

He led Maggie and Jake through a corridor, past a mirrored rooms full of treadmills, weights, and sweaty, well-muscled men.

"Your boy's done good for himself," Jake said, looking approvingly at the clean, well-appointed space. "I've got a few buddies who come here. They really like it. Say it has a good vibe."

"That's nice to hear. He's smart, my kid." Mark smiled, opening a side door. Maggie and Jake walked into the video room, where a man sat, watching a dozen or so monitors recording various areas in the gym.

"Hey, Danny," Mark called to the man who was watching the cameras. "Can you pull up the videos for Tuesday? And then give these two some privacy."

"Sure, Mr. Radley." The man pulled up the videos on the center console and then left the room.

"I'll give you a few minutes," Mark said.

Jake reached over and shook his hand again. "Thanks, brother."

"Hope you find what you need," Mark said. "And I mean it about those membership deals—we've got some good ones."

Jake smiled easily. "I just might take you up on that."

"Ma'am." Mark nodded to Maggie, and then closed the door behind him.

For a second, there was only silence and a muted darkness, the light from the screens flickering over Jake's rugged features.

She was caught in his gaze with no way out, and she shivered despite the warmth of the room. For the first time since Frank approached her in the park—God, it felt so long ago—her wrists didn't ache with phantom pain.

Jake's eyes—so deep and green—dropped to her lips, just for a moment, and then he shook his head, refocusing. He cleared his throat.

It was like that moment yesterday when they were talking and she'd let her emotions bleed through. His face had changed, softened, and he'd reached for her, unthinking, like it was an automatic thing.

Like it was a need instead of a want.

Maggie had never felt needed like that. She didn't think she was the kind of woman who inspired that kind of emotion. But standing there, just inches away from Jake O'Connor, unable to look away and break the moment, she felt the possibility of it . . . the bud of something shimmering between them. It made her want—need?—things she wasn't even sure were possible. It made everything in her body tighten in anticipation as images danced through her head. His strong hands bracketing her waist, then dipping lower to her hips. His lips running along the curve of her jaw with just the barest hint of teeth, enough to make her shiver.

God, what was wrong with her? Maggie tugged at the bottom of her blouse, looking away, trying not to breathe hard. She needed to focus. *That* was what she needed. Not Jake O'Connor and his daring smile. "We should get to watching."

"Right."

She took the chair closer to the main monitor, and he sat down in one next to her, pressing a few buttons to get the video started.

"I didn't know you were a Ranger," Maggie said quietly, keeping her eyes fixed on the grainy video that showed a scene in the lobby.

She wasn't sure he was going to say anything, but then, just as quietly, came his reply. "Sometimes it seems like another life."

Maggie didn't know what to say to that. The flash of realization, of kinship she felt in that moment was startling.

She never thought she'd have so much in common with Jake O'Connor.

She never thought she'd feel . . . God, whatever it was she was feeling. More than attraction? Desire? Connection? Recognition? All of the above?

Like recognizes like, after all.

She understood that feeling of being unmoored. The FBI had been her tether; negotiating had been her rock. She'd shaped her life around it because it was safer, sturdier than the foundation that her traumatic childhood kidnapping had destroyed. When she left, she blasted a hole inside her very being, obliterating her sense of self. The duty that had guided her no longer served as the convenient barrier from the trauma she'd been running from for so long.

What was Jake O'Connor running from?

"Hey, there he is," Jake said, straightening in the chair, pointing to the screen.

Maggie zeroed in on the monitor. Randy Macomb sauntered into the lobby, a baseball hat turned backward on his perfectly coiffed head. He scanned his card at the desk, talked for a moment with Mark and then headed to the lockers.

"Scroll ahead a few minutes," Maggie said.

Jake did, pausing the video when a second figure appeared in the lobby.

Maggie frowned, staring at the man. He was facing away from the camera, his hoodie obscuring his face.

"Can you get a better angle of his face on the other cameras?" Maggie asked.

Jake typed something into the keyboard in front of the main monitor, and the screen shifted from the lobby to the corridor they'd just been in. But the hoodie guy had kept his head tilted down just enough that the camera angles hadn't captured his face, and he disappeared into the locker room.

"Dammit," Maggie muttered. She was sure this was their guy, just because he was being so careful to avoid the cameras. Uncle Sam would've scoped out the place beforehand, memorized the camera angles so he could avoid them.

"Just wait," Jake said, typing a few more commands.

"They can't have cameras in the locker rooms!" Maggie said, knowing she sounded horrified.

"Of course not," Jake said. "But . . ." He hit two more buttons. "There."

The monitor shifted to another camera, this one pointed at a different angle on the locker room door.

"I noticed it when we were walking down the hall," Jake said. "They've got a few cameras that look like fire alarms. Probably to catch theft. It's not hard to case a joint you go to every day. Or figure out how to avoid the more obvious cameras."

"Do you think he didn't notice them?" Maggie was impressed. Even she hadn't noticed the extra cameras.

"Here's hoping he didn't," Jake said, and Maggie peered at the monitor eagerly.

A minute later, the locker room door opened, and there he was.

Jake paused the screen.

Maggie frowned, peering at the distant image. There was something familiar about the fuzzy angles of the man's face, but she couldn't quite place it.

"Let me zoom in," Jake said. A few clicks, and Maggie gasped, her heart kicking hard against her rib cage.

"Oh, my God."

"Shit," Jake said.

They looked from the monitor to each other, horrified at the realization.

"We have to get to that press conference," Maggie said.

Jake nodded grimly. "I'll drive."

Maggie grabbed her bag and headed for the door, casting one last look at the man's face on the monitor.

The kidnapper's face.

It was Max Grayson.

CHAPTER 23

"Are you carrying?" Jake asked as he raced through traffic, weaving in and out of lanes with such smooth precision it made Maggie wonder if he'd been a car thief in a previous life.

She reached into her bag and grabbed her Glock in its leather holster. She took it out and double-checked the safety and magazine. "I'm set," she said. "You?"

He patted his side. "All good."

Jake pressed harder on the accelerator, changing lanes to veer away from a slow-moving pickup without breaking a sweat.

"It can't be a coincidence, right?" Maggie asked.

"There's no way Grayson goes to a gym like that," Jake said. "He's one of those hipster health nuts. Adonis doesn't even offer yoga."

"Good point," Maggie said. "Okay. So not a coincidence."

"Definitely not," Jake said. "Fucking *Grayson*," he muttered.

Maggie bit her lip, concentrating on the road. She understood his anger. She was furious too. Mostly at herself.

How had she not seen this? Grayson had been right in front of her. But his presence in the Thebes household at least meant he could be keeping Kayla within driving distance—that was one small nugget of knowledge she could glean from what was quickly proving to be a potential powder keg that could blow up in their faces.

"How long has he been working for the senator?" Maggie asked, her thoughts racing in circles. Had he been planning this all along? Had he run into some kind of trouble, and the senator was the easiest target?

"We should fan out once we get there," Maggie said. "I'll get Frank to lock down the building." She punched in a few numbers on her cell, but put it down in frustration seconds later. "Dammit. He's not answering." She dialed Paul's number, but he didn't answer either. She shook her head in frustration. They'd probably be mingling with the crowd at the press conference, so she'd have to be fast and quiet when she clued them in to what was happening.

"And I'll secure Grayson," Jake said, his voice a dangerous rumble that made the hair on her arms stand up.

"We might need to tail him, instead," Maggie said. "To find Kayla's location. Otherwise he might use it as leverage when he's arrested."

"Trust me," Jake said. "I'll get him to talk."

They sped down Pennsylvania, narrowly missing traffic clogged by a diplomatic motorcade. Jake made a sharp turn down a side street, avoiding the sleek sedan with diplomatic plates. "We're almost there," he said, and Maggie had to press her hand against the window for balance as he made a sharp right, the tires screeching a little. Someone they cut off honked at them, but Jake just sped ahead, a man on a mission.

"We need to take him as peacefully as possible," Maggie warned. "The room's going to be crowded."

"I'm not going to kill anyone, Goldilocks," Jake said, his voice heavy with scorn. "I'm not stupid enough to go shooting into a crowded room. I hit my targets."

"As long as we're on the same page," Maggie replied. "We need him *conscious*. Who knows how long it's been since he's given Kayla her insulin? We have to get to her as soon as possible."

"Trust me, he'll be conscious," Jake said. "He might be hurting. A lot. But he'll tell us where he's got her. I'll make sure of that."

"Sounds good to me," Maggie said grimly.

"Here we are," Jake said, coming to a halt in front of the Hale Building, where the senator was holding the press conference. The large colonial edifice had been gutted and refurbished in the eighties, retrofitted for political conferences and other civic functions.

As soon as Jake hit the brakes, Maggie jumped out of the car, racing toward the arched entrance. She heard the other door slam behind her. With Jake hot on her heels, she charged through the double glass doors.

"Thebes press conference?" Jake asked the startled concierge.

"Conference Room B," he said. "It's almost over, though." He pointed down a wide hall, and Maggie darted forward, sprinting toward the room on the right at the end of the corridor. His legs so much longer, Jake overtook her, but she stayed close behind. Her gun pressed heavy against her hip as she ran.

She saw security before they saw her—they were too focused on tackling the six-foot-five-inch hunk of ex–Army Ranger charging them. Only Maggie was going to make it through the conference room doors, she realized with dread. "I'll get Grayson!" Maggie shouted over her shoulder, galloping past the four guards before they could register what had just happened.

She burst through the wide wooden doors, drawing her Glock, the doors slamming shut behind her, echoing throughout the room. The senator and the group of journalists all turned to stare.

Maggie's eyes scanned the surroundings, searching. There! Grayson was standing to the senator's far left, near the exit. Their eyes met across the distance. Her hands tightened on her gun. "Max Gray—" she started to shout, but then all the breath was suddenly knocked out of her as she was tackled to the floor. The impact jolted her. She struggled, her cheek jammed into the carpet, her neck tightly gripped by a strong hand.

"Gun, gun!" someone was shouting. "Protect the senator!" Footsteps pounded as frantic journalists began to run. Her Glock was knocked out of her hand and skittered across the floor. She reached helplessly for it, trying to push up against the punishing weight against her back. Confused shouting and footsteps filled her ears.

"Hey, *hey*, get off my agent!" Frank's scuffed shoes came into view, and a long second later, the weight lifted. Maggie rolled to her side, coughing.

"Frank," she gasped, struggling to sit up. "It's Grayson! Max Grayson!" she panted. She stood up, grabbing her gun. "*He* took Kayla. Where is he?"

She whirled around, desperately searching the now-chaotic crowd. Cameras abandoned, journalists piled toward the exit as security ran around in circles. She charged through the crowd, Glock at the ready, tracking through the mess of people with quick, measured steps. Someone clipped her as he ran past, nearly knocking her over. She stumbled, but kept a steady grip on her gun as she recovered.

"Sorry!" the journalist called over his shoulder, not even looking back.

Maggie swore, spinning in a slow circle as security barked orders and tried to control the situation—badly. She couldn't see a thing from this vantage point.

Goddammit, being short sucked sometimes. She had to get to the stage where the podium was—she needed the elevation to scan the crowd as a whole. She couldn't see Grayson anywhere. Usually he stuck to the senator like a second skin, but Thebes was being ushered away from the podium, looking bewildered and perturbed by the disturbance. Maggie fought her way through the mêlée and vaulted up onto the stage with a fluid movement. Her heart in her throat, she peered across the thinning crowd with a sinking heart.

It was too late. She'd missed him. He'd gotten away in the rush.

She felt like sinking to her knees right then and there. Let the defeat drum down into her like a thunderstorm. How could she have been so stupid? Grayson had been there the whole time, and she hadn't seen it. So much for her killer instinct. She was botching this job, just as she'd done at Sherwood Hills. What was going to happen to Kayla, now that they knew who Grayson was?

She felt sick at the thought. She'd failed Kayla. She'd had her kidnapper practically in hand, but she hadn't been fast enough.

But she still had time, Maggie reminded herself. No one was dead. Not yet. She could still turn this around.

She needed to turn this around.

"We've got to lock down the entire building," she told Frank, who'd finally caught up with her.

Frank paused for just a moment before he turned to the security guard who'd followed him. "You heard what she said—get to it! I want all entrances blocked. Every room searched. This bastard's been hiding right in our midst. He's been pulling fast ones on us since the start—it's time we do the same to him."

"Yes, sir!" In seconds, the officer was on his radio, barking orders.

Maggie rose to her feet, straightening her skirt, brushing her hair back from her face. Her shoulder ached from being slammed to the ground, but she ignored it.

"Press conference is over," she called loudly to the remaining journalists standing. "Please congregate in the lobby. Security will check your credentials there."

They filed out, leaving the senator standing there. Maggie glared at him, but he wouldn't meet her eyes. "Where's O'Connor?" she asked the remaining security. "Get him in here."

"What are you thinking, Maggie?" Frank asked.

Maggie rubbed a hand over her forehead, her mind picking at the puzzle like a bug bite. "They aren't going to find Grayson," she said. "He's too smart. He was the one who suggested this venue. He probably has a handful of exit strategies, just in case."

"You think he's that prepared?" Jake asked, loping up to

them. There was a small tear in his shirtsleeve, but even though she knew he had, he didn't look like he'd just taken on four security guards—and won.

"He knows everything we've been talking about," Maggie said, the realization sinking in. "He knows all of us. Knows how we interact, knows how we plan. He's been privy to it all. He's three steps ahead," she added bitterly, "and we didn't even know what game he was playing until just now."

"It's not your fault, Kincaid," Jake said softly, reaching out, his palm settling between her shoulder blades and pressing gently. It was an intimate touch, a gesture to comfort a lover, not a colleague. Warmth burst through her like a lit sparkler. She felt it down to her fingertips, and everything inside her wanted to lean into the touch, wanted him not to take the burden from her, but only to help her bear some of it. His shoulders were strong, and his eyes were warm and understanding. Maggie could get lost in them. She wished she could right now.

Frank cleared his throat, and Jake's hand dropped away, his cheeks reddening. Maggie felt the loss of his touch as a sudden, aching absence. She tried to put it out of her head—everything was heightened right now, she told herself. It had been a stressful few hours.

"I feel like an idiot," Maggie said, grimacing in disgust. She hadn't seen it. She should have.

"Something's weird about this case," Jake said.

"It does feel fishy," Frank agreed.

Maggie took a deep breath. She'd let Kayla down by not seeing through Grayson from the start. Well, no more. This wasn't going to end like Sherwood Hills. And Kayla wasn't going to end like Erica. Maggie would be damned if Kayla Thebes ended up being forever a girl in her loved ones' memories. An always-innocent who never got to grow up into a woman, all because a crooked kidnapper wanted something from her crooked father. Kayla deserved to grow up, to fall in love, to go to college, to get married, and have a career and family of her own. Maggie would do anything necessary to ensure that happened . . . that Kayla didn't become frozen at fourteen, like Erica was for her.

"Let's go find out what it is," she said. "And for Kayla's sake, let's do it fast."

CHAPTER 24

Kayla had lost track of time. Was it morning? She couldn't tell: The room was windowless, and the kidnapper—whoever he was—hadn't come back after he'd videotaped her reading the book.

She'd managed to undo the drawstring on the hood and pull it off and once she was free, the stale air against her face felt like the best thing in the world.

She was in a windowless gray room. It was almost like being in a box except for the door, which had an added iron-barred security door in front of it. Her eyes darted across her surroundings. She needed a weapon . . . *something*. He'd left a bucket in with her and she dragged it closer, wincing at the smell.

Blinking back tears, she tried to stay calm. Had the kidnapper contacted her parents? They had to have arranged a ransom or something by now, right?

She'd be rescued soon. Any second now. Her parents would make sure of it.

She licked her dry lips, muffling a sob, because she couldn't fool herself. What was she going to do? She didn't want to die. Her mom would never recover if she didn't come home.

She struggled to her knees, her bound wrists making it difficult. A wave of dizziness hit her as she straightened up, and her hands began to shake.

Her blood sugar was spiraling down fast. She needed to

check it and eat something. She needed her insulin. God, how long had it been?

Kayla pushed herself to her feet, circling the tiny room, searching for her purple pouch. Had he left her some?

But there was nothing. Just the rusty bucket and the sleeping bag on top of the mattress pad.

What was she going to do?

Then she heard it: footsteps coming closer. Kayla scrambled backward into the farthest corner of the room at the clink of keys.

The door swung open, and Kayla's heart leapt for a second when she saw it was Max, her dad's policy advisor. For one glorious moment she thought that he was here to save her. That her dad had sent him and he'd somehow found her.

And then she realized he was wearing the same hoodie as the kidnapper.

That he *was* her kidnapper.

Oh, God. How long had he been planning this? He'd been working for her dad for *years*!

The pit in her stomach grew. This was bad. This was *really* bad.

His hair was messed up, and he was panting hard, as if he'd been running.

Kayla cringed against the wall, her mind racing. What was going on? Why would he do this?

"What are you doing?" she asked. "You work for my dad!"

His mouth was a grim line of determination. "There's no use in pretending anymore, Kayla. The game's changed."

"Please, I didn't do anything. Didn't they pay you? If you talk to my mom, she'll make sure you get whatever you want. I promise."

"Strange you leap to your mother instead of your father," Max said. "Or maybe not, all things considered. Did little Kayla figure out what her precious daddy was up to?" he singsonged mockingly at her.

Her lip trembled, but she had to be strong. "I don't know what you're talking about," she said. "Please, just call my mom. She has money apart from Dad. She comes from a really rich family."

"There's always collateral damage, Kayla," Max said, pulling out the purple pouch that held her insulin. Kayla's heart leapt. No . . . he wouldn't. "Sadly, you're in the crossfire of a war you didn't even know existed, and it's time to dial up the pressure."

He threw the pouch onto the ground and stomped . . . hard. She could hear the bottle of insulin inside breaking under his foot.

Oh, God. Her hands shook harder. Sweat crawled down the back of her neck as she realized how bad this was.

He was going to kill her. Slowly.

Max Grayson looked at her, a gleam in his eye that made him look deranged. "Let's see how your father's hotshot negotiator responds to that."

CHAPTER 25

Maggie leaned against the wall of the long corridor leading to the kitchen. It was far enough away from the throng in the conference room that she could barely hear the buzz of voices.

She closed her eyes, tilting her face up to the ceiling, trying to let the anger churning inside her go. She had *had* him, dammit! And he'd slipped away, with every detail about her team in his disgusting hands.

"Maggie?"

Maggie's eyes opened. Jake was standing there, his green eyes concerned.

"Hey." She straightened. "I'm okay," she said, even though he hadn't asked.

"They asked me to bring you back," he said. "You ready?"

She looked up at him, everything inside her saying *no* even though she knew she had to say yes. It'd been an hour since Max Grayson had fled the press conference, narrowly avoiding FBI capture. Senator Thebes and his wife, plus the rest of her team, were on the other side of the doors, waiting for her.

Waiting for her to give them some answers.

How could she have not seen it? Recognized that Grayson was the very person she'd been hunting? Had she just let her automatic dislike of the callous, fast-talking politico cloud her instincts? How had she not seen the devious, criminal mind beneath the expensive suits and slick hair?

"None of us saw it, Maggie," Jake said quietly.

It took Maggie a second to realize she'd asked the questions spinning in her head out loud. Her cheeks burned, but her embarrassment faded when Jake smiled gently at her. His black hair was messy; he hadn't fixed it since his altercation with the security guards earlier. She felt a sudden urge to run her hands through it, to see if it was as thick and silky as it looked. She tried to push the distraction away.

"He must have slipped out to film the video."

"There were at least forty people running around then," Jake said. "It was easy to miss. This is more on me than it is on you. Your job is to negotiate. I'm supposed to notice security threats or breaches—and I didn't notice he was gone either."

It was nice of him to try to take on some of the guilt, but Maggie knew this was on her. She was the one trained in the criminal mind. She was the one people brought in on the tough calls . . . the tricky ones. She should've spotted him. Where was that famous instinct of hers when she needed it? It had failed her, just as it had at Sherwood Hills.

Had her instincts just atrophied? It was two years since she'd been in the field. Maybe Frank was wrong—maybe she wasn't the right person for this job. But it didn't matter. If they switched things up now, Grayson would know they were panicking. He'd use the weakness to his advantage.

"Grayson must've sent the second ransom ask using some sort of timed app," Maggie said. "We should have the techs look into that."

"We will," Jake said. "We'll figure this out. We'll get Kayla home safe and put Grayson behind bars."

"How can you be so hopeful?" she asked. She wanted to be that sure, that faithful, but after everything—those nights of terror and leaving Erica behind, leaving Erica to die, after Sherwood Hills and even more blood on her hands—she wasn't certain it was in her anymore. She felt like crumbling underneath the pressure—any other time, she'd be there already, in pieces on the ground. But here he was, standing there, telling her what she needed to hear, holding her up, holding her together . . . how did he do that . . . *again*? Know what she needed before she did?

He reached out, and normally the movement would make her flinch away. But instead, she found herself leaning into it as his thumb stroked over the soft plane of her cheek. She shivered at the contact, warmth pooling inside her.

"I'm hopeful because I've seen you in action now," he said. "You're fast on your feet. You think creatively. You don't let fear get the better of you. You can do this. You're the touchstone."

There was something about Jake speaking those words that bolstered her. "You're right," she said, and it came out a little shakier than she'd like, but he smiled.

He bent down and everything inside her froze, thinking he was going to kiss her.

Thinking she wanted him to.

She wanted to reach out and grasp those muscular arms, drawing him toward her, pressing his strong chest against the softness of hers. She wanted to trace every difference between them with her fingertips and lips, the strength of his jaw, the power in his shoulders.

He was so close, she could smell a hint of aftershave—something spicy and masculine—and then his cheek, rough with stubble and excruciatingly sexy, brushed against hers as his lips touched her ear.

"Go get 'em, Goldilocks," he said.

SHE WALKED THROUGH those doors like a new woman. The game had changed, and she wasn't sure it could be won. But she'd be damned if anyone stopped fighting for Kayla as hard as they could.

"All right, everyone, time to review," she said briskly, striding up to the center of the room.

Her agents and techs gathered, and Senator Thebes pulled up a chair for his wife, whose bloodshot eyes were smudged with blue-black shadows. She reached for her husband's hand, but after a moment of contact, he pulled away. Frank nodded to Maggie, his face grim. He understood how bad this was—Max Grayson had been privy to everything. He knew their people and their strategies. And now he was running scared.

It couldn't get much worse. Any hope of a peaceful resolution was gone. People were going to get hurt—and Maggie had to make sure Kayla wasn't one of them.

Maggie tried to ignore the way her wrists ached. She clenched her fists, resisting the urge to rub them. She looked up and saw Jake, towering over the group of FBI techs. He flashed her a quick smile, and the warmth it sparked inside her melted away the phantom pain.

Paul wheeled a whiteboard into the center of the circle of agents. Max Grayson's photo was dead center.

Maggie pointed to the image. "This is our kidnapper: Max Grayson. He's been working for the senator for almost two years as a policy advisor. His original ransom claim, the five million dollars he never followed up on? It was a distraction. This is not about money—it's about politics."

Maggie was all too aware of Senator Thebes scowling at her, furious at where she was heading. She swallowed, ignoring the fury radiating off him. It was for the greater good, she reminded herself. "What we now know is that Grayson really wants a classified file that only Senator Thebes has access to."

Mrs. Thebes looked at the senator, her brow furrowed in confusion, and he resolutely looked anywhere but at his wife. Maggie's stomach twisted, hating that it was the first time the woman had heard this bombshell. She hated that she had to be the one to break the news, but she knew better than to expect the senator to do it.

Maggie had to plead her case one last time to Thebes. It was a long shot, but maybe the outside pressure of all the agents and even his own wife staring at him would make him crumble. Maggie didn't care about his reputation. She didn't care if this lost him his job. She'd try anything. Kayla's life was hanging in the balance of her father's choices.

"Senator, Grayson's not only well prepared. He's not only two steps ahead. He's working with inside knowledge.

He's been around all of us. He knows us. He knows how we work, he knows all the theories. He's been manipulating this from the start, orchestrating it all. Outsmarting him without using the documents for bait is going to be difficult."

"There is no way I can obtain the file," Senator Thebes said. "We've gone through this, Kincaid. You need to find another way. Do your job. Get creative."

Maggie had to look away as Mrs. Thebes muffled a sob at her husband's refusal.

"Can you at least tell us *why* Grayson wants this file in particular?" Jake asked. He moved through the circle of agents and techs, taking his place next to Maggie. Instead of being annoyed by this move, she found herself glad to have someone beside her. She had to ramp up the pressure on Thebes.

"That would help," Maggie said quickly. "I need to understand his motives—what he's done, the lengths he's gone to infiltrating your world. Whatever's in that file is hugely important to him—more important than anything else. After years of planning, he's not going to be appeased with money or false promises."

"I don't know why he wants the file," the senator said. "How am I to know the inner workings of a madman's mind? I've clearly been the target of this man for God knows how long, yet you seem unable to do anything about it."

"Because you're keeping things from us," Jake barked, his voice ringing loudly through the room. Thebes grew still as a statue. Maggie could practically feel the people stiffening in anticipation of the senator's response at being called out so boldly. No one else would dare to confront Thebes like this—well, no one but her. Her admiration for Jake's take-no-prisoners attitude was almost as fast growing as her grudging attraction.

The senator leaned forward, lowering his voice. His cheeks were a mottled, embarrassed red as he rasped, "Are you calling me a liar, O'Connor?"

Jake seemed to grow even taller as he looked down at Thebes, contempt written all over his face. "If the shoe fits, Senator."

"Okay," Maggie interrupted before the man, whose face was rapidly turning purple, could respond. "Senator Thebes, why don't you sit down next to your wife?" She snapped her fingers, and an agent brought another chair, setting it down next to Mrs. Thebes. "Jake . . ." she said pleadingly, looking at him.

His face—the angry, skeptical expression—smoothed out as soon as she said his name. "I'll play nice," he said.

"Thank you." Maggie scanned the group of people watching her. Waiting for her to guide them. To save Kayla. She didn't know if she was worthy of such faith. In fact, she was almost sure she wasn't. "Our top priority right now—the only thing that really matters—is figuring out where Max Grayson has gone and where he's keeping Kayla. If we know that, the file doesn't matter."

"There have been no sightings," Paul said, coming forward. "I just called the police chief. He's got squads across the entire city, and we've got agents everywhere, but so far, nothing."

"What about his phone? Or phones. He had two last time I saw him," Maggie said.

"I've got techs tracing them both," Paul said. "But the signals are bouncing all over the world."

Maggie turned to the whiteboard photo, staring at Max Grayson's overly tanned face. Where was he? What was he feeling right now? He'd been so careful, he must have planned this for ages. What was so important to him that he'd do this? Throw everything he had—all the privilege, the power, the incredible income—down the drain for . . . what? What was in that file? What kind of information was so important that the senator wouldn't even consider giving it up to save his only child? Hidden missile locations? Nuclear plant codes? Evidence of a deal gone wrong in a major agency?

And why did Grayson want them so badly? If it was

merely a matter of acquiring information to sell on the black market, there were much easier ways of doing that. Especially with the access he had on the senator's staff. This kind of elaborate plan, this focus, meant Grayson's goals didn't just involve whatever was in that file. It was about the senator himself. But until she discovered what was in the file, she wouldn't know for sure.

Maggie was certain that the FBI getting the drop on him wasn't part of Grayson's plan. That's what worried her the most. Max Grayson was a control freak. And when control freaks have to deviate from their plans, they tend to panic. Panic was a powerful thing, Maggie knew all too well. It was what had fueled her that night Erica had convinced her to run. It'd been the claws raking her throat as she ran through the woods, sobbing, aching, and terrified.

Panic could change a person. It robbed them of rational thought.

Panic could turn a man into a murderer.

"I do have the report from the lab about the ransom video," Paul said, pulling it up on his tablet. "They can't tell us much about the location." He scrolled down the page. "But they did identify some bugs in the background."

"Bugs?" Jake asked.

"Yeah, they're some kind of water beetle," Paul said. "It could mean Kayla's being held near water."

"DC was built on a swamp," Maggie said, shaking her head. "That's not going to really narrow our search area. We need something more than that."

"I'll get the lab to get some entomologists on it. Maybe the water beetle is found only in certain spots. But it's a long shot," said Paul.

"We'll take what we can get," Maggie replied. Paul handed her the tablet and she began to look over the report herself, hoping something would leap out at her. But it was a whole lot of nothing. Common drywall, nondescript floors . . . even the sleeping bag was a generic one from Target. No indicators at all where he was keeping Kayla except for the beetles. Maggie's fingers clenched around the tablet. She wanted to throw it across the room and watch it shatter into a million pieces, but instead, she handed it back to Paul.

The double doors of the conference hall burst open, and a junior officer rushed in. "Ms. Kincaid!" He charged over to her, panting. "We found his car, ma'am. It looks like he hit the highway before you called for their closure; then he pulled off on the Hamilton Street exit."

"Was there anything inside?" Maggie asked urgently.

"His cell phones, minus the SIM cards. They were smashed to pieces. Your field techs showed up just as I was leaving to tell you."

"Jessa," Maggie said, pointing to the spiky-haired tech to her right. "Please go with this officer and oversee the techs going through the car. I want every part of that vehicle examined. Make sure they test everything down to the dirt in the tire treads, and I want to know everywhere it's gone. Look for hair strands, fingernails, anything that might give us some DNA. We need to know if Kayla's been inside it."

"I'm on it," Jessa said, following the officer out of the room.

So Grayson had a backup vehicle. How well prepared *was* this guy? How far had he thought ahead? Maggie rubbed at her wrists, trying to follow the path through the maze Grayson had led them into.

"What do we do now?"

Maggie turned. It was Mrs. Thebes. Her eyes met Maggie's, and Maggie saw the same fear that had been in her own mother's face when only one daughter was returned safely to her. She tried to banish the echoing memory, to keep her face neutral.

"We keep looking," she told Mrs. Thebes.

"What if you don't find him?" she asked shakily, as if she didn't even want to contemplate it. As if she was still holding out hope that maybe, even with her husband's unwillingness to compromise, Maggie could bring Kayla home safely. Maggie wished she could give her more than empty comfort. But she couldn't make promises—she knew better than to do that. If this ended badly, Maggie wasn't going to add the pain of broken promises to Mrs. Thebes' grief. She knew what that did to a person. It had eaten away at Maggie's own mother, spiritually and physically. Once a robust, upbeat woman, she was now quiet, thin, broken. She'd done her best in the face of insurmountable grief and had been an extraordinary mother despite it, but Maggie wouldn't wish her hell on anyone—not even her worst enemy. And Mrs. Thebes was clearly someone who defined herself as a mother first. It was her identity. Her calling. It was what she lived for.

Kayla was what she lived for.

"If we don't find him, he'll come to us," Maggie said. "He'll call us."

"How can you be so sure?"

Maggie looked at the senator, letting all her frustration and anger bleed into her face. "Because the senator's the only person who has access to what he wants. He won't let it go."

Grayson would call.

And Maggie would be ready for him this time.

CHAPTER 26

A bead of sweat trickled down his forehead. With an unsteady hand, Max Grayson wiped it away, staring down the hallway that led to the room he'd locked Kayla in.

He'd gotten away clean. That's what mattered, he reminded himself as his feet shuffled back and forth, as if they had a mind of their own. He couldn't stop moving. He felt like he was about to jump out of his skin, his nerves raw and sparking. God, what a rush. He couldn't believe he got away. For a second, he'd thought that woman was going to catch him, but there'd been so much chaos, he'd managed to fight through the throng and get out through the back.

Having an extra car waiting down the highway had been a lifesaver. You can never be too careful, he reminded himself, sitting down in one of the rickety chairs before jumping up and starting to pace again.

He was exhausted but exhilarated. He'd pulled it off so far, and exposure was . . . well, it was a snag, he thought bitterly. That fucking bitch Maggie Kincaid had figured him out. He hadn't counted on that.

But he could roll with it. He *had* to.

Max dug in his pocket, pulling out a metal keychain. He rubbed his thumb over the Harley-Davidson logo and held it tight.

This is for you, Joe. I said I'd make them pay for what

they did. We're almost there, buddy. Almost home free. Just like I promised.

There was a thumping sound from the locked bedroom. Max frowned, pocketing the keychain and walking to the sink to fill a glass of water.

He unlocked the door, closing it behind him. Kayla had dragged the mattress pad into the corner farthest from the door and was curled up on it. There were sweat marks on the drywall where she'd been banging her fists, trying to get his attention.

"Please," she said, her voice cracking. "I need my insulin."

Max walked over and held out the glass of water. She eyed it suspiciously before her thirst won out. She grabbed it, but her hands—and her entire body—were shaking so violently she spilled half of it down her front.

He didn't relish this. She was a kid. He'd done a lot of bad things in his life, but he'd never hurt a kid. He wasn't a monster. But she was the unfortunate means to the end he needed. He had no choice. He'd made a promise. And that promise was more important than Kayla . . . than anything.

"You're going to have to hang in there, Kayla," Max said, taking the empty glass away from her.

"Please, Max," she said. "Why won't you help me?"

"You'll be fine," he told her, even though she was pale and sweaty, her eyes half-lidded and hazy.

"No, I won't," she said. "This has happened before. I need my insulin. Please, just give it to me." Her voice cracked with desperation, her eyes wide with bone-deep fear. "You don't want me to die, right? You can't ransom me if I'm dead, Max. You won't get what you want unless I'm alive. I need my insulin to *stay alive*."

He turned away, steeling himself against the guilt rising in his chest.

Joe, he thought, and just his name strengthened his resolve.

"I won't get what I want unless I apply some pressure," Max snapped. "You're going to just have to hold on."

Tears—part anger, part fear—spilled down Kayla's face.

She looked so small on that bed. "They're going to find you!" she shouted after him as he stepped out of the room and locked the door.

He doubted it. He'd been careful. He'd planned for everything.

And now he wanted them to be afraid. He would hold off calling the senator. He didn't want to seem too eager, not with the way Thebes was stonewalling him. You would think taking a man's daughter would be motivation enough, but Max knew politicians were a special breed of scum. And Thebes was . . .

Well, Thebes was a monster. Max knew that better than anyone else. And soon, the whole world would too.

Let them worry. Let them wait. Let the press speculate and spin theories.

Let Maggie Kincaid chase her tail for a while.

Once she realized she wouldn't be able to find Kayla, she'd be ready to listen.

Then she'd realize who was in charge: *him*.

CHAPTER 27

They waited.

Maggie picked up a framed photo from the side table in the senator's library. Kayla was a little younger in the picture, twirling in a purple dress. She was beaming at the camera, obviously excited for whatever dance or party she'd dressed up for.

That's what Gretchen Ellis had been doing at Sherwood Hills that day, the day Maggie had failed her: shopping for a dress for her freshman dance. It'd been yellow. She would have looked beautiful in it.

All of a sudden, the picture in Maggie's hand felt like it weighed a hundred pounds.

"That was her first dance," said a voice behind her.

Maggie turned to see Mrs. Thebes standing behind her. The senator's wife, even puffy-eyed and terrified, was a beautiful woman . . . stately in how she carried herself.

"Purple's her color," Maggie said, setting the photo back down on the marble-topped table.

"I wanted her to go with pink or green," Mrs. Thebes said. "A pastel. But my girl . . . she likes to stand out."

Maggie smiled.

"Why hasn't Grayson called yet?" Mrs. Thebes asked. "You said he'd call. It's been two hours, and we've heard nothing. Were you wrong? What if . . ." She trailed off, unable to finish that sentence. For several moments, she tried to regain her composure, still her shaking hands, and keep the smooth mask of elegance on her face, but she was failing, bit by bit, minute by minute, as her daughter's captivity continued. Panic and fear leached into her face and voice, the fine tremor in her hands grew with each breath.

Maggie wanted to reach out and reassure her, but she knew it wasn't her place. She wondered who had done this for her own mother. Who was the agent that had comforted her, reassured her, while Maggie and Erica were bound in a closet, terrified for their lives? Was it as hard for them as it was for her to force the words out?

"He's playing games," Maggie said. "What you're feeling right now . . . the worry and fear? He *wants* us to feel that. He wants us to know he's in control. He wants us desperate so that when he finally does call—and he will, Mrs. Thebes—we'll give him whatever he wants."

"The file," Mrs. Thebes said woodenly. "The file my husband refuses to give him."

"Yes," Maggie said. "What about it?"

"What will Grayson do if he doesn't get it?" Mrs. Thebes asked.

Maggie could tell by the stony expression on Mrs. Thebes' face that she knew the answer already. But Maggie wasn't going to tell her the ugly truth. She wasn't going to shatter any hope that remained in the poor woman. "I can't tell the future, Mrs. Thebes," she said gently. "But it would really help if your husband was . . . more flexible about this."

Mrs. Thebes let out a short, harsh laugh that sent chills down Maggie's spine. "My husband is not a flexible man," she said.

"He needs to learn to be," Maggie said. "Fast."

Mrs. Thebes looked her up and down, a serious moment of examination that made Maggie shift, a little uncomfortable at the scrutiny. "I like you, Ms. Kincaid," Mrs. Thebes said. "You're a smart woman. A capable one. You don't falter much, do you?"

"I try not to," Maggie said.

"But you're not a mother."

Maggie shook her head. "No, ma'am, I'm not."

"That's my daughter out there," Mrs. Thebes said, fire in her blue eyes. "I carried her inside me. I brought her into this world, and my entire life has been about protecting her from it. Making sure she's safe and loved. If you tell me the only way to get my little girl back is to get that file, I'll tear the Capitol apart myself to get it."

"And I'll be right there with you," Maggie said. "But your husband might not be. I need something to go on. I need insight in order to understand Grayson's psyche and goal. The senator has the access—so he has to start talking."

Mrs. Thebes nodded, her eyes narrowing. "All right." She looked over at the senator, who was sitting near the fireplace, staring at the coals in silence, looking like he'd aged ten years in the last two days.

"I'll talk to my husband," Mrs. Thebes said, stepping past her. "Oh, and, Ms. Kincaid . . ."

Maggie looked back at her. "Yes?"

Mrs. Thebes drew herself up, stately, queenlike, almost terrifying in her lethal regality. "If something happens, if you make a mistake . . . if my daughter doesn't come home safe and sound, I will destroy you. Every part of your life, whether you deserve it or not."

Maggie let out a long breath. She almost wanted to let out an appreciative whistle. Mrs. Thebes stood there like a warrior, prepared to go to war for what she loved most. It reminded Maggie of her own parents. Her mom and dad would have broken the world apart if it could have saved Erica.

"Fair enough," Maggie said. If Mrs. Thebes wanted to play hardball, she'd lay out the reality of the situation for her. "You and I, we want the same thing, Mrs. Thebes. We want Kayla home safe. But your husband's reluctance tells me that isn't his first priority. You might want to think about that. Because if I were his wife, if I were Kayla's mother, I would do all I could to change that. Immediately."

Mrs. Thebes didn't stiffen in reaction to the shot Maggie had just taken—she was a politician's wife, after all. A Jackie, not a Marilyn. She knew control, just like Maggie did. So her face stayed smooth, unaffected, as anger mixed with doubt simmered in her eyes. She turned and walked away without another word.

"Well, that was friendly," came Jake's voice. "I could have cut that tension with a knife."

Maggie had been so focused on Mrs. Thebes she hadn't noticed him break off from talking with Frank about extra security measures and walk over to her. She smiled weakly at him. "She's just scared," she said. "Parents . . . sometimes they lash out. This—" she gestured around her, to the agents buzzing around, the thick fearful tension in the air "—is every parent's worst fear."

Maggie knew what Mrs. Thebes was feeling, how helpless she was, how she knew there was nothing she could do. That she had to let go of her control, let go of her daughter, and pray that Maggie was capable enough to bring her back to her.

Maggie truly understood that swamping, all-encompassing dread and fear. It'd been her constant companion since Erica pushed her out of that hole, urging her to escape. Sometimes she thought that feeling, more than anything else, was what spurred her toward the FBI and her career in negotiation. She'd never be able to find Erica. She and her mother would never have more than a marble headstone set over an empty grave. But at the very least, she could help others. Prevent it from happening to more families.

"I get it," Jake said, shaking his head. "I don't know what I'd do if I were a parent in this kind of situation."

"Arm yourself like you're going to war and go all vigi lante?" Maggie suggested.

She'd meant it as a joke, but the expression on his handsome face sank her like an anchor on the ocean floor.

"I protect what I love," he said. "Whatever the cost."

The way he said it, the promise in his voice, the truth of the words, rocked her to her core. It was an innocuous, almost teasing statement, but the sudden seriousness in his eyes made her want to be the person he protected—loved—most. "You're reckless," she countered.

"You like it." His mouth quirked up teasingly. He sat down on the leather chesterfield, beckoning to her.

After a moment of hesitation, she sat down, a few inches away, trying to ignore the heat radiating off him. She licked her dry lips, shifting, trying to get comfortable.

"So, what are we going to do now?" Jake asked. "I can't imagine your plan is 'sit around and wait for Grayson to make a move.'"

"Of course not," Maggie said. "I sent a forensics team and the best profiler in the FBI to Max's apartment. And I'm going to head over there to see what we can learn about him." She paused, unsure. "Do you want to come?"

Jake shook his head. "I wouldn't be any help to you. I'm not a science guy, and the profiling stuff is better left to the pros, I've found. I'm gonna do a little recon with some local guys I know."

Maggie was a little disappointed, but she knew he was right. "You'll call me if you get a solid lead?"

"You're the boss, Goldilocks."

She didn't even bristle at the nickname this time. Instead, she had to suppress a smile, and didn't quite manage to. "I'll see you later."

SHE'D HAD ONE of the junior agents call her a car, since hers was still parked at the Adonis Lodge. They'd taken Jake's SUV to the press conference. The walk down the Thebeses' driveway was long, but it gave her a few minutes to breathe. The day had begun to heat up. The sun felt good against her face, and she paused for a moment, letting it warm her skin. But she couldn't truly enjoy the moment. The situation was spiraling out of control, just like Sherwood Hills. She had to make sure it ended differently this time. She had to be cautious. Careful. Controlled.

She wasn't going to lose Kayla.

No criminal was perfect, not even Max Grayson, for all his smoothness and trickery and planning. She would find the crack, and she'd chisel away at it until the case shattered open. Hopefully, there'd be something at his apartment—a clue to where he'd taken Kayla, some sort of hint as to *what* was in that file he wanted so badly. If the senator wasn't going to volunteer the information, she would find it some other way—even if it meant getting it from the kidnapper himself.

Maggie rounded the last curve of the Thebeses' driveway, gravel crunching under her heels, and came to an abrupt halt as she saw the gate up ahead. Flashes of light filled her vision, and the sounds of shouting against a background of cameras clicking rose around her. A throng of journalists was grouped behind the gate, blocking the car—and her escape route.

She stumbled backward, and her childhood terror, the familiar feeling of being trapped, rose to the surface. For weeks after her parents had gotten her back, journalists had followed her around. They'd circled like vultures, ready to pick her off, until they'd found a fresher target. Her wrists ached, and she couldn't stop herself from rubbing at them as questions were shot at her from all sides.

"Agent Kincaid! Agent Kincaid! Can you comment on Kayla Thebes' kidnapping?"

"Is it true you left the FBI two years ago? If that's so, why are you in charge of this case?"

"Max Grayson's been a political fixture in the community for over two years. Any theories on why he would do something like this?"

Maggie squared her shoulders and strode up to the gate, careful to keep her face neutral. The journalists would read into every look, every frown, every smile. They'd pick it apart, analyze it, theorize on it, whipping everything up into a frenzy. She nodded to the security guard who manned the gate, and he opened it wide enough for her to squeeze through.

They descended on her, shoving their microphones and cameras in her face, their shouted questions overlapping, surging into a confusing cacophony. Maggie froze, panic exploding inside her, zipping along her skin in icy bursts. She was trapped, unable to move, as everything inside her screamed *run away, run away, run away.* People jostled her from all sides, a camera nearly clipping the back of her head. She wanted to collapse on the ground, her arms around her head, her knees clutched to her chest. Any second, her legs would give out, and the mob would trample her . . .

"Hey, clear out! Get out of my way!" Frank came muscling through the crowd, grabbing Maggie's arm and pulling her through the throng. He practically shoved her into the back seat of the car he'd just emerged from, shutting the door behind her. Inside, in the warmth and safety, she was able to breathe again, to calm the trembling of her hands. She let out a long breath, rubbing her hands up and down her arms, trying to rid herself of the cold.

"I've got this," Frank told her, leaning in through the half-opened window so he could see and hear her. "You going to Grayson's apartment?"

Maggie nodded and sank back into the leather seat, relieved at the sudden silence and privacy. Frank was always on her side. "I need a better handle on this guy."

"Get to work," Frank said. "I'll deal with this bullshit."

He straightened, a calm smile on his face. All annoyance at the press vanished as he turned to the crowd, ready to work it like the expert he was. "Ladies, gentlemen, if you'll just get out of the way of the car, I'll be happy to answer your questions."

"Let's go," Maggie told the driver.

Only when she was a good mile away did she breathe easier.

CHAPTER 28

Max's apartment was in a downtown DC high-rise called the Berkshire Arms. A tall, imposing brick building right in the thick of the action, it was the perfect pick for a man like him. Or rather, for the man he wanted everyone to think he was.

The degree of deception Max Grayson had pulled off was staggering. It made Maggie nervous, because it spoke to a high level of intelligence and organization. He would be hard—maybe even impossible—to manipulate unless she had leverage over him. And so far, he'd been steps ahead of her in every way.

Maggie still couldn't decide as she flashed her ID at the doorman and he directed her to the twelfth floor: Had this been a crime born out of opportunity, or had Max Grayson orchestrated his entire job with the senator for the sole purpose of accessing the mysterious file he wanted so badly?

Her gut told her it was too much of a coincidence for it to be the former. But she didn't want to take anything off the table—not with Grayson so far ahead of them.

It was time she got ahead of him.

Please let his apartment tell us something, Maggie thought as she punched the elevator buttons impatiently. It finally opened, and she stepped inside, riding up to the twelfth floor.

The Berkshire Arms had been built in the 1920s and had long, softly lit hallways with curved alcoves that held trailing ivy plants—a touch of life in a quiet, nearly sterile setting. Maggie couldn't imagine most of the Berkshire's residents spending much quality time in their apartments. Washington types, they were always out hustling. Home wasn't something to be treasured—it was merely a place to lay one's head.

She could relate, sadly. At least she had Thwonk, her cat.

Maggie stopped outside apartment thirty-eight, where police tape crossed the door and an officer stood outside. Automatically, she reached inside her coat for her badge, only to remember she didn't have one anymore.

"I'm Maggie Kincaid," she said. "I need to get in."

"I'm sorry, ma'am," said the officer. "I can't let you in without a badge. This is a possible crime scene. Law enforcement only."

Maggie bit her lip. "I'm the lead on this case, Officer. Please get Grace Sinclair, the profiler who's inside."

She got a blank, almost suspicious look from the officer. "Long hair, very pretty, well dressed, killer heels?" she prompted.

His eyes took on a glazed, enraptured expression as he remembered Grace. Maggie tried not to roll her eyes. "Oh, yeah, she's here," the officer said with more than a little appreciation.

"Please get her," Maggie said.

He went inside, and moments later, Grace came out. Even in blue booties and gloves, she looked perfectly put together. Her bright pink lipstick matched the angora sweater she'd tucked into her houndstooth A-line skirt, her long dark hair pulled up in a crown of braids around her head to keep it out of the way as she worked the scene.

"For goodness' sake, Arthur, let her inside," Grace said to the officer. "I said to keep out civilians, not Maggie."

"She doesn't have a badge, ma'am," the officer said, looking at Grace as if she was some sort of goddess.

"She doesn't need one," Grace replied, holding out a pair of blue plastic booties. Maggie slipped them on over the soles of her leather ankle boots, ducked under the police tape, and walked into the apartment. She snapped on the gloves Grace handed her, automatically keeping her elbows tucked in and her hands at her sides. It'd been two years since she'd been to a crime scene, but some habits were ingrained.

Forensic techs were milling about, using tweezers to place carpet fibers and hairs in evidence bags.

"Anything yet?" Maggie asked, stepping out of the way of an evidence tag.

The apartment was plainly furnished, with very few personal effects. Political magazines were strewn across the glass coffee table that was set in front of a beige couch that Maggie recognized from IKEA. A bowl of overripe fruit sat on the kitchen counter, a dirty blender soaking in the sink. A tub of protein powder was left next to the blender's base near the fridge.

"No sign Kayla's been here at all," Grace said. "All the hair samples that were taken to the lab are short, similar in color and texture to Grayson's. No blood spatter anywhere, no signs of violence or struggle. If he'd been keeping her here, he would've needed to soundproof the hell out of his spare bedroom—these old buildings have thin walls—but it's just full of gym equipment."

Maggie turned in a slow circle in the living room, getting a feel for it. She could picture Grayson sprawled on the couch, reading the magazines. There wasn't a TV in the living room. It must be in the bedroom. He'd have a TV, just to keep up with the news. She imagined him walking to the kitchen, opening the fridge. It was probably full of takeout and juices. Maybe his favorite kind of hot sauce. A typical workaholic's home.

"What do you think?" she asked Grace. "Can you give me a profile?"

"He's neat. Highly organized. Take a look at his desk." Grace led her down the hallway, into the second bedroom turned office where three flat-screen TVs hung on the wall. Grace picked the remote off the desk and flipped them on. Each one was already tuned to a major news channel.

"Notice how he has everything arranged," Grace said. In the center of the desk lay a yellow legal pad, a cup of pens, and a perfect row of pencils sharpened to fine points. Maggie bent down, looking closer at the legal pad. It was brand new, never used.

"Looks like your typical DC wannabe, right?" Grace asked.

Maggie nodded, but she had a feeling that Grace was going somewhere with this. "Yeah, it all seems to fit. What of it?"

"That's the thing," Grace said. "It fits *too* well."

Maggie frowned, looking around Max Grayson's home office. It looked exactly like she'd guessed it would, honestly.

"I've gone through the entire apartment," Grace said. "Come see." She led Maggie into the bedroom, where a king-size bed with rumpled sheets took up most of the space. A white end table next to the bed held nothing but a lamp and a spare phone charger.

"Every book he owns fits the profile," Grace continued. "Every movie—and the boxed *West Wing* DVD set, of course. His clothes, the sheets on his bed, even the premade meals in the freezer. Everything falls into the 'bachelor politico' profile."

"Okay," Maggie said. "And you're saying it shouldn't?"

"I'm saying that people, humans, we're messy," Grace said. "But this is perfect. No detail out of place. *Nothing* out of place. Nothing deviating from the profile—the persona—he wants to project. Regular people don't fit in every single box. There's always something off, something that makes us *us*. Even for a neat freak, there's always something that reveals an individual personality. You have that idiotic cat, for instance."

"Thwonk is very sweet," Maggie said.

"But you're so not a cat person, Mags."

Maggie had to give her that one. She wasn't.

"And if you looked at my life, you wouldn't immediately think 'Grace loves MMA fighting.'"

"So you think Grayson's pretending," Maggie said.

"Not necessarily," Grace said. "But he's so deliberate it makes me nervous."

"Is he a psychopath?" Maggie asked.

"I don't think so," Grace said. "I think he's a control freak with a mission. One that means a lot to him . . . maybe more than anything else."

Grace gestured at the space around them, at the carefully curated life Max Grayson had left for them to examine. "He's stripped his life of anything personal," Grace explained. "And it was clearly in pursuit of playing the part well enough to get this far without anyone suspecting or questioning him. That kind of dedication speaks to a deeply rooted motivation. An unbearable emotion, maybe an obsession. Or both. Whatever's in that file is something Max Grayson's willing to do anything for. He's prepared to die for it. More importantly, he'll kill for it."

"We have to get Kayla out," Maggie said.

"And soon," Grace agreed. "You messed up his plan. He's probably pissed and scared. Even though he must have planned for the possibility of getting caught, I don't believe he really thought it would happen at this stage. He expected taking Kayla would be enough to sway the senator. He didn't count on the senator refusing to hand over the file. He didn't count on you."

"Can I see the bedroom again?" Maggie asked.

Grace nodded, leading her back into the room. This time, Maggie didn't head toward the bed or its side cabinets. She went for the closet.

"I looked through it," Grace said. "Even the workout clothes are the right brands, but they're impersonal. There isn't one worn-out college tee or charity shirt from a 5K in his hometown. Nothing identifiable. It's just . . . it's too careful, Maggie."

Maggie peered inside the closet. There was a row of suits and button-down shirts, expensive Italian leather shoes. She pushed them aside to make sure nothing was stashed in the corners. She was about to step away and join Grace when she paused, peering at the back of the closet again.

It was too small, even for an apartment closet. The wall had been moved in several inches, as if to accommodate plumbing even though the bathroom and kitchen were on the other side of the apartment.

She smiled, shoving the suits out of her way, and stepping in. It was rare moments like this when being short came in handy. She fit easily in the tiny space without any awkward bending.

"Did you find something?" Grace asked over her shoulder.

"Give me a sec," Maggie said, tapping the wall with her gloved hand. About halfway up, the sound turned distinctly hollow. Running her fingers along the wall, she felt the hint of a seam in the drywall.

"There we go!" Maggie's heart skipped a beat. Hidden compartments meant secrets. Secrets that could lead her to Kayla's location.

Please, please let this be a lead, she thought.

"Get me a knife?" she asked. Grace hurried out of the room, only to return with three. Maggie smiled, appreciating her friend's characteristic thoroughness. She selected the utility knife and ran it along the seam in the wall, pushing hard to cut through the drywall in a square. With a delicate touch, she fished out the segment with the flat of the blade, revealing a hollow spot with a file folder tucked inside.

Maggie grabbed it and stepped out of the closet, away from the drywall dust and the suffocating presence of all those suits embedded with a trace of Max Grayson's overpowering cologne. Grace would probably have something to say about the brand and how it fit his fake persona.

"Well, well, well," Grace said as Maggie opened the folder. "Looks like Max isn't so smart after all."

The first thing Maggie saw were surveillance photos, shot from far away with a long lens. Kayla at school. Kayla at lacrosse practice. Kayla riding her horse at the stables. Kayla kissing Lucas in his car. Kayla with her parents. Maggie flipped past them to find a series of newspaper clippings and magazine articles, all about the senator and his family. In one clipping, a magazine profile about his reelection campaign, Grayson had underlined a passage about Kayla's diabetes.

Maggie silently handed the folder to Grace, whose face tightened with concern as she flipped through the pages. She glanced at Maggie in alarm.

"He's been planning this for more than two years," Maggie said.

"This guy plays the long game," Grace said, shaking her head as she returned her attention to the file. Maggie could practically see the gears of her mind working as she added all the information into the profile she was working to build, already analyzing how it changed the variables and might affect the outcome.

Kayla's outcome.

Maggie looked around the room. At the perfectly arranged—perfectly fake—life Max Grayson had created for himself. Frustration and confusion swamped her. What was going on here? She felt lost in the woods with nothing to light her way. Nothing to grasp, no solid leads to follow. There were too many secrets being kept, too many agendas to juggle. And at the center: an unsub she couldn't nail down.

"Who the hell *is* this guy?" she asked.

And how the hell was she going to beat him?

CHAPTER 29

Jake hurried up the steps of the Capitol Building, taking the steps two at a time. Walking past the tourists and students with cell phones extended as they posed for selfies, he took a right, heading toward security. He handed over the badge the senator had given him to the agent standing in front of the metal detectors.

"What's your business on the Hill today?" the guard asked.

"I'm a member of Senator Thebes' security team," Jake explained, tossing his phone, keys, and wallet into the tray to be scanned. "With all the chaos of the last few days, it took the senator until now to realize he'd left his briefcase in his office. He sent me over to pick it up."

The guard walked him through the metal detector and then a full-body scan—Jake had left his guns and knife secured in his SUV—and nodded an all-clear, allowing him to walk through the doors and down the hall into Thebes' office.

No matter how many times Jake had been in this building, the feeling of history always seeped into his bones. Great men and women had walked these halls, helping shape and protect the country he was so proud to serve.

He wasn't a complicated man: His faithfulness to his country, to his team, his family was paramount. It defined him.

And it pissed him off that Senator Thebes, the very man

he was supposed to be serving, was acting so unconcerned about his own daughter's safety. His decisions appalled Jake. They were not the choices of a great man. They weren't even the decisions of a good father. Something in those files mattered more to Thebes than his daughter's life. What was it? That question ate at Jake, and he was determined to find the answer.

The senator wasn't going to spill—if anyone could've gotten him to, it would've been the firecracker that was Maggie Kincaid. So Jake had to take matters into his own hands and find out what the hell was going on. Starting now.

Maggie would be pissed if he got the drop on her. Maybe she'd do that cute outraged thing with her mouth again. Her lips were impossibly, distractingly rosy pink, and he knew it had to be natural. She wasn't the kind of woman who'd bother with lipstick on a run. He liked that about her. DC was full of a lot of women who had perfect hair and perfect nails and perfect lipstick that never smudged. And he understood why—it was a way to be taken seriously and be considered professional in a world run by men who hadn't quite woken up to the twenty-first century when it came to women. His last girlfriend had been a lobbyist who hated the idea of his seeing her without makeup. He'd grown up on a ranch with country girls who wore mud spatters more than they did perfume. Maybe that was why the slight messiness to Maggie Kincaid—the natural brightness, her clear, dogged focus—lured him toward her like a sailor to a siren.

Jake slipped into the senator's office, using the key card security had issued him. The small, cluttered room had a desk outfitted much like the one in Thebes' home office, with pictures of Kayla and his wife set in frames. Legal texts filled a large bookcase, and a framed painting of the Founding Fathers stared down at him from the wall. But Jake wasn't here to go through the senator's things—his focus was on the side door that led to Max's office. Taking his keys out of his pocket, he twisted the top of a silver keychain that looked like a whistle. Pulling off the cap, he exposed a hollow interior and shook out a small tension wrench and a set of lock picks into his palm. With a light touch, he raked the pins inside the lock with the tension wrench, getting a feel for it before inserting the pick and pushing the pins up one by one. After a quick, practiced turn of the wrench, the lock sprang free, and the door opened.

Jake smiled in satisfaction, stepping into Max's office.

He knew men like Max Grayson. He understood the type. He'd been surrounded by them ever since the Army had slapped medals on him and sent him home to "advise on sensitive matters."

For politicos of Grayson's ilk, home was a place to sleep, but *life* happened at work. A guy like that felt more at home in an office than kicking back in front of the game on the TV. Jake knew Maggie would zero in on anything of note at the apartment, but it was better that he was here. Faster. They covered more ground apart, and he knew that with Grayson's apartment crawling with FBI, she'd be safe. Plus, she was armed and knew what she was doing. That was a load off his mind, especially with her habit of spouting off her opinions and jumping into situations on her own, without waiting for any cover. He'd be damned if he ended up chasing after her, trying to play catch-up when she went after Max.

Now that they knew her kidnapper was Grayson, Kayla's time was running out fast. The thought made him want to punch something—or someone, preferably the senator. That sweet kid wasn't going to die, he told himself firmly. Not with a woman like Maggie Kincaid fighting for her. And not with him watching Maggie's back.

It was strange to have that much faith in someone he'd just met, but Jake found that instead of retreating, he wanted to charge toward the feeling—toward *her*. Their connection evoked something he thought he'd lost when he'd been hauled back to DC, leaving his team, his men, behind. He trusted her: her intellect, her instincts, her fighting spirit. She was as smart as she was sexy, but it wasn't just physical attraction that drew him to her and made him want to skim his hands underneath that neat button-up blouse. There was something behind those big blue eyes, the deep kind of pain that has forged a person stronger than steel.

She would fight a hell of a battle to bring Kayla back, and he was determined to stay right by her side. Someone needed to watch her back. The FBI was full of guys eager to dismiss and discredit her. Jake smiled grimly. He bet she'd outgunned and outsmarted all of them when she worked there. She wasn't one to play nice, not with lives on the line. And there was a certain kind of man who was threatened by a woman like that, instead of intrigued.

Jake was the type to be intrigued . . . to say the least.

Grayson's office was plain and even smaller than the senator's, with a less opulent desk and a pair of locked cupboards behind it. Selecting a longer pick from his set, Jake got the cheap lock open in less than twenty seconds. File upon file spilled out of the cupboard—they'd been stuffed inside in no discernible order—which seemed a little weird to Jake, considering the stuff on Grayson's desk was so organized and neat. He brushed more files onto the floor, digging deeper through the ones remaining. Behind a stack of them, he caught sight of the square edge of a laptop.

He pulled it out from where it was jammed into the back recesses of the cabinet, scattering more papers and manila envelopes to the ground.

Walking over to Grayson's desk, he flipped the laptop open and turned it on, unsurprised when he was prompted for a password. Grayson wasn't stupid—he was a careful son of a bitch. But so was Jake. He dug in his pocket for his wallet and pulled out a slim USB drive tucked into one of the credit card slots.

It paid to have retired Army buddies who had turned to the private tech sector. This little baby had a hacker virus coded into it. The minute it was inserted into a computer, it began to unravel and read all the passwords, unlocking them one by one.

Nothing is safe. Nothing is secret. Not if you have the right code. Or the right friends.

It took only three minutes for the virus to unlock the computer, the screen flipping to the desktop. Multiple folders, labeled with titles like "Clancy Hearing" and "Senator's October Schedule," turned up a whole lot of nothing. As Jake clicked through the folders, every single one of them empty, he began to think he'd hit a dead end.

Pulling up the search bar, he typed in ".jpg." Maybe Grayson reserved the laptop just for pictures? He had to have scoped out the place he was keeping Kayla, after all. He hit Search, and a list of images appeared.

He clicked through the pictures—most were stock photos that came preloaded in the computer. He clicked on a file named "HarleyDavidson.jpg," but instead of finding a picture of a motorcycle, a spreadsheet appeared on the screen.

"Gotcha," Jake whispered with a smile. He scrolled down, finding copies of financial information, dates, times, and Grayson's passport photos.

Jake frowned. He knew what this was. He'd seen it before when he'd been stationed in Afghanistan. This was a ready-made identity. Professional level. It went back all the way to childhood medical records.

How could this be? He scrolled through the file again, just to be sure. But it was too extensive, too high quality. How had Grayson gotten his hands on this? *Who* had gotten his hands on this?

Max Grayson *wasn't* Max Grayson. Everything about him—everything they thought they knew so far—was a lie. Max Grayson didn't exist. He was a lie. A mask invented solely to get whatever was in that secret file of the senator's.

Jake leaned back in the chair, staring at the information in front of him. This was a new kind of trouble, a different kind of game to play.

Who the hell was this guy? And what was he planning to do to Kayla?

CHAPTER 30

"You ready for this?" Paul asked as Maggie walked down a hallway in the FBI headquarters for the second time this week. This time, she found it easier to ignore the stares and whispers that followed her. She even smiled neutrally at the people gawking, unable to hide their surprise at her return.

You're the touchstone, Maggie. She could hear Jake saying it in her head, how earnest and sure he sounded. How much faith he had in her. Strength built inside her. "I'm ready," Maggie said.

"You didn't think you'd ever be here again, did you?" Paul asked, his mouth flattening in concern.

He was always worried about her. She hated that he still carried that burden. That was one of the reasons why they had broken up. She wanted to tell him she was fine and she wanted him to believe it. She wasn't sure if they'd ever get there.

He needed to move on. To find a woman who deserved his goodness and sweetness. Who wanted to have him worry about her. To love her.

Paul needed the kind of softness she no longer possessed. Life had sharpened her edges and she'd learned not just to use those edges, but to like them.

"I meant it when I left, Paul," Maggie said. It was impossible to dismiss the double meaning of her words. She'd quit the FBI and then she'd quit him, and she'd known those had been the right choices. The FBI might have drawn her back in—temporarily—but Paul never could.

He smiled sadly, reaching to get the door to the conference room for her. "You'll be fine."

"Of course I will," Maggie said. "I have to be. For Kayla."

Chin up, she moved into the room with confidence. Ten or so agents were already waiting for her to debrief them and had gathered around a trio of whiteboards. Ignoring the unsettled murmurs that followed her, she walked briskly to the front of the room and turned to face her audience.

"Our unsub is no longer unknown," she told the agents grouped around her, pointing to Max's photo posted on the middle board. "Kayla Thebes' kidnapper is Max Grayson, the senator's political advisor. Agent Sinclair has put together a preliminary profile that you'll find in the files provided. Grayson is a highly organized criminal with a very specific end goal: to acquire sensitive material from Capitol Hill that only the senator has access to."

"Can't the senator tell us what it is?" asked an agent.

"He's not being forthcoming with that information," Maggie said. "He insists it's a matter of national security."

"And you believe him?" asked a skeptical voice.

No, Maggie thought. But she couldn't say that. She didn't want the agents distracted. She needed their focus on Grayson and his location. Kayla's time was running out.

"The senator deals with many classified issues," Maggie said, hoping she sounded convincing. "This is his child's life at stake. If he could tell us, he would. It's time we put the focus of our investigation on Grayson. I want to know everything about this guy. She pointed to three techs to her left, who snapped to attention. "Thomas, Wilder, and Eager—you're on financials. I want to know everything that man's bought and where. Gas stations, especially. Pullman and Smith, you're on phone records. Who's he called and who's calling him? I want every phone call traced and every email analyzed."

"We're on it," Agent Pullman said, already flipping open her laptop.

"Johnson, you're on pharmacy detail," Maggie said. "Grayson's been giving Kayla insulin—where did he get it?"

"Do you really think that's necessary?" Johnson, a hulking agent with a thick, overhanging brow who looked more Neanderthal than human, asked.

Maggie whirled around, a death glare on her face. "Considering Kayla's insulin dependency, yes, I do."

Johnson folded his arms across his chest, the picture of stubbornness. "Why should I take orders from a burnout like you, Kincaid?"

Before Maggie could say another word, Paul stepped forward, glowering. Johnson shifted nervously. Paul outranked him and he knew it. "Because I said so, Johnson," he barked.

Anger spiked through Maggie. She knew Paul meant well trying to defend her, but he wasn't helping her earn any respect. She could fight her own damn battles.

"Do your job, Johnson," she ordered. "You know how to do that, don't you?"

He glared at her, nodding sullenly after Paul shot him another quelling look.

"Let's continue," Maggie said. She had to keep this moving, keep them thinking. An investigative team was like a machine: All the moving parts had to be working in unison. One moment of delay and everything could fall apart. "It's clear from the evidence Special Agent Sinclair and I pulled from Grayson's apartment that he's been planning this for a long time. Years. That means we—"

The door opening and slamming shut startled everyone in the room, causing Maggie to stop midsentence. Jake hurried in, striding through the crowd of agents, who parted as he made his way up to her. An excited murmur followed him, and Maggie heard catches of muttered conversation. ". . . works for the senator . . ." and ". . . Special Forces, I think?"

"Can I talk to you?" he asked in an undertone.

She cast a nervous glance around the crowd of agents, already muttering at the disruption. "Can it wait?" she asked.

"You're gonna want to hear this," Jake said. When she hesitated, he said, "Trust me."

Such simple words for such a complicated request.

Did she trust him?

She wanted to. And not just because his touch seemed to be sex personified when it came to her.

"Take five, everyone," Maggie called. "Let's go into the annex," she said, gesturing to the small room that branched off from the conference area. He hesitated for a moment, and Maggie grabbed his arm. She didn't think she had any way of physically moving him—she was strong for her size, but Jake O'Connor was built like an infuriating—though sexy—brick wall. Still, at her beseeching touch, he followed.

She closed the door, catching one final glimpse of the curious and skeptical faces of the agents waiting.

"Did you have to do that?" she asked.

"This is a game changer," Jake said. "I figured you'd want a heads-up so *you* could break it to your team."

Maggie bit her lip. As bad as it looked to get pulled out in the middle of a case breakdown, she knew he was right.

"Okay," she said. "Thank you. Now tell me what's going on."

Jake set a laptop on the small desk inside the annex, flipping it open. "Max Grayson doesn't exist," he said.

"What?" Maggie asked, moving forward, hair rising on her arms at his words. "How's that possible?"

"It's an alias," Jake explained as she leaned over his shoulder and he began to open the laptop's files.

"I just pulled this from Grayson's office on the Hill," Jake said. "His real name is Roger Mancuso. Grew up in Charlottesville. Not the best childhood, if we're being generous. Parents dead, brother dead. No family. No one to identify him or mess up his plans."

"And this was all in his office?" Maggie asked. It made sense—it was safer than his apartment.

"Stuffed in the back of a cabinet," Jake said. "Under his real name, this guy's been busted six times for minor offenses. Drunken fights, disturbing the peace, that sort of stuff. His last offense was reduced to minor assault by a judge who should've known better. Five years ago, he broke parole and disappeared.

"To find out more, I started making some calls. Reaching out to my contacts overseas. Turns out right after Roger Mancuso broke parole, Max Grayson shows up for the first time, in Paris, for about a week. Next time he emerged, it was in DC, with an impressive resume that was apparently good enough to fool several background checks. He worked his way up the political ladder for three years before being hired by Senator Thebes."

"He's been planning this for five years," Maggie breathed. God, it was even worse than she thought. Dedicating two years of your life to a criminal plan was a commitment.

Five years . . .

Five years was obsession.

Jake met Maggie's gaze, his eyes solemn and worried. "Everything we think we know about this guy is a lie."

CHAPTER 31

"This is bad," Maggie said. Then she laughed, exhaustion and despair bubbling inside her. "God, that's an understatement."

"This guy's fueled by some kind of vendetta," Jake said. "And you and I both know, men like that . . ." He paused.

"Men like that don't play nice," Maggie finished.

"Men like that don't want money," Jake said. "They want power."

"And the senator has plenty of it."

"We need to go in and brief the team," Jake said.

Maggie hesitated, biting her lip as dread built inside her.

"What?" he asked.

"I missed this," she said.

"Hey, no," he said reassuringly. "You weren't looking for it."

"Yes, I was," Maggie said. "I was looking for it at his apartment. Grace said that his place was weird—like there was no actual indication of a personality there."

Jake frowned. "So you're going to beat yourself up because I got to his office before you? It would've been the next place you went, Maggie. And if you had beat me there, you would've found the laptop."

"I know that," Maggie said. "But the guys out there?" She gestured to the door. "They hate me. I'm the bitch who got the promotions they thought they deserved. When I screwed up, they acted like they were expecting it all along.

They're just waiting for me to screw up again. And this will be more ammo for them."

"Screw them," Jake said.

Maggie's mouth dropped open. "Excuse me?"

"You heard me," Jake said. "Screw them. You're the best, right? That's what everyone I called about you said. Every single person, Maggie. They said you were a pit bull . . . you never let go, never stop, never get tired. They told me that the best person to have on this case is you."

Her cheeks heated up, and she glanced back at the door to the conference room. "They'll try to undermine me," she said weakly.

"I'll have your back," he promised.

She'd heard those words before, countless times, from colleagues, from friends, from boyfriends.

But never had she believed them like this.

She reached up before she could stop herself. She had to go on her tiptoes because he was so tall, balancing herself with a hand on his shoulder as she brushed a kiss against his stubbled cheek. "Thanks, O'Connor," she said, softly.

She began to pull away, but he grabbed her waist, his fingers spread against the sensitive curve, five points of fire burning through her shirt. His glance dropped to her lips.

"I could kiss you right now," he said, his voice husky.

"You could," she said, feeling breathless. Could he hear how hard her heart was beating?

He raised his free hand, his thumb brushing the lushness of her bottom lip. She closed her eyes against the heat, tingling shocks dancing across her body. When her eyes drifted open, he was watching her like she was something beautiful and mysterious, like he wanted to spend hours, days, months puzzling her out.

"But if I do," he went on, "I'm not gonna be able to stop."

She smiled. "You should let me go then," she whispered.

"Is that an order?" he asked, boyish teasing in his eyes and grin. Her heart twisted inside her chest. How could he have so many different smiles? She wanted to discover all of them. To be their cause.

"Does it need to be?" she countered.

He let go of her, his fingers trailing off her body like they wanted to linger there. "You can order me around any day, Goldilocks."

She blushed, and his grin widened when he saw it.

"Okay, let's go do this," he said. "Be the big bad bitch they've built you up to be in their heads, Maggie. They won't know what to do with themselves."

"You've got my back?" she asked, because she wanted to hear it again. She wanted to *feel* it again; that warm, hopeful emotion that had sprouted and blossomed in her chest at his faith in her. This wasn't the time or the place to consider the depth of that emotion—where it came from, how it had taken root so fast—but it comforted her just the same.

"I've got your back," he promised.

She turned toward the door when her cell phone, set on the desk, began to ring.

Jake looked over to it as she grabbed the phone and looked at the screen.

"It's an unlisted number," she said.

"You think it's him?" he asked.

"Could be," she said.

"I'll get them to trace it." Jake opened the door to the conference room and got the attention of one of the techs, who scrambled to set up a trace as Jake returned to her side. The rest of the room had gone mercifully silent, and Maggie turned her back to them, steeling herself. She didn't need to see all those eyes on her. This call was too important.

She knew who Max Grayson really was. She was finally a step ahead of him. She needed to use that leverage carefully.

So far, he was flying high on his success. So far, he'd made it look easy. But now it was time to change the game. She needed to put a chink in his armor.

She didn't have a lot of time to think. She had to answer.

Her heart skipped nervously and her stomach swooped in a sick circle as she swiped the phone screen. After a deep breath, she accepted the call. "Hello?" Her voice was level and calm, without a hint of the desperation she felt.

"Hello, Maggie," Max Grayson said. Gone was the digitized voice. Instead, she heard the crisp, practiced tones of someone who'd spent years lying for a living. "Since the cat's out of the bag, we can cut out the middleman. This is nicer, isn't it? Just you and me. More private."

"Like that secret compartment in your closet?" Maggie asked.

Grayson laughed. "Searching through my stuff, are you? How's that going?"

"Did you call me just to gloat?" Maggie asked. "Because you fooled me. We can talk about that, if you want. Or we can talk about what you really want."

"You should be aware," Grayson said, a note of satisfaction in his voice, "that I've destroyed sweet little Kayla's insulin. She's got the shakes, poor thing. Her blood sugar, you know. I looked it up—WebMD says this kind of crash is pretty painful. From what I read, if she doesn't get help, it can cause permanent damage. She might slip into a coma and never wake up. It'd be quite the blow to her mother, don't you think? But I doubt her dad will mind as much. He doesn't seem to be the most *involved* father, if you know what I mean."

Maggie was livid at his casual cruelty, but managed to keep her cool. "I'll ask again." Her voice was tense. "Do you want to do business, *Mancuso*?"

There was an audible, sucked-in breath and a long pause.

"Oh, yeah," Maggie went on. "I know who you are. Roger Mancuso. Grew up at 345 North Street in Charlottesville. It costs a pretty penny to manufacture this extensive an identity. I must admit I'm impressed, *Max*." With the last word, her voice was heavy with sarcasm.

"It—it doesn't change things," Mancuso replied after a pause, his voice cracking. He was clearly rattled and hiding it badly. "I still have Kayla. You won't find her in time,

Maggie. Do you really want that on your head after your last case?"

Maggie's hand tightened so hard on the phone she was afraid she'd break it. She couldn't say anything—her voice would shake, her anger would come through. He would know he'd struck a well-aimed blow. She needed to breathe and gain some kind of control, she reminded herself sternly. This wasn't about her. It was about Kayla's safety. She wasn't going to botch this like she did at Sherwood Hills.

"You know, I listened to the agents talk about you," Mancuso pushed on. "How you burned out. They thought Edenhurst was crazy, bringing you in. Kept talking about how badly you screwed up two years ago. How everyone had to clean up your mess." Mancuso's voice deepened as he went in for the kill. "Do you want another mess, Maggie? Because I can make a big one. Bigger than you can even imagine."

Maggie couldn't stop the quick breath she sucked in. An audible sound that she knew he heard. She swallowed, her throat dry and tight. She couldn't defend herself. Not to him. Not to anyone. Not even to herself. It wasn't the time or the place. She wasn't the kind of person who'd try.

This wasn't about her. It was about Kayla. She had to ignore the hurt and doubt rising inside her like a tsunami. She had to hold steady. She was Maggie Kincaid, and she would not be shaken.

"Senator Thebes has until seven o'clock to get me the file," Mancuso went on, his voice rising. "He will drop the file in the garbage can right outside the entrance of Lafayette Square. Don't even try to get someone undercover in position. I will spot any law enforcement, Maggie—you know I will. I've outsmarted you once, and I'll do it again. If you send anyone else, Kayla's going to wish she slipped into a coma."

Maggie's heartbeat spiked at the determination in Mancuso's voice. He was escalating, and she didn't know what to do about it. Push him too hard and he'd snap.

Be too weak and he'd take advantage. God, what to do? What was the right choice?

She could feel the ropes tightening around her wrists, and she rubbed at the skin furiously, her mind racing.

"If you get the file, then I get Kayla's location," Maggie said. "And she needs to be in good health, Mancuso."

"*If* I get the file," Mancuso stressed. "You can have Kayla. But your fine senator hasn't been exactly forthcoming about all this, has he?" The venomous mockery in his voice made Maggie's skin prickle.

Jake scribbled something on a notepad, holding it up to her: *What's in that file?*

Maggie nodded to show she understood.

"No, he hasn't," Maggie said, a plan forming in her head as she spoke. Senator Thebes clearly wasn't going to tell her what was in that file—and getting him to hand it over would be even more difficult. Maybe Mancuso could give her the lead she needed. She softened her voice, her tone turning conversational, like she was a coworker complaining about an annoying boss. "It's been really frustrating, to be honest. I'm kind of pissed off. Typical politician, thinking he's more important than he actually is."

"I bet you tried to bust his balls and failed." Mancuso sneered.

Maggie could tell he wasn't convinced by her sudden change of tone. She needed to sell it. To create a thread of commiseration between them. "He's been very stubborn," Maggie agreed. "I mean, you worked for him. You know what I mean."

Mancuso snorted. "Yeah."

Maggie continued, encouraged by his reaction. They were building a rapport. This was good. "It's been incredibly difficult to get him to do anything, really. But you don't have to be like that. You seemed like an up-front guy when I met you. Slick as hell, but that's politics for you. You didn't beat around the bush like the senator does."

"Damn right," Mancuso replied.

"So you could help me out," Maggie said, encouraged

by the hint of pride in his voice. She was getting to him. "Help us both out, really. If I know some of your story, I can understand where you're coming from better. It must be pretty bad, right? Whatever's in that file? The senator seems determined to keep it quiet. I mean, you've got his *kid*, and he's not budging. I really need some leverage with him, Mancuso."

There was a long pause. Maggie felt a knot form in her stomach as she worried she'd overplayed her hand. But then:

"Ask the good senator about SouthPoint Oil," Mancuso said. "He'll know what I mean."

Jake whipped out his phone and began typing. He was probably Googling it.

"Anything else you can tell me?" Maggie asked, encouraged by the lead.

"If I don't have that file in hand by seven o'clock, you won't hear from me again," Mancuso said. "And Kayla gets her throat slit."

He hung up.

Horrified, Maggie looked up at Jake. But she couldn't let her fear and worry swamp her. It was time for action.

"We need to have another conversation with the senator," she said.

Jake nodded grimly. "It's not going to be easy. His kid getting kidnapped wasn't good enough motivation. I don't know what will light a fire underneath him."

"We've got to try. You still have my back?"

The warmth in his face made her feel as if she was standing in front of a long-burning fire. She realized that she could count on this man to back her up, whatever it took . . . a strange and comforting feeling of support, at the moment she needed it most.

"I've got your back, Maggie," Jake said, looking into her eyes. "All the way."

CHAPTER 32

"My wife is resting," the senator said stiffly as he led them into his office. The house seemed empty and echoing now that it wasn't full of FBI. Only two agents were stationed at the gates, along with the senator's own security.

His displeasure at seeing the two of them together again was apparent. He knew why they were here—again—and didn't like it one bit. He glowered at Maggie as they walked into his office, his icy silence saying it all. Maggie could practically see him gearing up for another battle.

"I'd ask you to sit, but I don't expect you to stay long," the senator said.

Very deliberately, Maggie sat down in one of the leather chairs facing his desk, raising an eyebrow until he sat down. He folded his arms across his chest, sticking out his chin like a petulant child.

"Max Grayson isn't who you thought he was," she said.

"Yes, Ms. Kincaid, that's clear," Thebes replied. "Do you have any new information for me, or are you just here to make more impossible demands?"

"She doesn't just mean Grayson fooled your security team's background check," Jake began.

"Max Grayson is an alias," Maggie explained. "Kayla's kidnapper is a man named Roger Mancuso. And he seems to have a very big grudge against you."

Maggie watched the senator closely, searching for any

flicker of recognition. His mouth flattened in disapproval, like this was her fault.

"This man kidnapped my daughter. I know he dislikes me," he snapped. "I'm a United States senator—there are plenty of people who feel that way. How did he get through my security?" He turned to Jake, accusatory. "He had credentials. Recommendations. They performed a background check. My security firm is the best in DC."

"The problem is, Senator, that Mancuso hired the best too," Jake said. "Whoever created this identity for him was the best of the best. Nothing would've pinged on their radar."

A mottled color rose in his cheeks, his lips tightening so much they practically disappeared. He turned to Maggie. "What's your plan here, Ms. Kincaid?" he demanded. "Because so far, I'm not seeing a clear path to getting my daughter back safely."

Because you're not helping her or *me!* Maggie thought furiously. She hated that he could fix this with one trip to the Capitol but wouldn't even consider it. Why? She had to find out.

"Mancuso's withholding Kayla's insulin," Maggie said. "He will use her illness as leverage until you give him the file he wants."

"We've gone through this," Thebes replied coldly. "I cannot give up the file. Find another way."

Frustration rose inside her, threatening to blot out everything else. She breathed deep. She had to stay in control. "Then tell me what's in the file, so at least I have a goddamn lead," Maggie gritted out.

The senator straightened in his seat, recoiling slightly from her obvious anger. She didn't care if he was offended. She cared about the scant breadcrumbs that might lead her in the right direction to save his daughter.

"It's impossible to share the file with you," the senator said. "You're not even an agent anymore," he sneered, the derision dripping from his voice. "Even if you were, you don't have the clearance."

Maggie's lip curled in disgust. She was done giving him any benefit of the doubt. She was done baiting. The bastard would let his daughter die before he put that file into Mancuso's hands. What was he so afraid of? She stared at him across the desk and dropped the bomb. "Tell me about SouthPoint Oil."

And there it was. The sign she was looking for: guilt mixed with surprise flashed across Thebes' face. Maggie knew it'd be there, she'd been sure of it, but the satisfaction that flooded through her was bitter. The senator had a lot to lose, and SouthPoint was at the core of it. He wasn't about to give up that file for anything—not even Kayla. It disgusted and horrified her. She could feel the revulsion in the back of her throat, a sour taste that lingered. Her hands fisted unconsciously, and she had to force herself to uncurl them.

Maggie's parents had done everything they could to bring their girls home safe. They would've paid any price. Her father would've chopped off his own hands if that was the ransom that had been demanded. But this man, this man who claimed to be a leader of people, a loving father and husband, wouldn't lift one finger to save his daughter. Not if it risked his reputation.

There was a special kind of hell for men like him. He didn't deserve Kayla. And she deserved so much more than him.

The anger inside Maggie was molten, bubbling, rising to the surface of her skin. She breathed through it, tamping down the imminent explosion. She needed to stay calm. She had to.

"What *about* SouthPoint Oil?" the senator asked. He was clearly trying to sound and look indifferent, but the sweat beading along his collar and the slight crack in his voice said otherwise.

"It's an oil company with headquarters in your state," Jake said.

The senator shrugged. "Maryland's a very pro-business state. You can't expect me to keep track of every company with headquarters back home."

"Stop lying," Maggie said between gritted teeth.

The senator's steely gaze cut to her, trying to wither her, but instead, it fueled her anger. She glared right back at him, standing tall—well, as tall as she could get while sitting. She stared at him resolutely, refusing to blink or look away.

"I'm not lying, Ms. Kincaid," he said.

She slammed her palms on his desk, exploding out of her chair and pushing into his space until their faces were just inches apart. He flinched at her sudden movement, but quickly recovered, fury boiling in his face.

But she wasn't afraid. She was fueled by an anger he could never understand, because she cared more about his kid than he did. Because she knew what Kayla was feeling right now. How scared she was. How she was sure her father was doing everything he could to get her home.

But he wasn't. He was hindering her safety. And Maggie wouldn't stand for it.

"I am sick of you trying to cover your ass instead of owning up to whatever the hell you did," she hissed right in his face. "This is your *daughter*, you crooked bastard. Your *kid*! Do you know what she's going through? Have you even *thought* about it?" Her voice was rising, trembling. Her wrists ached, the rope that was just a memory tightening, digging into her skin. "Kayla's in the dark—alone, scared, and *powerless*. She's sick, and she knows every minute that ticks by she's closer to death. She's sitting somewhere, terrified, waiting for her daddy to save her. She's sure you're coming for her. That you're doing everything you can to get her home. You could be the man she thinks you are, that she hopes you are, that she needs you to be—but you won't. And don't you dare try to feed me that national security bullshit, Senator. You're a horrible liar—and an even worse father."

Thebes stood up so fast that his sleeve knocked over the cup of pencils, which rattled across his desk. "Don't you dare speak to me that way," he spat out, his voice low and dangerous. His steely eyes narrowed in fury. "If you don't like how I'm handling this, you can go to hell. Get out of my sight."

Maggie looked him dead in the eye, unafraid, undaunted. "'Handling' this? You don't deserve that sweet little girl," she said. "You don't deserve her trusting you or loving you or calling you *Dad*. I'm going to find out what you're hiding, Thebes. I'm going to dig up every dirty secret and lay them all out. I'll destroy your reputation if it means getting Kayla back safely. The fact that you won't do the same makes you less than a man—it makes you scum . . . it puts you on my shit list, even below the kidnapper. And just wait until you see what I do to him."

Without another word, Maggie pushed herself away from the desk and stalked out of the room, through the entrance hall and out the big double doors, into the late afternoon. It seemed strange to notice how beautiful the day was when she was this furious. She half expected storm clouds and lightning to echo her mood. Energy buzzed under her skin.

She felt like beating the man to a pulp, but he'd call security before she could get in a decent punch, so that wouldn't help matters.

Walking. Walking was an option. Burn off some of her fury so she wouldn't march back inside and slug a United States senator. She began to move, rubbing at her wrists as she made her way briskly across the lawn.

Halfway down the expansive slope, heading toward the rose garden, she heard someone call her name.

She turned to find Jake jogging toward her.

She waited for him to catch up, and he smiled.

"That was a hell of a fight," he said, his eyes gleaming with respect.

"I don't want to talk about it," Maggie said. They arrived at the gravel walk that wound through the rose garden. Bright splashes of red, white, and pink stood out against deep green. She took a deep breath, trying to enjoy the flowers' soothing fragrance, the sound of bees buzzing lazily around them.

She finally stopped. They were out of sight of the house,

half-hidden by the towering blooms. Her heart was beating too fast, her skin was radiating heat. She wanted to sit down and bury her face in her hands.

"You okay?" Jake asked.

Her wrists ached, and her lower lip, to her great embarrassment, began to wobble. She felt frayed at the edges, like a rope stretched too tight. Any more pressure, and she would snap.

"Hey." He reached out, placing his hand over her fingers. They were wrapped tightly around her wrist, her nails digging into her skin, leaving half-moon marks. With a startling softness—who knew such a big, rough man could be so gentle?—he coaxed her fingers free from their grip until their hands rested palm to palm.

His fingers laced with hers, an intimate motion that sent a frenzied heat spreading across her cheeks, chasing away her anger with something even more powerful: desire.

Maggie could feel gun calluses on his fingers—calluses that matched her own.

It was like they fit together.

"Come sit," he said. He drew her to a marble bench set near the back of the garden, in a shady, ivy-covered alcove that provided some privacy. In the shadows, his expression softened, worry in his eyes.

Worry about her.

As soon as she was seated, Maggie let out a shaky breath. She hadn't realized how close her knees were to buckling. Was that from her confrontation with the senator?

Or from Jake's touch?

"So, you've been through some heavy stuff, I'm thinking," Jake said softly.

It was hard to think straight when he was touching her, when she could close the space between them in just one step, when his eyes were full of promises she wanted so badly to believe.

"I could say the same thing about you," Maggie said.

"I was trained for it," he said. "But you . . . you were young, weren't you?"

Once again, his perception was dead on. For a long moment, Maggie wondered if she could do this. When she'd told Paul, she'd divorced herself from her emotions and approached it like another case. She thought that would be easier for both of them. She hadn't wanted Paul to worry.

But that was what had ruined them in the end. That she kept running from the emotion. From the hurt. From the memory of Erica.

She'd *left* her. She never should have. She should have been there.

She should have died with her.

It was a horrible thought. A selfish thought, when she considered her parents; her mother especially, who'd lost more in her life than any parent should. But it was one of the dark truths in her soul. One that lurked in the back of her mind, only peeking out late at night, never voiced, hardly acknowledged.

"My father came from a very wealthy family," Maggie said. "He was a good man . . . a great man. When his father died, he inherited a lot of money. It made him a target. It made *us* a target."

Jake shifted toward her so they lined up, his shoulder pressing against hers, the dip of her waist resting against the strong, warm line of his. He squeezed her hand, lending her the strength to continue.

"My mom, she was always determined we grow up normal." Maggie smiled at the memory. "We took the school bus just like everyone else. She didn't want us to grow up snobby." She stared up at the heritage oaks that bordered the rose garden, their ancient branches casting deep shadows across the gravel walk. Then she took a deep breath and went on.

"It was a normal day. Everything about it was normal. Our house was a few miles out of town, so Erica and I were always the last kids on the bus at the end of the day. We didn't think anything was strange when there was a new driver. It happened sometimes."

She could see Jake piecing it together, the dread on his

face as he realized what she was about to tell him. Paul hadn't done that—it was almost like he'd shut down out of fear. He'd been scared to make leaps. At what it might mean if he really considered what happened to her.

There may have been dread in Jake's face, but there was also acceptance warming his eyes and his touch. It bolstered her in a way that Paul's concern and tiptoeing never did.

Maggie stared up at the sky, the fluffy clouds against the brilliant blue. She blinked back tears. "But the driver didn't brake at our regular stop," Maggie said, her voice thick with emotion. "We thought it was just a mistake. Erica got up to tell him, and then . . ."

She could still see the flash of the gun, the way Erica stumbled backward, how she ran to shield Maggie with her body as the bus rocked back and forth, and the driver—some man their kidnapper paid off—yelled at her to stay still. The memory made her want to curl within herself, to hide, even now. But Jake's presence made her brave. It filled her with an openness that had eluded her grasp for so long.

"He drove us to a deserted spot, where the man was waiting for us. He gave the driver his money and blindfolded us, and threw us into the trunk of a car," Maggie said.

"Maggie . . ." Jake's rough voice wasn't full of pity, as she'd feared. Instead, there was a dawning realization in his voice. An understanding of the incident that had made and broken her.

"He had us for five days," Maggie said. "Erica . . . she was always the strong one. She didn't trust him, didn't trust that he'd let us go. We knew Mom and Dad would pay whatever money they had to, but the days kept passing and we knew something had gone wrong. Something had changed . . . we knew we had to do something before . . ." She swallowed and then went on.

"Erica was tall. She took after Dad. There was this hole in the closet he kept us in where the wood was rotted away, and we managed to kick the space open big enough for me to wiggle through—but only me. I didn't want to leave her behind. God, I never wanted to leave her behind . . ." Her voice cracked as she remembered the desperation that swamped her, the pleading in Erica's face, her insistence it was the only way. Had she known she was as good as dead? Would it have mattered?

Maggie knew it wouldn't have. She knew it was likely that, in her older-sister wisdom, Erica understood what her choice would entail. And it hadn't mattered to her.

She had sacrificed herself so Maggie could live—and look how Maggie had repaid her. She'd failed at doing the one thing she'd dedicated her life to. Maggie blinked back tears, shaky with the truth she was baring so trustingly to Jake. It should have frightened her, but he made her feel safe. Understood.

He understood pain. He was haunted too.

"Leaving her behind . . . running through those woods . . . it was the hardest thing I ever did," Maggie confessed. "I remember her exact words. Erica told me, 'No matter what happens tonight, you and I are in this together.' But we weren't, Jake. I left her behind. I left her, and when I went back . . ."

She couldn't finish. She couldn't tell him. She couldn't go back there, to that room full of blood, to the awful evidence that her sister was dead.

That she'd left her to die.

"What happened when you went back?" Jake asked softly.

Maggie looked away from the acceptance in his eyes; the understanding. She didn't deserve it, no matter how much she wanted it.

"There was blood," she said shakily, the memory of it creeping into her mind. "Her blood, it was everywhere. But she was gone. He . . . he didn't even leave her behind for us to bury. Her headstone's on an empty grave, and my mother goes and sits there every Sunday without fail because it's the only thing we have. And it was my fault. I left her. I should never have left her."

Tears gathered in her eyes. She tried desperately to blink

them back but was determined not to hide them when she failed. They trickled down her cheek, and Jake reached out, brushing them away with his thumb, the tenderness in his touch causing a different kind of ache inside her.

"You did what she asked of you," Jake said softly. "You were a good little sister, Maggie. You listened to her, just like you should have. Just like she needed you to."

"I couldn't save her," Maggie said, feeling the cracked and heavy words build a barrier of guilt around her.

"But you let her save *you*," Jake said, cupping her cheek, his palm strong and rough against her soft skin. "She knew you were going to be safe. That you got away. That's so important, Maggie. I'm pretty sure that was everything for her."

She met his gaze, and the earnestness she found there, the truth of his words, warmed her to the core. It made her almost believe him.

It made her *want* to believe him.

"She was a hero," Jake said.

"She was *my* hero," Maggie said. "Afterward, I tried to make it up to her—to us. To the girls we were . . . to the woman she never got to be. I worked hard in school. I focused on getting into the Academy. It was all I wanted . . . all I thought about. I drank, slept, and ate negotiation. I needed to understand criminal motivation. To control it. I needed to . . ." She looked away, his hand falling from her cheek. She didn't know how to voice it. That burning inside her, her compulsion to understand the criminal mind, to dissect it, so that if she learned the right combination, she could unlock the truth about what had happened to Erica. "I needed to somehow find a way to undo it," she said. "Undo what happened to us. Undo leaving her behind. Undo even getting on the bus that day. And I thought if I could get other kids back safe, maybe some part of me could break free too. Maybe one night I wouldn't close my eyes and find myself back in that closet, tied up like an animal, terrified of every sound."

"Why did you leave the FBI?" Jake asked.

Because I got a girl killed.

Maggie didn't know if she could bear to tell him. Would the softness in his eyes fade to disgust and disappointment?

"Two years ago, I got called in on a high-risk hostage situation," Maggie said. "A man named Daniel Branson had developed an obsession with a teenage girl. Gretchen Ellis. She didn't know he'd been stalking her, she was just . . ." Maggie's hands clenched. "She was just a normal teenager," she said, her voice cracking. "Branson was a sex offender who thought she was his soul mate. God . . ." Maggie shook her head, trying to banish the disgust and revulsion so she could go on. "He was delusional. He followed Gretchen and her best friend to a local mall—Sherwood Hills—and while they were in a boutique, shopping for a dress for her freshman dance, he walked up to her. Started talking about how much he loved her and how they were fated to be together. Gretchen was confused and then scared—and when she rejected him, he lost it. She'd shattered the fantasy in his head when she tried to get away from him. He couldn't handle it; he'd built an entire world hinged on her. So he pulled a gun."

She looked down at her palms, thinking about how much better she felt when his hand was in hers, as if his strength filled missing pieces of her soul. Old wounds she tried not to disturb, that only came alive in her dreams.

"Gretchen was fourteen," Maggie went on. "Just like Erica. And there was something about her . . ." She blinked back tears, letting out a shaky breath. "It wasn't just that they looked alike, even though they did, *so* much. It was what . . . what she did. Gretchen pushed her best friend out of the way. To safety. Just like Erica had done. That's why Branson was able to grab her and put the gun to her head. Because she didn't try to save herself, she saved her best friend."

"Like your sister saved you," Jake said softly. Maggie nodded, her face twisted in agonized memory.

"I thought I had control," she went on in a stricken voice. "I thought I was over it, what had happened to me. I thought I could do my job and it wouldn't affect me. That it would *help* me. Inform me in a way that no other agent could be. But I never thought about what would happen if I were ever in a situation where my memories took over and made me ruin everything. But it happened. Gretchen looked so much like Erica; she acted so much like Erica . . . and instead of taking time to suss things out, I—I sent SWAT in too soon. I thought it was the right call. That Branson needed to be shown extreme force. I thought it'd reaffirm how in over his head he was. I thought he'd buckle. But I was wrong . . . I was so wrong. I didn't realize he would rather kill Gretchen than give her up. I should've taken my time instead of pushing. Grace wanted me to wait for a more detailed profile—I wanted to get Gretchen out of there as fast as possible. But SWAT made him panic. Violently. He shot her in the head before turning the gun on himself."

For a moment, Jake's entire body tensed; she could feel his shoulder hard against hers. Then his hand squeezed her fingers gently as he looked into her eyes. She saw no blame or judgment there; instead, only a deep well of sympathy and pain that echoed her own. His lips softened, quirking up at the side, encouraging her, telling her she was safe. Somehow, it lent her the strength to go on.

"I quit the FBI the next day," Maggie said, straightening in her seat, trying to sit tall, to sound confident. Like it had been the right idea. It had, hadn't it? "I walked away and I told myself I'd never come back. I really thought I was done. I told myself I was. But then Frank showed up and dragged me back in, and now . . ."

"Now we're here," Jake finished for her.

"Sometimes I feel like I'm losing my mind," Maggie confessed. "I'm not up to this. I'm just too broken."

"Maggie," he said gently. It was just her name, but for some reason, it was what made her want to break. To lean into him and take the comfort he seemed ready to offer. He placed his hand on her leg, not squeezing, but resting there, a reassuring strength. After a moment's hesitation, she brushed her hand over his. He smiled at the small gesture.

"With jobs like ours, there are going to be failures," he

said quietly. "People will die. Sometimes it's our fault . . . sometimes it isn't. Sometimes life just screws with us, and even though we did everything right, followed all the rules, and hit the right targets, sometimes people still die. It's always harder when it's a kid, I know. Trust me, I know." The catch in his voice and the way tension seeped into his muscles made something deep inside her ache. He understood pain.

He understood *her.*

What a feeling—to lay yourself bare, to put everything out there, and to be *known.* It was liberating. Exhilarating.

Healing.

"I've made mistakes too," Jake continued. "Big mistakes. I've screwed up so bad that good men . . . and even children have died. And I have to carry that, just like you carry Gretchen and Erica. That sort of weight, it breaks us; it does. But here's the secret, sweetheart: When we put ourselves back together, we're stronger. You are strong, Maggie. Hell, you're the strongest woman I know, and I was raised by an Army wife."

She smiled.

"Look at you," he said, reaching out and cupping her cheek. A frisson of electricity shot through her, and she wanted so badly to close her eyes, to embrace the feeling, but she couldn't look away from him. From the way he touched her like he wanted to know all of her—the good, the bad, and the beautiful. "You're amazing," he whispered, leaning forward, his lips brushing against hers.

He kissed her like it was the last thing he wanted before he left for war. Like she was air and light and sound.

She kissed him back. Deeply. Desperately. Wantonly. Suddenly, she needed everything. Her fingers wove through his hair, relishing its silky feel against her skin. All she could think of was having nothing between them, her bare skin against his, the aching drag of his mouth sliding down her neck, her collarbone, her breasts, her stomach. Lower and lower, to the core of her.

She shouldn't be doing this. There was a case. She should

be—what, exactly? She couldn't think with Jake's mouth on hers, his taste enticing her. The warmth pooling inside her was almost unbearable.

What was there left to do? She was fired for sure, not that she'd ever been officially hired in the first place. The senator would be certain she didn't go near the case. She was done.

But she could have this. She wanted this. She wanted *him*. She craved him with a need that should frighten her, but consumed her instead. She wanted to push him against a wall and drink her fill. To take the comfort he offered. To feel the indulgence his eyes promised.

She made up her mind. Pulling away from Jake, she rose to her feet. And when she got up and held out her hand, his eyes simmered with heat.

They would have to be quick, but she could have this. She could have him.

"You sure?" he asked.

"I'm sure," she said.

THERE WAS A greenhouse set behind a thicket of trees to the west of the rose garden; a small glass building with slanted windows and roughly hewn tables holding rose starts and orchids. As soon as they were inside, Jake fell upon Maggie like a starving man. His mouth was back on hers, his hands slipping under her shirt, tracing over her rib cage, palming the weight of her breasts, his thumb brushing over her nipple through her bra, making her gasp.

"God, you're so perfect," he said, kissing her hard, his fingers making quick work of the buttons on her blouse. He pushed it off her shoulders and for a moment, he just looked at her. The awe and anticipation in his face made her feel cherished. His practiced touch, the easy way he flipped open the hooks on her bra, made desire coil inside her stomach. Warm air hit the sensitive skin of her breasts, and her nipples peaked, aching for contact.

She needed to see him too. With fevered urgency, she flipped the tables on him, grabbing his shoulders and pressing *him* against the glass. He grinned at her sudden display of dominance, his eyes daring her to do her worst.

She tore his shirt off. His body was like a Greek statue, broad and beautifully defined. She hadn't been wrong about those washboard abs. She dragged her fingertips lightly up his stomach to rest her palm against his chest, which was sprinkled with a thick thatch of dark hair. She could feel his heart racing under his skin at her touch.

She'd made that happen.

"Look at you," he said. "God, Maggie." He kissed her like it was his only recourse. With his hands cupping her breasts, his lips trailed down their gentle slopes. The warm shock of his mouth against her nipple made her gasp, shocks shooting through her as her fingernails dug into his shoulders. "Sweet girl," he murmured. "So beautiful."

Normally she would have scoffed over such words, but instead, she found herself fueled by the ardor in his voice. She wrapped her legs around him, and he grabbed her waist, lifting her easily. He spun them around until her shoulders pressed against the cool glass of the greenhouse as he trailed kisses down her neck. She closed her eyes against the slow, gentle, maddening assault of his tongue, trying to clear her spinning head, and failing as lust swamped her. God, it felt so good not having to think. To just *feel*.

But his touch was like a drug, leaving her aching. Desperation building inside her, she hitched herself up higher on his body so she could get at his belt. She shivered in anticipation when his sinful hands stroked her bare back, tracing her skin like a map.

"You've been driving me crazy," she told him, fumbling with the buckle, pulling it free. With shaking fingers, she managed to unbutton his pants, and they fell in a pool at his feet. "This is all your fault," she gasped—because it was true, and he laughed at the annoyed tone of her voice. But the laugh turned quickly into a moan when she brought her palm against the strained material of his boxer briefs, rubbing in a slow circle.

"You're gonna be the death of me," he swore. "Always arguing." His thumb flicked open the button of her skirt. She strained up against him, needing his hands, his mouth, any kind of friction. Her skin was too tight, too hot. She needed him to release her. To quench the fire that had been raging between them since the moment they met. "Always contradicting me." He dragged down the zipper, the noise unbearably loud in the greenhouse. "Always going off without backup." Her head lolled back against the heavy glass wall as his fingertips traced the lace edge of her bikini panties. *Please, please, please.*

"What's that, sweetheart?" he asked, smiling against her skin, his fingers teasing, slipping along the lace, but never quite reaching where she wanted it to. "Tell me what you need."

She wriggled against him, trying to gain leverage, trying to think. But she was drowning: His touch was an anchor, pulling her down, down . . . She needed . . .

God, she needed him.

"Please," she gasped.

His tongue traced the edge of her ear, making her choke back a sob. She was on fire and he was the only cure.

"Please what?" he said, the insufferable, beautiful, sexy, maddening man. She was going to *kill* him after this.

First, though . . .

"Please touch me," she gasped out. "Please."

She looked up to see the satisfied, primal smile on his face as he stripped away the lace covering her like it was nothing, baring her to his gaze.

"God, Maggie," he whispered her name like a benediction. His fingers parted her, and she trembled when she felt how wet she was for him. "Wanted this from the start," he whispered in her ear, his fingers rubbing in circles, building the tension inside her until she was gasping each breath, on edge. Right before she was about to spill over the edge, he pulled his hand away, and she honest-to-God *whimpered* over the loss.

"I've got you," he said. "Don't worry . . . this is all for you, beautiful." Then he was back, his chest pressed against her breasts, his cock resting right against her core. She tightened her legs around him, trying to push down, desperate for him. But he gripped her hips, keeping her from moving.

"Look at me," he said softly.

Dazed, wanting, she struggled to focus, but when she did, when her eyes met his, everything else faded away as he slid inside her. Her head fell back at the sensation of being filled, of finally being complete.

"Oh, God," Jake groaned, moving inside her, sparking sensations that spread through her body, from the top of her head down to her toes. Every part of her was alive and singing with pleasure. "Wanted to be inside you," he gritted out, his eyes drifting shut as the feel of being inside her took him over. "Wanted to be with you. Wanted you to drive me crazy. So fucking hot. So fucking stubborn. Wanted to make you mine."

She could feel her orgasm building inside her, her body tensing and tightening, ready to shatter. Her fingers dug into his shoulders as her hips moved against his, desperate to chase the feeling. She gripped his shoulders tightly, her nails digging into his skin as their mouths crashed together, the sweetness of his lips against hers singing through every part of her. She gasped as the pleasure rose inside her, and he pulled away, his lips dragging along the sensitive line of her jaw.

"That's it, sweetheart," Jake murmured against her ear. "Come for me."

He reached down between their joined bodies and pressed firmly down on her clit.

She had to muffle her scream. Light danced along the edges of her vision, and she gasped against his skin, trying to bury the sound in his shoulder. She went still in his arms as pulsing pressure shattered through her, and she clung to him, knowing he wouldn't let her fall, but needing to be closer than close.

She never wanted this moment to end.

"So fucking beautiful," Jake whispered, brushing her hair off her face as he began to move inside her again. She twisted in his arms, the aftershocks of her orgasm making her almost unbearably sensitive. She was even more aware of him, her body clenching around him as he thrust fast and deep, finishing with a sound that was half groan, half her name.

He'd been right, she realized with the clarity that followed impulse: this kind of desire, this level of want . . . this man was going to be the death of her.

But God, what a way to go.

CHAPTER 33

Maggie's entire body was so relaxed—sated, really—that she didn't want to move. Jake had found a lopsided settee in the far corner of the greenhouse, tucked away among the orchids. He'd carried her there, laying her down next to him on it like a prince in a fairy tale. If they weren't pressed for time, she was pretty sure they'd be going for round two right now.

Damn, the idea was tempting.

But she had to get up. She knew that. Before it got awkward. Before her doubts grew louder. God, it had felt so good. Insanely, gloriously hot. Part of her wanted to dive for his mouth again, to let the sensation of his tongue against hers drown out all her doubts. She wanted to pin him back on the settee and wrap her legs around his waist, and just *have* him again.

She shouldn't. She licked her lips.

She couldn't. She straightened, sitting up and buttoning up her shirt, running a hand through her unruly curls.

Jake shifted on the settee, propping his head up on his arm, and her eyes met his. He smiled, a lazy, catlike quirk of his lips that looked so self-satisfied, she was torn between swatting him and kissing him.

She stood up instead, smoothing her skirt. "Well," she said, hoping something to say would come to her, but finding she had nothing. "At least we're good at that."

He let out a short bark of laughter. "I'm good at a lot of things," he said.

She rolled her eyes. "Don't get too high on yourself, cowboy."

He reached out, trailing a finger down the side of her neck. She shivered, leaning toward him almost involuntarily. "I'm high on *you*," he said.

She tried to make herself breathe normally. God, this was idiotic. She was being silly. "I should go first," she said. "Wait a few minutes after I leave, okay? Just in case?"

"You ashamed of me, Goldilocks?" He raised an eyebrow.

"Do you really want to talk about feelings? Now?" It was a surefire way to get a man to shut up or want to flee. She wasn't above using it in this situation.

He shook his head. "Fair enough. I'll wait . . . be your dirty little secret."

She shot him a glare, and his eyes sparkled at her, telling her he wasn't really angry at all. The insufferable tease. She knew she had to regroup and get back to business, but despite herself, her stern look softened into a smile.

She turned on her heel and hurried out of the greenhouse, heading back toward the mansion, refocusing on the crisis at hand. She was probably fired, but she could work around that. She was going to get Kayla home safe no matter what. She felt reborn; more determined than ever. Jake's openness, his caring, had filled her with a renewed faith.

But she had to find a way to talk to Mrs. Thebes, the only person who might be able to convince the senator to give up the file. Maggie knew without a shadow of a doubt that she loved her daughter, that she'd do anything to get her back. A mother was the backbone of a family; the heart. The fiercest warrior a child had on their side. If anyone was up to this fight, it was Mrs. Thebes.

As Maggie walked past the rose garden, she saw a figure heading toward her from the senator's mansion. She slowed to a stop on the sloping lawn when she realized it was Paul.

Uncomfortably aware of her flushed cheeks, Maggie had to stop herself from reaching up and trying to fix her hair, which was still a tangled mess.

It wasn't as if Paul didn't know what she looked like after . . .

Her cheeks got even redder. *Please, please let him not notice.*

"There you are! I was looking for you," Paul said. "I just finished calming Thebes down." He smiled proudly. "I know he's being an ass, and I'm sorry. I think the stress is just getting to him. I made sure he knew how instrumental you've been every step of the way. And I stressed that at this point, changing negotiators would be next to impossible, especially since Mancuso's calling your cell. He's formed a connection to you, and to change the game now would be disastrous. He understood."

Relief rushed through her already incredibly relaxed muscles as Paul said, "You're still on the case."

Maggie wasn't sure if she should be thankful or hang on to her anger at the senator's behavior.

She could do both. She was thankful because she would have pursued this even if she'd been dumped, but not being fired made things easier. And she was angry because Paul was right—she had been instrumental, and no one bothered to see it.

Frank had brought her in because she'd been the best, and she'd be the best for Kayla.

"I hate how upset this has been making you," Paul said, reaching out and squeezing her shoulder. "I know it must be so hard, and I want to help, Mags. I *always* want to help. I just never seem to do or say the right thing." He sighed, dropping his hand. "I guess that's why we didn't work out, isn't it? There were always parts of you that you could never show me. Parts of you I could never see."

In a way, it hurt to hear it out loud, the thing that she knew, that she had hoped he'd someday understand. But inside the hurt was relief, the bone-deep kind, that he was coming to terms with the fact they'd never quite fit.

"You are an incredible man," she told him. "You were so good to me."

"I—" Paul began, but then he broke off, frowning at something over Maggie's shoulder. She turned to see what he was looking at.

Jake had just left the garden shed, heading in the opposite direction, his back to them.

Paul's mouth snapped shut as he glanced back at Maggie, taking in her rumpled clothes, messy hair, and pink cheeks. His eyes widened, and she saw the dawning of understanding, followed by deep hurt.

Maggie's heart twisted, and heat crawled up her face. She hadn't wanted this to happen. She had never wanted to hurt Paul. Not when she'd broken off their engagement, and not now.

"Oh," he said, and she had to bite the inside of her lip to keep looking at him. She couldn't act ashamed.

And she wasn't—even though she felt terrible that he'd been slapped in the face with this raw evidence of her moving on. That wasn't fair to anyone, but especially Paul, who had been nothing but good and strong and honest and faithful.

"Paul—" she began, and then found she didn't know what to say.

He took a deep breath, holding out his hand to get her to stop. "Let's . . . not. None of my business."

"I meant what I said," she told him. "You are such a good man. And . . . I still need your help."

He let out a breath that was almost a laugh. "God, you and your laser focus," he said, shaking his head. "I always admired it. You never lose sight of the case." He pulled out his phone. "What do you need?"

"Information. Probably classified. And I need private access, so nobody else knows I'm investigating. Can you do that for me?"

"That's against regulations," Paul said.

"I know," she replied. "I wouldn't ask if it wasn't important. And I *know* you know some guys. Like your poker buddies." He'd never talked much about his weekly game, but she knew some of the players had access to highly classified information. It might cost him some major favors, but his connections could work.

Paul nodded. "I can get information for you. What do you need to know?"

"I'm looking for the connection between SouthPoint Oil and Senator Thebes."

He frowned. "Well, I can do that without going through back-channels," he said, after a moment. "SouthPoint Oil is the senator's biggest campaign contributor. He and the CEO Carl Dessen go way back—they went to Harvard together. During the last election, they were all over the TV. They cut ads together about the Maryland economy. Don't you remember them?"

Maggie could suddenly see the commercials clearly in her mind. The senator and Carl striding down a small-town street bordered by quaint old buildings, discussing the importance of tax cuts and business growth.

"Yes, I remember," she said. "See if there's anything else you can dig up for me. Anyone who's heard anything, I want to know. Thank you, Paul. Really."

Any other time, she might've reached up and kissed him on the cheek. But she knew that wasn't possible anymore. It would just cause more hurt.

"Wait," he said as she turned to head toward her car. "Where are you going?"

"I'm going to SouthPoint headquarters," she called over her shoulder. "To get some answers for myself."

CHAPTER 34

Kayla's eyes opened, the hazy room coming slowly into focus. She licked her lips, wincing when her tongue hit the corner, where the skin was so cracked it had begun to bleed. The tang of copper filled her mouth, and she spat weakly onto the ground, trying to get rid of the taste.

She'd curled up on the lumpy mattress pad, her knees drawn close to her chest. She couldn't stop shaking, no matter how tight a ball she tucked herself into. Sweat crawled along her back and chest, and she didn't even want to think about what she smelled like. She breathed through her mouth, panting shallowly.

She was so tired. Everything took effort. Her entire body hurt and felt too hot. Her head ached, and every time she moved, dizziness closed in and dark spots floated in front of her eyes.

She knew what this was. When she was seven, she and her mom had been with her dad on the campaign trail, and the week had been so busy, no one realized she'd missed a few shots. She'd passed out right in the middle of her dad's speech and had been rushed to the hospital.

After that, her mother had an app designed, synced to all their phones, that would send reminders if she was even five minutes late with a dose.

She remembered the feeling. The dizziness. How the world swung around her when she tried to sit up or stand.

She wanted her mom. The thought made tears leak out

of the corner of her eyes. She wanted her mom so badly it hurt almost as much as her body shutting down. Would she ever see her again? What would she do if Kayla didn't come back? Would she be okay?

Kayla kept trying to think about the last thing she said to her. She couldn't pinpoint it. They'd been at breakfast that morning—how many days ago had that been? Kayla had no idea. Mom had been on her way to a meeting with one of her charities and she'd said something about moving their weekly ride to Tuesday. Kayla remembered being annoyed.

Oh, God, what if she'd said something snotty? What if that was her mother's last memory of her before . . .

She whimpered, trying to muffle her sobs. She didn't want to die. She wanted to go home and sleep in her bed and have her mother stroke her hair back like she did when Kayla was in the hospital.

She was going to pass out soon. This time, she wouldn't wake up to worried parents and doctors and nurses, an IV in her arm and her blood sugar regulated.

This time, she might not wake up at all.

Her skin prickled, and she made up her mind.

She only had a little time. She had to get out of here. Make a run for it. Something.

Anything.

She knew her chances were slim. But her mom needed to know that she at least had tried to get back to her.

She dragged herself to her feet and, leaning on the wall, made her way to the door. She banged on it, yelling Max's name until she heard footsteps and the scrape of a key in the lock.

"What do you want?" he demanded. "You need to stay quiet."

"My bucket's full," Kayla lied. "Can I please use the real bathroom? I feel sick." She pressed a hand to her stomach. That was no lie, she thought. "I might throw up all over you."

His face wrinkled in disgust, and his eyes flicked to her bound hands, like he was trying to measure her capacity for damage.

He obviously didn't think she could do much, because he yanked her by her wrists, dragging her down the hall and into the bathroom.

For a moment, he just stood in the room with her, and she flushed in embarrassment. God, was he going to *watch* her?

But then he gestured at her. "Hurry up," he ordered. And closed the door.

The bathroom was tiny and typical. Shower, bathtub, sink, toilet, mirrored medicine cabinet over the sink. Kayla scrambled for the cabinet, blinking hard, trying to get her eyes to focus. Her head felt like spikes were being hammered slowly into her temples. She needed to get free. She needed . . . something—a tool. With her hands bound, she was useless. She needed something sharp.

"Sharp," she whispered to herself, trying not to make any noise as she pawed through the medicine cabinet. She kept having to stop and lean against the sink, the black spots dancing in front of her eyes.

There was a knock at the door. "You have one more minute."

"Just a second," Kayla called.

"You don't need this long," Grayson said.

"I'm a girl," she said back, closing the medicine cabinet as softly as she could and bending down, carefully easing the sink cabinet door open. Please, please, let there be something. "I'm taking care of girl stuff. You don't have any pads."

There was a pause. She hoped she'd grossed him out, the jerk.

"Fine. Just hurry."

"I'm trying," she said. Her fingers closed around something cool. Something metal.

Scissors.

They were kind of small, like from a sewing kit. But she could make them work. She had to. She grabbed them, straightening up from her crouch too fast in her excitement.

The world swayed. It felt like the floor was dropping out from underneath her.

No. *No.* She couldn't pass out. Not yet.

Kayla desperately tried to blink away the darkness. She needed to hide the scissors on her. She needed to tuck them into socks or her skirt or . . .

Her knees began to shake so hard they buckled. She hit the floor with a badly muffled cry.

"What's going on?" Grayson asked.

The doorknob began to turn.

Kayla's fingers tightened around the scissors.

No . . .

CHAPTER 35

Maggie hated awkward car rides, and unfortunately, her drive with Jake to SouthPoint headquarters was one of the most awkward she'd ever had. He'd been waiting for her in the driveway, clearly wanting to talk about what they'd just done, but when she'd told him about the connection between the senator and the SouthPoint CEO, he switched gears instantly.

He had insisted on driving, and she reluctantly agreed. As they drove farther from the town, the awkwardness had reached its breaking point. The knowing kind of tension combined with an acute awareness that he'd given her the best orgasm of her life made Maggie squirm in her seat. When they both reached for the radio dial, their hands had brushed and she'd gone bright red, wanting nothing more than to thread their fingers together, to relish the feeling of his skin against hers.

She had to do something. There was only so much commenting on pretty trees and local historic landmarks she could do before it became obvious she was just trying to fill the silence. But what else could she do? *Should* they talk about what had just happened? Or should she just focus on the case? If she hadn't gotten a new tip, would he have just gone home—or would he have been waiting at her car because he wanted something more?

As time stretched on, she reached forward and started to fiddle with the radio just for something to do, anything to break the silence. After scanning through a few stations, she settled on classic rock.

Jake snorted.

"What?" she demanded.

"Rock, really?"

"Let me guess," she said. "You like country."

"Yes, ma'am," he drawled. If he had been wearing a hat, she was sure he would have tipped it. She wondered if he'd spent his childhood riding horses and roping cattle, or if the drawl was merely for show.

She had a feeling nothing about him was for show. He was 100 percent grade-A American cowboy turned soldier turned security specialist. An interesting career trajectory, to say the least.

An interesting man. In so many ways. Being in his arms had made her feel more exciting, more alive than she'd felt in years.

"I bet you and the Man in Black could trade some stories," Maggie said.

He grinned, and she couldn't help but smile back at getting it right. She liked it, this bickering, this surprisingly effortless teasing.

"Johnny Cash knew love," Jake said. "The good and the bad."

"He certainly put June through a lot," Maggie agreed.

"Some people are worth fighting for, don't you think?"

She glanced over at him, the seriousness in his expression making every part of her tighten with awareness. He was the type who would fight for his woman. Who'd make her the center of his world.

"We're here," Jake said, before she could decide how to respond.

Maggie looked away from him and out the window, startled. He'd pulled up to a warehouse where greasy oil drums and muddy oil drilling trucks were lined up in rows behind a chain-link fence. Jake drove through the open gates and parked. Several single-story prefab metal buildings stretched across the property, most of them locked up tight.

Maggie got out of the car with him, and they headed across the lot toward a two-story building that looked like an office.

"Hey," someone called behind them. "Can I help you?"

Maggie turned and looked the man up and down. He was older, with salt-and-pepper hair, and wore a flannel button-up shirt with the sleeves pushed up. He had on a hard hat, and there was a black smear of oil across his forearm.

"Let me take care of this," she said to Jake in an undertone.

Before he could respond, she smiled at the man, walking up to him. "Hi, I'm Special Agent Kincaid with the FBI." She flashed her wallet at him so quickly he didn't have time to look closely. "I'm looking for the manager of this facility."

"My boss is out for lunch," he said. "You're gonna have to come back later."

Maggie wasn't that easily dismissed. "This is time sensitive, so we'll have to ask you some questions right now. What's your name?"

"Tom Jennings," the man said. "Look, what's this about?"

"An investigation," Maggie said. "Do you know who Senator Thebes is?"

"Sure," Tom said, nodding. "I voted for him."

"Have you ever seen him around here?"

He frowned, looking genuinely confused. "Why would a senator come here?"

"What about the name Max Grayson?" Jake said. "Does that ring any bells?"

Tom shook his head.

"How about Roger Mancuso?" Maggie asked.

Again, Tom shook his head, looking even more bewildered.

"Are you sure?" Jake asked, pulling his phone out of his pocket and swiping the screen until he'd located Mancuso's photo. He held it out to Tom. "Have you seen this guy around?"

The man took the phone, squinting at the screen for several seconds. "He does look kinda familiar," he said.

Maggie's heart leapt. She wanted to pounce, but forced

herself to remain quiet. It was never a good idea to apply pressure when someone was trying to remember something.

Tom took off his hard hat and scratched his head, handing the phone back to Jake. "He looks a lot like Joe. Same eyes, same chin, same big nose."

"Who's Joe?" Maggie asked.

"Guy who used to work here. Good guy. Great worker. Always picking up the slack. Always pulled overtime. Never complained. It was really sad what happened. He got killed over in Riyadh, working on the pipeline."

Killed? Maggie's mind raced. Was Mancuso's plot all centered around revenge? Or was he trying to cover up a murder?

"How did he die, exactly?" Jake asked.

"Car accident," Tom said. "It sucked. He was one of my best guys. If I'd had ten of him, this place would be running smoothly."

"Would you happen to have his file still?" Maggie asked.

Tom looked at her, eyes wide. "That's private, miss."

"Tom," Jake cut in with a smile. "What would it take for it to be not so private anymore? Three hundred? Four?"

Before the man could answer, Jake had pulled out four hundred-dollar bills from his wallet and handed them over. Tom took the money automatically.

Jake's method was smart, Maggie thought approvingly. Once someone has cash in hand, it's that much harder to give it back.

Tom looked down at the bills with a surprised expression. "I—I don't—" He stuttered.

"Five hundred then," Jake said, as if he was being hardballed. He placed the final note in Tom's hand, and the man's fingers closed around it.

They had him.

"No one has to know," Jake advised him.

"Well, okay," Tom said, pocketing the bills. "Come on."

He led them into the building, where they followed him down a hall and then into an office filled with file cabinets.

They stood in silence, waiting for a few minutes while he looked through one.

"Here it is." He turned, taking a file folder out of the cabinet and handing it to Jake. He pointed to the copy machine in the corner. "It's an old one, so you have to do it a page at a time. I'm heading out. I didn't see you, okay? Lock the office door behind you when you leave. I can give you fifteen minutes. Then I'll come back to set things straight and secure the building."

Tom left. Maggie could tell he just wanted to get out of there. Good. That meant he wouldn't talk, especially if he felt ashamed or nervous about taking the bribe.

"Okay," she said. "Time to copy." She flipped open the folder, marked "Joe Tiller." Walking over to the copy machine, she positioned the first page on the glass. A shadow fell over her, and Jake's arm brushed up against her.

"You have it upside down," Jake pointed out.

Maggie had to force herself to hold still. All she could think about as he reached over, the warmth of his body pressed along her back—who knew there were so many nerve endings in her shoulders?—and flipped the piece of paper over.

"You okay, Goldilocks?" he asked, and she didn't have to turn around to know he was smiling that cocky, self-assured smile. He knew he was affecting her—and he liked it.

She wanted to punch him in the face.

She wanted to push him against the wall and kiss him.

The problem was, she couldn't figure out which she wanted more.

CHAPTER 36

"Can I see the copy of the newspaper article about the accident again?" Jake asked.

Maggie handed it over.

They were sitting in the back seat of his SUV about two miles down the road from the SouthPoint headquarters. After copying the folder's contents and locking the office behind them, they'd hightailed it out of there before Tom returned. Once they were far enough away, Jake had pulled over so they could pick through Joe Tiller's file.

They'd spread the files out on the back seat, sitting so close their knees kept brushing as they sifted through the papers. He kept looking down each time they touched, and even fumbled with the papers in his hands when she leaned over.

"Am I distracting you?" she asked, an eyebrow arched.

He grinned, sheepish. "Always."

She rolled her eyes, secretly pleased as she scanned the calendar in front of her. She frowned as she mentally added up the hours.

"Damn, this guy worked a lot of overtime," she said, glancing up at Jake. The look on his face made her pause. "What?"

"I'm reading through the report on the accident that killed Joe," Jake explained. "It seems like a hit to me."

Maggie straightened in her seat, papers slipping all over her lap. She leaned forward, inhaling the subtle spiciness that seemed to cling to his skin. “Really?” she asked. Who in the world would want to put a hit on a blue-collar oil worker?

“I’d put money on it,” Jake said.

Maggie took the article from him, reading through it. “I don’t see it,” she said. It seemed like a normal article reporting a tragic car accident. “What am I missing?”

“It’s too clean. There’s no follow-up by law enforcement. It was just . . . dropped. Because all the details were just right. Tidy. Perfect. All of this, actually.” He gestured to the papers spread across the front seat and dashboard. “This entire file.”

Maggie frowned. “That’s what Grace said about Mancuso’s apartment.”

“Grace?” Jake asked.

“The FBI profiler,” Maggie clarified. “She’s great. Without even knowing it, she keyed in on Grayson not being an authentic persona. She told me that everything about his place was too perfect to be real . . . like he was playing a part.” She looked down at Joe Tiller’s work schedule. “You think Joe was playing a part too?”

Jake nodded. “I don’t think Joe Tiller’s his real name. Spooks don’t use their real names.”

“What?” Maggie couldn’t help but scoff. “You think he was a *spy*?”

“I spent a long time in the Middle East, Maggie,” he said, his voice so serious her skin began to prickle. “I worked mostly covert ops. I have a lot of experience working with intelligence pros. You learn how to spot the signs. And when I was over there, I saw hits like this go down all too often.”

“Are you sure?” Maggie asked. She looked at the article again, trying to read between the lines and see the clues he’d found. “We’re not in a movie. And this guy is dead. Unfortunately, Mancuso’s not.”

“Tom didn’t say the picture I showed him *was* Joe,” Jake reminded her. “He said it *looked like* Joe. Roger Mancuso had two parents and a brother, remember?”

"So . . . maybe Joe was Roger's brother—a spy who was killed in the Middle East?" Maggie said, trying to follow him down his theoretical rabbit hole. She shuffled through some papers, pulling up one of Joe's travel schedules. "He did spend a lot of time over there."

"Joe Tiller is actually Joe Mancuso, Roger's brother. The fake name, the job at SouthPoint was probably his cover," Jake said.

"Or maybe his *mission*," Maggie offered, her eyes lighting up. "If investigating SouthPoint was the assignment, then that file Mancuso wants so much will tell us why—and lead us to who killed him."

Jake nodded.

"Whatever the senator's hiding about SouthPoint must be incredibly corrupt—something big that will dirty a lot of hands—including Thebes'. If Mancuso's brother was a threat to exposing that, killing him would be seen as an easy solution to a problem."

"So this is very personal for Mancuso," Jake mused. "Family's always personal."

She nodded. "It's about revenge and justice. That's why it never felt like it was about money or Kayla—it's all about Senator Thebes. He's involved in something big and crooked with the company. Mancuso blames him for his brother's murder, just as if he was the one who drove Joe off the road," Maggie said. Thebes had proven repeatedly he was ruthless when it came to protecting his reputation. "I mean, for all we know, Thebes could have ordered or paid for the hit on Joe."

"It's entirely possible," Jake said. "But what does that mean for the profile?" Jake asked.

Maggie licked her dry lips. "It means Mancuso will do anything," she said in a hushed voice. "He'll justify any act—killing Kayla, shooting a cop, even his own death. He'll do anything to ruin Thebes. He's got tunnel vision. Even if Mancuso was just your average petty thief before his brother's death, he suspects Thebes is somehow involved in Joe's murder. So he's got a powerful motive.

You've got to love someone a lot—like a brother—to go to war for them like this."

Jake swore under his breath. He reached out, his arm settling around her shoulder, drawing her closer. She let him, closing her eyes for a moment, wanting nothing more than to sink into his warmth and never leave. She pressed her cheek against his chest.

"He's all in," she whispered, her heart sinking.

Jake pressed a kiss on her temple. "I know," he said.

Kayla was just collateral damage at this point. Mancuso may not fit the standard kidnapper/murderer profile, but he'd do anything to accomplish his goals. He might not slit her throat, as he'd threatened to, but if Thebes didn't give in, he'd kill her somehow. She was just a pawn in his bigger game of revenge.

He'd do anything to take his brother's murderer down. Sacrifice anyone.

Even himself.

CHAPTER 37

The Royal, an old-school, exclusive restaurant, existed only to serve important men doing important things over expensive scotch. The booths were made of studded leather, the cigars cost more than Maggie's electric bill, and the oysters were imported from Australia at a hundred bucks apiece—wholesale.

"Miss! Excuse me, *miss*!" The hostess tried to stop her, but Maggie ignored her as she and Jake breezed past her station and into the dining room. The opulent burgundy rugs were so plush that her heels sank in a good inch deep. It made her feel slightly unsteady, as if she was walking on a sponge.

"There he is," Maggie said, pointing to the corner booth where Frank was sitting with a man so neatly put together that the part in his hair looked like he'd combed it with a ruler. She was pretty sure he was the head of the Armed Services Committee. Crap. Frank wasn't going to be happy with the interruption, but desperate times . . .

"Miss!" The hostess had caught up with them.

"I'll take care of her," Jake said. "Go on." He turned to the hostess and flashed her a smile.

Of course he'd go for the charm. Annoyed but grateful, Maggie rolled her eyes and walked over to the booth, clearing her throat. Frank looked up midslurp, an empty oyster fork at his lips. He coughed. "Maggie, what in the world are you doing here?"

"I need to talk to you," she said.

He gestured to the table and his companion. "Can it wait?"

She shook her head. "I'm sorry, sir," she said to his lunch partner. "But it's time sensitive."

"My apologies, Jeremy. I'll be right back as soon as I talk with my agent," Frank said.

"It's fine, Frank," the man said. "I know you're in the middle of a case."

"Come on." Frank put a hand on Maggie's back and guided her out of the restaurant. Jake was waiting for them outside the entrance, having dissuaded the hostess from chasing after Maggie. Frank nodded at him. "O'Connor."

"Sir."

"That was an important meeting, Maggie," Frank said.

"I'm sorry," Maggie said. "But this is important too."

"What's going on?" Frank asked. "Paul called to tell me you'd gone off on a wild goose chase."

"It's no wild goose chase," Maggie scoffed. "I discovered a connection between Senator Thebes and SouthPoint Oil. Jake and I were just at their headquarters. We found out that Roger Mancuso's brother worked for them, and he was killed in a car accident that probably wasn't really an accident."

"Mancuso's brother was intelligence, sir," Jake said. "I'm sure of it. I've spent a lot of time in the Middle East, and I know a hit when I see it. A man like you understands how cut-throat the oil business is. Killing a guy who got too close to revealing corruption is just a regular day for some of these companies."

"We think that while he was working for SouthPoint in the Middle East, Mancuso's brother got a message to Mancuso. Something that tipped him off to the senator's involvement in the company. Then he was killed in the 'accident.' So Mancuso adopted one of his brother's old aliases—an identity called Max Grayson—and began planning to kidnap Kayla. He infiltrated Thebes' staff and just waited for the right time. This speaks to an extraordinary level of commitment and patience, Frank," Maggie said. "You know what that means."

"I do," Frank replied grimly. The wrinkles on his face deepened as he considered the situation. Frank had a brilliant and flexible mind, but cases involving children were always the hardest. The only time Maggie had ever seen her mentor break was at the end of a twenty-seven-hour standoff that had involved a six-year-old hostage. After the little boy had been returned safe and sound, her mentor had excused himself abruptly, and she'd heard what she was sure was the sound of relieved sobs coming from the bathroom he'd disappeared into.

"We have to figure out what's going on here right away," Jake said. "We're running around blind, sir, and we have been since the start. We need to find out what Mancuso's brother knew. We need to understand exactly what was going on at SouthPoint Oil, why Joe Mancuso died for it, and what Thebes has to do with it."

"You've always told me information is a weapon," Maggie said. "This is the only trail we have to follow. The situation is bad, Frank. We both know it. The news is going wild, the press is speculating, and we're running out of time. This is being whipped up to a fever pitch, and if Mancuso doesn't get that file by seven tonight, he'll kill Kayla. He's committed, Frank—he has a mission. He may not be a natural killer, but if he doesn't get what he wants, he's going to start killing. And he may not stop at Kayla. It could escalate."

"You're thinking a mass hostage situation?" Frank asked.

She nodded grimly. "Or he could just go after the senator. Or Mrs. Thebes. Or anyone else who stands in his way," Maggie said. "He's a wild card. The only steady thing about him is his motive. He'll adapt in any way to stick to his mission."

Frank rubbed his droopy eyes, looking worried. "I'm damn glad you're back, kid," he said.

"You'll help?" Maggie asked.

"Of course," he said. He pointed to the file in Jake's hand. "Anything in there that might help you find an address?"

Jake looked down at it. "What do you mean?"

"I mean, follow the money," Frank explained. "His pay stubs—they're in there, right?"

Jake nodded.

"Where did they send them?"

"Oh, God," Maggie said. "I can't believe I didn't think of that."

"You've been out of the game for two years," Frank said. "I forgive you, even though I trained you better than that. But you—" he looked at Jake with a skeptical eye "—what's your excuse?"

"I'm a soldier, not a pencil pusher," Jake said, looking slightly embarrassed.

Frank snorted, and Maggie had to hide her smile, grateful she had his help, and not only because he was so thorough that he'd point out the obvious things that are often overlooked.

CHAPTER 38

The address on Joc's pay stubs was in Silver Spring, Maryland. Frank promised to make some calls and headed back inside the Royal while Maggie and Jake walked back to his SUV.

"Why don't you let me drive this time?" Maggie asked.

Jake grinned. "Funny. I don't think so," he said.

"I'm a good driver! I aced my defensive driving course at Quantico."

"Goldilocks, you could drive for NASCAR on the side and I still wouldn't let you," Jake said, swinging up into the driver's seat. "I have a feeling you're a terror behind the wheel. My SUV, my rules."

"You're such a caveman," she muttered, hopping into the passenger seat and grabbing the seat belt.

"Me Tarzan. You Jane," Jake grunted, and her annoyed expression melted.

"You're ridiculous," she said primly, trying to hide her amusement.

He leaned over, his fingers tilting her chin so he could press a quick kiss to her lips. He pulled away, just inches, his green eyes shining.

"I think you like it," he said.

A thrill went through her. She did like it. She'd never been teased like this before. People usually took her seriously and acted accordingly. Even men who were interested in her.

She reached up, and this time, she kissed him. And this time, it wasn't quick—it was one of those long, languid kisses that lasts forever, the kind that hint at wicked things to come. His hand tangled in her curls as he kissed her deeper, as lost in her as she was in him.

She pulled away reluctantly, breathless, her entire body flushed and tingling. All she wanted to do was pull him back. But they had work to do.

"I do like it," she whispered, her lips brushing against his ear, teasing, because two could play that game.

"You distract a man, Goldilocks," he said, his eyes darkening to a forest green as he pulled back. He buckled his seat belt and turned the key in the ignition. They headed into the flow of traffic toward the tangle of highways that would lead them out of the city, toward Silver Spring.

"Have you really worked with a lot of spies?" Maggie asked.

Jake shrugged. "There are all sorts of power players jockeying for position throughout the Middle East," he said. "And they all have their men—or women—on the ground over there. You get a sense for some people. You pick up stuff." He smiled, and it was bittersweet. Like he was remembering the action, the adrenaline, and wishing he were back in the thick of it.

"You sound like you miss it," Maggie said.

"Sometimes." He flipped his turn signal and merged onto the highway. The time of day was perfect, with incoming city traffic clogged and nothing but clear roads on the way out. They'd get to Silver Spring in record time. "I liked knowing what I was about. What the mission was. But now, this work for politicians . . ." He paused, shaking his head in disgust. "Well, they're not the most honest people," he finished.

"And you like honest." He was a black-and-white sort of man, she could tell. No room for gray. Trustworthy. Stalwart.

And sexy as hell. Like some sort of medieval knight who took things like vows and protection seriously—and backed it up with his life.

"I like knowing all the facts," Jake said. "In the military, things are straightforward."

"And out here, it's anything but," Maggie said.

"What about you? Do *you* miss it?" Jake asked. "I just got a job change. You left altogether."

Maggie sighed, looking out the window at the blurring traffic. "I miss being sure. And I miss . . . you know that feeling, after the adrenaline's finally settled down, after the job's been done, after everyone is safe and everything went the way it was supposed to, and you may be battered and bruised, but you're not . . . scarred?"

Jake nodded.

"I miss that," Maggie said. "That feeling of knowing I defused the situation. That I saved someone. That I was part of that." Jake nodded again in agreement. They both felt an unusual but growing sense of camaraderie. They had both faced major crises and saved lives, and drew the same deep satisfaction from it.

"When Frank said you'd come back, you didn't correct him," Jake pointed out.

"I can't think about that now," Maggie said, but he shot her a skeptical look. "I can't. It's not because I don't want to—well, maybe, a little. But we need to focus on this." She pointed to Joe's folder. "If we don't get Kayla back soon . . ."

"I know," Jake said, reaching over with his free hand and squeezing hers. "Don't worry. We'll be there in a few minutes."

He pressed harder on the accelerator.

SILVER SPRING WAS a small town with a run-down atmosphere. Lawns weren't kept up, and it seemed as if every other business on the main drag was shuttered, their GOING OUT OF BUSINESS signs still hanging in the windows. But every few blocks, there was a house whose residents clearly hadn't given up yet, as evidenced by a neat, green lawn, fresh paint job, and an American flag hanging from the porch.

The house Jake pulled up to wasn't one of those. In the driveway, a rusted Oldsmobile was propped up on cinderblocks, leaking oil onto the asphalt. A yellowing patch of tall weeds that looked like it hadn't been mowed in months filled the front yard. Paint was peeling in big strips off the sagging porch rails.

"This is the ex-girlfriend's house?" Maggie asked.

Jake nodded. "Doesn't look like much."

Maggie shrugged, getting out of the car. She walked up to the porch and knocked on the door. A dog started barking, and then she heard a female voice swearing at the creature before the door opened.

The woman had bottle-blond hair with a good inch of dark roots showing, circles under her eyes, and a cigarette hanging from tobacco-stained fingers. "Yeah?" she asked, looking Maggie up and down. "I'm not interested in any preaching."

"I'm Maggie Kincaid," Maggie said. "Are you Barbara Kent?"

"That's me."

"I'm with the FBI. We have some questions about your ex, Joe Mancuso."

Barbara's expression darkened further. "What about him?" she asked suspiciously. "Joe's dead. He's been dead for years."

"We're aware," Maggie said. "Can we come in?"

Barbara sighed, as if she was greatly put upon. "I guess." She waved them inside.

The inside of the house was dated—very eighties, in a bad way—and reeked of tobacco. Maggie perched on the edge of the hideous couch, trying to ignore the overflowing ashtray on the coffee table. Jake sat down next to her, and Barbara sprawled in an armchair, popping open a can of Pabst Blue Ribbon.

"So, what do you want to know about Joe?" she asked.

"What was he like?" Maggie asked.

"He was a son of a bitch," she said, taking a long sip of her beer. "He never hit me, at least. But he was never around. Always taking 'business trips.'" She nearly dropped her beer doing air quotes with her fingers. "Lied to me all the time. I'm sure he was cheating, but I could never catch him. I tried. Bunch of times. But he was tricky. Always prepared. He would've been one of those prepper types if he wasn't so busy cheating and lying."

"Did he leave anything with you?" Maggie asked. "Papers? Personal things? Pictures?"

Barbara shook her head. "He hardly even slept over or let me come to his place. I always had to meet him in a motel."

Jake held out his phone, pulling up the photo of Roger Mancuso on the screen. "Does he look familiar?"

Barbara glanced at the phone, her lip curling.

"That's Roger, Joe's brother," Nancy said. "God, Joe was bad, but Roger was a whole other level. I pity the woman who gets saddled with him."

"What was so bad about him?" Maggie asked.

"He was a total loser," Barbara said. "Always coming around, distracting Joe. Always broke, never could hold down a job. Him and Joe . . . they were close. Hell, Joe paid more attention to him than he did to me, the bastard."

"Have you seen Roger since Joe's death?" Maggie asked.

"Nah," Barbara said. "I made sure he understood how I felt about him, so he knew better than to come around. I didn't even go to Joe's funeral. I had to focus on me, you know? Nurture myself in my time of grief."

"Of course," Maggie said. Obviously, this woman didn't know anything. She was bitter, but clueless. A spy probably didn't make the best boyfriend, after all.

"Thank you for all your help." Maggie smiled. "We should get going."

Jake rose to his feet, and Maggie was almost out of the living room, desperate for fresh air, when she heard Barbara mutter, "I swear to God, I wish I'd burned down that fishing cabin just to show them."

Maggie paused, turning around, lingering in the tobacco-scented air for the greater good. "What fishing cabin?" she asked.

"Did you not know about that?" Barbara frowned. "I thought you FBI types knew everything, what with the government spying on American citizens all the time."

Why was Maggie not surprised she was a conspiracy theorist? "Why don't you tell me?" Maggie asked, trying to be patient.

"Joe and Roger were always up at that place," Barbara said. "Bro-time. He never once took *me* up there. And I like nature . . . in small doses. Anyway," she stepped forward, opening the front door. "You said you had to get going."

Jake's eyes narrowed as Maggie shot him a "do something" look. "Hey, Barbara," he said, shooting her that smile of his. "Did you ever get any of the settlement money for the accident?"

Barbara's sour, pinched expression completely changed. A calculating eagerness lit up her eyes. "What money?"

"I can give you the details in a moment," Maggie said. "But first, tell us a little more about this cabin. Where is it located?"

CHAPTER 39

Sweat trickled down Mancuso's neck. He wiped it away, ignoring the thumping sound coming from the room he kept Kayla in.

His fingers ran compulsively over the Harley-Davidson keychain in his pocket. He was going to put this right for Joe. Roger had stood over the grave and watched his brother's coffin lowered into the ground. He'd made a silent vow to make sure the senator got what he deserved.

Joe had always been stronger than him. Not just physically, but in every way. Their dad had beaten the shit out of them as kids, and Joe always took the worst of it, always stepped in front of the angry, drunken fists, protecting his little brother.

Now it was Roger's turn to be strong.

All he could think about was Joe's letter, full of details about Thebes' corruption and SouthPoint Oil's shady dealing. By the time it arrived, Joe was already dead in the supposed "car accident."

Roger saw his death for what it was: an assassination. In the letter, Joe had told him that he'd discovered the collusion between SouthPoint and oil smugglers. That they'd made an illegal deal that got the nod from the board of directors and beyond, all the way up to Thebes. The CEO of SouthPoint got Thebes to help fund the whole thing, and the senator's international connections were essential to the smuggling operation. The collusion between the company and its powerful friend went deep—and Joe had died trying to expose it.

Now Mancuso was determined to make sure his brother hadn't died in vain. He would get his proof exposing SouthPoint and the senator. The whole country needed to know what kind of man they'd elected into office . . . and the kind of business Americans unknowingly supported in their own backyards.

The thumping from Kayla's room had stopped. Mancuso couldn't help but worry. He'd never spent much time around her, but she'd always seemed like a genuinely nice girl. Which, considering what a bastard her father was, surprised him.

He hadn't wanted to take her. But with a man as crooked and corrupt as the senator, a man who didn't value human life, who had helped fund the murder of his brother, Mancuso could take no chances. The only things that mattered to a man like that were his reputation and his family. But Mancuso had underestimated the senator's cruelty. When it mattered most, Thebes had decided to protect his reputation over his kid.

Mancuso wished he could give the girl some insulin. He checked his watch. It was nearly five o'clock.

Just two more hours playing the tough guy. He had to think like a professional.

He had to be like Joe. Just be like Joe, and everything would work out.

He heard a sound . . . almost like a whirring. Was it a helicopter? He hurried across the living room and cracked the thick curtains to peer up at the sky. Nothing.

At least not yet.

But it couldn't hurt to be careful. He went through the house, turning off all the lights. When he returned to the living room, he sat down in the well-worn armchair. Closing his eyes, he thought about spending time up here with Joe. How Joe would clean the fish they'd caught, and they'd talk as the fire slowly died out.

Mancuso had rigged tripwires in the woods with fishing

line and bells. If anyone came through those trees, he'd be ready for them.

Everything was riding on this.

He gripped the arm of the chair.

For Joe, he told himself.

For Joe.

CHAPTER 40

We've been waiting for you," Frank said, walking up to Maggie and Jake as they passed through the security desk. "We've got everything set up on the second floor. Come on."

"Who's leading the SWAT team?" Her heart was pumping like she'd been running at full tilt. Things were falling into place. There was a chance that they were finally one step ahead of Mancuso. Maggie might be able to get Kayla out safely. She felt deep down that Mancuso probably didn't want to hurt the girl, but she was worried about what would happen if he was pushed.

The kind of bond he clearly had with his brother was hard to break. If Joe was still alive, she might have been able to play the brothers against each other, but with his death, Joe had turned into a martyr. In Mancuso's eyes, he'd become more than a man, more than a brother—now he was a symbol of mythic proportions. Trying to break that bond would be next to impossible—and too dangerous to attempt at this point.

"Mike Sutton was the only one available," Frank said, and she could hear the apologetic tone in his voice. Working with Mike at Sherwood Hills had been a disaster, but Maggie smiled reassuringly at Frank. She wasn't going to let Sutton and their bad blood get in the way of this. She couldn't second-guess herself now, not with the clock ticking down and the FBI closing in on Mancuso. There was only one chance to get this right—and she *had* to get it right.

"Everyone else is already assembled?" Maggie asked.

Frank nodded. "We're ready to go."

She couldn't let her nervousness make her falter. She was in control, she reminded herself. She could do this. She'd faced much worse than a roomful of men who resented her. "Let's get to it, then," she said.

Frank opened the conference room door, and she walked in like she owned the room. Mike Sutton was standing next to Paul, examining the images projected on the screen. Aerial images of thick trees and a cabin's rusty tin roof set in a small clearing filled the room. The Thebeses were sitting at a table in the corner, the senator's arm around his wife's shoulders. She looked as if she hadn't slept in days. Now that Maggie knew he was involved in oil smuggling and partly responsible for at least one man's murder, she had difficulty hiding her disgust as she met Thebes' eyes. The obvious fact that his reputation was more important than his child's life made her want to scream at him. To shake him. She hated that she couldn't fully confront him, not now. Maybe not ever.

Mike Sutton looked over his shoulder, his mouth twisting into a sneer when he saw Maggie. She ignored him and walked up to stand next to Paul, Jake following her. "Where are we?" she asked.

"Images from the surveillance chopper," Sutton said, pointing to the screen. "As you can see, it's a thickly wooded area. Coming in from the north, it's uneven terrain, and not a lot of visibility. The southern approach—" he pointed to the bottom of the picture "—is a little clearer because of the river. But it adds to our trek time by fifteen minutes.

"The park's been condemned for years," Sutton continued. "So we'll be dealing with major overgrowth, fallen trees, obstructed trails. Even the rangers rarely patrol out there anymore. We've already sent them an alert so they know we'll be going in."

"When the chopper got close, the lights in the cabin went out," Paul said. "So we know someone's in there."

"We've got no visual confirmations that Mancuso's in the cabin," Sutton said. "Or the girl. The chopper's too high to get an accurate body heat scan," he said, his brows drawn tight in frustration. "Whoever's in there, it could just be squatters. I'm sure there are a lot of them this time of year."

Maggie shook her head, coming forward to examine the photo. It looked like a peaceful place—Mancuso probably had good memories of it. But it also meant he was surrounded by memories of his brother. Nancy said the brothers spent most of their free time there, so maybe the cabin was a shrine of sorts. A representation of their fraternal bond.

If Mancuso wanted to go down in a firefight, the cabin would be the perfect place.

Maggie rubbed at her wrists, trying to think. What would be the best approach here? Send in SWAT, guns drawn, and hope for the best? She could tell Sutton wasn't thrilled about the terrain, and neither was she. A lot could go wrong.

Too much.

Kayla was in that cabin. Maggie knew it.

"She's inside," Maggie said.

"How can you be sure?" Paul asked.

"Mancuso values his brother over everything else," Maggie explained. "Look at everything he's done to bring his murder to light. The cabin is the place the brothers shared. It's where he feels the connection to his brother the strongest. It's also remote, in a thickly forested area. He'd keep her there. It's ideal. Isolated. He'd probably need only minimal construction to drywall over the windows in one of the rooms to keep her from escaping. It's close to the river."

"Which would explain the water beetles we found in the video," said Jake, picking up on her train of thought. "Maggie's right. This is the place."

"I agree," Paul said. "That means we need an attack plan in place."

"What are you thinking?" Jake asked.

"I'd hit the cabin hard and fast," Paul said. "From multiple sides, so if he's got an escape route ready, he'll have nowhere to run."

Sutton nodded and said, "I've got a team of twenty geared up and ready to go."

Maggie didn't look at them, but kept studying the aerial photos. She could see why they wanted to rush in. She really did. Time was ticking down.

But Mancuso had planned this too well. If he felt cornered, if things began to truly unravel, there was no telling what he'd do.

She'd gone in too fast at Sherwood Hills. She hadn't taken the time to look at the situation from all angles. She needed more time here, so she wouldn't make the same mistakes.

"No," Maggie said.

"Excuse me?" Sutton demanded. Even Paul was looking at her like she was crazy. The only person who didn't seem startled or angry was Jake. He just gazed steadily back at her, reaffirming her decision.

"We have to wait until he contacts us again," Maggie said.

"He's made it clear he's not *going* to contact us again," Paul said quietly. "Remember what he said? He said he'd slit her throat."

Maggie pressed her lips together. She understood Paul's take, but she knew in her gut it was wrong. "He needs proof. He needs that file. He's not going to screw up his one piece of leverage," she said. "I know why he's doing this now. I have a profile. I understand his motivation. We can keep him talking, keep him distracted. We can work this out."

"Did Sherwood Hills turn you crazy?" Sutton demanded. "Since when are *you* gun-shy? We have only a short window here, Kincaid."

"Watch it," said Jake, glaring at Sutton, who glared back, squaring his shoulders angrily.

"Look, Maggie," Paul said. "I understand the instinct, I

do. You want everyone out safe. But we're out of time. We know where Kayla is. It's time to go in fast and hard. We can distract him with flash bombs. He won't even know what hit him. He'll be on the ground and cuffed before he can draw."

"I agree with these two fine agents," said the senator.

Maggie turned to him, her lip curling and her eyes darkening with disgust.

"Senator," Jake said. "You should trust Maggie's instincts. We wouldn't have made any of this progress without her. These guys—" he gestured to Sutton and Paul "—would still be chasing their tails."

"I think it's time for the professionals to take over, O'Connor," Thebes said.

"If that's how you feel," Jake said. "Then send *me* in. Send me in alone. You know I have stealth training. This kind of terrain is nothing new to me, and frankly, no offense, but I'm trained for this." He jerked his thumb at Sutton. "Storming in with a team of twenty is going to spook Mancuso so badly he'll have no choice but to come out shooting. I can get in unnoticed and dismantle the threat before he even knows I'm there. Kayla will be safe."

"No," the senator said, his eyes glittering with a bizarre, almost crazed light. "I want the team. I want this guy wiped off the map." He glanced at Maggie dismissively. "You're done, Ms. Kincaid. Thank you for your help."

"This is a terrible idea," Maggie said, her anger sparking inside her like a firecracker. This was his daughter—but to hide his corruption, he was willing, even eager to risk her life. She shook her head in disgust. "You seem to just be full of them."

Thebes refused to even look at her, but instead went back to stand with his wife. Mrs. Thebes looked at Maggie, and Maggie thought for a moment she'd side with her, that she'd try to reason with her husband, but then the woman turned away, leaning into the senator.

Maggie couldn't watch them, fearing that her fury would spill over. She needed to talk sense into someone, though.

Paul. Paul *had* to listen to her. "Don't do this," she said to him in an undertone. "Please, Paul. You said before that I'm a natural. That my instincts are a gift. Trust those instincts, then. Trust *me*. There is a better way to do this. A safer way."

Paul sighed. He wouldn't even meet her eyes. "This has nothing to do with trust, Maggie," he said, the clipped tone in his voice hurting her more than she expected. "This is the right play. You and your new boyfriend did good work. Now leave it to us to handle the rest."

He turned away deliberately, showing her his back. The physical act angered Maggie even more than his pointed words.

Fine. Fine. If these idiots were going take this bullshit macho approach, she wasn't going to watch them march off to what could easily cost them not only their own lives, but Kayla's too. She couldn't do it.

She couldn't watch more people die.

She needed air, and she needed it now.

She backed away from the men so deep in discussion that they didn't even notice as she slipped out of the room and down the hall, heading out of the building.

But the distance didn't help. With each step, dread built in her chest. The same words looped inside her mind, that instinct in her screaming, *This is a mistake, this is a mistake, this is a mistake!*

CHAPTER 41

Dusk approached, the hum of the city was rising with the moon. The rush of traffic, people coming and going, heading home, heading out for a night on the town. Maggie closed her eyes and breathed it in, letting it carry her away for a moment before reality kicked in.

She looked up at the sky, trying to calm herself, to block out the memories. She swallowed, trying to banish the tight feeling in her throat. She couldn't cry. She had to be strong.

She pulled out her phone and dialed a number.

"Hey, honey." Her mother's normally cheerful voice was concerned. "I saw you on the news."

"Hey, Mom," Maggie said.

"You went back." The statement was no accusation. Maybe it should have been. Maggie knew that when she'd quit the Bureau, her mother had been overjoyed. Maggie couldn't blame her for that: She'd lost one daughter, and Maggie dove headfirst into danger to cope. It would wear on any mother . . . especially hers, who had already lived through the worst kind of agony.

"I know why you took this case," her mother continued, when it was clear Maggie couldn't say anything. Her throat was choked with emotion.

"I had to," Maggie forced out.

"I know," her mother said, her voice softened, full of warmth and praise. "You, my sweet girl, are just like your father. Hell-bent on justice. He'd be very proud."

Maggie smiled. It was bittersweet, being compared to her father.

"Are you okay?" her mother asked.

Maggie shook her head, trying to regain control. "I'm fine," she lied. She knew her mother wouldn't believe her, but Maggie prayed she'd let it go. Just this once.

"Are you close to finding whoever did this?"

"Yeah," Maggie said, "and I'm gonna bring the girl home safe."

Was she? Or had she condemned Kayla by not putting her foot down? By not finding *some* way to get Paul and Sutton to understand that a full-out assault was the worst kind of fire to light in this situation?

"Yes, you are," her mother said proudly. "Honey, come up and visit after all this is over, okay? Just for a few days."

Maggie could see Jake heading toward her across the courtyard. Excitement and worry fizzed inside her. Had SWAT moved out already? Or had he gone searching for her because he was worried?

"I'll think about it, Mom," she said quickly, her throat getting tight. "Listen, I've got to go. I love you."

"I love you too."

She hung up, blinking back whatever tears she had left before Jake reached her. But she must have done it badly because he reached out, brushing her curls off her face. His arms wrapped around her and he drew her close, pressing her cheek gently into the softness of his shirt. She breathed in the faint smell of his aftershave—a hint of something rich and earthy—and felt the tension uncoiling at the base of her spine, spreading through her body.

"They're making a mistake," she mumbled into his shirt, because she couldn't bear to look in his eyes and have him confirm what she knew was true.

"They're trained," Jake said. He was clearly trying to look on the bright side, but the strain in his voice revealed his concern.

"He's going to panic. Mancuso's desperate enough. Add the pressure of SWAT breathing down his neck? It'll trigger anything. What if he has a backup plan?" Agitated, she pulled away from Jake, pacing up and down the sidewalk.

"This is a terrible idea," she said for what felt like the millionth time. "I hate this. I hate that there was an easier, safer solution they ignored." Her shoulders slumped in defeat. "I hate that they won't listen to reason. And I hate that Thebes is going to get away with *murder*. He shouldn't be serving our country. He's not a patriot. He's not even a good father. And most of all, I hate that Kayla . . ."

She was breathing hard, her chest heaving, her blood spiking hot. She couldn't go on. She felt all the fight trying to leave her like water down a drain, and she tried to keep her hold on it. She *needed* to fight. Kayla needed her to fight.

"Hey." Jake reached out and caught her hand, wrapping it in his. Her breath caught, and the strength and desire he inspired filled her, making her bold. How was he so *warm*? All she wanted to do was sink into him, let him envelop her in his arms. Being held by him felt safe. It drove everything else out of her thoughts until it was just him and her, their breath, their bodies, the memories of those moments in the greenhouse, his skin against hers, his body moving against hers, the choked words breathed like a prayer against her ear.

"Kiss me," she found herself saying. And she didn't have to ask twice. His lips were on hers, that glorious feeling—hope, warmth, and something else, something she wasn't ready to name—filling her. She stroked the slope of his broad shoulders, down the hard breadth of his biceps, remembering vividly how strong he'd been, holding her up against the greenhouse wall. It had felt like he'd hold her up through anything.

And it felt like that now. Like no matter what happened, he would see it through.

He was a man who kept his promises. And he'd promised Kayla would be all right.

She'd be a fool to believe him completely, because you can never predict the outcome of cases like these.

But maybe, in his arms, she could be the fool. She could believe. In herself. In him.

In *them*.

She couldn't save Erica. She couldn't save Gretchen.

But maybe, with Jake's help, she could save Kayla.

CHAPTER 42

Kayla blinked slowly. When she licked her lips, she could taste blood on them.

She was back in the gray room Max had been keeping her in. He must have dragged her back in here when she'd passed out in the bathroom.

The bathroom! She pawed at her side, breathing a sigh of relief when her fingers came in contact with cool metal. She'd managed to tuck the scissors into the waistband of her skirt, and they were still there.

With clumsy hands, she pulled them out and began to saw at the ropes binding her hands. She was shaking so badly. Disoriented from the lack of insulin, it took a good ten minutes to get through all of them. When she managed, she nearly sobbed in relief when the tight ropes loosened.

A loud sound—like an alarm—went off. Kayla started, dropping the scissors. What was that? Was someone coming? Was she finally rescued? Her heart leapt and then fell to the pit of her stomach when she heard footsteps coming toward the room. Panicking, Kayla kicked the scissors under the sleeping bag just as the door burst open. Max's eyes were shining with a scary light, and his hair was a mess, like he'd been running his hands through it.

He stalked toward her like a lion closing in on its prey. Kayla scrambled away, looking desperately—uselessly—around. But she knew there was no escape. Terror spiked inside her, swamping out everything else. Oh, God . . . Oh,

God. Was he going to kill her? Her heartbeat roared in her ears, and black spots clouded her vision as the room swayed around her.

She screamed as he grabbed her arm. Screamed like she'd never screamed before. He winced at the sound, but continue to pull at her. She went limp, hoping it would stop him. Instead, it seemed to make him angrier. He slapped her across the face, a move that was so unexpected it left her silent and gasping, her cheek throbbing as he dragged her out of the room.

"It's time," he said.

CHAPTER 43

Paul moved steadily and swiftly through the woods in a half crouch, his gun making slow, even sweeps as he neared the structure.

Mancuso's cabin rested by a river in Potomac Overlook Park. Overgrown and unkempt, the park trails were more a hindrance than a help. He and the SWAT team moved as silently as possible through the woods off trail, approaching the cabin from the north. His footsteps crunched through the forest floor as he navigated around trees, hopping over a fallen log. He scanned the woods around him as he moved, his footsteps assured, his breathing steady. The sun was beginning to set, and they had to pick up their speed. A firefight in the dark was the last thing they needed.

Being in the field had always felt more natural to him than the conference room. So much so that he'd considered SWAT after graduating from the Academy. Direct action had an order that assured him, that made sense.

"Alpha One, the cabin is in sight. I repeat, cabin is in sight," said Sutton over the radio. "Awaiting your green light, Alpha One."

"Confirmed, Alpha Two," Paul replied. "Approaching now."

He scaled up the last slope, clearing the top in minutes. The shadow of the cabin—all the lights turned off—came into sight. The sun was sinking fast. They needed to do this. Now.

Paul's stomach tightened in anticipation. Adrenaline might be rushing through every part of his body, but he had to keep his hands and mind steady. Focused.

"Visual confirmation on the cabin, Alpha Two," Paul said. "Alpha One is in position."

He waited until the other five SWAT members had moved into place and confirmed it over the radio. He counted silently in his head, eyeing the exact positions of his teammates in his field of vision. They were ready. It was time.

His muscles tightened, coiled like a tiger ready to spring on his prey as he gave the order. "Alpha Team, you have the green light. I repeat: you have the green light."

The seven men moved toward the cabin in unison, like parts of one body. Paul kicked the front door down, his gun at the ready.

"Freeze!"

"FBI!"

"Down on the ground!"

But they faced nothing but an empty room. The men broke apart, turning the lights on as they went, searching the other rooms.

"Clear!"

"Clear!"

"Clear!"

"It's all clear, sir!"

"Omega Team One and Two," Paul said into his radio. "Cabin is empty. Stay sharp. Suspect has fled. I repeat: Stay sharp. He's out there and most definitely armed. Use extreme caution. He might have the girl with him." He switched off his radio, gesturing to two of the SWAT team. "Set up a perimeter," he ordered.

He glanced around the living room. The furniture was old and rickety. A faded high-school pennant was stuck on the wall, next to a tapestry of a black bear. A fraying carpet lay crookedly across the floor.

Paul turned to Sutton. "What went wrong?" he asked.

"Maybe he saw us coming," Sutton said. "Dammit!" He kicked the wall.

The lights cut out.

"Shit!" Paul heard someone say. Then a thumping sound, like a body dropping.

"Sutton? Rhyne?" Paul called, scrambling for the light on his gun, raising it. The beam fell on the agent's unconscious body.

"He's in here!" Sutton shouted. "Hidden door!" There was a scuffling sound as Sutton moved toward the hallway, then the muffled, sickening sound of metal hitting skull. Sutton fell to the ground.

Paul swore, forcing himself to turn in a slow circle despite every instinct screaming at him to move quickly. He needed to watch for movement. He needed—

The gunshot echoed so loudly that pain spurted through his head. He felt something whiz by his ear, embedding in the wall, casting a spray of wood splinters everywhere.

A bullet. Near hit. God, that was close.

Then he felt something even worse: the pressure of a hot gun barrel against the back of his neck. The click of the hammer being pulled back filled Paul's ears.

"Don't move," said a voice.

Shit, Paul thought. *Maggie was right. This was a terrible idea.*

CHAPTER 44

Maggie and Jake were almost to the conference room when Frank came hurrying down the hallway, his face gaunt.

"Something's gone wrong," he said, jerking his thumb behind him. "We're needed downstairs, in the basement."

Maggie and Jake turned to follow him to the stairwell as Frank gave them the facts. "They got through the woods, the approach was smooth, everything looked good. They breached the doors, and initial examination of the cabin interior brought up nothing."

"It was empty? Did Mancuso get away?" Maggie had to half jog to keep up with the two men as the three of them wound their way through the maze of hallways. They were heading toward the back of the building, where the armory and surveillance equipment was stored.

"No," Frank said, a dark expression settling over his face. "The bastard got the drop on them. I don't know how he did it—visual and radio access were cut off as soon as shots were fired."

Maggie's stomach clenched. "Was Paul leading the raid?"

Frank looked down, away from her. It was all the confirmation she needed.

"Oh, my God," she said, covering her mouth with her hand. "What do we know? Is he alive? Is he okay? Frank, *tell* me."

"We don't know," Frank said.

Maggie bit back a horrified sound. Why hadn't he listened to her? If he died because of this, she'd never forgive herself. Was there something she could've said to convince him? She should've been stronger. More argumentative. *Anything*.

"What we know is there are three agents inside that cabin," he said. "We've got the place surrounded, but . . ."

"Christ," Jake swore. "What a mess."

"And Kayla's still inside with Mancuso," Maggie said.

Frank sighed. "Your instincts were on point again, kid. Going full tactical assault was the wrong choice."

Duh, she wanted to snap at him. Fury wrapped in fear sparked inside her, but she pushed it down. She had to keep her cool. Now Mancuso had *more* hostages. The FBI had practically handed them to him on a silver platter. This might empower him. Give him an ego boost and confidence. Emotions would be high on all fronts.

"We need to get you suited up," Frank said grimly. "They have a vest in your size."

He opened the door to the armory, where equipment of all kinds sat in giant metal cages, waiting to be used. Several techs were running around, placing guns and other equipment on the table in the center of the room.

"I found it! Sir! I found it!" A young woman with short black hair triumphantly held up a bulletproof vest. "Agent Kincaid—" she held it out to her "—here you go."

Maggie took the Kevlar from her, the weight of it familiar in her hands. She remembered the first time she had to wear one, when they were training in Quantico. It had been too big for her, bulky and ill-fitting on her petite frame. When she had graduated, Frank had given her one specially fitted for her as a gift. "Just in case you're ever in a pinch," he told her. "Better safe than sorry."

"Maggie?" Jake's soft prompting pulled her out of her daze. "You're up."

Her fingers clenched around the Kevlar. She pulled on the vest, snapping it into place.

She was up.

"Let's go," she said.

BY THE TIME they arrived at Potomac Overlook Park, night had fallen. Stealth was no longer a priority. It didn't matter if Mancuso heard them coming, they were already there. Frank, Maggie, and Jake drove through the forest in a Gator, a tricked-out all-terrain vehicle painted in camouflage colors that sailed over rough territory like it was asphalt.

Choppers circled above the treetops, beaming bright lights down on them, illuminating the cabin garishly, like a movie set. Positioned every ten feet, SWAT members surrounded the cabin, shields at the ready, guns drawn. Out of shooting range, on the south side, SWAT brought in a ring of armored trucks, using them as both shields and impediments to Mancuso's escape.

Maggie hopped out of the Gator and walked confidently toward the group of men standing behind the trucks.

"Who's lead here?" she demanded.

A man with a mustache and a slightly panicked expression cautiously raised his hand. "Um, me. I guess."

"You guess?"

"Agent Sutton is on his way to the hospital," the man said. "Mancuso tossed him and Agent Rhyne out the front door about ten minutes ago. They were both unconscious, but alive."

Why in the world would Mancuso give up hostages? Unless . . .

Oh, no. Dread built inside her, filling her chest, rising up to her throat, choking her. "What about Agent Harrison?" Maggie asked.

"He's still inside," the man said.

"Okay," Maggie said. "Okay," she repeated, trying to gather her thoughts. "You." She pointed at Sutton's teammate. "Name?"

"Agent Collins."

"You'll be taking your orders from me," she said. "You good with that?"

He looked relieved. "Yes, ma'am."

"I need to reestablish dialogue with Mancuso. He's got not only one, but two hostages now. He has the upper hand, and he knows it. He'll want to gloat."

One of the agents went running, coming back with a megaphone, which she handed to Maggie.

Maggie clicked it on. "Roger Mancuso," she said into it, her voice booming through the clearing. "It's Maggie Kincaid. I've discovered some things about Joe. About your brother. Why don't you give me a call and we can talk about it?"

Within seconds, her phone buzzed. Handing off the megaphone to Collins, she pulled it out, unlocking it.

"Oh, my God," she whispered, her stomach sinking. Mancuso had texted her a photo.

A photo of Paul, stripped of his tactical gear and Kevlar vest, bound to a chair, with what looked like C4 explosive wired in an M112 block taped to his chest.

"I need the bomb squad out here!" Maggie shouted. "*Now!* Frank." She looked at her mentor. When he'd seen the amount of C4 in the block, his skin had taken on a gray sheen. He had trained Paul just like he'd trained Maggie. This was personal for him.

"That's enough to blow us all to kingdom come," Frank breathed.

Maggie swore. Jake's hand settled on her shoulder, and he squeezed, a quick, comforting touch that helped her breathe through her worry.

Her phone buzzed again. This time, it wasn't a picture, but a call from an unknown number.

Maggie stared down at it, wanting desperately to pick it up immediately, to scream at Mancuso. But she forced herself to wait. She was in control. She needed to convey that message. Paul's and Kayla's lives might depend on it.

She picked it up after the third ring.

"Hello, Mancuso," she said, fighting to keep her voice level. He couldn't find out how worried she was about Paul; he'd use it against her.

"You don't keep your promises, Maggie," Mancuso said. He was breathing heavily into the phone, like he'd been pacing.

"I'm really sorry I wasn't able to get you the file," Maggie said.

"You have to be lying," Mancuso shouted. "If you know about Joe, that means you must have seen it."

"No," Maggie said. "Trust me, that would've made my life a lot easier. I've been chasing leads all over Maryland today. I went to SouthPoint, Roger. And I talked to Nancy, Joe's ex. I put it together, but these jerks overrode me and messed up. I understand, Roger. I know what you're trying to do. You need to make sure your brother didn't die in vain, right?"

"Joe was *murdered*," Mancuso hissed. "And that bastard Thebes was the one who orchestrated it. People have to know! He has to be held accountable for what he's done. He's a murderer!"

"I understand," Maggie said. "And I'll help you. But what's the point of blowing up Agent Harrison and Kayla—and *yourself*? That'd bury the truth so deep no one would ever know."

"I have to do this," Mancuso said, his voice breaking. "I have to."

"Look—" Maggie started.

"No!" He shouted into the phone, sounding truly unhinged. Was she going to lose hold of this? Was he going to snap? He was on the verge. She could feel it. Dammit. Why hadn't they listened to her? Or at least sent Jake in alone? Paul would have been safe right now. Kayla would be on the way home. If anyone could've gotten her out solo, it would've been Jake O'Connor.

"It's time for *you* to listen to *me*. Okay, so the senator won't get the papers." Mancuso was clearly thinking out loud, all plans abandoned. "That's fine . . . that's fine. I don't need the file. I want a national news crew here in one hour, plus a ride to the airport and a private plane chartered with a one-way trip to Andorra. And I'll take that five million dollars—in cash—too. Unmarked bills, Maggie. And no funny business."

So Mancuso wanted to tell his story. Okay. That was something she could use. A new bargaining chip. "I can work on getting the news crew here," Maggie said. "But it might take longer than an hour. It's getting pretty dark out here."

"I don't care!" Mancuso barked. "Do what I say in the time frame I've given you. Otherwise, you won't like what happens."

Maggie's hand tightened around the phone, sweat crawling down her neck. "I'll get working on that right now," Maggie said. "Can I talk to Agent Harrison?"

Mancuso snorted. "You think I'm stupid?"

"What about Kayla?" Maggie asked, checking her watch. God knew how long it'd been since she'd had food or insulin. She didn't trust Mancuso's word that he'd given her any—or that he'd crushed the remaining supply. "Can you give her some insulin? As a show of good faith?"

Mancuso laughed, a high-pitched, almost maniacal sound of a man cornered. "It's your agent who's got a bomb strapped to his chest, Maggie, not me," he said. "You aren't in control here. Give me what I want. And if you double-cross me, if anybody comes within fifty yards of the cabin, I'll blow it up and take all of you with me. I got the drop on your SWAT team. I can kill you all. If I have to, I will."

With a click, the phone went dead.

Maggie looked up at the men surrounding her, staring.

"Agent Kincaid, what do we do now?" Collins asked.

Maggie looked over her shoulder at the darkened cabin. It looked quaintly rustic, almost charming—if you didn't know how much C4 was inside.

"We keep the dialogue open," she said. It was the only way she had any chance of getting Kayla and Paul out of there alive. Mancuso was too far gone, and she . . . she had to guide him. She had to be the touchstone, even if every irrational part of her was screaming to send SWAT into the cabin, no matter the consequences. She must stay in control. She pushed down the surge of panic and worry rising inside her. "Then we figure out a way to get in, get everybody out, and dismantle that bomb . . . before he blows us all up."

CHAPTER 45

The beam of the floodlights glared down on the cabin, making the shadows of the trees stretch freakishly long across the clearing. Jake had done a slow circle around the perimeter as SWAT set up teams. It was secure—for now. The forest line started a good fifty feet away from the cabin—no matter where they tried to hide, Mancuso would be able to spot them.

"O'Connor?" Agent Collins said.

Jake turned from where he was staring at the cabin, working through the potential approaches in his head. "Yes?"

"Agent Kincaid asked me to keep you apprised," Agent Collins explained. "We've cut the power. Omega Teams are patrolling the perimeter."

"They should stay sharp," Jake said. "Mancuso's probably thinking he's invincible right now. And he's got a good vantage point."

Agent Collins nodded. "We're being careful."

Jake didn't want to say what he was thinking, which was that "careful" should've happened before they stormed the cabin. But the guy didn't need that on him. He hadn't made the call. He had superiors, just like Jake did. Instead, he gave a short nod of dismissal to Collins, who went back to his team to give them the hourly update.

The moon had begun to rise in the night sky, adding to the floodlights beaming down on the cabin. Choppers swung in tight circles above their heads, and Jake looked up for a moment, tracking them.

His instincts were on red alert, his body tense for action. The weight of the gun on his hip was a comfort, because this situation was teetering into catastrophic territory. Jake knew catastrophe well.

It had been almost an hour since Mancuso had issued his demands. In that time, SWAT had brought in one of their mobile units through an overgrown access road, along with a slew of trucks. The bomb squad had arrived, and an impermeable perimeter had been established.

Mancuso wasn't going anywhere.

The cabin was dark. Floodlights were strategically positioned around it, giving the SWAT team patrolling the perimeter good visuals while serving the double purpose of blinding anyone who tried to leave the cabin.

They had Mancuso boxed in, but no amount of firepower would save them from that bomb strapped to Agent Harrison's chest. Jake had picked up enough knowledge working with the bomb squad in the Middle East to know that amount of C4 was trouble. Big trouble. Especially if Mancuso built it himself. He was a slick operator, no doubt, but no one became an expert bomb builder in just a few years. The explosives in the device could be unstable, the trigger or wiring faulty. There were too many things that could go wrong.

Jake felt for Agent Harrison, but he knew the man was trained for this. Kayla Thebes wasn't. The girl must be terrified—if she was even conscious at this point.

It set his teeth on edge, his body thrumming for quick action and solid resolution, but there was nothing he could do. Not without Maggie's go-ahead. She was running the show—as she should be.

He smiled at the thought. He'd never met anyone like Maggie. The memory of her in the greenhouse, the long line of her throat as her head fell back, reveling in her release, would haunt him for the rest of his days. She wasn't just sexy as hell; there was this barely contained fire inside her—a mix of passion and a thirst for justice pulling him toward her. He wanted to know everything about her. To break down all those walls she put up and discover the real woman beneath.

She was tougher than any civilian he'd ever met. She'd been through so much, so young. She'd gone from a little girl locked and bound in a closet, forced to leave her sister behind, and had become the kind of woman you'd fight wars for. Tough, empathetic, self-assured. Anyone would be impressed by a person with Maggie's history managing to have a normal life. But normal wasn't enough for a driven woman like Maggie Kincaid: She didn't just overcome the evil she'd been forced to endure so young, she faced reminders of her trauma from all sides and instead of crumbling under the pressure, she gained strength from it. She may think she was a failure because of what had gone wrong at Sherwood Hills, but Jake knew that she'd done everything possible. That was the kind of agent—the kind of person—she was. Maybe calling in SWAT too soon had been a mistake—but who was to say the situation wouldn't have escalated further if she hadn't? That was the problem he understood too well: In the dangerous work they both did, they could never know the what-ifs—and he was sure that fact was as torturous for her as it was for him.

Sometimes, horrible things happened. Sometimes, they could stop them—but the other times . . .

It took a special person to not break under that kind of pressure. Jake had lost a lot of people in his life—that was the nature of war—and some losses were harder than others. He closed his eyes, trying to drive away the unbidden memory that rose to the surface of his mind. Bullets whizzing over his head, blood staining the golden sand, boots protruding from under an overturned, bombed-out Humvee.

He shook his head. He wasn't going to think about that.

"O'Connor," said a voice behind him.

Jake turned, finding Senator Thebes standing behind him, illuminated in the light beating down on the clearing.

About time he showed up, Jake thought with more than a little derision. He kept his face neutral instead of showing his revulsion. He was still technically working for the man, after all. He had to remain professional.

The senator looked awful—as if he'd aged ten years in three days. His eyes, heavy with dark circles underneath, had a wild glint that made Jake nervous. He didn't trust this guy as far as he could throw him. His actions had been deplorable, and he didn't even seem to know it.

"Senator." Jake nodded his head in acknowledgment.

"I'm glad you're here," Thebes said. "That woman—" he glanced over at Maggie, the disgust practically seeping out of his pale skin "—is not forthcoming with me."

She's been nothing but forthcoming, Jake thought. *She just won't play your fucking game because she thinks saving your daughter is more important than your precious reputation, you crooked bastard.*

"I know I can trust you," the senator went on, leaning forward and clapping a hand on Jake's shoulder. "I need you to keep the lines of communication open," he continued. "If that woman gets too . . . hysterical, I'm relying on you to reel her in. There are so many moving parts here. I need you to be my eyes and ears. Can you do that? I need you to protect what's important."

Jake raised an eyebrow. "And what is it you deem important, Senator?" he asked. "Your daughter or your career?"

Senator Thebes' mouth twisted, offended by the bold question. "My daughter, of course," he said.

Jake wanted badly to ask, *Are you sure about that?* The anger and distaste rising inside Jake was like a tidal wave. He knew better than to show it. Getting fired from this job meant he was off the case—and Maggie needed his help. She might never admit it, but she needed his support.

"I'll take care of it for you, Senator," Jake said. "Don't worry. We'll get Kayla home safe."

The man's suspicious expression faded at Jake's words. He truly thought he was going to get away with this—but Jake knew better.

But first things first, Jake thought, turning his attention back to the cabin. It was a shabby building, no more than a glorified shack, really. The porch was sagging in the middle and the plaid curtains in the split windows were frayed, but pulled tightly closed. Tall pines surrounded it, casting it further in shadow. It stood there, dark, lonely, and dangerous.

They had to get Kayla Thebes out of that hellhole. To do that, he had to find a way in—and fast.

Jake looked over his shoulder at the group of agents clustered around Maggie. He couldn't get to her without drawing too much attention. And anyway, he didn't want her to get any of the blame for what he had planned.

Casually, he made his way toward the pines, pulling his cell out of his jacket and pulling up a file to email Peggy before dialing her number.

"Hey, boss, what's the situation?"

"Has it hit the news yet?" Jake asked.

"A few vague news reports of police activity in the area. Nothing big yet. Police scanners are going crazy, though. The reporters will be heading out your way soon—if they haven't already."

"Okay, I need you to call Mark O'Brien at CNN," Jake said. "Give him all the information in the file I'm sending you. Tell him I'm sure."

"Got it," Peggy said. "I'll text you when it's done. So, you're pulling the trigger, huh?" Her normally cheerful voice had a hint of dread in it. He didn't blame her. The general wasn't going to be happy.

"I'm bringing that little girl home alive," Jake said. "By any means necessary."

He turned back toward the cabin. "Whatever it takes," he said under his breath.

CHAPTER 46

Maggie hugged her elbows as she watched the camera crews setting up just beyond the cordons the police had hastily erected.

"What the hell are *they* doing here?" Maggie demanded. She could see news vans pulling up from the service road. "Who called them?"

Frank looked over his shoulder, shrugging when he saw them. "It's public land, kid. They'll stay behind the cordon, but we can't really prevent them from recording. It's news."

"Didn't you at least issue a no-fly zone for this area so they can't send choppers up?" Maggie asked.

Frank shot her a look. "Do you think I'm stupid?"

"Sorry," she said, realizing how snotty she sounded. The stress was starting to get to her—as the minutes ticked on, her hands shook so badly she had to shove them in the pockets of her jacket.

Mancuso's deadline was closing in.

"Let's go into the command center," Frank said, taking her arm. Maggie followed, glad to get away.

The SWAT mobile unit was enormous, built like a deadly, bulletproof RV on wheels. Inside, computers and radios ran at full speed, and the bomb squad huddled in a corner, their heads bent as they conferred.

Maggie knew better than to bother them. She'd met with the head of the squad when they'd arrived, but she'd gotten out of their way as soon as they provided her with a basic breakdown. They'd give her an extensive report as soon as they knew the details—there was no point in rushing them. But she needed all the information she could get on the device wired to Paul's chest.

Her heart clenched at the thought. She would always care about Paul. She loved him, like she'd love a friend. He was a good, solid man who deserved a good, solid life. It's one of the reasons she'd left him. Because she wanted him to have that. Because he deserved someone who looked at him like he looked at her.

The idea of having to go to his family with the news of this . . . if this was how his life ended . . .

No. She shook the thought from her head, her fists clenching at her sides. Absolutely not. She wasn't going to think about it.

No one was getting blown up today. Everyone was getting out alive. She would make sure of it.

"Agent—I mean, Ms. Kincaid?"

Maggie looked over to Agent Collins, a tall, reedy man standing in a small group of SWAT team members. Alpha Team Two, she realized as they turned toward her—they'd been the agents patrolling the perimeter when Mancuso had captured Paul and Sutton inside the cabin.

Collins' boyish face was still white and drawn. She recognized the guilty expression in his eyes—he felt that Mancuso getting the drop on them was his fault. That he should have reacted faster or better, or somehow *known* what was going to happen before it did.

She recognized the emotion. But she didn't have time for it. They needed to focus on the future, not on past mistakes. It was go-time, and the decisions they made now were about life—or death.

"Update?" she asked.

"We've cut the electricity," Agent Collins said, ticking it off on his fingers. "And the techs have gotten the phone company to disable all calls from Mancuso's cell except for those to your number. I've got four snipers in the trees, waiting for the order. Alpha Team Three is positioned around the cabin. Bomb squad is analyzing the picture of the device inside the second mobile unit; they should have a report for you soon."

"Good," Maggie said.

"We should go in," said the man next to Collins. "Hit him hard and fast. We can take him. An overwhelming display of force."

Several of the other SWAT members shifted, a few nodding in agreement.

Maggie looked at the man who had spoken, exasperation fluttering in her stomach. He was tall, with a head that looked a little too small for his broad shoulders. He wore his dark hair cropped close to his skull, and she could see a thick scar on his neck. But she wasn't going to be overruled by a man's opinion like this.

"What's your name?" she asked, keeping her voice calm and level, almost friendly.

"Agent Grant," he said with a sneer.

"Okay, Grant," Maggie said, picking up a tablet from the table, bringing up the photo Mancuso sent earlier. "Come here."

Rolling his eyes, he shuffled forward, looking at the tablet in her hand.

"You see this?" With a touch of her fingers, Maggie zoomed into the mess of wiring in the center of Paul's chest.

"So what?" he demanded.

Maggie quirked an eyebrow. "You don't see it?" she asked. "Maybe you missed your classes in explosives at Quantico. But I didn't. That right there." She tapped the photo, circling the corner where Mancuso's hand was visible. "See what he's holding?"

He leaned forward, squinting.

"It's a dead man's switch," Maggie said, the unspoken *"you moron"* hanging in the air between them. "Do I have to educate you on that topic?" she asked sternly. "Mancuso's got the bomb's trigger in his hand at all times. If he drops it or releases the trigger, the bomb goes off. That means if you charge in there, showing your 'overwhelming display of force,' you'll get *everyone* blown up—including Kayla, Agent Harrison, and the rest of your team."

Grant ducked his head, his cheeks burning in embarrassment over missing such an obvious risk.

"So maybe take a step back, follow my orders, and remember that not everything can be solved by putting a bullet in an unsub's brain," Maggie concluded.

Grant wouldn't meet her eyes, but she could tell he was scowling, humiliated at her dressing him down so neatly. Well, it served him right, she thought.

"How did he get his hands on this kind of tech?" Grant asked, his confidence turning into confusion.

"This guy knows what he's doing," Maggie said. "You've underestimated him every step of the way, and now you've fed his confidence. He just took on the FBI and succeeded in getting *another* hostage. All because you guys thought you knew who you were dealing with better than I did! Look where we are now: He's got explosives, he's got weapons, and he's got more than one hostage. *Stop underestimating this guy.*" She stared at them, waiting until they met her eyes sheepishly, then continued.

"Stop assuming that your regular tricks are going to work. This guy has a mission, and nothing's going to get between him and his goal—not even his own death. He has nothing to lose, and your little raid just pissed him off further."

"What if we send in a tactical team disguised as the press?" Collins suggested. "You say he has a mission. That's to tell his story, right? So why don't we tell him he can have that? Send in agents disguised as journalists, get him talking, defuse the situation before he even realizes he's been tricked."

"That would never work," Maggie said. "Mancuso's spent two years working with the press professionally. He knows them. He'd recognize a Trojan horse like that right away."

"Then what *do* we do?" Collins asked anxiously. "One of our own is in there!"

He wouldn't be if you all had just listened *to me*, Maggie thought with frustration. But there was no point in dwelling on it. They were in this situation now, and she had to make the best of it. She had to find a way through.

"We find another way," Maggie said.

"But—" Collins stopped talking when the mobile unit door opened. A tech climbed inside, Jake following behind her.

"You might want to turn on CNN," he said to Maggie.

Maggie reached over and flipped the TV on. The senator's face filled the screen as the anchor continued, "This is Mark O'Brien, with a special report. Senator Thebes, a three-term senator from Maryland, has been implicated in alleged illegal activities involving the company SouthPoint Oil. Rumors began when news broke that the senator's teenage daughter Kayla was kidnapped earlier this week. Now, reliable sources indicate that the kidnapping was directly related to Senator Thebes' close association with SouthPoint's board of directors, a connection that allegedly involves oil smuggling, price rigging, and even assassination of uncooperative company operatives. Stay tuned for more details after the break."

The screen switched to a commercial. Maggie frowned. How in the world had they gotten all that information?

She looked over at Jake, whose face slipped into a quick, sly grin before returning to his normal, tough-guy exterior. He wouldn't . . .

But the satisfied gleam in his eye said otherwise.

"Did you do this?" she asked him in an undertone.

"Do what?" he asked innocently, that sly grin flashing at her again.

"You're a piece of work," she muttered, but as she looked around, she saw that no one else had realized what he'd done.

She knew she should be angry that he had seeded the story without consulting her first. But she couldn't be—not really.

The man was clever, she'd give him that. Reckless, but

clever—and effective. His move had just given her the one thing she desperately needed: a way to reestablish some trust with Mancuso.

Maggie looked at the screens on the wall of the mobile unit, camera feeds from each SWAT member's position, showing multiple vantage points inside the darkened cabin. It felt like a hand was closing around her throat, making it hard to breathe.

Calm, Maggie, she reminded herself sternly. *Stay in control. Stay strong.*

She balled up her fists to hide the trembling.

Kayla was inside. Paul was inside. The danger was immeasurable. Mancuso was a wild card.

She had to lure him out and rescue his hostages. And Jake O'Connor had given her a way to do it.

It was time to make another phone call.

CHAPTER 47

I need silence!" Maggie said. "We're going to be making another call. Jessa, please start recording," she told the tech sitting in the far corner, her headset firmly in place.

"Yes, ma'am."

Maggie pulled out her phone and dialed Mancuso's number. As it began to ring, her heart kicked in her chest like an angry horse. She wanted to reach out for Jake's hand, to squeeze it, to let the warmth of him give her strength, but she knew she couldn't. Instead, she met his steady gaze, and he nodded in encouragement as the phone rang and rang.

Wasn't Mancuso going to pick up? God, what if he didn't?

Sweat sprang up along the edge of her forehead, and she wiped it away, trying to breathe through the nerves.

Should she hang up? Try again? It'd been ringing too long.

Then there was a click. Her heart leapt and fell as the silence stretched out. Then, finally: "What do you want, you bitch?" Mancuso yelled.

Relief bolted through her, followed quickly by alarm at the anger in his voice. She could just picture him in there, sweating in the dark, listening to the choppers above, ducking the searchlights sweeping past the windows, and trying to gather the presence of mind to do . . . what?

She needed to solve this. Now. Fury paired with a dead man's switch was a recipe for disaster. Even if Mancuso didn't mean to, he could accidentally drop the trigger if he was startled. Stress did bad things to a guy's motor skills. Especially when he wasn't used to this level of panic.

"You cut my lights, you cut my phone, and now you expect me to trust you?" Mancuso demanded. "I should just—"

"Mancuso," Maggie interrupted. "Roger. Can I call you Roger? There's been a development. Something that I think will make you really happy. The SouthPoint scandal has just broken on CNN. It's been connected to the senator, Roger. His face is all over the media, and they're talking about how he's crooked. That he's deeply involved in criminal activity—including murder. It's just a matter of time until a dogged reporter finds out the specifics about Joe—about what Thebes and SouthPoint did to him. The full power of the press is focused on digging out the truth behind this. If the senator's guilty, they won't just find out. They'll destroy him."

There was a pause. A moment where Maggie thought—hoped—that she'd hooked him. *Please let it be enough*, she thought. *Please let him be satisfied.*

But then: "That's not good enough," Mancuso burst out. All of Maggie's hopes shattered. She felt like throwing the phone across the room, but instead, she kept listening, kept quiet, kept him talking.

"If all I wanted to do was create a scandal, I would've leaked the information myself. You don't get it, Maggie," he scoffed. "You're naive. Men like the senator are snakes—he'll wiggle free. He'll get out of this unscathed. Maybe his political career is over—and that's a big *maybe*—but I know how this town works. I know how politics work. I've lived and breathed them for years preparing for this. I've seen it all. That bastard will end up working for some think tank, making millions. Or he'll serve on a corporate board somewhere. Men like him don't stay down for long. He'll rise out of this like a phoenix. He'll hurt more people."

"*You're* hurting people, Roger," Maggie said seriously. Maybe if she appealed to his sense of justice, she'd get through to him. He wasn't a natural killer; she was positive of that. He was just a guy on a mission. A guy she'd trapped in a corner with no escape. "Kayla is innocent in this. You know that. She's just a kid. And Agent Harrison was just following orders."

"There's a price to be paid," Mancuso said coldly. "My brother paid the ultimate price. He was an American hero. He uncovered a massive scheme worth billions, and Senator Thebes and his friends had him killed for it! Someone has to pay!"

Maggie straightened in her seat, her eyes widening. "What do you mean *'and his friends'*?" she asked.

Mancuso snorted. "I thought you were smart, Maggie," he said. "Thebes is a senator. Do you really think he's going to order a hit himself? Of course not. It's too risky. And he's not going to have those kinds of connections. Someone bigger than Thebes—someone who's just as deep into this—gave the order. I'm not going to rest until I know the faces of the bastards who killed my brother. I want their names splashed all over the news and the papers and the Internet. I want them *punished*."

Maggie thought very fast. He was right. Thebes probably didn't order the hit. He likely just informed whoever was in charge of the threat Joe Mancuso posed. Thebes had plenty of reasons to keep this covered up, but the real power behind this mess? They had even more motivation to keep their misdeeds under wraps. And they clearly weren't shy about pulling a trigger when it served their purposes.

"Roger," she said. "You're a smart guy. Hell, I would say brilliant at this point—"

"Don't try to flatter me to make me trust you," he snapped.

"I'm not," Maggie said—and she wasn't. He *was* smart. He had to be, to get this far. And he was dedicated. That's why she *had* to sway him toward trust. It was the only way to get everyone out safely. "But if you're right about the kind of men who are behind this, you know they're not going to let you expose them."

"That's not my problem," Mancuso said. "It's yours."

"Roger—"

"No," he said. "You're supposed to be the best, right? Then go *be* the best, Maggie. Kayla doesn't have a lot of time left."

"Is she conscious?" Maggie asked, images of a pale and dying Kayla filling her head. Her wrists burned, as if rope was still chafing them. She flinched, unable to rub at the skin, to banish the feeling.

Dammit.

"Last time I checked." Mancuso sneered.

"Okay," Maggie said, running through the scenarios in her head. She needed someone to check on Kayla. She had to know the girl's condition before she made any big moves. She hated playing fast and loose with Kayla's health. But if Maggie had a time frame to work with, she'd be able to time her negotiation better. She'd have more control. She needed to know if Kayla was at immediate risk medically or if Maggie had some time to work with before she was in real danger. "I want to send a doctor in to look at Kayla."

"No way!"

"Roger, I've been frank with you," Maggie said, going in for the kill. She needed this. She needed to know the girl was okay before she executed her plan. "I could've fed you lies about the men who killed your brother. I could've given you false names or promises. But I didn't, did I?"

There was a pause, a suspicious one. Maggie's hopes spiked in the silence, her heart beating fast. He was listening. He was thinking.

He was considering.

"We need to establish some trust here," Maggie said. "On both sides. So we can all get through this, we can all get what we want. All I want is to send in a doctor—not to give Kayla insulin, but just to look her over. If you let the doctor in to check on her, then I'll give you electricity. You can watch the TV. You can see for yourself what's happening—how the press is gearing up to destroy Thebes. Isn't that what all this is about? You want to see that, don't you?"

Another pause. This approach may have been a thin thread, but it was a strong one. Please, *please* let Mancuso agree.

"I want my phone working again too, then," Mancuso said. "I want to be able to make outside calls to people other than you."

Relief flared in Maggie's chest. He'd jumped at the bait. They were making progress—finally! She took a deep breath and went on. "I can get the electricity back on, but I can't do the phone, not yet," she said. "Look, you've seen me work. You know how I operate. I'm not going to try anything funny with the doctor. I'm not here to pull the wool over your eyes and send in a SWAT member in a lab coat—you and I both know you're too smart for that. I'm not here to trick you, Mancuso. I only care about Kayla's safety and well-being." She didn't want to emphasize her concern about Paul, because she knew Mancuso would leap on that, try to use it to his advantage. An FBI hostage was valuable, maybe even more valuable than a senator's daughter, but Mancuso hadn't realized that. He was operating on panic and instinct right now. He had no backup plans. He was on his own, no plan—no blueprint, just instinct. It was probably terrifying for a control freak like him. Maggie had to keep that in mind. Fear was a great motivator. The problem was that it sometimes pushed people in the wrong direction.

She had to guide him in the right direction in order to get the hostages to safety.

"Fine," Mancuso said. "But no one else is allowed in. No matter what happens tonight, you and I are in this together."

For a moment, it almost didn't register. For an impossibly long moment, she thought she'd heard wrong. She had to have heard wrong. He couldn't have said what she thought he did . . .

But he had.

Having those familiar, haunting words spoke to her again felt like falling off a cliff. The bottom of her world dropped away, she was hanging in midair, panicked, spiraling down. She was back in the woods, twelve years old and running, running, her feet bloody and torn, her hands still bound as she tripped and fell. She was back in the shed, Erica's shoulder pressed against hers, her sister's whispering voice filling her ears. Begging her to run. Begging her to leave her. Maggie nearly dropped the phone as she croaked out, "What?"

No answer.

"Mancuso! Mancuso? *Roger?*"

But Mancuso had already hung up, leaving her with the pieces.

Leaving her broken, like the little girl she'd been so long ago.

CHAPTER 48

The phone fell out of Maggie's hand, clattering to the floor. Everyone else in the mobile unit faded away as Mancuso's words—*Erica's* words—spun in her head over and over.

How had he known? Was it just a coincidence? Was she going crazy? Reading into things? Had she even *heard* him right? Yes. She had. She knew she had. She was sure of it.

She felt sick to her stomach, about to fly out of her skin. She rubbed at her wrists, unable to stop, unable to rid herself of the painful itch under her skin.

Erica . . .

"Maggie?"

She started, blinking furiously, trying to collect her thoughts as her heart kicked against her rib cage. *Run, Maggie*, it said. *Run. Run. RUN!*

There was nowhere to run. No one chasing her. She wasn't twelve anymore.

She took a deep breath. *Calm, Maggie. Control.*

"Agent Kincaid?" Agent Collins' blond brows furrowed, his mouth a flat line of concern as he peered at her. "You're not really going to turn the electricity on, right? That was just a bluff?"

Maggie took another deep breath, forcing down the panic. She couldn't think. She *needed* to think.

Get it together, Maggie.

"We need to establish trust," she said.

"That's ridiculous," Agent Grant snorted. "We need to establish control. Let him know who's in charge here." Irritation grated inside her, distracting from the panicked confusion that threatened to overtake her entire being. She latched on to the irritation, the frustration, letting it fill her and drive everything else out.

"It seems to me that *you* are having trouble remembering who's in charge here," Maggie snapped. "I am. And I know what I'm doing." But doubt rose in her. What if she was wrong? What if she got everyone killed? Just like she got Gretchen killed . . . just like she got Erica killed.

"She's right," Jake said, coming to stand next to her. Concern was written on his face, but he was by her side. He was *on* her side. It bolstered her, helping to quell the panic and questions spinning in her head. "You really want to startle a guy holding a dead man's switch? Do you want to be responsible for making the call here? Because if you choose wrong, Harrison's and Kayla's deaths are on *you.* Agent Harrison is one of your own. Kayla's not even old enough to drive. Start acting like you understand the risks here instead of focusing on some action-movie rescue you've got in your head."

Agent Grant scowled, the prominent ridge of his forehead making him look even more like a caveman, but mercifully, he shut up.

Maggie turned to Frank, who was sitting near the computer station. She glanced at the screen, at the transcript of her call. Right there were Mancuso's words—no matter what happens tonight, you and I are in this together. Maggie stared at them for a moment, her mind spiraling down again into the dark memories of her childhood. She was barely keeping it together, and any second, Frank would realize it. She had to get out of here. She needed space to breathe. Freak out. *Something.*

"We need a doctor," she told Frank. "And we need one fast. Someone we can trust. No affiliation with the Bureau, but it would be good if he had some sort of combat training, just in case. Ex-Army or -Marine is preferable. He goes in, unarmed, just to assess Kayla's health. We have to play this straight, Frank. It's the only way."

Frank pulled his cell phone out. "I'll get someone. Might have to fly him in by chopper, but I'll get it done."

Maggie nodded curtly. "I'll be just a moment," she said, her voice strangled with the emotion rising in her chest. Before Frank could protest, she marched out of the mobile unit, walking as fast as she could into the cover of the trees, a good seventy feet away from all the law enforcement and flashing lights. It was getting cold, and she pulled her jacket tighter around herself, shaking not from the chill, but from shock. She could hear frogs croaking in the distance against the groan of wind in the tree branches. When she came to a stop, far enough away that no one could see her, she began to shake.

Oh, God. What was going on? She pressed her palms against her eyes, trying to stop the tears. She needed to *move*. Her skin buzzed with adrenaline as her mind circled frantically, trying to make sense, trying to keep calm—trying and failing miserably.

"Maggie?"

She whirled around. Jake stood there, illuminated by the moonlight, his eyes worried. He walked up to her, cupping her cheek, drawing her close. She shut her eyes, the fire in his touch soothing the restlessness under her skin.

"What's going on?" he asked, concern written all over his face. "You went tearing out of there. Mancuso . . . did he say something to you? You seemed really freaked out suddenly. What am I missing?"

She looked up at him, stricken, wanting nothing more than to lean into him. To let how he made her feel—alive, excited, hopeful—force everything else to fade away.

But Mancuso's words echoed through her like a horrible warning. She had to tell someone.

"Mancuso," she said haltingly. "The last thing he said."

"About being in this with you?" Jake asked. "That's good, right? It shows you built trust."

Maggie shook her head, closing her eyes tightly, trying to

find her strength. She knew she was going to sound crazy. Like she was looking for connections in a random phrase spoken by a panicked man. But Mancuso had repeated her sister's *exact* words. And he'd said them so deliberately, so knowingly. How did he know? Why did he say it? She'd never told anyone but Jake. Not even her own mother. Logic told her that it was just a coincidence, but her gut said otherwise.

And her gut wasn't wrong.

"Hey." Jake's voice softened. He tucked a curl behind her ear, his thumb resting against the flutter of her pulse. His eyes solemn and wide, he said, "Tell me."

She took a deep breath and decided she had to tell him. To trust him. "He said, *'No matter what happens tonight, you and I are in this together.'* And that—that's *exactly* what Erica said to me the night I escaped. Word for word, Jake. It's like . . . it's like he knows or something. And he couldn't know!"

She broke away from his touch, pacing, restless. Moving with erratic energy, pacing in circles, trying to calm herself. She rubbed at her wrists compulsively, not caring if he noticed, not caring about anything but answers. "Nobody could have known. I never told anyone the exact wording. Not even the police or the agents who interviewed me when I was little." She jerked a shaky hand through her curls, flipping them out of her face, trying to stop the trembling. She needed to get a hold of this. She needed control.

But she couldn't get a hold of it. Not with this. Not when it came to Erica.

She'd spent so long trying to find her. The first two years after Maggie had become an agent, she followed every lead, she went through every file she had access to. She was determined to find her sister's body and bring her home, to give her mother more than an empty grave to visit. And she'd failed. She'd forced herself to let it go. To concentrate on the living, the hostages she could help. She told herself that's what Erica would've wanted. That her big sister would have been so proud of her.

Had she just been lying to herself? Was their kidnapper

still out there? The man who ruined her life? Who killed her sister? Was he watching her? Waiting for her?

Her mind spun with the questions; her wrists burned as if rope was cutting into her skin, rubbing it raw and bloody.

"There's only one person who Erica could have told before she died," Maggie said. "And that's our kidnapper. They never caught him, you know." She should have found him. She should've kept her focus, stuck with searching for answers. It was why she been drawn to join the FBI in the first place. How could she have given it up? Given up on Erica? She should have made sure he'd never do it to anyone else. She should have made it her life's mission.

"Okay," Jake said. "Let's think this through, step by step." He reached out, stilling her, grasping her by both shoulders and forcing her to look at him. What she found in his face—the warmth, the worry, the determination—made something inside her unwind, spreading calm within her. "You were twelve when you were taken." She nodded. "And Mancuso's only a year older than you," he pointed out. "When you and Erica were kidnapped, he was a thirteen-year-old punk in Virginia."

"I know," Maggie said. "I know it's stupid. It's not rational. It could just be a coincidence. Do you . . . do you think it is?"

Jake frowned. "It's a common phrase. He could've been just trying to show solidarity. But I don't know for sure," he said. "And if your gut is telling you something else, Maggie, I trust your instincts. They're good. If you think something's up, then it's worth pursuing."

"What if I'm just losing it?" she asked. His hands tightened around her shoulders, like he expected her to start pacing again. "Maybe I'm the wrong person to be doing this." She gestured uselessly around her, to the mobile units and SWAT trucks parked everywhere. "This is just like Sherwood Hills. I'm reading into things too much. My memories are messing with me. Ruining my focus."

"Your experience as a hostage makes you *strong*, Maggie," Jake insisted, drawing her closer to him, his green eyes earnest. "You have a perspective from both sides that no one else does. If I were Kayla, I'd want you on my side. And if I were your ex-fiancé, I'd know there was no one better, no one smarter, to get me out of there alive."

"You knew Paul and I were engaged?" Maggie asked.

Jake shrugged. "It's part of my job to assess anyone coming in close contact with the senator."

"It's been over for a long time," Maggie said. She didn't want him to think she'd just jumped into bed with him after a broken engagement. Those moments in the greenhouse meant more to her than a quick fling. She'd felt . . . well, she'd never felt that way before. Jake brought something out in her that she didn't know existed.

"I know," Jake said. "And Paul's a good guy. He's lucky to have you fighting for him."

Maggie felt calmed by his matter-of-fact manner. The last thing she needed was jealousy or drama.

"I don't know how to do this," she confessed quietly. "Every time I think I've got a handle on things, that I'm making progress, something happens that throws a wrench into all of it."

"And you're rolling with the punches," Jake said. "You're playing it right. Buying time and building trust. You're taking it step by step instead of charging in and messing up."

Maggie looked in his eyes, calmed by the confidence she saw there. Confidence that soothed her worries . . . and helped her to refocus on the urgency of the moment. She shook her head, as if shaking off her panic. Coincidence or not, she had no time to think about anything but Kayla. She had to push Mancuso's words out of her head. This wasn't the time or the place. If he was using them deliberately, he was doing it to rattle her. She couldn't give him the satisfaction. She wasn't going to play into his hand.

"There's only so much time we can buy," she said. "Because if we send in that doctor and he tells us that Kayla's out of time, the plan has to change."

All bets would be off. And Maggie would have to decide. The problem was, she wasn't sure what the solution was.

CHAPTER 49

As Maggie and Jake made their way back to the mobile unit, she saw two more news vans through the trees. The press had been corralled, but it wasn't stopping them from lining up behind the barriers. They had a good view of the cabin from their spot, but were far enough away from the trucks and cordons that they weren't in the line of fire, in case Mancuso came out shooting. There was a small chance the journalists could get hit with falling debris if Mancuso set off the bomb, depending on where in the cabin Paul was when it was activated. It made her nervous that the blast radius of the bomb was an unknown. They could estimate the best they could and keep everyone as far away as possible. But without being aware of Paul's positioning or Mancuso's bomb building skills, there were a lot of unknowns. Maggie looked up to see bright flashes of light—journalists talking into cameras, reporting live. Uneasiness settled in her chest, wrapping around her heart.

"We're still in restricted airspace," Jake reassured her as he caught her scowling at the vans.

"I know," Maggie said. "I just wish they'd back off. They're like vultures."

"Part of the job," Jake said. "Crappy part, though."

"Understatement," Maggie said as an SUV pulled through the cordons and up to them. Grace stepped out. She made a face when her heels sank into the dirt, but her expression disappeared when she caught sight of Maggie. She hurried over.

Maggie couldn't help but glance at Jake out of the corner of her eye, waiting for Grace's beauty to hit him and the all too familiar worshipful look men always got when she was around. But he barely looked at her other than to give a short nod of acknowledgment.

"Maggie, I need to talk to you," Grace said.

"I'll be right back," Maggie told Jake.

"Take your time, ladies," he said. "I'll go make sure Agent Grant doesn't stage a coup."

"Appreciate it." She shot him a quick, reassuring smile, and he smiled back.

"You got this," he told her before walking back to the mobile unit. Her cheeks heated, and when she looked at Grace, she saw her friend's perfectly shaped eyebrows rise in an unspoken question. Maggie's blush deepened. Why, oh why did her friend have to be an expert in human behavior, of all things?

"Oh, my God," Grace said with a wicked grin. "We'll talk about whatever *that* was later. Over wine, and after this is all over and everyone's safe." She straightened, tugging at the hem of her gray peplum top. "But right now, we've got to talk. I've been going through everything, putting together a profile—and I think we have a problem."

"What kind of problem?" Maggie asked, ushering her into one of the empty SWAT trucks. She sat down on one of the seats, and Grace settled in one across from her, legs neatly crossed, looking troubled. She pulled out a folder from her leather briefcase, handing it to Maggie.

"The profile I put together speaks of a self-sacrificing personality," Grace explained. "His mission is paramount. The lack of any personal touches in his apartment kept getting to me, though. For a guy who is so focused on his brother, you would think he'd keep *something* around to remind him of his mission. But there was nothing; nothing at all. Then when I got a transcript of your call when he listed his demands . . ." Grace leaned over, her delicate lips, painted a bright coral, twisting in concern. "He knows he's not getting out of here, Maggie," she said. "He knows there's never going to be a ride to the airport or five million dollars. He was just spouting off whatever he could think of. He's buying time. And not to form a new plan. He's trying to get up the nerve."

"To do what?" Maggie asked.

"To die. From the beginning, he's never expected to make it through this," Grace said, the worry in her eyes clear now. "He doesn't care about surviving. All he cares about is exposing the men who killed his brother. This is a suicide mission."

Her stomach sank, her hands twisting in her lap. Maggie wasn't surprised that Grace had reached this conclusion. It was something that she had suspected and dreaded. But she had wanted Grace to tell her she was wrong.

In a way, as someone who had lost a sibling, she almost understood Mancuso. Hadn't she spent her life trying to make up for Erica's loss? Wasn't Mancuso essentially doing the same thing for his brother—just in a more harmful way?

"I know you're right," she said quietly.

"Then what are you going to do?" Grace asked. "What's the plan? Because the scenario changes when the unsub's planning suicide by cop. You know that. Do you really think you can pull him back from the edge? You're fantastic, Mags, but I'm not sure anyone's *that* good. This guy's dedicated. He's got tunnel vision."

Maggie didn't know what to say. All of her training and her instincts still told her that the best way to get Kayla and Paul out of there alive was to keep Mancuso talking, building trust with him until an opportunity appeared. She knew he was trying to buy time—but so was she. Mancuso wasn't the kind of person who took pleasure in killing. He had to be pushed into it. If she could just keep from pushing him . . .

There was a knock on the door of the SWAT truck, and Grace got up and opened it.

"Ms. Kincaid?" asked a deep voice.

"She's inside," Grace said.

"I'm coming," Maggie called. She got to her feet.

"Think about what I said." Grace squeezed her arm, stepping back to allow her to get out.

"I will," Maggie said, stepping down and onto the ground, blinking in the bright lights at the figure in front of her.

A tall, lean, dark-haired man stood in the beam of the floodlights, his shadow stretching out menacingly on the ground. He seemed slightly out of place in a t-shirt and jeans, considering the park was swarming with people in tactical gear.

"I'm Maggie Kincaid," Maggie said, holding her hand out. "You are . . . ?"

"Mr. Black," he said with a neutral smile, not taking her hand. She felt like an idiot for extending it, but she quickly realized that was the point.

This was someone who preferred his adversaries off-kilter from the start.

Maggie looked him up and down. She knew he couldn't have gotten past the barriers without a badge. He wasn't FBI, she was sure of that. Homeland Security, maybe? Or had the senator hired another expert to mess with her?

"And what agency do you work for?" Maggie asked.

"That doesn't matter," he said in a level, detached voice.

Maggie frowned. "Yes, it does," she said. "I don't allow people with unknown affiliations on my active crime scenes."

"There are national security issues at stake here, Ms. Kincaid," Mr. Black said. "My job is to protect and eliminate threats. I'm here to observe and watch out for the larger interest."

"Are you in business with SouthPoint Oil?" Maggie asked, her instincts working overtime. This guy was suspicious as hell. What kind of badge did he flash to get through the cordons? It had to be something high up; SWAT wasn't stupid. They weren't going to just let anyone in.

"As I said, it doesn't matter," he replied.

Irritation pricked inside her like a swarm of hornets. She did *not* like this man. Every part of her was screaming not to trust him. "Actually, it does matter," Maggie said. "If your job is to protect a bunch of high-ranking billionaire criminals, our goals aren't the same. So if that's your aim when you talk about 'national security issues . . .'" She used air quotes and was rewarded with his calm mask faltering just slightly. ". . . you might want to step aside. The only things that matter are the hostages. I'm not interested in cover-ups or protecting corrupt men."

"There's no need to get emotional, Ms. Kincaid," Mr. Black said, the bland smile still pasted on his lips.

Maggie's eyes narrowed. "I'm not being *emotional*, Mr. Black," she spat viciously. "I'm doing my job."

"I know that the hostages are the priority. I also know you have a personal connection to Paul Harrison in particular," he continued, and Maggie kept her face impassive as he studied it, searching for a reaction. She wasn't going to give him one. "I'm merely here to help."

His smile, that maddeningly calm, superior smile, widened as he went on. "In fact, there are quite a few people in some very high places who wanted you off the case. I'm sure you understand, after the unfortunate way your last case turned out. They didn't have any faith in your abilities. They said you were washed up. But I stuck up for you. Defended you. Told them to give you a chance. I think you have potential, Ms. Kincaid."

Maggie didn't need Grace's help to know she shouldn't trust this guy.

Mancuso had been telling the truth. His brother's murder was just the tip of the iceberg. There were some very powerful people involved here. The kind who thought murder was a convenient solution to their problems. What if they decided it was more convenient to let Mancuso kill the hostages if it meant killing himself too?

She had more than Mancuso to worry about.

"I don't need my ego stroked, Mr. Black," she said. "And I don't need your kind of assistance, whoever you work for."

"I'm not an enemy, Ms. Kincaid," the man said. "I'm here to help. Think of me as your friend."

Maggie raised an eyebrow. "I trust my friends," she said. "And I already know I shouldn't trust you."

She turned on her heel and stalked off, leaving him behind, hoping it wasn't a mistake.

Hoping he wouldn't be as trigger-happy as she feared.

CHAPTER 50

Sweat dripped down Paul's upper lip, and his muscles tensed at the tickling sensation. He was aware of every part of his body, every movement, every breath as he desperately tried not to move. The weight of the bomb strapped to his chest pressed against him like a ton of bricks, and the zip tie was punishingly tight around his wrists.

The room was dark, but his eyes had adjusted. Cracks of light from the copters flying above flitted through the windows, casting shadows across the room. He could hear Kayla moaning softly in the corner on the couch. Mancuso had dumped her there earlier. Paul had managed to get a good look at her then. She'd been pale as a ghost and drenched in sweat, her blond hair a tangle around her face.

She didn't have much time.

"You okay, Kayla?" he asked into the dark.

"Hurts," she whispered in a cracked voice.

"Just hang on," he told her.

"My mom," she said. "Have you . . . is she all right?"

"Yeah," Paul assured her. "She's fine, sweetie. She's gonna be really glad when she sees you. Just focus on that, okay?"

More sweat trickled down his face. He wanted nothing more than to duck his head, try to wipe off some of the sweat with his sleeve, but he knew better than to move too much. He had buddies on the bomb squad, and he knew there were a million mistakes an amateur like Mancuso could have made in rigging this thing. The thought made him stiffen further in his chair.

Goddammit, don't move, Paul!

"It's gonna be okay, Kayla," he said. He hated giving false hope to the kid, but it was better than telling her the truth of how bad this was. She'd suffered enough. He glanced at her out of the corner of his eye, trying not to turn his head too much. He frowned at her stillness. Had she passed out?

"Keep talking to me," he directed softly, moving his head a fraction to get a better look at the dark lump on the couch. She was curled up tight in a fetal position. Every few seconds, she'd jerk, as if her muscles were in spasm.

He needed to keep her awake. He didn't know much about diabetes, but he knew if she fell unconscious, she might not wake back up. "You ride horses, right?"

"Yeah . . ." Kayla's voice floated, shaky, across the room. "I have a horse. Star."

"That's a great name," Paul said. "I rode when I was a kid. I had this gorgeous palomino. He was stubborn as hell. Knew how to unlock the stall door. You ride Western or English?"

"Both," Kayla said. "My mom wanted me to focus on English, but Dad said it wasn't American enough."

Paul let out a short laugh, the irony not lost on him. The senator was concerned about his daughter's patriotism when it came to saddles, but not his own when it came to screwing over his own government.

"I thought it was silly too," Kayla said.

"What about school?" Paul asked. "Tell me about school. About your favorite class. Who's your best teacher?"

As the girl haltingly began to talk about her history class, Paul tried to relieve the pressure on his shoulders by stretching his head forward a little, trying not to shift too much.

He couldn't believe he was here. He hoped to God the other agents Mancuso attacked were okay. Had Mancuso killed them and stashed their bodies somewhere? They were gone by the time he came to, bound tight with the bomb already strapped to his chest.

He prayed they were safe. He didn't get along with Mike Sutton and likely never would, but the guy had twin daughters. They didn't deserve to be orphaned.

The cabin was small, he reasoned with himself as he prompted Kayla to tell him about lacrosse. There wasn't any blood that he could see. Mancuso probably dumped the agents he didn't want outside. After all, he only had one bomb vest, so he only needed one hostage.

If he got out of this alive, the guys were never going to let him hear the end of it. Letting a unsub get the drop on him was bad enough. Getting rigged with explosives was another. He'd be trying to live this down until his retirement.

If he got to retirement.

He tried to push down the fear, but it was real, and it was there. He'd be stupid not to be scared.

But he had a chance. He had a great chance.

He had Maggie. Maggie and that square-jawed security guy she was apparently sleeping with.

Not my business anymore, he told himself, but the hurt was there, dull and muted beneath his hammering heart.

The door opened, and the shuffling of Mancuso's boots filled the room. Kayla's weak voice silenced immediately, and she whimpered, shifting on the couch, trying to curl up in a tighter ball. Paul's stomach clenched in sympathy. The poor kid. She didn't deserve any of this.

Paul squinted in the darkness as Mancuso walked forward. His body tensed—*don't move too much, dammit*—as Mancuso brushed past him, sitting down on the chair across from him.

Paul looked out of the corner of his eye at Kayla, now that he could see her better, he could see how hard she was trembling. *It's okay*, Paul mouthed at her, before turning his attention back on Mancuso.

Mancuso straddled the chair, setting a battered LED lantern on the ground. A soft glow filled the room, lighting his face. He leaned forward. "Time to start talking, Harrison," Mancuso said. "Let's discuss your ex."

Paul swallowed, his throat unbearably dry. "Which one?"

Mancuso rolled his eyes. "Let's stop playing games, okay? If you're honest, things will go faster. And maybe you'll get out of this alive. Maggie Kincaid. I know you two were gonna get hitched."

"How do you know that?" Paul asked. It wasn't common knowledge. Sure, family and close friends had known, but Maggie had broken it off before they'd even started looking at venues. He'd spent a week at the bottom of a tequila bottle until a series of bank robberies had called him back into work. It had forced him to pull it together and stop mourning the loss of the life he'd pictured with her.

"It's on the Internet," Mancuso said.

"No, it's not," Paul said. "We're FBI. We don't broadcast stuff online."

"It doesn't matter how I know," Mancuso snapped, his face twisted in frustration. "I know. So now you're going to tell me about her, or I'll kill you."

Kayla whimpered behind them.

"It's okay, Kayla," Paul assured her. "Close your eyes, honey. Block it out. Think about Star."

"Stop talking to her!" Mancuso demanded, grabbing Paul's chin and forcing his gaze to his.

Paul gritted his teeth as Mancuso's fingers dug into his jaw. It was hard to resist the automatic urge to jerk away. *Don't fucking move! Who knows how unstable this bomb is?*

"What do you want to know?" he asked, trying to avoid revealing anything.

Mancuso released him, settling back in his chair. "She good at her job?"

"She's the best," Paul said. "She came out of Quantico with more know-how and skill than anyone the Bureau had seen in years."

"She wants to send in a doctor," Mancuso said, suspicion creeping into his voice. "If I let her do that, is she gonna send in some burly guy with a gun hidden in his lab coat?"

"No," Paul said firmly. A doctor! Thank God. Kayla needed one. He was worried as hell about her. She clearly needed insulin or sugar or *something*. Mancuso was playing fast and loose with her life, and nothing pissed Paul off more. He hated that he was frozen, stuck in one spot, unable to help, unable to attack. If he didn't have this shit strapped to his chest, he would've taken Mancuso down by now. But he couldn't risk it. Not with Kayla in the room. He had to wait for Maggie to execute her plan and save him. God, he hated being reduced to a victim who needed saving. But at least it was Maggie who was doing the saving. He wouldn't want anyone else.

"Maggie's not stupid," Paul said. "And more importantly, she knows *you're* not."

Mancuso straightened a little at the blunt compliment.

"Maggie knows you'd see through it if she tried to double-cross you," Paul continued. He figured this guy needed a little ego-stroking—his nerves were clearly getting to him. He'd rather have a confident unsub than a nervous one. Confident unsubs were bold, but they made mistakes. Nervous ones just panicked, succumbing to their fight-or-flight instinct. And if Mancuso tried to fight or tried to run, it wasn't going to be pretty.

"Maggie's not gonna pull anything on you, Mancuso. She'll play it straight. She won't gamble Kayla's life on something so reckless. You can trust her."

Mancuso looked at him closely in the muted light, and Paul was uncomfortably aware of the knowing expression on his face. The understanding. Mancuso was good at reading people—it was the only way he could've gotten so far in Washington. Had Paul revealed too much? Had he laid it on too thick? Had he given Mancuso some sort of ammo?

Did it matter, considering the explosives wrapped around him?

"You really love that blonde pain in the ass, don't you?" Mancuso asked.

Paul didn't say anything, but he could feel angry heat rising up his neck to his face. He squared his jaw, trying to show no emotion. Trying not to show how deep that blow went. How deep a truth that was.

"How sad for you," Mancuso said pityingly. "She obviously doesn't feel the same way." He leaned forward, his elbows on his knees, his eyes lighting with curiosity. "Now, how about you tell me about Sherwood Hills?"

CHAPTER 51

Maggie?"

She looked up. Frank was standing in the door of the mobile unit, his bulldog face solemn. "Doctor's here."

"I'll be right there," she said, closing out of the transcript from her last call with Mancuso. She'd been pretending to go over it, but really, she'd just been staring at his final words, obsessing.

She hurried outside, where a balding older man was standing with Agent Collins and Jake. The doctor fidgeted as she approached, looking nervous. "Dr. Aaron James, ma'am," he said, holding out his hand. She shook it.

"I'm Maggie Kincaid. I'm in charge," she said. "Has Frank filled you in on the situation?"

"You've got a diabetic teen in there. She's been without insulin for how long? What's her usual protocol?"

"She uses up to a unit a day, administered over three or four doses," Maggie explained. "Her mom said she was a good candidate for an insulin pump, but Kayla didn't want it because she was worried people would stare. She's an athlete, so there were locker room concerns. You know how teenage girls are. We believe the unsub—the kidnapper—was originally administering insulin, but we have no way to know for sure. He claims to have destroyed her supply, if he did and was giving it to her before that, it's been at least half a day, maybe more, since her last dose."

He nodded. "That's not good," he said. "Especially if she's dehydrated and under stress. Do you know if he's been feeding her?"

"I don't think so," Maggie said. "The unsub's been busy and . . . not happy with how things are turning out. He's withholding medication because he thinks it'll get him what he wants faster."

"Was she still conscious when you last made contact?" Dr. James asked.

"I can't confirm," Maggie said. "The unsub said she was, but at this point . . ."

"He might be lying," finished the doctor. "I understand. What am I allowed to bring in?"

"Nothing," Maggie said.

"Not even medical equipment? The girl's going to need insulin and fluids immediately. The risk of diabetic coma is high."

"I know," Maggie said. "But this guy's on edge. You reach for a syringe in your pocket and you might end up with a bullet in your head."

"Then what do you want me to do?" Dr. James asked. "If I can't give her medication, there's not a lot I can do for her."

"I need you to examine her and tell me how much time I have to get her out of there before there's any permanent damage," Maggie said. "If you tell me five minutes, I will make my move, but I risk Agent Harrison dying in any crossfire. If you tell me five hours, I have more time to talk Mancuso out of this and put together a strategic plan that gets everyone out safe and sound."

"Understood," Dr. James said, nodding. "I'll do what I can."

"While you're in the cabin, try to get a sense of the layout," Agent Collins said. "We haven't been able to pull accurate blueprints of the building. Take note of any weapons visible, the bomb trigger—"

"Collins," Maggie said firmly. His mouth snapped shut. The doctor looked between the two of them, clearly confused. "Don't worry about the layout or getting a feel for the situation," Maggie said. "That's not your job. Your job is the girl. Go in. Don't make any sudden movements. Make sure your hands are always visible. If you're going to reach into your pockets, inform the unsub before you do. Examine the girl. Estimate a time frame—how long she has before she's in real medical trouble. Once you know, you get out of there. No heroics. No panicking. You got it?"

Dr. James smiled reassuringly at her. "I've been in a few of these situations," he said. "I know the drill."

"Okay," Maggie said. "Then I'm going to make the call. We'll be sending you in right after."

She pulled out her cell and dialed Mancuso's number. After two rings, he picked up.

"Roger, it's Maggie," she said in a clear voice, praying he hadn't changed his mind about letting the doctor in. "I have the doctor here, like we discussed. Can I send him in to check on Kayla?"

"What about the power?" Mancuso asked. "You promised to turn it back on."

"You're right," Maggie said. She snapped her fingers at one of the techs, mouthing *Turn on the power* to them. They went running.

"They're doing it right now," Maggie promised. She wanted desperately to ask him about how he'd thrown Erica's last words at her. But she knew she couldn't. She needed to be patient. This wasn't the time or place.

But she'd make sure to create a time and a place. And soon. She was going to get answers if it was the last thing she ever did.

A few seconds passed, and the lights inside the cabin blinked on.

"There we go," Maggie said into the phone. "If you turn on the TV, you'll be able to see what they're saying about the senator on CNN."

She heard shuffling and then the muted sound of a voice on the TV. Mancuso sucked in a ragged breath as the anchor talked about Senator Thebes and the rumors of corruption. Maggie smiled to herself. Validation would make Mancuso trust her more. This was exactly what she needed.

"Can I send in Dr. James now?" she asked after giving him another moment to soak in this victory. She needed him feeling good to get the doctor in and out safely.

"Yes," Mancuso said. "He needs to be alone and unarmed. I have a gun and I'll shoot any of your SWAT team who takes a step toward this cabin, you understand?"

"I understand, Roger. No funny business. Just the doctor checking on Kayla. I promise. I'm walking with him right now." Maggie motioned for the doctor to follow and they moved through the convoy of SWAT trucks until they were in front of the cabin, a good thirty feet away from the door. She could see a flutter of a curtain in one of the cabin windows, and she knew Mancuso was watching them.

"I see you," Mancuso said. "Send him in."

He hung up.

"Go ahead, doc," Maggie said. "Just a straight line to the door. In and out. Calm and steady and slow, like we talked about."

Dr. James began to make his way toward the front door, and Maggie watched him, trying not to wring her hands. Mancuso was watching, she was sure. She needed to appear in control and confident. If she didn't believe in herself, he'd never believe in her ability to get him what he wanted.

"Should we get the press away?" Jake asked, nodding to the throng of journalists in the distance who were watching with rapt attention.

Maggie shook her head. "If there's shooting, they're out of the line of fire," she said. "Bomb squad said they'll be out of the blast radius if everything goes to hell. They're annoying, but they keep everyone playing by the rules," she said. "If Mancuso is right about how high up this goes, those journalists might be the only thing preventing someone from faking a gas explosion and blowing us all up."

Jake snorted in disgust. "You're probably right," he said. He glanced away from Maggie, toward the cabin, freezing. "Shit."

Maggie whirled, her eyes widening in horror. "What is he doing?"

The doctor wasn't making a beeline for the front door of the cabin. He was veering to the right, approaching the cabin from an angle, moving in a low, guarded crouch.

Moving like a goddamn soldier.

Oh, God. No. No. No. *No!*

Panic rose inside Maggie almost as fast as the dread. She was stuck to the spot, unable to shout, to move, to do *anything*, as she realized she'd been double-crossed. Ice flooded her veins as she watched, sure any moment the world would erupt in a bomb blast, shedding fire and debris everywhere.

The doctor was clearly Special Ops. As he reached the door, he pulled a gun from his waistband. Even this far away, Maggie could see the silencer on it.

"Shit, shit, shit," Jake muttered. Maggie couldn't tear her eyes away from the disaster unfolding in front of her, but she knew his face carried the same horrified expression as hers.

They were screwed.

She wanted to scream. She wanted to run for the door and knock the good "doctor" to the ground. She needed to stop this. But she knew it was too late. At this point, moving in would be even more dangerous.

Dammit! She had *done* it. She'd established a connection, she'd made him trust her! She was going to get everyone out safe and sound. And now . . . and now . . .

She was helpless. No safety. No trust. No control.

Paul and Kayla were as good as dead.

She needed to make sure her team was safe. The bomb—oh, God. They needed to pull all the agents back—fast.

"Recall all the teams. Get everyone back," she said to Jake. "Out of the range of the bomb blast. Do it quietly and *fast*."

"On it," Jake said, disappearing between two SWAT trucks.

Maggie stayed where she was. It was like watching a car accident in slow motion, knowing there's nothing you can do. The doctor knocked, and when there was no answer, he tried the doorknob.

It was unlocked. He stepped inside.

The air felt heavy around her, suffocating and dark. It made her want to run. To hide. But she couldn't. She was locked to her spot, staring, waiting for disaster.

For a long, tense minute, Maggie just breathed. Breathed and prayed. There was nothing else to do in that moment that seemed to stretch out forever. And then . . .

Gunfire. Muted, but to her trained ears, evident. Several shots, fired in quick succession.

Behind her, she could hear Jake corralling people away from the area, to safety, just in case the bomb went off. But her focus was on the cabin. On the silence settling like a storm cloud over the cabin in the echo of gunshots.

She knew she should run for cover behind the SWAT trucks in case Mancuso activated the dead man's trigger. But she couldn't. Not without knowing. Not without trying *something* to help Kayla and Paul.

What had happened? Had the doctor botched it? The cabin was still standing. That meant Mancuso was still alive, holding the bomb trigger, or. . . .

Maggie's phone rang. She jumped at the sound, nearly dropping it. She tried to calm her shaking hands as she unlocked it and answered.

"Hello?"

"You lied to me, you bitch!" Mancuso said, his voice shaking with anger. "You said he was a real doctor!"

"Wait—" Maggie begged, desperation rising, choking her voice, making tears prick at the corner of her eyes as she watched all the control, all the leverage she had swirl down the drain.

"No!" Mancuso shouted. "I'm going to kill your ex. Maybe that'll make you listen."

"Please, Roger," Maggie said, fear spreading inside her as her legs nearly buckled. She locked her knees, determined to stay upright. "I didn't do this. I got screwed over. I promise you. I did not know. I would never have done this. It's stupid. It's an insult to your intelligence. I know how smart you are. They didn't, clearly. Look at how you proved them wrong. I was playing this straight, I promise. I had nothing to do with this."

She was losing control, her rapid-fire excuses coming out of her mouth in a flood, her voice rising, filled with fear. She tried to breathe, tried to grasp the thin threads of control she had left, but Kayla was inside there. Paul was inside there. Mancuso had thrown Erica's words at her like weapons, designed to weaken her, make her question herself.

This was personal.

"Too bad," Mancuso said. "You got screwed over, I got screwed over. You're a liar like the rest of them, Maggie. If there's not a news team in here, broadcasting live, in one hour, I'll kill Paul and Kayla—I'll blow this cabin to bits on national TV."

CHAPTER 52

Anger didn't even come close to describing what Maggie felt right now. She stalked toward the mobile unit, her legs still shaking. People scattered when they caught the rage in her face. She burst through the door, surveying the agents inside.

"Who the hell sent a shooter into my hostage negotiation?" she demanded.

"That would be me," said a clipped, clear voice. Mr. Black stood up in the back of the unit, his face still that smooth mask of indifference.

Now that she had a clear target, Maggie rounded on him. Who the hell did he think he was?

"How dare you . . ." Maggie stalked toward him, her shoes making angry clicks against the floor. So much fury radiated off her that she was surprised he didn't recoil from the heat. "Are you a complete idiot?" she snarled, right in his face. "You sent an active shooter into a building with one of our agents inside with a *bomb* strapped to his chest. Who trained you, that you would do something so stupid?"

Her voice rose steadily, and the agents in the unit were shifting uncomfortably, unsure of their place. "Mancuso will never trust me again," Maggie went on. "You understand that, right? You've destroyed any chance of this not ending in a bloody mess. What if Mancuso released the trigger? Those SWAT members around the perimeter would've been in the blast radius! Paul and Kayla would have been blown to bits! And those journalists hanging around wouldn't just get the story of a lifetime, they would have been hit with debris! What the hell is wrong with you?"

"I made a judgment call," Mr. Black said coolly.

"It's not your call to make!" Maggie shouted. Everyone around them was staring, mouths agape.

"Well, it's done," the man said in an almost offhand manner. "I will accept responsibility."

"Really," Maggie scoffed, jerking her thumb to the side, where the news was playing on a TV. "That's rich, because it's *my* face on the news right now."

Mr. Black looked over at the screen, and sure enough, there was a photo of Maggie, her Academy portrait, superimposed over footage of the fake doctor approaching the cabin.

Mr. Black shrugged. "I didn't mean accepting responsibility publicly. My involvement in this situation is classified."

"Get out," Maggie demanded, gesturing at the agents around her. "Now!" she snapped, when they were slow to move. She glared at Mr. Black. "Mr. Black and I need to have a *classified discussion*."

The agents filed out, one by one, and Maggie slammed the door shut behind them, turning back to Mr. Black.

"You're going to talk," she said. "And tell me what the hell is going on."

"Or what?" he asked, an eyebrow quirked, as if he was amused.

Maggie pulled her phone out and snapped a picture of him before he could react. "Or I take this to the media. Whatever agency you work for, I'm pretty sure your higher-ups wouldn't be too pleased with your face on the news in connection with this."

Mr. Black's calm, controlled expression faltered, just for a moment. Triumph burst through Maggie. This guy didn't want his face anywhere. He was the kind who operated in the shadows. Whose job relied on anonymity. He was calm and bland and nondescript. He had a face that wouldn't be remembered. He was a man who could blend in so well he'd never be found.

He was more than dangerous—he was skilled.

And he had motives that didn't line up with hers.

"What the hell is in those SouthPoint papers?" Maggie asked. "Who are you protecting? What's the real reason Mancuso's willing to kill himself and everyone else?"

Mr. Black reached out with blinding speed, grabbing her wrist and twisting painfully. Maggie cried out, as her bones ground against each other. The phone dropped out of her hand into his waiting palm. She tried to snatch for it, but he held it over her head with a mocking smile, like a schoolyard bully. She glared at him while he erased the picture she'd taken.

"Let me make one thing perfectly clear, Ms. Kincaid," Mr. Black said, his voice going dark, almost deadly. A shiver ran down Maggie's spine. Her wrist throbbed dully. She wasn't egotistical enough to think she could take him in a fistfight. He was too strong. And he was probably the type who would hit a woman and enjoy it.

"You don't need to know what is in those papers," Black said. "It's not your job to even wonder about it. You are here to secure the release of the two hostages, not to investigate an alleged murder in the Middle East. So do your job. And don't do anything else. Or you might find yourself in the kind of trouble Joe Mancuso got into."

Maggie drew herself up, resisting the urge to rub at her aching wrist. She couldn't let him see he'd hurt her. She wasn't going to give him the pleasure.

"You think I haven't dealt with invasive government agencies before?" she asked. "I know your type, Black. You don't value human life—you value secrets. Using them. Keeping them."

"Your point being?" the man asked, looking bored.

"It's not a point," Maggie said. "It's a warning. Because as far as you're willing to go to protect powerful men's secrets? I'm willing to go ten times farther to save that girl.

You think you can get me in line? You've obviously never met a woman on a mission before."

She stalked out of the mobile unit, leaving him behind in the wake of her anger. She wasn't going to be intimidated by a man who thought he knew better than she did. She wasn't going to fail Kayla. Even if it meant destroying every man Mr. Black kept secrets for.

It was starting to get cold outside, mist rising from the nearby river. Maggie shivered, pulling her jacket closer around her, searching for Jake. He was standing in a group of agents, deep in conversation. She hurried over and tapped him on the shoulder. "Can we talk?"

He nodded, following her a distance from the trucks and crowds of people. The smell of pine hung rich in the air; she could hear the rush of water, punctuated by the chirp of crickets. It was pretty out here, she thought idly, trying to distract herself from the nightmare spiraling out of control. What could she do, what kind of progress could she make if she had Mr. Black subverting every decision she made? What was going to happen to Kayla without any medical attention?

Maggie couldn't see an escape route. That's what troubled her the most.

She'd always been able to see a way out. The last time she felt like this . . .

The last time she felt like this, she was twelve and tied in a closet, begging her sister to let her stay.

"What happened?" Jake asked. "You were pretty pissed at Black."

"Aren't you?" she asked, her voice cracking. The stress was getting to her. The lack of sleep, the adrenaline. She couldn't remember the last time she ate or even drank anything but coffee. God, what she wouldn't do for a hot bath and a steak.

"Yeah," he said. "He screwed up. Majorly."

"Does it feel . . . does it feel like we're even working with the good guys right now?" Maggie asked. She ran a hand through her hair, her fingers snarling in the curls. She probably looked terrible. She should splash some water on her face or something.

Jake sighed. "It doesn't seem like there are any good guys—just crooks and victims."

"I feel like I can't trust anyone," Maggie confessed. Who did she have? Had Frank known Black was pulling this? Or had Black gone over even his head? She hated to think her mentor might have let this pass, but she couldn't think straight anymore. She was surrounded by men who didn't trust her and she didn't really trust them. Who was on Black's side? Who was on hers?

"Hey," Jake said softly. He reached out and grasped her hand, tugging her forward. Her free hand braced on his broad chest as she tilted up, her lips meeting his.

Their fingers entwined as their kiss deepened. She sighed, surrendering completely. She wanted nothing more than to draw the kiss out, to lose herself in him, in the heat of his skin and the power in his touch. But she knew they couldn't linger.

When they pulled apart, Jake brushed a straw-colored curl off her forehead. "You can trust me," he said.

"I know," she said, because it was true. It was real. It was maybe the truest thing she'd ever known. She looked over her shoulder, making sure no one was listening to them. "I need something," she said.

"Name it."

Relief blossomed inside her. Jake would have her back. He'd do what needed to be done, and she wouldn't have to worry about him. He could more than take care of himself—and her.

"I want you to go back into investigation mode," she said. "You got me Mancuso's real identity. I need you to do the same for Black. I need to know who he is. Who he works for. It has to be someone powerful, since he just strolled onto our crime scene and took charge. I need to know everything that these people are trying to protect. How deep it goes. How high up it goes. Whoever Black works for is dangerous. They clearly aren't interested in anyone else's well-being, they just want to keep their own secrets."

"I'll dig up the dirt," Jake promised.

He leaned over and kissed her again. She sank into him, not caring that people might see them, not caring that it wasn't the time or the place. All that mattered was his belief in her, his willingness to defy, to protect, to understand. His lips lingered against hers like he was reluctant to pull away, and she knew the feeling all too well.

But chaos was happening all around them. Danger loomed, and thc clock was ticking down.

It was only a matter of time before Mancuso snapped.

And Maggie had to make sure Kayla and Paul were out of that cabin before that happened.

CHAPTER 53

Jake was a man on a mission. After making sure Maggie was safely back inside the mobile unit, he slipped through the protective barrier formed by the SWAT trucks toward the area where the SUVs and other vehicles were haphazardly parked.

The moon was high in the cloudless sky, the stars shining brightly. It was a beautiful night, but the whirring of the copters in the sky and the blinding burn of the floodlights swinging over the cabin marred the pretty picture.

Jake strolled casually over to the clearing where they'd put the vehicles, his hands in his pockets. He nodded to a few police officers he passed, slowing down as he approached the officer standing in front of the cars.

"Kincaid needs some papers from her car," he said to the officer.

"She got you playing errand boy?" the officer asked.

Jake had to stop himself from rolling his eyes. "Women," he said with a shrug.

The officer laughed. "She seems like a handful," he said. "Go ahead. Wouldn't want to get you in trouble with the little lady." Jake walked past him, thinking how a dated, backward ass like that could never even spark an interest in a strong, independent woman like Maggie Kincaid. He'd never understood men who were threatened by women who matched them. Who challenged them. Where was the fun in someone you could run circles around?

Ten minutes arguing with Maggie was hotter than ten hours in bed with anyone else. She made him rise to the challenge in the best way. Revved him up, got him going, got him thinking. He liked that about her.

Jake strolled down the row of cars, checking over his shoulder to make sure the officer wasn't watching. He'd already turned his back, not paying attention to anything Jake was doing.

Perfect.

He'd watched Black park, because noticing that type of thing—that type of person—was part of his job. Black's sleek gray SUV was top of the line, but he hadn't bothered to lock it—assuming it was safe behind the cordons, guarded by the cops. Jake sneered at the guy's hubris. What an egotistical idiot. He obviously thought he was untouchable. If Black wasn't already on his shit list for pissing off Maggie and pulling the stunt with the fake doctor, his carelessness would've earned him a spot.

No matter what, you should stay sharp. He'd learned that the hard way in the Middle East. Looked like he'd be teaching Black that lesson tonight, Jake thought with a smile. Anything that screwed that guy over or got him in trouble was fine by Jake. Black was an ass. A dangerous one.

Jake ducked into the front seat, shutting the door softly behind him. The plush leather was still heated from the seat warmer, and the dashboard was spotless. Jake ran a finger along it—not even a speck of dust.

Figures that Black would be a neat freak, Jake thought. He didn't think the man had a military past—he didn't carry himself the right way. Whatever agency he was with, he'd clearly been stripped of all defining characteristics. He was someone who could blend into a crowd, an unassuming figure until you were too close to run. He'd unlearned everything he'd been taught in order to become something anonymous and secretive.

Jake knew how it went. He'd had friends go into intelligence. It was a hard life, full of danger and darkness and a lot of lies. You wouldn't be able to pay him enough to live a double, sometimes triple life. He liked things black-and-white—and the spy game was all about the gray.

Jake ran his hands under the dashboard and the seats, searching for bugs or hidden electronics, but the SUV was clean. So he reached over and opened the glove compartment, coming up with a wallet and nothing else.

"No registration or insurance, naturally," Jake muttered to himself.

The brown leather was well worn, and when Jake flipped it open, he found only a stack of clean, crisp hundred dollar bills. No credit cards, no driver's license. Not even a badge.

Okay, then. Maybe not as careless as he originally thought. No matter. Jake had other ways of finding out who the hell this guy was.

Was the money for a bribe? He thumbed through it, noticing the serial numbers were sequential, filing that away in his mind, just in case it turned out to be important.

Jake checked out the back of the SUV, but it was pristine. Crawling onto the back seat, he pulled up the flap that hid the spare tire, running his fingers underneath.

Clean again.

He returned to the front, nearly hitting his head on the ceiling—crawling around in an SUV wasn't exactly a graceful exercise. Using the dim light from the screen on his phone—the flashlight might call attention from Officer Sexist over there—Jake found the VIN where the dashboard met the windshield.

Slouching in the front seat, he dialed Peggy's number.

"Did you get her out yet?" Peggy asked instead of saying hello like a normal person.

"Working on it," Jake said. "Thanks for tipping off CNN."

"No problem," Peggy said. "Mark told me to say hi, and thanks for the tip. Dad call you yet?"

Jake winced, thinking of how pissed General Hoffman was going to be. This entire situation was messy—a far cry from the clean operations he usually ran. He probably would ream Jake out for throwing the senator under the bus—but Jake would convince him it was the only way. Once Kayla was safe and the bomb was deactivated, the general would soften and see the logic behind Jake's choices.

"Not yet," he said. "I need you to run a VIN for me," he said.

"Who are we going after now?" Peggy asked.

"New player showed up," Jake explained. "Calls himself Mr. Black. He's throwing himself around like he owns the place."

"Uh-oh," Peggy said. "Okay, I'm in the DMV databases. What's the number?"

Jake gave it to her, the tapping sound of her keys increasing as her fingers flew across them. "Huh," she said, sounding surprised.

"What?" Jake asked.

"All it says is 'Government Issued,'" Peggy explained. "No specifics. That means it's under some sort of protection. I could probably hack a few firewalls—"

"No need," Jake said. "I have a pretty good idea what kind of person requires that kind of protection."

"This isn't good, is it boss?" Peggy asked.

"No," Jake said grimly. "Listen, I gotta go. If the general wants me, he can call. But I'm bringing the girl in safe—no matter what Mr. Black does. You tell the general that."

"Why do I feel like you're going to be in *so* much trouble when you get back?" Peggy asked.

Jake smiled grimly. "Probably because I am," he said, before hanging up.

Black was making this hard on him, but he still had options. He already knew that Black had to be working for some sort of government agency—the question was which one. He had his suspicions, but he needed some sort of confirmation before he took the full leap down the rabbit hole. He looked down at his phone, an idea forming.

Black's phone was likely connected to the sound system through Bluetooth. If he could get the car started, he might be able to access the phone without Black realizing it.

Peering out of the window, he watched as Officer Sexist moved toward the north end of the clearing. Good, he still wasn't paying attention. If Jake was patrolling, he'd be wondering why the guy he let through hadn't returned with the papers he was supposed to be retrieving.

Sometimes people's incompetence worked in his favor.

He had time.

Jake pulled his knife out of his boot, using it as leverage to yank out the paneling under the steering wheel, exposing the ignition wires. He carefully stripped two of their protective coating, exposing the live wires underneath. He twisted them together, and the engine purred to life.

He grinned, straightening. He turned on the radio and waited for the system to boot up. A long minute stretched out as the screen blinked, trying to connect with Black's phone. Just when Jake was about to give up hope, there it was. The signal was weak, but it might be enough.

Using the radio dials, he keyed through Black's recent calls, landing on the last incoming number. He dialed it into his own phone and pressed *Call.*

His body tense with anticipation, he waited as it rang. Once. Twice.

Would they pick up? Or was this just a crapshoot and he would have to return to Maggie empty-handed?

The receiver clicked, and a woman's voice answered. "Director Hedley's office. How may I help you?"

Jake hung up immediately, without saying a word. With that one sentence, he'd learned all he needed to know.

Shit.

This was bad. This was really bad. He needed to get out of this SUV. He needed to get to Maggie.

Everyone who worked for anyone important in DC knew Hedley's name.

Timothy Hedley was the director of the CIA.

Jake had assumed Black had been working Homeland Security. Maybe the NSA.

But the CIA?

Christ. If the Agency was violating its legal mandate to work only outside of the U.S., this must go all the way to the top. That meant the director himself might be corrupt.

Who could they turn to for help? There was no one to trust. Anyone could be involved. Anyone could be crushed underneath the CIA's heel.

He needed to tell Maggie. Now.

Jake turned, reaching for the door. But before he could touch the handle, it was yanked open. With no time to react, his hand on his phone instead of his knife, Jake lunged forward, but the twin prongs of a Taser caught him in the chest. He saw sparks, and then his vision went black.

CHAPTER 54

Maggie leaned over the sink in the tiny bathroom of the mobile unit. The entire mobile unit was outfitted in sterile white and shiny chrome. It made her feel like she was in a hospital, except there was no noise. Frank had cleared everyone out of the unit, leaving her alone.

The silence was a blessing and a curse. A respite from the arguments and accusations, but an opportunity for the memories to creep in.

She couldn't shake the uneasy, sick feeling settling in her chest. She was certain that Mancuso's parroting Erica's words was no coincidence. It was worse than a bullet to her chest. More damaging. Because, at this crucial moment, her attention had been split . . . her focus scattered.

Erica . . .

No! Her fingers tightened around the edge of the sink. She stared at herself in the mirror. Kayla. She had to concentrate on Kayla and Paul. On how to get around the mysterious Mr. Black and his disastrous interference.

God, Paul. Guilt twisted through her like a tightened noose. She'd broken his heart and now his life depended on her. She had to save him. She had loved him—it wasn't the right kind of love, not for the forever he wanted, and it had taken her too long to realize that. She'd always regret that so much, saying yes, even though she had meant it at the time. She had truly thought it was right for both of them. It had seemed right—they understood each other's work, their mutual passion for the law, for protecting people. But they came at that passion in such different ways—for Paul it was a way to do good.

For Maggie, it was a way to drive out the bad.

Now, with years between them, she could see she should never have agreed to marry him. Not when she couldn't bear to show her real self.

Who was that, really? She'd been a sister, and now she wasn't. She'd been a fiancée, and then she ran. She'd been an FBI agent, and she threw it all away.

She wished she had never agreed to go with Frank that morning. The second she saw him, she should have just turned around and walked straight to her car. Then she wouldn't be here on the edge of losing everything. Again.

Part of her wished she'd run for the fake doctor, tried to tackle him, stop him, heedless of the danger. Had Mancuso killed him or just wounded him? If he'd killed him . . . she worried about what that meant for his state of mind. He was already on the edge, ready to snap. If he'd taken a life . . .

He must have thought of it. He was obsessive. He'd probably considered all the outcomes, considered each carefully, deemed them worth the risk.

But when it came to killing, thinking was different than doing. It changed you for the worse. Some people were consumed by the horror. Others found a taste for it.

That's what she feared the most, if Mancuso had killed. If he'd already taken a life in his mission to avenge his brother, then taking another might be easier now he knew he could actually pull the trigger. Some people couldn't. They didn't have it in them.

But Mancuso might be capable of it. Was he a good enough shot to take down Mr. Black's agent? Had he just been lucky? Or was he a better marksman than she'd originally assumed?

What would she do if he killed Kayla? How could she face Mrs. Thebes?

Frank had been the one to inform the parents after Sherwood Hills. She had already turned in her badge, unable to face it.

She'd been a coward.

She wouldn't hide this time, no matter what happened.

Her skin felt stretched too tight and hot, so she turned on the faucet, letting the water flow over her hands before she bent down to splash water on her face. The cold shock of it cleared her head for a blissful moment.

It happened fast: Just as she was beginning to straighten, water dripping down her chin, a hand covered her face, pushing a cloth against her nose and mouth.

Maggie's entire body seized up as a strong arm wrapped around her waist when she tried to rear back. Panic coursed through her before her training kicked in. She sucked in a breath, the sickly sweet smell of the chemical-soaked cloth filling her senses. She kicked uselessly. Her head spun as she tried hard not to breathe. She had to fight back. She gritted her teeth, planting her feet and tensing her neck. She jerked her head back *hard*. There was a muffled sound of pain as her skull hit her attacker's face, but his hands remained punishingly tight around her. She kicked out desperately, sputtering for breath. Blackness began to seep along the edges of her vision.

She needed . . . she needed . . .

Her attacker's hands fell away as he crumpled and dropped to the floor behind her. Maggie coughed and gasped for untainted air. Her throat felt raw and abused as she turned to lean against the wall. She stared down at her now-unconscious attacker, a burly man with a shaved head and a five-o'clock shadow.

Jake stood above him, his fist still raised. "Sorry I'm late," he said, his casual tone belied by the worry shining in his green eyes.

Maggie stared at him, mouth burning from the chemical-soaked rag. "What the hell just happened?" she asked hoarsely. Her question died in another sputter of coughing, tears streaming down her face as she fought for air.

"You all right?" he asked.

She nodded, wiping away the moisture staining her cheeks. "Yeah," she said. "I just . . . I didn't see him. I didn't even *hear* him."

Pulling a zip tie out of his back pocket, Jake secured the man's hands behind his back and then looked up at her. "What do you want to bet that our new friend Mr. Black knows this guy?"

In a second, Maggie's fear and panic morphed into hot and blinding anger. Black. How dare he? He'd sent someone to attack her on her own *crime scene*?

Before Jake could stop her, she stepped over the unconscious man and stormed out of the mobile unit, heading toward the command tent that SWAT had set up. The wind had picked up, and it sent her hair flying. She pushed it impatiently out of her face, wincing as she licked her lips. They felt cracked, almost burned, from whatever the hell that rag was soaked in. Her throat was dry and raw from the coughing, and her lungs ached as if they'd shriveled up.

Driven by the furious anger inside her chest, she marched toward the tent, branches and leaves snapping beneath her feet.

Frank stood under the flapping canopy, talking to one of the techs. He caught sight of her, at the wild spray of her curls, the tear tracks down her face, the redness around her lips. His mouth tilted in concern. "Maggie, are you okay?"

But Maggie marched right past him, ducking underneath the command tent door flap and making her way through the agents milling about. She had eyes for only one person, and he was standing over a table in the middle of the tent, SWAT members surrounding him like he was their god.

"Black!" Maggie shouted.

His head shot up, his steely eyes sparking for a moment before his normal, disinterested expression settled in them.

"Surprised to see me?" Maggie sneered.

"Can you give us some space?" Black asked the SWAT agents. They scattered like obedient schoolboys, refusing to meet her eyes. Maggie glared at them, disgusted at the way they were acting. What the hell was wrong with everyone? Couldn't they see what a danger this man was to the case? He'd throw Paul's life away in a second if he thought he could get his hands on Mancuso. They should realize that he only had his own interests in mind, not the hostages'.

"Why would I be surprised to see you?" he asked. "You can't seem to stay away."

"One of your cronies just attacked me in the mobile unit," Maggie said. "Care to tell me why you felt the need to chloroform me?"

"My cronies?" Mr. Black asked, frowning. "Whatever gave you the idea that I'd send someone to hurt you?" He looked her up and down, and a smile spread across his face. A horrible, menacing, shark-like smile that showed his true nature. A chill ran down Maggie's spine. "Doesn't look like they did a very thorough job. *My* men are thorough."

The not-so-subtle threat hung between them like smoke. Maggie's fists clenched. She felt a sharp sting near the corner of her mouth. When she licked her lips, she tasted blood.

"Not as thorough as Jake, it seems," Maggie said.

"Mr. O'Connor does seem like the heroic type," Mr. Black said. "Following you around like a lapdog, I see." He looked meaningfully over her shoulder, and she didn't have to turn to know Jake was there, near the edge of the tent, ready to help her if needed.

"You've been looking into things you're not supposed to, Ms. Kincaid." Mr. Black moved away from the table and stalked toward her as if she were prey. "I warned you, but you didn't listen. You've given me no choice."

He pointed at Jake behind her and looked at the circle of agents who were milling around nervously, pretending not to listen. "Gentlemen, please take Mr. O'Connor into custody. He broke into my car, and I'd like to make sure he doesn't get into any more trouble."

Agent Collins moved forward tentatively, a pair of handcuffs dangling from his hand. Maggie glared at him. "Collins, you do not work for Black—you work for me."

"I'm sorry, ma'am," Collins said. "We've got orders from the director himself."

Maggie's eyes widened, horrified at the implication. He hadn't—he *couldn't* . . .

"Ms. Kincaid," Mr. Black said, brushing an imaginary speck off his shirt. "You're fired. I've been given leave by the FBI director to take over this case. Special Agent Edenhurst has also been relieved of his duties—and reprimanded for bringing in a former agent who clearly still suffers from PTSD. Really, Frank," he scoffed. "I don't know *what* you were thinking. I know you have a fondness for her going all the way back to Quantico, but she never struck me as anything special."

Maggie whirled around, looking at Frank, his wrinkled face somber and regretful. He gave her a quelling look, telling her all she needed to know. He was powerless.

She was powerless.

She watched in horror as Agent Collins slipped the cuffs on Jake's wrists. Jake tensed, and for a moment she worried he'd fight Collins off. In a fair fight, Jake would win, but he couldn't take *all* of them on. She had no idea what Black was capable of. He clearly had no regard for human life. He'd already sent someone to attack her under the noses of dozens of FBI agents. There was clearly no line he wouldn't cross. She couldn't risk Jake. She couldn't let him get hurt because of her. Because he protected her.

She looked at Jake, silently begging him to remain calm, to not do anything stupid. Jake sighed, nodding his head to her silent request, letting Collins snap the cuffs shut without protest.

"This is insane," she told Mr. Black. "What evidence do you have to arrest Jake?"

"I don't need proof," Mr. Black said smoothly. "One of the perks of being me."

"Jake—" Maggie rushed forward, but two agents muscled in front of her, blocking her.

"You're heinous," she hissed at them. "Your own team leader is in that damn cabin, and you're playing lapdog to *this* guy?" She jerked her thumb at Black. "Where's your loyalty?"

"We're just following orders, Kincaid," said one of the agents.

"Don't worry about it, Maggie," Jake told her as Collins led him away from the tent. He smiled reassuringly at her, which just made her feel worse. "Concentrate on Kayla," he called over his shoulder.

"That won't be necessary," Mr. Black said. He held out his hand. "I will be needing your phone."

Maggie glared at him. "What are you going to do?"

"I'm giving Mancuso one hour to surrender," he replied. "Then I'm sending a team in, guns hot."

"That's a terrible move," Maggie said flatly. "He'll blow that cabin—and everyone in it—sky high."

Mr. Black shrugged. "Let us hope the SWAT team is better at neutralizing a slightly above-average thug before he drops the trigger."

"How did your undercover operative fare against him?" Maggie said. "Because I'm pretty sure your 'doctor' is dead somewhere in the cabin. What do you bet, Black? Do you feel any remorse? You made a bad situation ten times worse. You could care less about body count here. Even if it includes one of your own!"

"Our jobs carry risk." Mr. Black shrugged. "He was aware of that."

"You're a sociopath," Maggie said, contempt dripping from her voice. "And you're not even a smart one. Mancuso's willing to die," Maggie said. "Look at his profile. You send someone in there, he will sacrifice his life for his mission. Or is that what you're counting on, Black?"

Mr. Black's placid face didn't even twitch with emotion. God, what a monster. Maggie felt like spitting. Or slugging him.

"Your phone, Ms. Kincaid," he said, his hand still extended.

Maggie made no move to give it to him.

"Don't make me force you," he said quietly.

The expression on his face, the muted anger hiding in his eyes, sent chills spreading through her body. She stood tall, refusing to look away. She would not show her fear. That's what he wanted. "You sent one man after me and it didn't work," Maggie said. "How dangerous could you be?"

"I've kenneled your bodyguard," Mr. Black pointed out.

"He's a threat, isn't he?" Maggie asked. "He got the drop on you." A smile spread across her lips, making the cracked skin break and bleed, but she ignored it. "He's good, you're right. But I'm better. You haven't begun to see what I can do."

"Trust me, you don't want to find out what *I* can do," Mr. Black said, and the dark promise in his voice made the bad kind of goose bumps prickle across her skin. "Just give me the phone, Maggie, and leave like a good little girl, or I'll have you escorted out in cuffs. The journalists would love that."

She slapped the phone down hard on his palm, hoping it hurt.

"This isn't the last you've seen of me," she said.

"You better pray it is, for your sake," Mr. Black replied, the warning clear.

She knew she should be scared of him. If Jake hadn't intervened, she would probably be tied up in a car trunk on her way to a CIA black site by now.

But she was done with fear.

And she was done with Mr. Black.

CHAPTER 55

Two agents silently escorted her to her car. They refused to meet her eyes, and for the entire walk, Maggie seethed, furious at how easily they'd been swayed. Even if she'd been an underling, even if she'd gotten a call from the director himself, she never would have fallen under Mr. Black's thumb so easily. She knew better. Frank had taught her better.

Even Frank was powerless against Black.

But she wouldn't let herself be.

"Thanks for the escort," she said sarcastically as they got to her car. "I can take it from here. Maybe go concentrate on saving Agent Harrison's life, if that even matters to you."

They walked away, shame in their eyes. Maggie unlocked her car and got inside, gunning it out of the clearing because if she went slowly, she knew she'd turn back. And then Mr. Black would probably arrest her—or kill her.

Her headlights cut through the darkness as she made her way out onto the main road, driving away from the wilderness and toward civilization. The farther she drove, the harder it hit: the exhaustion, the panic, the worry. Everything that she'd been pushing down and pushing down, trying to ignore so she could do her job—now she had no excuse to ignore it.

Now she was free to scream and cry and throw things.

Kayla Thebes was going to die. She was going to die—and it was Maggie's fault.

A car honked wildly at her, and she gasped, yanking the steering wheel to the right. She'd almost drifted into the other lane, distracted by her thoughts. The car sped past her, still honking.

She couldn't take it anymore. This wasn't safe. She'd been driving for only fifteen minutes, but when she saw the neon sign for a roadside diner, she pulled into the parking lot.

It was a kitschy place, with black-and-white checked tile floors and rickety Formica tables. She headed to the pay phone in the back, and with tired hands and a heavy heart, she dialed a number.

"Hello?"

"Hi, Mom," she said.

TWENTY MINUTES LATER, a Buick pulled into the diner's parking lot, and her mother, a petite woman with a shock of curly blond hair and brilliant blue eyes, got out.

"Sweetheart," she said when she walked into the diner and found Maggie sitting in the far booth, a cup of coffee on the table in front of her.

"You look awful," she said bluntly. It made Maggie smile. Her mother had never been one to beat around the bush. "When was the last time you ate?"

"I couldn't eat anything right now," Maggie said.

"I'm guessing your case didn't end well," she said, sitting down across from her daughter.

"It hasn't ended yet." Maggie's voice shook. "It's still going on. I just got fired." Her face crumpled, hot tears pricking the corners of her eyes. "They're going to die, Mom. And I can't even be there to try to stop it. Just like Erica died because I wasn't there to stop it. Because I left her behind."

Her mother's expression, her gentle face, full of warmth, flickered with concern and worry. "Sweetheart, that's not . . . that's not what you think, is it?"

Maggie stared at the depths of her coffee cup because she couldn't look at her mother while she said it. While she admitted it. "I can't forgive myself for what I did," Maggie said in a hushed voice, her heart tearing in little pieces at the thought of Erica, of what she did. "I left her. I shouldn't have."

"Margaret." Her mother reached over and grasped both her hands in her own, holding on tight. "Look at me."

Maggie forced her eyes to meet her mother's, terrified of finding blame there. Terrified she'd find all the hate she'd directed at herself for so long.

But she found none. There was unwavering love and sympathy in her mother's eyes—nothing else.

"Losing Erica was the most devastating thing that could have happened to any of us. It's not something I will ever be able to understand or justify or be at peace with. The only thing that would've been worse is if I'd lost *both* of you. Sweetheart, it was *never* your fault. The man who took you? This was *his* fault. His choice. His evil. You were a little girl. You did what your big sister told you to. And the fact that in her final moments, she knew you were running to safety . . . that you were going to be okay? That must have brought her—and will always bring me—more comfort than anything else ever could. You were so brave, Maggie. You did everything you could have to save her. I was so proud of you then—and now. Of the woman you've become."

"I failed," Maggie said. "I never found her. I tried, and I *failed*. So now you and I visit an empty grave next to Dad's, and I—" She couldn't continue, tears trickling down her cheeks.

"The point is that you tried," her mother said, her eyebrows drawn tight in concern. "You looked for her for years. You didn't give up."

"But it doesn't make me feel better," Maggie said. "It doesn't change things. It doesn't change *me*. And now I'm sitting here, miles away, while Kayla Thebes' life is in the hands of a man who couldn't care less about it."

The powerlessness, like being a bear in a trap, was overwhelming. Her wrists ached, her forever reminder. She didn't even bother trying to hide her compulsive rubbing from her mom.

"Sweetie," her mom reached out, placing her hands over Maggie's, stopping the movement. Maggie's cheeks burned. "I know it hurts," she said quietly, brushing over the tops of Maggie's fingers lightly. A light movement that soothed in the way only a mother's touch could.

"If Kayla's still alive, there's still a chance, Maggie," her mother said. "If she's still alive, you haven't failed yet, have you? Go back there. Be the woman I raised you to be. The woman Erica wanted you to be."

Maggie looked at her, strength blossoming inside her. She couldn't help but remember Black's warning.

But she was done with warnings.

It was time for action.

CHAPTER 56

Jake had been escorted to one of the empty mobile units by agents who wouldn't even meet his eyes. One of them cuffed him to the seat, and then they slinked out, the shame coming off them obvious.

Jake shook his head in disgust. There was following orders—and then there was just plain wrong. And Black was *all* wrong. He felt it in every fiber of his being. Jake couldn't help but wonder if he was going to end up at some sort of CIA dark site after Black botched this case—probably on purpose.

The worn vinyl bench he'd been tossed on was cool to the touch. There was a big rip in the middle of the seat, and for a moment, Jake considered digging through the vinyl to locate a spring, use it to pick the cuff locks.

It was a bad idea. He might be able to get out of the SWAT truck without being noticed, but getting past the cordons was nearly impossible. Black and his cronies would grab him before he took more than a few steps.

Jake's hands clenched behind his back, trying to banish the pins-and-needles creeping up his arms. He needed to keep his blood circulating, just in case he had to fight.

He'd fought cuffed before, though he didn't exactly relish the idea of doing it again. There were only so many moves you could make with such limitations. Brute force—the kind that killed—was usually necessary to win. And he knew Black would shoot him before trying to fight hand to hand. He was the type of man who relied on his gun more than his guts.

God, this was a fucked-up situation, Jake thought hopelessly. But he'd been in worse in the Middle East, and he knew there was no use in panicking. It wasted energy he might need.

He would try to stop Black, and he might succeed. But they were at the end of the line, and he knew it. Black had control, and he wasn't going to give it up. It would have to be taken from him.

At least Maggie was far away. He knew she was probably going crazy because she'd been tossed off the case. He knew, with a sinking feeling, that her absence reduced the chances of getting Kayla out alive. Harrison was as good as dead. Mancuso wasn't going to let anyone go free, and Black wasn't going to give Mancuso what he wanted.

Despite that reality, a part of him couldn't help feeling relieved that Maggie wouldn't be around when whatever happened went down. Catastrophic damage, lost lives, Jake could see it all looming ahead of them. All because of Black.

He didn't want Maggie to go through another trauma like losing her sister. Or losing the girl at Sherwood Hills. He knew how much these tragedies had marked and defined her. How they haunted her.

He understood being haunted like that.

But Maggie was out of Black's line of sight. There was some relief in that, even though watching her fight, watching her try to reason with Black and his cold response, had made Jake shaky with rage.

It was as if Black was deliberately ignoring expert advice. Almost like . . . like . . . he *wanted* a bloodbath.

Jake straightened, his eyebrows drawing together. Could that be it? Did he *not* want a peaceful outcome to this? Mancuso dying in a blast might solve a lot of Black's problems.

Did Mancuso have the goods on Black too?

He needed to get out of here. Jake jerked on the cuffs,

but they didn't give. He was looking around for something to use as a tension wrench so he could pick the lock when the sound of the door opening and closing made him stop.

Black strode toward him, his face blank, but his eyes glittered with triumph.

"Let me guess," Jake said. "You made some calls about me."

Black sat down on the bench across from him, interlacing his fingers and gazing at Jake over them. "I must admit, you have an impressive record," he said. "So many medals. So many commendations."

"I'm good at my job," Jake said. God, he wanted nothing more than to punch this guy. He was everything he hated about covert operatives. There were two types of people who were suited for the work: those who came naturally by deception, and those who had to learn it.

When you have to learn it, you learn empathy. Morals. Right and Wrong.

When it's as natural as breathing, it's a problem.

"So what's the plan, Black?" Jake asked, planting his feet firmly on the ground, just in case. He wasn't going to put anything past this guy. He was sneaky. Underhanded.

"I've spoken to your superiors," Black said.

Jake's grin was slow and slick. He chuckled, imagining the look on the general's face when some CIA hard-ass called him up. "How'd that go?"

"You have a very loyal team," Black said.

"Damn right," Jake said with pride. He and the general didn't always see eye to eye, but he wasn't the kind of man to bow under any pressure.

"It'd be a pity if something happened to them."

The emotion fled from Jake's face in an instant. His heart turned to ice and he leaned forward, the cuffs cutting deep into his wrists with the movement. He didn't even feel the pain.

"You touch one hair on my team's head, and there'll be nothing left of you for your spook buddies to find," he said, his voice low and full of a deadly promise that they both knew he could fulfill.

"You really shouldn't show your hand so easily," Black commented, getting up from the bench.

It was exactly what Jake needed. He slouched down in his seat, straightening his legs, and in a lightning-fast movement, hooked them around Black's ankles. With a practiced twist, his hands still bound, he yanked Black's feet from underneath him, and the man went flying, his face slamming into the floor of the SWAT unit. He let out a surprised grunt as Jake pressed his boot against his neck.

"I could break your neck right now," Jake told him calmly. His heart pounded from the exertion and strength it took to keep Black pinned with only his legs. The cuffs cut deep into his skin, and he could feel blood trickling down his arms. "You decide to play the tough guy and threaten my team? For that alone, I should lay you out. But you also sent that man after Maggie. And that was a big mistake." Jake pressed his boot harder into Black's neck. "There I go again, showing my hand," he said pleasantly, like they were buddies having a beer. "You or any of your goons touch Maggie again, and you'll be begging me to stop."

"You gonna go all Goldlake on me?" Black sneered.

For a second, shock took over him when Black used that expression. He couldn't control it. And Black was ready for the chink he'd made in Jake's armor. He twisted, grabbing Jake's foot and pushing it backward, hard. Jake slammed into the bottom of the bench as Black leapt to his feet, coughing and red faced. Blood trickled down his forehead and he wiped it away, flicking it onto the ground.

"Fucking animal," Black spat at him. "I know all about you. All about that week in the desert."

Jake fought hard to keep his anger off his face—but from Black's triumphant expression, he knew he was failing.

No one was supposed to know about Goldlake. The mission had been completely off the books—or so he'd thought. Fury twisted in his chest, and he fought hard against the memories that threatened to spill into his head. He couldn't think about the past now. That's exactly what Black wanted.

Kayla's safety was what mattered. And Jake needed to fight for her. With Maggie gone, there was no one else here on her side who was willing to do that.

Black marched over to the door, yanking it open. Jake could hear him shouting for someone to come and cuff his legs. And a few minutes later, an agent scurried in and secured his legs, tightening the cuffs.

"Sorry," the agent muttered when he saw how torn up his wrists already were.

"What happened with Agent Kincaid?" Jake asked in an undertone. "Did she leave?"

The agent—some guy with red hair—hesitated. And then he gave Jake a short nod before hurrying away, leaving him alone in the mobile unit.

Jake slumped back on the bench as far as his bonds allowed.

At least Maggie was safe, away from this madness.

But that meant this was on him to fix. He allowed himself five seconds, just five seconds of worry and anger, and then he took a deep breath and straightened in his seat.

First step: He needed to find a way out of here.

And then he was going to show Black exactly what kind of man he was.

CHAPTER 57

She'd gone insane. That's the thought that spun around in her head as she crept through the woods. The trees provided great cover, the overgrown trails barely visible in the dark. A few times, she stumbled in the dark, nearly falling flat on her face once when her boot caught on a particularly gnarled tree branch. But she forged ahead through the underbrush. She was determined.

She had to be because she was about to take the biggest gamble of her life.

It was unnerving, being this deep in the woods again. She had to go off-trail to make her approach. She'd never admit this to anyone, but she avoided landscapes like this. She ran in well-lit, manicured parks instead of on hiking trails. It helped her avoid the memories of bloody bare feet, every panicked step taking her farther and farther away from her sister.

But now she had no choice. So she sucked it up, pushed down the memories, the guilt.

Erica was gone. But Kayla wasn't. There was still time.

There was still hope. If her plan worked.

Maggie approached the cabin from the north, where there were only two SWAT officers patrolling. It was the perfect angle, and the line of journalists stubbornly waiting the story out had a prime view, just in case. She reached the final slope, wiggling up it in a crouch so she wouldn't draw SWAT's attention.

She lay there, frozen still, flat on the ground, watching them. It felt as if every cell of her body was on fire. Part of her wanted to run away, her flight instinct appealing to the lost twelve-year-old inside her instead of the woman she'd become. She didn't have to do this. She was off the case. No one would blame her.

But if she didn't at least try, she'd never be able to stand tall, to look Jake in the eye without shame.

She refused to be a coward. She would be brave, like Erica had begged her to be. Crazy, but brave.

Crouching in the bushes, she waited until both of the SWAT agents' backs were turned. Maggie leapt to her feet, thankful her legs were burning from exertion rather than trembling. She needed all the strength she could muster up. All the speed she could summon. This had to happen. Fast.

Maggie moved quickly, with a confidence she didn't feel. Her entire body was tensed, half expecting to get shot at any second. Brush and dry pine needles crunched beneath her feet as she hurried toward the cabin.

Oh, God. Oh, God. *Oh, God.* This was crazy. This plan was against all her training. But she couldn't care. There was too much at risk with Black in charge. She needed to put a stop to it, and this was the only way she knew how.

Jake would be furious if he knew what she was doing. She hoped he wouldn't blame her, that he wouldn't be too mad—because if this crazy plan worked, she was going to need him.

"Hey!"

They'd caught sight of her. Maggie tensed, but pressed on, surefooted. She was sure any second a bullet would pierce her back, her shoulder, her skull. Her stomach lurched sickly with fear, but she didn't even look up—if she did, she might stop. So she kept going, concentrating on the door.

Keep moving, she told herself. People are indecisive when they're surprised, even when they were trained as well as the Omega Teams. SWAT knew who she was, so they wouldn't shoot her. Probably.

God, please don't let them shoot her. Thank God for the press—they were recording everything. Black wouldn't give the order to shoot, knowing it'd end up on live TV . . . would he?

There was a confused murmur, then shouting, as the reporters caught sight of her. Her stomach tightened, knowing that every camera they had was on her. That her insanity was being broadcast all over the world.

She just needed to get to the door. That's all. Only a few more steps.

"Ms. Kincaid!" Black's voice boomed over a megaphone. Maggie flinched but accelerated her pace, not even bothering to look over her shoulder at him. She knew he was there. She knew he was furious. She didn't need to see it. Screw him and the CIA. Kayla meant nothing to them: They cared only about covering up their own misdeeds.

She was done with him and his callousness. He had his priorities, but she had hers.

She was going to show him exactly what it meant to cross a woman like her.

"Ms. Kincaid, you're in violation of orders. Return to the perimeter immediately!"

But it was too late: she'd reached the door.

With a shaking hand, Maggie knocked. "Mancuso!" she shouted. "Mancuso, it's Maggie. Let me in!"

There was a pause, an impossibly long second when she was sure she'd end up tackled to the ground and cuffed. She was sandwiched between two horrible options: the cabin full of C4 or Black and his men, clearly ready to shoot to kill. Either way, she might end up dead. But she would die trying to help Kayla. She closed her eyes, waiting for it. For the darkness to engulf her. For it to be over. For *her* to be over.

Then she heard the scrape of a lock, and the door opened slowly. Maggie held both hands up so he could see she wasn't going for a gun.

"Why are you here?" Mancuso demanded, his hand clutching the dead man's switch.

"Let me in before they shoot me," Maggie hissed.

Rattled and sweating, Mancuso stepped aside.

"Don't you dare go in that cabin, Kincaid," Mr. Black shouted over the megaphone.

She glanced over her shoulder at him. He stood near the edge of the clearing, his legs spread wide, clutching the megaphone as if he wished it were a gun. He kept looking over at the journalists who were watching with rapt attention, their cameras trained on Maggie.

Maggie barely resisted the urge to flip the jerk off before she rushed inside the cabin, slamming the door shut behind her.

For a moment, she and Mancuso just stared at each other in the dim light. He looked terrible. Dark circles ringed his eyes, his normally coiffed hair was drenched with sweat, and his tanned face was gray and drained.

"I'm just here to help Kayla," she said.

"You're fucking crazy," Mancuso said flatly. "What the hell was that?" He kept looking her up and down, like any moment he expected her to pull a gun. Maggie watched as his fingers tightened around the dead man's switch.

She needed to start talking fast.

"That was me taking a risk," Maggie said hurriedly, eyes still on the switch. "I'm willing to sacrifice to get you what you want, Mancuso." She met his eyes determinedly. "I'm willing to risk my life so we can make a deal. That should breed some trust."

Mancuso stared at her like she was an alien. "They wouldn't have shot you," he said uncertainly.

Maggie shrugged. "Don't be so sure," she said. "Thanks, by the way. I owe you."

"You're wasting your time trying to suck up to me," Mancuso hissed. "I'm not going to make a trade."

Maggie looked around the cabin. They were in what looked like a mudroom. There were boots in a row near the door and a rickety coat rack with a few scarves and a plaid jacket hung from it. The floor was a worn, scarred oak that looked like it hadn't been cleaned in years.

She couldn't see Kayla or Paul; they must be in the front room. She needed to get in there. Paul was trained for these high-stress situations; he would keep it together. But Kayla was a kid. The stress was likely making her worse.

"I know you won't make a trade," Maggie told Mancuso. "But you also know that there's no way in hell Black's going to send a news crew in here to talk to you. So it looks like both of us are kind of stuck, aren't we?"

Mancuso frowned, confused. "Then why are you here?"

"To help you get what you want," Maggie said.

"You've gone rogue?" Mancuso sputtered. He yanked his free hand agitatedly through his hair, staring suspiciously at her. Maggie eyed the trigger in his other hand, but his fist remained clenched tight. "But you just said—"

"I have my priorities," Maggie interrupted. "The guy who'll be calling you in a second? He has his. He and I are not on the same page. If you're going to trust anyone, Roger, don't let it be that guy. He'll use it against you—and then he'll probably kill you. He's not interested in helping you. He's interested in eliminating threats. And you're a threat."

As if on cue, Mancuso's phone rang. He dug in his pocket with his free hand, checking the screen. "It's from you," he said, looking confused. "What's going on? I told you, no tricks . . ."

"They took my phone when they fired me," Maggie explained.

He looked shocked, and then whistled. "They *fired* you? What the hell did you do?"

"Challenged authority," Maggie replied. "Pissed off the wrong guy." She held out her hand. "Let me answer it."

"Why should I do that?" he asked, suspicion rising in his voice.

"Because I'm better at negotiating than you," Maggie said brusquely. "And I'll get us both what we want."

CHAPTER 58

Jake had almost worked the spring out of the seat when the truck door opened. He settled himself over the torn upholstery, looking relaxed and bored as Black and two men he didn't recognize marched inside. He wanted nothing more than to lunge at Black, to crack his skull hard against the bridge of his nose, breaking it—and then finish him off.

Black stared at him icily, keeping his distance. Jake smiled to himself. He'd clearly learned his lesson about getting too close.

"You done already?" Jake asked sarcastically. "I didn't hear a bomb go off."

Mr. Black's normally placid expression had vanished, replaced by stormy, barely contained anger. Jake raised an eyebrow, leaning back in his seat. Something had happened. Something that Black wasn't happy about. This could be good. Or really horrible. Or both.

God, what a mess. The CIA screwed everything up.

"Uncuff him," Black ordered.

The men scurried to obey, and Jake frowned as they unshackled him.

"Leave us," Black said to his men.

Only when they were alone, did Black hold out a phone. Jake looked down at it, puzzled when he realized that it was Maggie's cell. He recognized the red case.

"She says she'll only talk to you," Black said.

"She . . ." Jake frowned, his gut churning with dread. No. She wouldn't. She wouldn't do that. She wouldn't be *that* reckless.

Right when he'd felt some relief that she was safe, out of the fray . . . He should have known she'd never give up. Like a little pit bull . . . He pressed his lips together, his worry sparring with his deep, however grudging, admiration for Maggie's outsized—and outrageous—courage. What a woman.

He was going to be pissed at her when this was over, but dammit, was she brave.

"Your girlfriend is in the cabin," Mr. Black said slowly, his voice barely containing his fury. "She's turned. She's taken over for Mancuso and she says she won't talk to anyone but you."

Jake reached for the phone. If Maggie had a plan, he needed to know it. Black leaned down, hissing in his ear, "Don't mess with me on this, O'Connor. I will kill you. Creatively. Painfully. You've been in the Middle East. You know what men like me can do."

"Got it," Jake said brusquely. He knew he should be scared—any rational person would be, because Black was right: He knew what men like him did—he knew it up close and personal, all too well.

But he was too goddamn pissed off to let the fear in. And he had to make sure Maggie was okay. She was inside a cabin with a bomb and a madman. It made him want to sweat. To scream. But he couldn't lose it.

She was counting on him.

He was the touchstone, now. Her touchstone.

He couldn't fail her. Not when he . . .

Not when he loved her the way he thought he could.

The sudden realization gave him strength, filling him with a faith he thought he'd lost years ago, back in the desert. She was a piece of him that he hadn't realized was missing, and now that he'd found her, he'd be damned if anything—or anyone—would stand in their way.

He tapped the phone onto speaker. "Well, Goldilocks," he sighed. "Looks like you're in the thick of it now."

For a second, he could almost see the shaky smile on her face—then her voice, all business, interrupted his memory. "Here's what I want, Jake," she said, clipped and quick. Despite the bravado in her voice, he knew she was scared out of her mind. "I want a car to the airport. And not just any car. I want one from the senator's fleet, one with bulletproof windows. And I want a private plane waiting on the runway, ready to take off immediately. With a clear flight path."

Jake looked at Black, who shook his head violently, his frown deepening. If Maggie hadn't been inside a building with a madman, a bomb, and two hostages, Jake would almost be amused at how she had screwed up Black's takeover so spectacularly. That was Maggie Kincaid for you—always surprising. But this was insanely gutsy, even for her.

"Black says we're going to need a show of trust," Jake said.

"When the car arrives, we'll hand over Agent Harrison," Maggie said.

So she was going to keep Kayla with her. Smart. Who knows what Black might do to Kayla. Jake didn't trust him to make sure she was all right—who knew what she'd overheard inside that cabin? Black might consider her a liability. Neither he nor Maggie could risk that.

"We can have the car ready in an hour," Black said in an undertone.

Jake almost rolled his eyes, but caught himself. Who did Black think he was dealing with? Black gestured for Jake to relay the information, impatience seeping into his stern expression.

"The car will take about an hour to get here, Maggie," Jake said obediently, thinking about how nice it'd be to pummel Black's face. Just one punch. That's all he wanted.

"That's a bullshit timeline, and you and I both know it," Maggie spat back. "Tell Black that delaying me isn't going to happen. I'm not some rookie criminal he can run roughshod over and leave dead in a ditch to be forgotten.

I'm the best damn negotiator the FBI's had in decades, and I know his tricks. I see through him. So—fifteen minutes. If the car's one minute late, Mancuso's going to kill me. That'd be a great story for the journalists outside. Former FBI agent dies trying to save a senator's daughter 'cause the CIA botched the job so badly. There'll be Senate hearings for months. Does Black really want that? I know you're listening, Black."

Mr. Black's eyes sparked with fury, his lips nearly disappearing as he pressed them tightly together. "I need to talk to the girl, Ms. Kincaid," he said finally.

"You weren't worried about her before," Maggie snapped venomously. "No need to start pretending now. Stop stalling. Clock's ticking, Black. Fifteen minutes. Or tomorrow's headlines are going to tank you—and everyone you're protecting."

She hung up.

Jake handed the phone back impassively to the man, trying not to let his confusion—and his concern—show on his face.

What was she up to? She had to have a plan. She always had a plan.

He just needed to figure it out. He traced the conversation back in his head. Pretty standard demands. Maybe that was the point? Could they be a red herring to hide her actual plot?

"What's she doing, O'Connor?" Black asked. "Did you two cook this up together? That insane do-or-die run she made to the cabin? I could've had her on the ground bleeding from a dozen bullets in three seconds flat."

Jake rose from his seat, towering over Black. The man's Adam's apple bobbed as he swallowed hard. Jake stared him down, anger radiating from his narrowed eyes.

"Bet you're regretting taking those cuffs off me," Jake said.

Black swallowed again, clearing his throat. "You don't scare me," he said coolly.

"I should," Jake promised, stepping forward. "Think

about it before you draw that gun," he said, his eyes going to Black's hip, where his holster rested. "Think about what you've read in my file. You miss, the bullet's going to ricochet." He gestured to the SWAT truck's thick, armored steel walls. "And Black?" Jake smiled, all predator, showing his teeth. "I'll make sure you miss."

Black's eyes narrowed as he considered his options.

Jake watched. He waited. He was ready.

He was a soldier, after all. Spies may have tricks up their sleeves, but soldiers have hearts of steel. And this soldier would do anything to protect Maggie.

"Sit back down," Black finally scoffed, with a lot more bravado than he clearly felt.

Jake sat back, relaxing a fraction. He was getting to the guy.

Good. Nobody could threaten his woman and get away with it.

He needed to have Maggie's back, no matter what. She was in that cabin with a madman and a bomb, with the CIA ready to finish her off. Both just as angry, just as dangerous. The CIA might be the worst of the lot. Mancuso hadn't shot her yet, which gave Jake hope that Maggie had calmed him. Jake was pretty sure Black would shoot her the second he knew there were no eyes on him.

Jesus. Jake needed to be free. To be ready.

He needed to be strong. For her.

CHAPTER 59

Maggie let out a shaky breath, dropping the phone onto the bed. A faded, hand-stitched quilt was spread across it— a strangely homey, personal touch that made her stomach twist. She could hear the choppers outside, circling in the air. The steady whirring of the helicopter blades was like a warning heartbeat.

Mancuso tossed something at her. Automatically, she caught it, looking down at the thick zip tie, looped wide enough for her to slip her wrists through.

"Put it on," he demanded.

She didn't want to. Fear—the base, animal kind—stirred to life inside her. But she couldn't hesitate. She couldn't falter. She had to ignore the fear.

Maggie obediently slipped it over her hands and tightened it, but she angled her wrists to provide some space without him noticing. She'd been bound and helpless once before, and had sworn to herself it'd never happen again. That meant an almost obsessive fascination with learning how to break free of various bonds. With just that little slack, she knew how to snap the zip tie if she had to, by bringing her wrists down onto her bent knee with a sharp, swift movement. But she needed Mancuso to feel in control. Tying her up was the first step.

Now that she'd made a step toward making him less nervous, it was time to get something *she* wanted.

"Can I please check on Kayla?" she asked Mancuso.

He nodded sharply, pushing her down the hall into the living room. Maggie scanned the room; Paul was tied to a chair in the center and Kayla was lying on the sagging seventies couch, her blond hair spread like silk over the ugly orange-and-brown plaid.

"Maggie!" Paul's eyes widened in horror. He looked frantically around her, as if he expected SWAT to be following right behind. His face fell when he realized she was alone. "Oh, honey," he said, the horror in his face melting into anguish and worry. "What have you done?"

"It's all right, Paul," she said, making a beeline for the couch. Kayla lay there unconscious, her breathing reduced to a shallow shuddering.

"Oh, God," Maggie said, bending down and feeling the girl's forehead. She was clammy and cold. "How long has she been out?" she asked Paul, trying to count a pulse. Frantic beats fluttered against her fingertips. Much too fast.

"About thirty minutes," Paul said. "I tried to keep her up, tried to keep her talking. It worked for a while. But she kept getting weaker and slower to answer. And then . . ."

"It's okay," Maggie said quickly. "You did good."

She looked up at Mancuso, who was staring at the room like it was the first time he'd seen it. His shoulders slumped, like the exhaustion was finally overtaking him. How long had he been up? Was it finally hitting him, what he'd done? She looked around the room, and she didn't see the "doctor" Mr. Black had sent in. Where was he? She almost wanted to ask, but she worried if she did, it'd be a trigger—a reminder of what Mancuso had done. What he was capable of.

"Roger," she said. "Please let me give her the insulin. You have plenty of leverage. You don't need to keep holding her life in the balance."

Mancuso's cheeks reddened, his eyes flashing with guilt. "I crushed it."

"What?" Maggie and Paul exchanged worried glances.

"I just . . . look, she'll be okay," Mancuso assured her. He sounded like he was trying to convince himself more than

Maggie. "I had an aunt with diabetes. She hardly ever took her meds. Always ate whatever she wanted."

Yeah, and she probably died at forty, Maggie thought, rage and fear rising in her chest.

She needed to get Kayla out of here. Fast. She checked her watch. Black and Jake had thirteen minutes to get her a car. They'd better hurry.

Maggie walked over to Paul. "What have you done?" he asked in an undertone. "Why aren't you . . ."

"I'm just checking on him," she told Mancuso, who had stepped forward as she approached Paul. "Vitals and stuff. I'm not going to mess with that much C4, Roger. I'm not stupid." She reached for Paul's wrist carefully, to make it look like she was feeling for his pulse.

"You'd better not," Mancuso said, holding out the dead man's switch to show who was boss. Paul tensed in his seat, and Maggie wanted to put her hand on his shoulder, to somehow soothe him, but she knew what a bad idea that'd be.

Mancuso kept pacing near the window, peering through the small crack between the curtains every few seconds. Maggie needed to take advantage of his distraction.

"Something big's going down," Maggie said to Paul quietly, bending down to check his pupils. They were blown wide from stress and adrenaline, but thank goodness they weren't uneven. No head injury. "The CIA's taken over."

"What?" Paul looked at her like she was crazy. "That's . . . ridiculous."

"The director's given control to a man named Mr. Black," Maggie said, keeping a close eye on Mancuso. "Jake figured out he works for the CIA. Mr. Black arrested him and fired me. So I took matters into my own hands."

"You just . . . walked in here? Maggie! What the hell were you thinking?" Paul whispered angrily.

Maggie glared at him. "Whoever the senator's working with to cover up SouthPoint's crimes is willing to sacrifice *all* of us to keep it secret. So I knew I needed to do something to change the game."

"What are you talking about?" Mancuso asked suspiciously from the window.

"I'm just filling him in on the senator's bullshit," Maggie said casually.

Despite the clock ticking down and the adrenaline shooting through her body like fireworks, there was a part of her that wanted nothing more than to grab Mancuso and demand that he tell her why he had parroted Erica's words at her. How could he know about her? About what she said? But she mustn't think about it, she told herself firmly. It wasn't the time. Thinking about Erica was what led her to the tragedy at Sherwood Hills. That couldn't happen again.

Kayla needed help, and she needed it fast. And Maggie had to get it for her. By any means necessary.

Taking advantage of Mancuso's current focus on Kayla, she turned back to Paul. "The press is crawling all over outside," she said softly. "So I'm using them. To get out of this alive, we have to keep things interesting enough to keep the cameras rolling and *live*. A lot is going to happen—and it's going to happen fast."

Paul's face hardened, going into field-agent mode. She could practically see the shift in his mind. "Okay," he said. "What do you need?"

Maggie wanted to hug him or thank him. Because what she was about to ask wasn't going to be pretty.

She took a deep breath and told him.

CHAPTER 60

"Sir, the car's arrived." One of the agents Jake didn't recognize—was he one of Black's men?—ducked his head inside the SWAT truck.

"Come on, O'Connor," Mr. Black said, yanking him to his feet. Jake shook him off, glaring, but following him outside. A sleek black Lexus had driven through the cordons and was waiting, with a clear exit out of the park. Jake had to hand it to the senator—he had good taste in vehicles.

The phone in Black's hand rang. He handed it to Jake, who answered, his stomach tight with anticipation. What if he couldn't figure out what she needed him to do? What if he screwed it up? Made the wrong assumption? Botched her grand plan?

"Hey, Maggie," he said, opting for casual. "Car's here, but I guess you know that."

"Tell the driver to leave the keys in the ignition, get out, and walk back to you," Maggie directed.

Black gestured at the driver, who hastily got out of the car and hurried behind the cordon.

"Are you going to drive?" Jake asked, praying she'd say *no*. Praying she'd find some way to get out of this unscathed, safe. The idea of her being hurt made his heart clench dangerously. It was a shocking, visceral feeling that took his breath away. A world without Maggie Kincaid in it suddenly didn't seem possible to him. He'd spent over thirty years not knowing she existed, but everything was different now that she was in his life.

"I'm not driving," Maggie said. Relief shot through him, only to crash and burn when she said, "You are. No guns. No knives. No weapons. See you in a second."

She hung up before Jake could reply.

"Absolutely not," Black snapped, snapping his fingers at his cronies, issuing orders at a rapid-fire pace, getting them in position.

"Think again," Jake said, grabbing his arm. Mr. Black looked down at his hand disgustedly, stepping to the side. But Jake was unswayed, thinking fast. Maggie needed him to drive, so he was going to be in that driver's seat. Even if he had to beat Black unconscious to get there.

"I can do this," he said seriously. "She wants me to do this, and I'm sure there's a good reason why. I can help defuse the situation. I'm good at what I do. I know you've dug into my record, Black—you know where I've been, what I've done, how good I am. Think about it. If the hostages die, they'll be investigating for months. Internally and publicly. Those journalists out there in the clearing will dig and dig, and they'll find threads leading them to the men you're protecting. Nothing can stay hidden forever."

Mr. Black stared at him, eyes narrowed, trying to read his face, his motives. Jake looked back levelly, trying to look as sincere as possible. He *was* sincere. He was also determined to make sure that Black paid for what he'd done. How much he'd fucked this up. How much he'd endangered Kayla, Maggie, and Harrison. Jake's blood boiled at the thought, but he had to keep calm. He had to get Black to agree.

Maggie needed him, and he'd be damned if he didn't have her back the whole way.

"Fine," Black said after a long moment. "But if you try to pull anything . . ."

"I just want the hostages and Maggie out of there and safe, Black," Jake interrupted him. "You can do whatever the hell you want with Mancuso once he's not a danger to them anymore. I'm not interested in your secrets or spy games. I'm a soldier—I care about innocent lives."

"Go," Mr. Black ordered.

Jake made his way across the clearing toward the car. Behind him, he could hear Black calling off his men, returning them to the perimeter, out of the blast radius, just in case. Jake came to a stop next to the car, turning to face the cabin, in full view of the front window. He opened the driver's door.

The plaid curtains fluttered, then the cabin door swung wide.

Jake's heart seized up with a kind of fear he'd never felt before. Hot, consuming, terror flooded him as Maggie stepped out of the cabin.

She had the bomb vest strapped to her chest.

Shit. Shit. Shit.

His mind raced with scenarios and solutions, staccato bursts through his brain. He wanted to run over there and tear that thing off her. He wanted to tackle Mancuso to the ground, his fist over Mancuso's hand, preventing him from releasing the dead man's switch. But he couldn't make a move. He had to be patient.

Maggie met his horrified gaze.

Trust me, her eyes said.

Trust her. Trust her. He had to trust her. This woman, so brave, so reckless—she knew what she was doing.

God, she'd better. Or they were all dead.

Maggie made her way slowly toward the car. The press rumbled and fretted to her right, every camera trained on her. SWAT paced restlessly along the perimeter, reined in by Mr. Black's orders. The lights from the choppers flooded Maggie in an eerie white glow as she came to a stop next to Jake.

She smiled weakly. She looked impossibly small and terrifyingly strong in that moment. A beautiful, brave contradiction.

"I'm going to be mad if you blow yourself up before we have a real first date," he said, trying to alleviate some of the fear he saw in her eyes. He didn't want her to see his own—he needed to be strong for her.

The touchstone needed a touchstone now.

"Yeah, that'd really suck. So I'll try hard not to," she said, holding his gaze.

Mancuso followed next, Kayla in his arms, one of his hands still clutching the remote trigger. Jake could barely tear his eyes away from it. What if Mancuso lost his hold on Kayla? If he shifted wrong, his grip loosened, Maggie would be gone. Jesus. This was a mess. It was all he could do to stop himself from leaping into action, but he knew that would bring on a disaster.

Trust me, her eyes begged. And so he did.

Jake hurried to open the rear doors of the car, and Mancuso put Kayla in the back seat, getting in to sit beside her.

"You keep your hold tight on that," Jake told Mancuso, nodding at the switch.

Harrison came out last, free of the vest, free of the danger, his hands firmly zip-tied behind his back. He hurried toward the car. "Maggie, please, take me with you," he said, his voice shaking with emotion.

"You have to stay, Paul," Maggie said earnestly. "That's the deal. If we don't keep our word, none of this will work."

"Maggie—"

"You promised," she reminded him firmly. "Please, Paul."

He sighed. "You'd better be right," he said.

"I usually am," she said, with a forced smile. "Now go," she added gently.

Paul looked at her as if it was the last time he'd ever see her, his brown eyes desperate, trying to memorize her. "You get her back safe, O'Connor," he said under his breath as Maggie got into the front passenger seat gingerly, mindful of the C4.

"I will," Jake promised.

As soon as Harrison walked behind the cordon, Jake slipped into the driver's seat and started the car. He turned to face Maggie, who was looking pretty damn calm for a woman who had explosives strapped to her chest.

"You know there's no plane at the airport, right?" he asked in an undertone, trying to keep Mancuso from hearing.

"I'm not stupid," she said. "And Roger knows we're not going to the airport."

"Of course we aren't," Jake replied, unsurprised. "Care to fill me in where we *are* going?"

"In a second . . . do you have my phone?" she asked.

Jake dug in his pocket, holding it out. As she reached for it, she slipped him a folded piece of paper, careful not to let Mancuso see. Her phone in hand, she turned in her seat. "Mancuso, you doing okay?" she asked.

"Yeah," Mancuso said.

"How's Kayla?"

"I think she's all right," Mancuso said. "Maybe if you two stop flirting and start driving, we'll get somewhere."

"Just a sec," Jake said. He unfolded the note, scanning Maggie's neat handwriting.

Maggie Kincaid's exquisite instincts were no joke. The second Jake read the words she'd written, he had to hold back a spontaneous low whistle of approval.

Instead, he let out a little huff of breath, impressed, maybe even a little frightened at her superhuman savvy. Thank God she was with the good guys. He didn't want to even think about what would happen if this woman had turned her smarts to the criminal side of life.

"You ready?" Maggie asked.

"Remember when you were lecturing *me* about taking risks?" Jake asked.

She let out a laugh, a short, almost frantic sound that revealed her nervousness.

Jake reached out and squeezed her hand. "I've got you," he told her.

She grabbed his hand, her fingers tightening around his. "Let's do it," she said.

Jake pressed down on the gas.

They drove.

CHAPTER 61

What the hell does this bitch think she's doing?

Mr. Black's frustration was pouring off him in waves as O'Connor pulled away onto the dirt road, heading out of the park. From the beginning, this situation had been badly handled. He didn't *do* messy. He was clean. He was in and out. No trace. No bodies. No press.

But Maggie Kincaid didn't play by his rules. She'd trampled over them, gleefully, willfully, all because of her mushy feelings about some stupid kid and a man she couldn't even be bothered to marry.

As he and the caravan of SWAT trucks and news vans tailed the car down the service road, out of the forest, and onto the highway, Black could feel his lip curling in disgust. What in the world was Kincaid's plan? She had to know there was no way out. She was mouthy and didn't know her place, but she wasn't stupid. She must know they put a tracker in the car. Wherever she drove, he'd have ten cars on her. It was standard in a situation like this.

Or was she just leading them on a wild goose chase while she tried to come up with a plan on the fly? Black hit the accelerator, changing lanes to keep the car in sight. He glanced in his rearview mirror. The caravan of news vans was still following them, and he heard choppers in the air close behind. He gritted his teeth. His bosses weren't going to like all this press attention. But he'd find a way to contain the journalists. To manipulate them. He'd have them dismissing Mancuso as an aggrieved brother who'd lost his mind down the conspiracy-theory rabbit hole. He'd find a way to spin it, to weasel out of telling the truth. It might involve silencing a few people—maybe permanently—but he never minded that part of the job.

Which is why he was so angry over his obvious gaffe. He'd made a big mistake not disposing of Mancuso after he'd taken care of his brother in Riyadh. It was sloppy to leave a loose end. He knew better. Now he had to deal with these ridiculous heroics from people like Maggie Kincaid.

It had been messy. He'd thought Joe was smarter than that. That he cared about his brother enough to not involve him in this. But he'd been wrong.

Suddenly, the car veered across three lanes. Taking a quick turn, it merged onto the highway that led downtown and sped off.

A smile crept across Black's thin lips. So they wanted a chase, did they? He jammed down the accelerator. With a sharp jerk, he skidded through empty lanes, chasing them. In the rearview mirror, he could see the news vans faltering. They were too cumbersome and heavy to react in time. Good. He didn't need more witnesses. Most of his men hadn't recovered fast enough—he'd need to have a discussion with them later. But a few SUVs managed to make the turn. And the police chopper was still in the air.

Black pressed harder on the gas, his car jerking forward, tires squealing, as he raced after them.

The game was on.

And he was going to win.

CHAPTER 62

"You're driving like a maniac, O'Connor! Where the hell are we going?" Mancuso demanded, hanging on to the back of the driver's seat. He gulped, looking a little green. Jake swerved in and out of traffic with an expertise that impressed Maggie despite her jangled nerves. She shifted uncomfortably in her seat, trying to stay as still as she could. She was all too aware of the deadly cargo strapped to her chest. The vest felt like a lead weight crushing her heart.

They sped by blocks dotted with high-rise buildings. She felt sick every time they passed a building or house, knowing how much danger she was putting the public in by bringing a bomb into a populated area.

You had no choice, she told herself. *Stick to the plan. It's the only way.*

Jake glanced in the rearview mirror. "We've lost all but three of the cars," he told Maggie.

"The chopper's still with us," she said, peering out the window at the sky. "Mancuso, calm down. And don't throw up. Check Kayla's pulse. Is it still rapid?"

Mancuso gulped, pressing his hand against the unconscious girl's neck. "It's pretty fast."

"This wouldn't have happened if you hadn't thrown a fit and broke the insulin," Maggie snapped.

Mancuso glared at her. "Maybe remember who's holding the trigger, Maggie," he shot back.

Maggie pressed her lips together disapprovingly. "Just make sure she's strapped in tight."

She turned back to Jake. "Can you lose the other cars?"

"On it," he said.

The light switched from green to red as they approached the intersection. But Jake didn't slow down; he accelerated. The SUV zoomed through the intersection, narrowly missing getting T-boned by a sedan. Honking filled the air. Maggie's eyes widened, an involuntary shriek rising in her throat as Jake slammed hard on the gas. The SUV jerked forward, approaching two semis, one beginning to merge into the left lane. He wasn't . . . he couldn't . . .

But he did. Maggie's hands gripped the dashboard, her face turned away. She braced for impact as Jake jerked the wheel. They shot forward, pulling in front of the merging semi, inches away from clipping it. Another jerk and a surge of speed, and they were aligned in the lane, safely sandwiched between the two trucks. Temporarily hidden from Mr. Black and the other tail's view.

Maggie took a deep breath and looked over her shoulder. A silver SUV was gaining ground in the next lane. "Black's still on us," she said, grimacing as they zoomed down the street. The other SUV had been run off the pavement and skidded onto the shoulder, with no way to catch up.

"One down," Jake said as they whizzed past a sign that read WELCOME TO DOWNTOWN DC.

"We're almost there," Maggie said breathlessly. Her pulse was probably beating as fast as Kayla's. Would this work?

It had to.

"Where are we going?" Mancuso demanded, sounding nervous.

"There's an area around the Capitol that's prohibited airspace," Maggie said. "Even for the police."

Mancuso's mouth dropped open in surprise. "So the chopper can't follow us?"

"That's right," Maggie said, peering up at the sky. The chopper was still there, looming in the sky, the spotlight illuminating their car, making it hard to see.

"Hang on!" Jake called, braking suddenly. Maggie's hands slammed down on the dashboard, her seat belt cutting into her chest, dangerously close to the explosive pack. She froze, sure that any second they would all be consumed in the blast. But the C4 held, the wires connecting the device staying stationary. Nodding to her in warning, Jake made a sharp turn from his dead stop. The gray SUV following their car shot past them.

"Two down," he said, wiping sweat off his forehead, glancing at the rearview. "It's only Black following us now."

"Gun it," Maggie ordered. As the car surged forward, she looked at Jake's chiseled profile, a picture of determination. No matter how this ended, she knew he'd do all he could to follow her plan and to save Kayla, even if it endangered his own life. Maggie was grateful, because if something happened to her, if Jake survived, he'd be the only thing standing between Kayla and Mancuso, and Kayla's only protection against Mr. Black.

They flew down the street, Maggie turning her eyes to the sky. As they hit downtown, just as she predicted, the police chopper veered away.

"Jake," she said, nodding upward.

It was time. Her stomach leapt.

It'd work. It was crazy, but it had to.

She had Jake by her side. He'd make sure they succeeded.

He glanced over to her, and she nodded again.

"Hey! Mancuso!" Jake said loudly. "Look at me. I'm going to need your help in a second."

Mancuso's focus shifted to Jake. It was just enough time, just the right opening. Maggie twisted in her seat, leaning back. Lightning fast and smooth as hell, she snatched the switch out of the startled Mancuso's hand, keeping it shut.

"Got it!"

"Hey!" Mancuso protested, scrambling forward. Maggie jerked her elbow up, catching him hard on the chin. His head popped backward, and he slumped in his seat, dazed. Her fist clenched tight on the switch, she curled her body around her hand, protecting the trigger from any more pressure. For a moment, she thought they were home free, but Jake's eyes had been on her and Mancuso for a moment, not the road.

The bumper caught the concrete barrier with a horrible crunching sound as it, the fender, and the side panel collapsed, jerking them back and forth as the car spun into the middle of the street.

Dizzy and disoriented, Maggie took a deep breath of relief as Jake gained control of the car again and slowed to a stop, pulling over off the lane, onto the shoulder. Unfastening her seat belt, she tried with her free hand to open the door. But it was partially smashed in, so she rolled down the window and climbed carefully through the twisted opening, clutching the switch. Jake heaved himself through the window after her. As soon as she was on the street, he rushed over to help her wriggle out of the bomb vest. Swiftly walking a safe distance away, she gently set it on the ground. Jake bent down, examining the vest as Maggie kept her fist clenched around the switch.

"Can you disarm it?" Maggie asked.

"Give me a sec," he said. "Go check on Kayla. And keep holding that thing shut." He nodded at the trigger.

She raced back to the car, jerking the back door open. Kayla was still unconscious—but she was alive.

"Got it!" Jake called. She turned to see him gingerly remove two red wires connecting the C4, her breath in her throat, terrified that he might have chosen wrong. He jogged over to her and they positioned themselves behind the car, just in case. "Moment of truth," he said, nodding to the switch in her hand.

Maggie didn't want to let go. What if they were wrong? What if Mancuso had built in fail-safes?

Slowly, carefully, her heart in her throat, she released the dead man's switch.

Nothing blew up.

Oh, thank God. Maggie sagged against the car in relief as Jake shot her a huge grin.

"See, no sweat, Goldilocks," he told her. "We'll get bomb squad out here to do the disposal."

Just when she thought they were in the clear, she heard a screech of brakes, and whirled around to see Mr. Black's SUV skidding to a halt in front of them. "I need an ambulance!" she shouted to him as Jake dragged Mancuso out of the car.

But when Black got out of the SUV, his gun was drawn.

"Black, wait!" Jake called out as the man pointed his Glock at Mancuso. "Maggie!" he shouted in warning.

She started to move forward, toward Kayla, but Black pointed the gun at her. She froze.

"Hey," she said, holding her hands up, thinking fast. She needed Kayla safe and away. That was the priority. "I'm just getting the kid out of your line of fire, Black. You don't want her hit by a stray bullet."

"I never miss," he replied, but pointed the Glock at Mancuso. Stripped of the dead man's trigger and all of his power, he cowered, defeat twisting his gray, sweaty face, blood trickling down his cheek from a cut on his forehead sustained in the crash. Maggie leaned into the back seat and grabbed Kayla in a fireman's carry. Pulling her out of the car, she walked swiftly to the side of the road, setting the girl down at a safe distance.

"Come here now, Ms. Kincaid," Black demanded.

With a shaky breath, Maggie straightened and walked slowly back to the wrecked car. She couldn't help but feel like she was walking to her death sentence, that these were likely to be her final moments. She bit the inside of her lip, her wrists burning. She wanted to reach for Jake's hand, but she knew she shouldn't. She had to be ready to fight, just like he would be.

They'd go down fighting. It was who they were.

"You idiots drove to a spot with no witnesses and no press," Black sneered, advancing toward them with confident strides. "My job is to contain the information—and that's what I'm going to do."

"Mancuso's unarmed, and he's not a danger to anyone

anymore," Maggie spat out. "Look at him." She gestured at Mancuso, who was hunched over and dazed, blood still dripping from his wound. "If you do this, it's murder."

"Yes, it is," Black agreed. "Just like with his brother."

Mancuso stiffened, wincing at the pain the sudden movement caused. "*You* killed Joe?" he shouted. "You bastard!"

He tried to lunge forward, but Jake caught him with an arm to the chest, holding him back.

"Don't be stupid," he warned.

"I didn't anticipate your rat of a brother contacting you," Black went on with a cold smile. "It was a significant breach of protocol. I should have realized it. I should have killed you then too, just to be safe."

"You bastard!" Mancuso yelled. "I'll kill you! You took him away from me! Just for telling the truth! For doing the right thing! All he wanted to do was work for his country—he was a patriot!" Maggie watched as tears of fury filled his desperate eyes. Mancuso had no recourse; they all knew it. Black had him.

Black had all of them.

Dread swirled inside her, mixing with fear and sadness. If it ended this way, at least Kayla was alive. Black would make sure of it, just for publicity's sake. But regardless of the motive, she'd get the help she needed.

She and Jake wouldn't die in vain.

"Your brother didn't see the whole picture," Black continued, clearly relishing finally having the upper hand. "When he uncovered the smuggling, he was focused on the senator's involvement. He didn't realize he was implicating his own bosses at the CIA too. We had no choice. I had my orders."

"So the CIA killed their own agent?" Maggie asked.

Black shrugged. "It's unfortunate, but sometimes it's necessary." He raised his gun, just feet away from Mancuso, aiming between his eyes. "And so is this."

"You're wrong about one thing, though," Maggie said, her voice ringing out clearly in the empty street.

Black frowned, his eyes skittering to her for a moment.

She pulled her phone out of her pocket, holding it up. "There *are* witnesses," she insisted. "While I was carrying Kayla to safety I speed-dialed the *Washington Post*. Care to elaborate on the CIA's cover-up, Mr. Black? Andrea Yates, the *Post*'s editor-in-chief, is listening."

Black's face drained of all color, and then just as swiftly, a red haze filled his cheeks. "You *bitch*!" he exploded, swinging his gun arm toward her, his finger closing around the trigger.

Maggie froze. She had no weapon. No time to run. This was it.

The end.

At least everyone was safe. At least everyone knew.

At least she'd be with Erica again.

She closed her eyes.

Bang.

She expected to fall back, to recoil from the piercing pain of a bullet in the chest, to feel the blood, the life surging out of her.

But when she opened her eyes, it was Black who was on the ground . . . Black who was bleeding.

Jake stood above him, a peashooter clutched in his right hand. He kicked Black's Glock out of the way, bending down to check the man's pulse. He looked up at Maggie and nodded conclusively. Black would never harm anyone again.

"You good, Goldilocks?" he asked, glancing up at her, his mouth a hard line of determination and grit.

She nodded, her heart felt as if it was beating right out of her chest.

Kayla.

As sirens began to ring in the distance, Maggie ran to her, falling to her knees beside the unconscious girl.

"It's okay, sweetie," she told Kayla. "You're safe now."

CHAPTER 63

As the sirens grew louder, Mancuso began to shift nervously.

"I'm not going to get out of this free, am I?" he asked Maggie.

Maggie looked up at him somberly. She wasn't going to lie to him. "I promised you I'd help you get what you wanted," she said. "And I did. I kept my promise. Everyone will know what Joe died for. That he was a true American patriot. And no matter what you did, you did it so that people would know that. That's what you wanted."

Mancuso stared at the headlights of the SUVs in the distance, fast approaching. His fingers twitched nervously as he wiped blood off his face.

"Is your head okay?" Maggie asked.

He nodded. "I've had worse," he said.

"You weren't planning to survive this and go free, were you?" Maggie asked, because she could see the wheels turning in his mind. The fight-or-flight instinct that was deeply embedded in every human.

"You're right," Mancuso said, his eyes darting back and forth around him. "But still, can't hurt to try."

He reached into his jacket, and Maggie dove to shield Kayla. A gunshot rang out. Jake jerked backward, falling to the ground. Mancuso ran, heading toward the expansive park down the street.

Shit.

Jake was on lying his back, bleeding. Maggie ran over to him, kneeling down.

"Where is it?" She pawed at his shirt as he tried to brush her hands away.

"Just my shoulder," he told her through gritted teeth. "Go! Ambulance will be here in a second. I'll take care of Kayla. Here—" he pressed his gun into her hand "—go get him, Goldilocks."

She didn't take the gun, though. Instead, she reached down, grabbing his face with both her hands and pressing a desperate kiss against his lips. She could die today—in just minutes—and she wanted him to know that she . . .

She pulled back, just inches from his face, from those brilliant, beautiful green eyes.

"Jake, I—" she started to say. She licked her lips, unable to say it yet, even though she wanted to. Oh, how she wanted to. But there wasn't time. She had to go. "Don't bleed to death," she ordered, grabbing the gun.

He grinned. "I'll try not to."

MAGGIE RAN, VAULTING over the cement divide and heading down the street. Her footsteps pounded on the pavement as she made a quick right, racing through the gates of the park. Mancuso had already disappeared among the trees lining the cobbled path, but she headed in, gun raised, every sense on high alert.

The park was empty; a sign she passed said it was closed for cleanup. She made a mental note to keep an eye out for maintenance workers. She didn't want to accidentally shoot an innocent guy who was just there to pick up trash or trim the shrubbery.

She made her way to the thicket of trees set on top of a hill near the center of the park. Mancuso would want cover, as much as he could find. He'd want the element of surprise on his side. That's where he'd go.

She had to be ready for him.

The sun had just started to peek up along the horizon, the gray light of dawn obscured by the dense spread of oak trees Maggie approached. Her leg muscles burned as she tried to move as steadily and swiftly as she could across the wet ground. The incline steepened as she headed toward the trees. Good. She needed the vantage point the hill provided. She'd never get anywhere without better visuals. She'd lose him or end up knocked out—or worse, shot in the back.

She crested the top of the hill, her lungs burning, Jake's gun held tightly in both hands. She had a better view from here, and she scanned the park below, tracking the walks and trails for movement. Where was he?

For long moments, she could hear only the rapid thud of her heartbeat echoing in her ears. But as she moved swiftly and surely along the edge of the hill, searching the park, her heart calmed, her focused narrowed, and her senses sharpened.

This is what her childhood had wrought: instincts honed by knowledge, by courage, by strength. This was what she had been born to do.

The long shadows of trees, statues, and benches stretching across the park in the rising sun made her edgy. Flickers out of the corners of her eyes made her jump, but she realized they were only branches moving in the wind. As she hopped over some fallen branches, her steps made little rustling noises, acorns breaking under her feet.

She came to a stop, turning in a slow circle, trying to get her bearings. Where would Mancuso go? Had he run out of the park already? It was huge; he couldn't have. He wasn't fast enough. Would he hide?

Would he circle back?

A branch snapped behind her. Instead of freezing or whirling around, which every part of her body screamed to do, she began to walk forward instead. Crouching as if she'd heard something up ahead, she moved quickly across the top of the hill, toward the north, waiting, waiting.

There it was: the telltale sound of footsteps.

He was behind her.

Every hair on her body raised, the prickle down her

spine made her want to shiver, but she had to stay calm. She couldn't give her ruse away.

Play it cool, Maggie, she told herself. *Let him come to you.* The footsteps grew closer.

She pretended to stumble, knowing he'd try to take advantage of her clumsiness. But instead of falling, she ducked and twisted in a smooth, quick movement. And before Mancuso could recover or retreat, she charged, tackling him to the ground. The gun flew out of his hand, and she pressed her knee against his stomach, hard against his diaphragm, making him wheeze and cough as she leveled Jake's peashooter right in his face.

"Stay where you are," she ordered as he raised his hands in the air.

The gun trained on him, she rose carefully and retrieved his weapon, unloading it and pocketing the clip.

"You shouldn't have run, Roger," she told him.

He let out a near-hysterical laugh. "Wouldn't you have run if you did what I did?"

Maggie didn't know. Keeping the gun on him, she stood over him.

"Are you gonna kill me?" he asked.

"I'm not Mr. Black," she said. "But I will shoot you if you make a wrong move."

He sagged against the ground, defeated. "I had to try," he muttered.

"You really didn't," Maggie said. "But I don't want to talk about that," she said.

She had to know for sure. She had to understand why he knew Erica's last words. How he knew them. Why.

She needed answers.

Something gleamed in Mancuso's eyes, shimmering in the early-dawn light. "What *do* you want to talk about?" he asked.

"I want to know why you said that to me on the phone," she said.

"Said what?" he asked innocently.

The slow burn of irritation lit inside her. He was still

playing games, after all this time. As if he didn't know how to stop. Didn't know who he was, now that his brother's death had been exposed and avenged.

"You know what," she said. "Don't mess with me. I'm the one with the gun." She raised it so it was right in his face, careful to keep her finger on the trigger.

"You already said you weren't going to kill me," he scoffed. "But I already knew that. You're not the type."

"I said I wouldn't kill you, not that I wouldn't shoot you," she said. "Now, *tell me*." She hated the brutal intensity in her voice, but she had to know. She had to understand. She had to stop that voice in her head that still screamed *Save her!* after all these years. "Why did you say that?"

"You mean why did I repeat your sister's last words to you?" Mancuso sneered.

Maggie's hand tightened on Jake's gun, the decades-old panic rising inside her. "How do you know?" she demanded in a trembling voice. "You're too young to have been involved. Who told you?"

Mancuso smiled—not his slick, politico smile, but the desperate, trapped grimace of a man who knows he doesn't have much time left. He struggled to his elbows, meeting Maggie's eyes.

"I got a phone call," he said. "Before you cut off my incoming calls at the cabin. The person on the line, he sure knew a lot about you, Maggie. He was very helpful, very informative. Very interested in assisting me. In getting to you. He told me how much you loved Erica. How that was the key to rattling you. He talked about how he'd used it against you before." He straightened his arm, sitting upright.

"He—What do you mean . . . *before*?" Maggie asked, her voice shaking, tears forming in her eyes. She had to hold on to the gun with both hands to steady herself. "*Who* called you? *Tell me!*"

Bang.

Mancuso's entire body jerked, his eyes open and blank as blood trickled down his forehead. A horrible gurgle came from his throat as his face went slack and he collapsed on the ground, dead.

Maggie spun around, her gun raised.

"Maggie, it's me!" Paul came hurrying up the hill, lowering his pistol. "Don't shoot!"

Maggie looked from Paul to Mancuso, dead on the ground, lost to her. All the answers she needed—*lost.* Just like Erica. Just like Erica's killer.

"What did you do? Why did you kill him?" Maggie asked, fury roaring through her like a wildfire. She crouched down to check Mancuso's pulse, but she knew it was no use.

He was gone.

"I got a ride in one of the cars following you," Paul explained. "Jake said you ran into the park after Mancuso. He told me to go after you since the EMTs wouldn't let him. Kayla's okay. On her way to the hospital."

"Why the hell did you shoot him?" Maggie demanded. "He was just about to—" She wanted to scream. What was Mancuso going to tell her? Did he have the name of this person who knew so much about her? Who was he? Had he been watching her? Was she in danger? She had to know. Erica's killer . . . she was *this* close to finding out his identity—she *had* to know who he was.

She had to know where Erica's body was.

"He was reaching for a knife, Mags," Paul said. He bent down, rolling Mancuso's body over onto its side. Sure enough, there was a knife on the ground.

Maggie let out a breath. She couldn't be angry at Paul. But if only she had had a few seconds more . . .

Frustration and relief twined inside her as she sagged onto the ground, all the fight draining out of her. Paul had probably saved her life. But he'd also prevented her from discovering the one piece of information she'd spent her life trying to find.

"Come on, Maggie," Paul said. "We should get you to the hospital."

He reached out a hand to help her up, but Maggie rose

to her feet on her own, straightening, her body aching with pain now that the adrenaline was starting to fade.

"Are you okay?" Paul asked.

"Yes," she lied, staring out into the distance at the lights of the city flickering in the gray dawn.

But nothing could be further from the truth.

He was still out there. The man who abducted her. The man who killed Erica.

The man who took her sister from her.

She knew that now for sure. And he had meddled in her life for the last time.

She was going to find him.

And she was going to make him pay.

CHAPTER 64

The hospital's fluorescent lights hurt Maggie's eyes as she made her way through the halls, looking for Jake's room. She'd been up for who knows how long, too jittery to sleep. Her body was one giant ache, but she was unhurt other than a few bumps and bruises. She was more worried about Jake.

She knocked lightly on the door before ducking her head into his room.

He was lying on the bed, his eyes half-closed. His dark hair was tousled boyishly and his tan skin was paler than usual, but otherwise he looked remarkably good for a guy who'd been shot just a few hours ago. Though she was a little biased, she'd admit. Jake O'Connor would probably look good after crossing a desert with no water or sunscreen.

"Hey, cowboy," she said, her heart contracting at the sight of him looking so uncharacteristically helpless.

He smiled at her, a bit lopsided, as if he was still a little loopy.

"They give you the good pain pills?" she asked, setting the flowers she'd brought on the table next to his bed.

He shook his head. "Nah, I don't like that stuff. Don't need it, anyway; it's no big deal."

"You got shot," she said. "It *is* a big deal."

He shrugged. "It's happened before, and I got over it," he insisted. Then he looked at the table and chuckled. "You brought me . . . flowers?" He looked up at her with a wry smile.

She blushed with embarrassment. Flowers seemed like such a weird thing to give a tough guy like him, but she didn't know what else to bring. "Black poplar," she explained. "I told the woman at the flower shop to find me something manly. She said they symbolized courage, so I thought it was fitting. You were mighty courageous out there."

His grin widened. "I think you like me, Ms. Kincaid," he teased her. "And you're pretty crazy brave yourself, ma'am. When I get out of here, remind me to get you your own black poplar bouquet."

Maggie rolled her eyes, not bothering to hide her amusement.

"Come sit," he said, patting the bed next to him. She did, trying to hide her worried expression when she got a closer look at the thick wad of bandages on his shoulder.

"Did anyone update you on the case?" she asked, because they could talk about flowers for only so long.

"Frank stopped by, but he got a call and had to run before he got into it. Fill me in?"

"Senator Thebes has been arrested. The grand jury is sure to indict him. And there's plenty of evidence to put him away for a nice long sentence—maybe life."

"That's where that bastard belongs," Jake said.

"And there's going to be a massive investigation into the CIA director's practices," Maggie said. "I think the only reason they haven't fired him instantly is because they have to weed out who was loyal to him and Black before they select his replacement. Frank said the intelligence community is really pissed."

"They should be," Jake said, a tinge of anger in his voice. "There used to be honor among spies."

"I guess times change," Maggie said. "But Kayla's awake," she went on in a happier tone. "And she's going to be all right. No lasting damage, thank God. The hospital is keeping her one more day, just for observation. I spoke to

Mrs. Thebes. She's already hired the best divorce lawyer in DC, so I think she plans to take the senator to the cleaners, which is just what he deserves."

"Smart lady," Jake said. "And good mom."

"Yeah," Maggie said. "Kayla's going to need her. After this nightmare, getting back to normal won't be easy, but it'll be better with her mom backing her up."

"You know that from experience, don't you?" Jake asked.

"Something like that," Maggie said, thinking about her own mother, of how hard she'd fought for Maggie after she got home. Every little thing had terrified her, from the traffic outside to her father's footsteps in the hall. Her mother had never acted as if her fears were silly. She'd been there every time Maggie woke up screaming from a nightmare those first few years.

"So what's next?" Jake asked, nudging her with his leg.

Maggie hesitated, looking out the hospital window for a long moment. "I don't know," she replied, turning back to focus on Jake's face, wearing a serious expression. "Frank . . . he wants me to come back."

"To the Bureau?"

Maggie nodded.

Jake leaned back, his eyebrows scrunched thoughtfully. "So, you gonna do it?" he asked, looking at her intently.

Maggie wanted to laugh, because he asked the question as if he already knew her answer.

"You know, if you'd asked me that a week ago, I would've laughed in your face," Maggie said. "But now . . ."

"Things are different," Jake finished for her, nodding his head in comprehension.

She smiled, the warm comfort of his understanding wrapping around her.

"Everything's different," she said frankly, hoping he'd know what she meant.

He reached out, caressing her cheek with a rough, warm palm. "For me too," he said.

She turned her head so her lips pressed against the callused skin.

"I think I'm going to take Frank up on it," she said. "It felt good, having that sense of purpose again, you know?" Despite its rough and rocky path through this mission, her self-confidence was far less shaky now—she was confident that she could do good work again. And she had another, even more compelling reason: She had been wrong to set aside pursuing Erica's killer. Now that she knew he was still out there, she wouldn't rest. She couldn't.

She would bring him to justice—at the end of her gun.

"I do," Jake said. "Completely. A woman like you . . . well, let's just say you're no slacker, are you?"

Maggie laughed. "Definitely not. But, speaking of slack . . ." she said with a mischievous smile. "You know the funny thing about federal employment? I said I quit, but technically, I'm just on extended leave. Frank's tricky like that. So that means my vacation days didn't disappear."

Jake's grin widened as he caught her drift. "How much time do we have?" he asked.

Her smile was bright. Happiness flooded her at the sound of that *we*. "Five weeks," she replied.

He leaned forward, ignoring the pain. "Come here," he said softly.

She closed the space between them, her lips meeting his. It was a sweet kiss, gentle, because she didn't want to rile him up *too* much. But the feeling spread through her like sinking into a hot bath: the anticipation, the excitement, the affection.

This was the start of something good. Really, really good.

He rested his forehead against hers. "So, Goldilocks," he said. "What's our first destination? I know an amazing little island off the east coast of Bali . . ."

Next month, don't miss these exciting new love stories only from Avon Books

Blame It on the Duke by Lenora Bell

Nicolas, Lord Hatherly, never intended to marry, but now he must honor his father's debt to a social-climbing merchant or lose the family estate. Alice Tombs has spent the past three seasons repelling suitors like the wild marquess so she could explore the world. Until Nick proposes a tempting arrangement: just one summer together. It'll be easy to walk away after a few months of make-believe—won't it?

Ride Rough by Laura Kaye

Maverick Rylan won't apologize for who he is—the Raven Riders Motorcycle Club Vice-President, a sought-after custom bike builder, and a man dedicated to protecting those he loves. So when he learns that the only woman who has ever held his heart is in trouble, he'll move heaven and earth to save her.

The Enforcer by HelenKay Dimon

Security expert Matthias Clarke's latest prey is the sole survivor of the massacre that killed his brother. Kayla Roy claimed she was a victim, but then she disappeared. Matthias thinks Kayla may be the killer—and he wants justice. Kayla never lets a man get close, but keeping Matthias away might be impossible, as their mutual attraction feels overpowering—and very dangerous.